"Fair enou
"Everyone is

In her heart, she had known that he would find her. And she had a very good idea of what might happen. There was a small part of her that wanted this—wanted to prove that she was not too old, not so unappealing that someone would leave her to die on a cliff.

Alexander Barclay sat down beside her, his elegant black velvet footwear gone, his fashionable stockings cast off as well, below his evening knee breeches of black satin. He dangled his lower legs in the water beside her.

She felt the warmth of his palm cover her hand, resting on the moss between them.

She turned to stare at him, only the sliver of moonlight guiding her vision. His brown eyes were black in the evening shade, his skin shadowed white.

She inhaled and leaned toward him. "Kiss me," she whispered.

"I thought—"

"Stop talking," she interrupted softly.

Suddenly, strong arms drew her across his lap, and she didn't care that the hem of the gown was getting wet.

By Sophia Nash

BETWEEN THE DUKE AND THE DEEP BLUE SEA
SECRETS OF A SCANDALOUS BRIDE
LOVE WITH THE PERFECT SCOUNDREL
THE KISS
A DANGEROUS BEAUTY

Coming Soon
THE ART OF DUKE HUNTING

Sophia Nash

BETWEEN THE
Duke
AND THE DEEP BLUE SEA

AVON

An Imprint of HarperCollinsPublishers

AVON BOOKS
An Imprint of HarperCollins*Publishers*
10 East 53rd Street
New York, New York 10022-5299

Copyright © 2012 by Sophia Nash
Excerpt from *The Art of Duke Hunting* copyright © 2012 by Sophia Nash
ISBN 978-0-06-202232-5
www.avonromance.com

First Avon Books mass market printing: March 2012

Avon Trademark Reg. U.S. Pat. Off. and in Other Countries, Marca Registrada, Hecho en U.S.A.
HarperCollins® is a registered trademark of HarperCollins Publishers.

Printed in the U.S.A.

10 9 8 7 6 5 4 3 2 1

To nobody but you.

Acknowledgments

Great thanks to all who inspired me: Peter and Alexandra Nash, Georgiana Warner Kaempher, Arthur and Kim Nash, Philip and Renata Nash, Philip Mallory Nash, Jean Gordon, Len Lossaco Fogge, Laurie and Eddie Garrick, Philippe and Christina Gèrard, Kim and J. P. Powell, Le Comte et Comtesse d'Aurelle de Paladines, Barbara Kehr, R. T. Williamson, and to a very special circle of girlfriends: Anne Kane (many thanks for reading the first draft), Amy Conlan, Mary Lee Reed, Cathy Maxwell, Jeanne Adams, Kathryn Caskie Parker, Annie Abaziou, Lanette Scherr, Pam Scatteragia, Lisa Schleifer, Irene Schindler, Kathy Weber, and Heather Maier.

And to the two people who guide me through the publication process with such expertise: Helen Breitwieser of Cornerstone Literary, and HarperCollins Executive Editor, Lyssa Keusch. Special thanks to Liate Stehlik, Carrie Feron, Pam Spengler-Jaffee, Mike Spradlin, Susan Grimshaw, John Charles, Michelle Buonfiglio, and Emily Cotler for your continued encouragement.

And to my children for continually showing me the meaning of joy and life.

Prologue

A new duke always had hell to pay.

Oh, it had been all well and good when Alexander Barclay, now the newly minted ninth Duke of Kress, had walked into White's Club in Mayfair and been pounded on the back by a blossoming number of friends a fortnight ago.

And it had been *very* good last week when he had met his new solicitors and removed from his cramped and moldy rooms off St. James's *Street* to palatial Kress House, Number Ten, St. James's *Square*.

However, it had gone from the first bloom of bonhomie with the *crème de la crème* of the most privileged societal tier in the world to near pariah status overnight. Alex's avalanche from grace had all started last eve at the Prince Regent's Carleton House, where he provided the spirits to toast His Grace, the Duke of Candover's last evening as a bachelor.

His own induction into the circle that same night, he could not remember.

Alex should have known better. Had not the sages throughout history warned to be careful of what one wished? Barons, viscounts, marquises, and earls would have given up their last monogram-encrusted silver spoon for entrée into the prince's exclusive circle, and all for naught as one had to be a duke of England to be included. For two centuries, the dukes in the peerage of Scotland had pushed for inclusion in the royal entourage to no avail. And one did not speak of the Irish dukes' efforts at all.

Yes, well. Being a duke was anything but entertaining right now. More asleep than not, Alex shivered—only to realize his clothes were wet, and even his toes were paddling circles in his boots. Christ above, he would give over a large portion of his newfound fortune if only someone would lend him a pistol to take a poorly aimed shot at the birds singing outside like it was the last morning the world would ever see.

Sod it . . . What on earth had happened last night? And where in bloody hell was he?

The fast clacking of heels somewhere beyond the door reverberated like a herd of African elephants. A sharp knock brought stars to the insides of Alex's eyelids before the door opened.

"Hmmm . . . finally. Thought we'd lost you," shouted a familiar feminine voice.

Footsteps trampled closer and Alex pried open his eyes to find a blurry pair of oddly golden peepers and coils of brown hair floating above him. Ah, the young Duchess of March, the only female in the prince's entourage. Alex wished he could make his voice box work to beg her to stop making so much noise.

"Although, you," she continued, looking at Alex's valet stretched out on a trundle bed nearby, "are not Norwich. Come along, then. The both of you. Prinny is not in a mood to wait this morning—not that he ever is." Isabelle displayed the annoying habit of tapping her foot as she stared at Alex.

When he did not move, Isabelle had the audacity

to start pulling his arm. Dislocation being the worse of two evils, Alex struggled to regain full consciousness and his feet as his man did the same with much greater ease.

Ah, at least he had one question answered. They were still in the prince's Carleton House. *Thank the Lord.* Any debauchery that might have occurred had at least remained within the confines of these gilded walls. There had been far too much gossip lately of the immoderation of their high-flying circle.

"Look, if we're not in His Majesty's chambers within the next two minutes, I cannot answer as to what might happen," the duchess urged. "Honestly, what were you and the rest thinking last night? There must have been quite a bit of devilish spirits to cause . . ."

He held up his hand for her to stop. Just the thought of distilled brews made him wince.

"Must have been the absinthe," his valet, Jack Farquhar, said knowingly. "Englishmen never have the stomach for it."

"You're English," Alex ground out, his head splitting.

"Precisely why I never imbibe. But you . . . you should be *half* immune to that French spirit of the devil incarnate."

Isabelle Tremont, the Duchess of March, had a lovely warm laugh, but right now it sounded like all the bells of St. George's at full peel.

"We *must* go. You too." She nodded to Jack Farquhar, before she continued. "Kress, do you have the faintest idea where Norwich is? Were you not with him during the ridiculous bachelor fete? You two are usually inseparable."

Alex made the mistake of trying to shake his

head with disastrous results. "Can't remember . . ." As the duchess pulled them both forward, Alex's toes squished like sponges inside his now not so spanking white tasseled Hessian boots.

The effort to cross the halls to the Prince Regent's bedchamber felt like a long winter march across Europe to St. Petersburg. Alex looked sidelong toward his soon-to-be dismissed valet. "Absinthe, *mon vieux*?"

" 'Twas the only thing in your new cellar . . . eighteen bottles. Either the last duke had a partiality for the vile stuff or his servants drank everything but that—in celebration of his death."

To describe the pasty-faced, hollowed-eyed jumble of gentlemen strewn around the royal bedchamber as alive was a gross kindness. Four other dukes—Candover, Sussex, Wright, and Middlesex—as well as the Archbishop of Canterbury formed a disheveled half-circle before Prinny's opulent, curtained bed where the future king of England reclined in full shadow.

"Your Majesty would have me recommence reading, then?" The pert voice of the duchess caused a round of moans. "I'm sorry, but Norwich and Barry cannot be found, and Abshire is, umm, indisposed but will arrive shortly." She blushed and studied the plush carpet. "As His Majesty said, there should be no delay in a response to these outrageous accusations." She waved a newspaper in the air.

Alex swiveled his head and met the glassy-eyed stare of the bridegroom, the Duke of Candover, who turned away immediately in the fashion of a cut direct.

"Uh . . . shouldn't you be at St. George's?" Alex would have given his eyeteeth for a chair.

"Brilliant observation," Candover said under his breath.

"Late to the party, Kress." The Prince Regent's voice was raspy with contempt. "Haven't you heard? Candover has been stood up by his bride on this wedding morning. Or was it the other way around, my dear?"

"It appears both, Your Majesty," the duchess replied, scanning the newspaper with what almost appeared to be a hint of . . . of *delight*? No, Alex was imagining it.

"Lady Margaret Spencer was tucked in an alcove of the church, but her family whisked her away unseen when Candover did not appear after a ninety-minute delay," Isabelle read from the column.

"Why wasn't I woken?" Candover grasped his wrenched head in obvious pain.

"James Fitzroy," the duchess replied, disapprobation emanating from every inch of her arched back, "you should know. Your sisters and I woke to find every servant here on tiptoe. You, and the rest of you"—her eyes fluttered past the prince in her embarrassment—"commanded upon threat of dismissal or, ahem, dismemberment that you were not to be disturbed."

"I remember that part very well," inserted Jack Farquhar.

In the long pause that followed, Alex imagined half a dozen ways to dismember his valet. He was certain that every duke in the room was considering the same thing.

"Continue reading, Isabelle." The royal hand made a halfhearted movement.

"Let's see," the duchess murmured, her eyes flickering over the words of the article. "Uh, well, the columnist made many unfortunate assumptions and . . ."

"Isabelle Tremont, I order you to read it," ground out the prince.

"Majesty," she breathed. "I—I just can't."

John Spence, the Duke of Wright, who at seven and twenty was the youngest of all the dukes, chose that moment—a most opportune one—to sway ominously and pitch forward onto the future king's bed. Without a word, the Duke of Sussex hauled Wright off the royal bedclothes and laid the poor fellow, who was out stone cold, on the floor.

Alex strode forward and grasped the edges of the paper from the pretty duchess's nervous fingers.

"Ah, yes, much better," the Prince Regent said sourly. "Might as well have the man"—his Majesty's hand pointed to him—"who is to blame for the ruin of us all, read it."

Head pounding, Alex forced his eyes and mouth to work. " 'In a continuation of the regular obscene excesses of the Prince Regent and his *royal entourage*, not one of the party made an appearance at St. George's earlier this morning, with the exception of our Princess Caroline, darling Princess Charlotte, and Her Grace, the young Duchess of March. His Majesty's absence and that of the groom and groomsmen caused all four hundred guests to assume the worst. And, indeed, this columnist has it on the very best authority, partially one's own eyewitness account, that not only the august bridegroom, His Grace, the Duke of Candover, but also seven other dukes, one archbishop and the Prince Regent himself, were seen cavorting about all of London last eve on an outrageous regal rampage. Midnight duels, swimming amok with the swans in the Serpentine, a stream of scantily clad females in tow, lawn bowling in unmentionables, horse races in utter darkness, wild, uproarious boasting, and jesting, and wagering abounded. Indeed, this author took it upon himself to retrieve and return to White's Club their infamous betting book, which one of the royal entourage had had the audacity to remove without even a by your leave. In this fashion we have learned that the Duke of Kress lost the entire fortune he so recently acquired with the title, although the winner's name was illegible . . .' "

Alex's voice stumbled to a halt.

"Happens to the best of us," the Duke of Sussex murmured as consolation. That gentleman was as green about the gills as Alex felt.

"And the worst of us," mumbled the Duke of Middlesex, as he finally gave in to the laws of gravity and allowed his body to slide down the wall on which he was leaning. He sunk to the ground with a thud.

"Don't stop now, Kress. You've gotten to the only good part." Candover leaned in wickedly.

Alex had never tried to avoid just punishment. He just wished he could remember, blast it all, what his part had been in the debacle. He cleared his throat and continued, " 'Even the queen's jewels were spotted on one duke as he paraded down Rotten Row. Yes, my fellow countrymen, it appears the English monarchy has learned nothing from our French neighbor's lessons concerning aristocratic overindulgence. As the loyal scribe of the Fashionable Column for two decades, you have it on my honor that all this occurred and worse. I can no longer remain silent on these reoccurring grievous, licentious activities, and so shall be the first plain-speaking, brave soul to utter these treasonous words: I no longer support or condone a monarchy such as this.' " Alex stood very still as the last of the column's words left his lips.

At precisely the same moment the other dukes cleared their throats, and one valet tried to escape.

"If any of you leave or say one word, I shall cut off your head with a . . ."

"Guillotine, Majesty?" Isabelle chirped.

In the silence, a storm brewed of epic proportions.

Thank the Lord, the chamber's gilded door opened to divert His Majesty's attention. The Duke of Barry, a Lord Lieutenant of the 95th Rifle Regiment, stepped in, almost instantly altering his unsteady gait with expert precision. Only his white face and the sheen of perspiration on his forehead gave him away. Mutely, he stepped forward and laid a dueling pistol on the foot of the cashmere and silk royal bedclothing.

"Dare I ask?" His Majesty's voice took on an arctic edge.

Barry opened his mouth but no sound came out. He tried again. "I believe I shot a man. He's in your billiard room, Majesty."

The Duke of Abshire entered the royal chamber behind Barry with the hint of wickedness in his even, dark features marred by a massive black eye. Known as the cleverest of the bunch, good luck had clearly deserted him on this occasion.

"I thought you were leaving, Abshire. Or do you need me to show you out?" Candover's usually reserved expression turned thunderous.

Alex leaned toward Sussex, and almost fell over before righting himself. "What did I miss?"

"Trust me," Sussex whispered. "You do not want

to know. You've got enough on your dish, old man."

Alex raised his eyebrows at Sussex and missed Abshire's dry retort directed at the premier duke, Candover. There was no love lost between those two. Then again, Candover's remote, holier-than-thou manner grated on just about everyone.

Middlesex, still on the floor, tugged on Alex's breeches and Alex bent down to catch the former's whisper. "I heard a lady shouting in chambers next to mine, then two doors slammed, and Candover came out rubbing his knuckles."

Alex shook his head. Could it get any worse?

The black-haired duke, Abshire, clapped a hand on the shoulder of the most respected and most quiet duke of the circle, Barry. "Is he dead?"

"Yes," Barry replied.

"Are you certain?" Sussex asked, eyes wide.

"I think I know when a man is breathing or not."

"But there are some whose breath cannot be detected," Middlesex croaked.

"Rigor. Mortis," Barry replied.

An inelegant sound came from the duchess's throat.

"Please forgive me, Isabelle," Barry said quietly. "Your Grace, I do not know the man."

"Just tell me you locked the chamber when you left it," the prince said dryly. When Barry nodded, the prince continued darkly. "I had thought better of you, Barry. What is this world coming to if I cannot count on one of England's best and brightest?" The prince, still in full shadow, sighed heavily. "Well, we shall see to the poor, unfortunate fellow, as soon as I am done with all of you."

"Yes, Your Majesty," Barry replied, attempting to maintain his ramrod posture.

"Now then," His Majesty said with more acidity than a broiled lemon. "Does not one of you remember what precisely happened last night?"

"I remember the Frenchified spirits Kress's man"—the Duke of Sussex looked toward Jack Farquhar with pity—"brought into His Majesty's chamber."

"I must be allowed to defend . . ." Farquhar began and then changed course. "Yes, well, since three of you locked me in a strong room when I voiced my concern, I cannot add any further observations."

"Is that the queen's coronation broach, Sussex?" the imperial voice demanded suddenly.

The Duke of Sussex, now pale as the underbelly of a swan, looked down and started. Hastily, he removed the offending article and laid the huge emerald-and-diamond broach on the end of the gold-leaf bed frame, beside the pistol.

Alex just made out Middlesex's whispered words below. "Very fetching. Matches his eyes to perfection."

Alex felt a grin trying to escape as he helped Middlesex to his feet.

"Just like the wet muck on your shoulder compliments your peepers, Middlesex," retorted Sussex.

Ah, friendship. Who knew English dukes could be so amusing when they dropped their lofty facades? Last night had probably almost been worth it. It was too bad none of them could remember it.

"Well, at least the columnist did not know about the unfortunate soul in the billiard room," Isabelle breathed. "Did you all really swim in the Serpentine? I declare, the lot of you are wetter than setters after a duck. I would not have ever done anything so—"

"You were not invited," the Duke of Candover gritted out.

"And whose fault was that?"

"Enough," the Prince Regent roared. The royal head emerged from the gloom and Alex's gasp blended with the rest of the occupants' shocked sounds in the room.

His Majesty's head was half shaved—the left side as smooth as a babe's bottom, the long brown and gray locks on the right undisturbed. None dared to utter a word.

Prinny raised his heavy jowls and lowered his eyelids in a sovereign show of condescension. "None of this is to the point. I hereby order each of you to make amends to me, and to your country. Indeed, I need not say all that is at stake." His Majesty chuckled darkly at them. "And we have not a moment to spare. Archbishop?"

A small fat man trundled forward, his head in his hands, his gait impaired.

The future king continued. "You shall immediately begin a formal answer to this absurd column—to be delivered to all the newspapers. And as for the rest of you—except you, my dear Isabelle—I order you all to cast aside your mistresses and your self-indulgent, outrageous ways to set a good example."

"Said the pot to the kettle," inserted Sussex under his breath.

"You shall each," His Majesty demanded, "be given your particular marching orders in one hour's time. While I should let all of you stew about your ultimate fate, I find . . . I cannot. I warn that exile from London, marriage, continuation of ducal lines, a newfound fellowship with sobriety, and a long list of additional duties await each of you."

"Temperance, marriage, and rutting. Well, at least one of the three is tolerable," the Duke of Abshire on Alex's other side opined darkly and discreetly.

Alex could not let this farce continue. "Majesty, I appreciate the invitation to join this noble circle of renegades but—"

"It's not an invitation, Kress," the Prince Regent interrupted. "And by the by, have you forgotten your return to straightened circumstances if this column is correct? You shall be the first to receive your task."

"An order is more like it," the Duke of Barry warned quietly. The solemn man wore a distinctive green military uniform that reminded Alex of his own dark past. A past that would infuriate the Prince Regent if he but knew of it.

Prinny glanced about the chamber in an old rogue's fit of pique. "Kress, you shall immediately retire to your principal seat—St. Michael's Mount in Cornwall. Since a large portion of the blame for last evening rests squarely on your shoulders, I hereby require you to undertake the restoration of that precious pile of rubble, for the public considers it a long neglected important outpost for England's security. Many have decried its unseemly state."

A departure from London was the very last thing he would do. He hated any hint of countrified living. The cool lick of an idea slid into his mind and he smiled. "But, according to that column, I've no fortune to do so, Your Majesty."

Prinny's face grew red with annoyance. "You are to use funds from my coffers for the time being. But you shall repay my indulgence when you take a bride from a list of impeccable young ladies of fine lineage and fine fortunes"—Prinny nodded to a

page who delivered a document into Alex's hands—
"within a month's time."

Candover made the mistake of showing a hint of teeth.

Alex Barclay, formerly Viscount Gaston, with pockets to let in simpler times, felt his contrarian nature rise like a dragon from its lair, but knew enough to say not a word. The ice of his English father's blood had never been very effective in cooling the boiling crimson inherited from his French mother.

"And you, my dear Candover," the prince continued, "shall have the pleasure of following him, along with Sussex and Barry, for a house party composed of all the eligibles. While you are exempt at the moment from choosing a new bride, as homage must be paid to your jilted fiancée, I shall count on you to keep the rest of these scallywags on course."

Candover's smile disappeared. "Have you nothing to say to His Majesty, Kress?" The richest of all the dukes coolly stepped forward to face Alex and tapped his fingers against a polished rosewood table in the opulent room seemingly dipped in gold, marble, and every precious material in between. The rarefied air positively reeked of royal architects gone amok.

When Alex's silence continued, all rustling around him eventually stopped. "Thank you," Alex murmured, "but . . . *no thank you.*"

Candover's infernal tapping ceased. "*No?* Whatever do you mean?" A storm of disapproval, mixed with jaded humor erupted all around him.

Oh, Alex knew it was only a matter of time before he would capitulate to the demands, but he just hadn't been able to resist watching the charade play out to its full potential.

The Prince Regent's face darkened from pale green to dark purple. It was a sight to behold. "And let me add, Kress, one last incentive. Don't think I have not heard the whispers questioning your allegiance to England. If I learn there is one shred of truth to the notion that you may have worn a frog uniform, I won't shed a single tear if you are brought before the House of Lords and worse. Care to reconsider your answer?"

It had been amusing to think that life would improve with his elevation. But then, he habitually failed to remember that whenever he had trotted on happiness in the past, there had always, *always* been *de la merde*—or rather, manure—on his heels in the end.

The only question now was how soon he could extricate himself from a ramshackle island prison to return to the only world where he had ever found peace . . . London.

Chapter 1

◦◦◦◦◦

Falling off a cliff was not the way Roxanne Vanderhaven had ever imagined she would die. It was far too dramatic for someone who led such an unremarkable life as she.

This absurd thought filtered through her mind as the sodden precipice high above Kynance Cliff gave way beneath her feet. She twisted and clawed at the jagged face of the crag during the terrifying descent toward the crashing surf far below.

Miraculously, her hand caught a stunted piece of scrub thirty feet down as a shower of stones pelted her. "Lawrence!" she gasped. "Oh, God, help me."

"*Roxanne, Roxanne, where are you?*" Her husband's voice echoed high above her.

She coughed, barely able to breathe for all the dirt. "Help," she choked out, her heart in her throat. Grime burned her eyes but she didn't dare close them.

"If you can hear me, darling Roxanne," Lawrence called out to her, "I'm off to find help—or a bit of rope."

Just then the roots of the half-dead bush loosened and she slipped a few more inches downward, her feet finding purchase on a small jut of rock. A moment later, a large boulder plummeted past her shoulder, glanced off one of the ancient fragments of rock standing tall in the violent sea, and disappeared into the swirling depths.

Lord, she really was going to die.

The roaring in her ears almost blocked out the faint neighing of one of the carriage horses as the pair presumably galloped away under Lawrence's hand. She was paralyzed, barely daring to breathe lest her perch disintegrate.

Roxanne darted another glance below the crook of her arm and quickly shut her eyes against a burst of dizzying nausea. Her favorite hat, the lace blue confection her father had given her on her wedding day, lost the fight to gravity and fell from her head only to crash below. She dared not look.

Why, oh, why had she ventured so close to the edge? She was such a fool. Everyone knew to stay clear of cliffs, especially after a storm. It was just that she adored her dog and had not been thinking properly when he went missing.

Not five minutes ago, her husband had stopped the curricle and looked at her sadly. "I'm so sorry, my dear, but I really do think dear Edward went over. See his trail in those grasses over yonder? You know how he loves to give chase to the rabbits in the warrens here. So many dogs perish this way each year. Perhaps we should have a look?"

Desperate, Roxanne had run into the thick sea oats bordering the edge, her love for her dog overcoming her good sense. A gust of wind at her back had fluttered the loose ribbons of her hat before . . . Oh, she wished she could turn back time.

Roxanne sagged against the cliff face and clenched

the prickly branch tighter, refusing to acknowledge the numbness already invading her arms. How long could she hold on? How long before the rock she stood on might give way? She began to count seconds, then minutes, in an effort to retain her sanity. She concentrated on the rich scent of the minerals and earth so familiar to a miner's daughter. Oh, how she wished she was stuck in a mine. At least there she would find calm in the familiar darkness.

Her muscles burned from the effort to remain motionless. Surely, it would not be much above a half hour before Lawrence returned. The minutes ticked by with maddening sluggishness.

At first she thought she imagined it . . . but, no . . . There it was again, sounds drifting above her. Lawrence was surely back.

No. It was Eddie's raucous yowling that pierced the air. A few pebbles trickled past her, and she glanced skyward only to see her dog's clownlike piebald face looking down at her. He howled.

"No, Eddie! Go away." She urged him to quit the dangerous rim, but he would not. Lord, it was severely concave below the long ledge, only the tight weave of tall grasses had held the edge intact when the rains had eaten away at the cliff. In her effort to see better, one foot slipped and her leg swung wildly before she found a better foothold in one of the deep cracks of the hardened clay.

She bit back any further words. She had to concentrate on not moving.

It could have been an hour, perhaps two. Lord knew, it felt like twenty, but at some point Roxanne had the uneasy sensation that too much time had lapsed. The intervals between Eddie's rounds of barking and silence grew too long. If she hadn't been so scared, she would have cried. It appeared even her dog was giving up hope.

What could have happened to Lawrence? The lane from here to Paxton Hall was a straight, easy distance without any hint of danger. The horses were dependable. Could her husband have suffered apoplexy in his distress? Her mind considered a thousand different possibilities, all increasingly ridiculous. Lawrence was in exceptional good health for a gentleman in his third decade. Surely at this minute he was gathering a troop of people to help and devising a brilliant scheme to rescue her.

She could no longer feel any portion of her hands and arms. It was as if they had become petrified. Even her legs, which were strong from long walks along the sinuous paths of her childhood, began to tremble with fatigue.

And then she realized she had made a critical mistake. The tide was retreating. She might have had a better chance if she had shoved away from the cliff face earlier and fallen into the sea. Now it was becoming shallower by the minute. She closed her eyes. She was going mad. With those jagged rock formations below, she would not have had a prayer of a chance.

When the first gust of cooling wind cut through the languor of the long, hot summer afternoon, Roxanne's mind reeled with the realization that Lawrence was not going to return.

And he had probably known all along that the ledge would easily give way. Had he not walked to the nearby promontory point only yesterday in his never-ending horticultural quest to find the rare Kidney Vetch? He must have seen the precarious state of the cliff from that vantage point. And had he not suggested she take a closer look?

Sod it all.

She had to face the cold, hard truth. She was married to a handsome, blackhearted, calculating, murderous clod.

Hope whimpered one last time. Nothing made sense. She ran the estate with care and precision, took an interest in every detail from sheep shearing to soap making. She arranged country balls for neighboring noble families, brought baskets to the poor and infirm, and oversaw the creation of a school for less fortunate children in the parish. Most importantly, she saw to Lawrence's every need before he even realized he wanted something. Her husband had only to engage in the gentlemanly pursuits he favored—his horticultural experiments, riding to hounds, evenings with neighboring members of the peerage, and reading journals.

Her aim in life was to provide Lawrence his ease, anticipate every need in the household, oversee the entire estate during Lawrence's trips to search out new, exotic plants, and to do him proud as his countess. The worst thing that could be said was that she was not of noble birth, but she had thought her immense dowry eight years ago had helped Lawrence overlook her father's very prosperous tin and copper mines. Then again, he'd never liked the *stink* of trade.

She was being ridiculous. Had he not always called her his *perfect* wife?

Oh, she was perfect all right. Perfectly *stupid*.

The Duke of Kress halted at the end of the eastern sandy path and dismounted his favorite new possession, Bacchus, a fine prize of a beast. He had purchased the striking black stallion before the night of debauchery because the steed gave the appearance of a brave, yet elegant warhorse suitable for someone on his way up in the world.

But during the endless ride down from London, Alex had determined three things. First, he should have taken a carriage. Second, the stallion might be a looker, but he had the most bone-jarring gait of any creature foolish enough to carry a man on his back. And thirdly—and perhaps worst of all—the animal was an out and out ninny-hammered, vain *coward*.

The horse refused to allow his hooves to be dirtied by a single drop of muddy water—not even the smallest puddle would he cross. The animal did not like to travel long distances and complained long and loud if the bedding and feed were not to his liking. Bacchus shied from anything and everything that moved in the countryside—birds, leaves, other horses, even, it appeared, small, harmless dogs. His horse, in short, reminded him of . . . almost every *female*, Alex thought with a half-smile.

He liked him very much.

The mongrel, dashing in circles around them, produced the most godforsaken howling noises in between those high-pitched yips and yowls. Bacchus's ears lay flat, and his raised hind leg promised swift corporal punishment.

The dog stopped to dance a jig in front of him, as if he were bred for herding. The mongrel was truly the ugliest canine in creation. Wiry white hair covered the short-legged creature, save for one large patch of black encircling his eye—his *only* eye. Lopsided ears framed his uncomely head—one stood up at attention, the other drooped in retreat.

"Away with you," Alex demanded halfheartedly. "Go on, then."

The dog sat down and cocked his head.

Alex removed his hat and raked back his hair. Damn, but it was hot. And now he was lost yet again. It had been madness to embark on this trip without a forward rider at the very least.

It had been absurd. But he'd had little choice given the Prince Regent's fury. Indeed, he'd been ordered to decamp Town within an hour of that memorable morning-after audience.

Well, he would just have a look at the coast for a recognizable landmark—not that he knew a bloody thing about Cornwall—and then he would return the way he had come until he found a signpost or a person to guide him.

He made a motion to remount, and the dog immediately lunged and closed his ineffective jaws around the ankle of Alex's boot. The cur made an awful whimpering sound, and dug in his paws in an effort to drag him away from Bacchus.

While he could not feel the dog's teeth, this made for another perfect moment to add to another wretched day on a journey that would not end. "Let go, damn you," he said with a laugh.

The dog obeyed at once and emitted a long whine that ended on a yawn as he sat back on his haunches.

"Stay," he ordered, and then sighed when the animal whined again. Alex turned and strode along the path parallel to the cliff, searching for a better vantage point. Strangely, the dog did not move. Oh, but the howling. The hound sounded like a dying cat.

The trail curved outward to the sea, toward a lower promontory point, and he followed it. After many minutes, he stepped onto a secure rocky ridge and scanned the vast wild beauty of the coastal landscape and crimson rays of the setting sun. Not twenty miles to the southwest, he could see his future—St. Michael's Mount. The magnificent castle was perched on an outcropping of granite, rising from Mount's Bay. All was swathed in an eerie, golden mist.

A long-dormant emotion pushed past the hard edges of Alex's heart and a sudden sense of déjà vu filled him. He forced the emotion back into the compartment he rarely opened.

Throwing out his arms, he embraced the strong wind that had traveled all the way across the Bay of Biscay from France and now whistled past him. What in hell was wrong with him? He was not normally given to such theatrics. He abruptly dropped his arms. Lord, he hoped this was not one of the effects of becoming a duke. He would have to guard against it in future.

His eyes suddenly caught on the bobbing white form of the dog higher up on the cliff to his right. A blue and gray length of material fluttered near the edge. His gaze moved lower.

Christ . . .

He started running before his mind could form words. A female was clinging to the cliff face, her skirts billowing. "I see you," he shouted as he ran, yanking off his gloves and coat. "Damn it, don't let go—don't bloody move."

Alex stripped Bacchus of every last bit of tack and quickly cobbled together the oddest length of salvation. A pair of reins buckled end to end and attached to the saddle's cinching, followed by a lead shank. The dog danced and yipped, urging his efforts. He added the durable portion of the bridle and breast strap for good measure.

Crawling, like the former Hussar he had been,

toward the edge where the dog danced and howled, he hoped for the kind of luck that always eluded him. "Hey, ho . . . Can you hear me?"

"Here," a hoarse voice called out. "I'm here. Oh, please hurry I'm . . ." The rest of her wispy voice was carried away by the wind buffeting the coast.

"Lowering a line," he barked, putting his words into motion. "Shout when you see it."

He continued to let out length after length of buckled leather and cinching.

"A little to the right and . . ."

And what? He hoped it was to *her* right. He adjusted the angle and stopped.

"I've . . ."

He lowered a few inches more of the breast strap. His muscles tensed.

" . . . got it."

He let out his breath. "Wrap the end around your arm and secure it." He gave her as much of the rest of the makeshift line as he dared. "I'm going to pull at your signal. Whatever happens, don't let go. Shout if you need me to stop."

The dog was in a frenzy, running to and fro, but thankfully now silent. Alex moved as far away as the end of the line would allow and dug his heels into the moist, grassy earth.

"Ready." The word floated on the same updraft a gray and gold falcon used to rise and troll the cliffs.

Lord, he hoped she wasn't stouter than the line could bear. It was going to be hellish as it was. He gripped the end around his arms and wrist to anchor it and then slowly he backed away from the precipice.

He erred on the side of speed over care. He just didn't trust the makeshift roping or her ability to properly secure the line about herself. He had been wrong in the end. Not about the method, but about her ability.

At the sight of her hands at the ledge, he slowed so she could angle onto the edge.

She was breathing hard and coughing, but God bless her, she had pluck.

He dragged her a few more feet forward and then rushed to pull her completely to safety. He had to peel her hand from the reins.

The damned dog was delirious and dancing all over her. Alex pushed him away and leaned her against his saddlebags.

She looked like a reclining statue come to life— all covered in gray clay and dust. Her tangle of hair was especially, ahem, *exotic*. He wasn't sure if she was five and twenty or five and fifty.

He left her but for a moment to retrieve his flask. He was at least grateful that Bacchus, amid the fracas, had not reverted to his usual skittish nature. The stallion eyed him with disdain and continued to munch on a thicket of delectable grass.

Alex removed the top of the flask and brought it to her lips. She swallowed a mouthful only to sputter. "Wha-what is this?"

"Blue Ruin."

"Blue *what*?"

"Sorry. Brandy's all gone. This is all they had at that unfortunate inn in the last village."

"No water?" Her voice was all dust and gravel churned together.

"Water? Why ever would I want that? Dangerous stuff, don't you know? Tea, coffee, wine, spirits are the only . . ." He stopped. "Care to tell me what happened?"

She paused. "I fell."

He waited.

"Off the cliff."

"Yes, I figured out that part," he said dryly. "All by myself." Perhaps she had hit her head during the fall.

She took another sip and managed not to cough.

"If you give me directions to your home, I shall go fetch someone to carry you." There was not a chance of making Penzance by nightfall now.

"No," she answered too quickly.

"No?"

"No."

"'No,' you cannot remember the directions to your house, 'No,' there is no one there, or 'No,' you have no residence?" Please Lord, say it was not the latter. He might have saved her today, but he didn't want to be responsible for her tomorrow.

"Of course, I have a home," she murmured. "A quite lovely, large one."

"Really?"

"Yes, really." She bit her lip, and then spit out the dust quite inelegantly. "It's just . . ."

"Yes?"

"I don't want to go there." She picked at her dirty gown. *"At present."*

"But someone must be worried about you. Must be waiting for your return."

She refused to comment.

"I'm sorry. I haven't even asked if you're all right."

"Oh, I'm perfect."

Her voice had that high keening to it that made men long to go in the opposite direction.

"Perfectly fine."

Uh-oh. These words were the inevitable prelude to every feminine lecture he had heard over the years.

"Yes. How could I not be? I thought my dog dead. I searched the cliff only to have it give way. I then had the joy of contemplating the merits of death by drowning versus splattering onto jagged rocks. And . . ."

"Go on. Best get it all out now."

"And . . . and I am married to someone who is in all likelihood sitting comfortably in his library drinking wine *I* purchased, in boots *I* polished since he likes the way I do it, and reading his horticultural journals, which *I* took care to lay out for him this morning."

"That was very nice of you."

"I'm a *very* nice person," she insisted. Her eyes, which he now discerned were quite blue, sparked in annoyance.

"Of course you are."

"*Stop*"—she ground out—"agreeing with me."

Yes, this was the way all his conversations went with females. In the past, however, he'd had the pleasure of knowing them a minimum of a fortnight before the ranting began. Well, at least her anger was directed toward another man. *Perhaps*. It was hard to tell.

"You must think me mad," she said, dejected.

"No, not at all."

"Yes, I can tell you do."

"You just told me to stop agreeing with you."

"Yes, but in this case you should deny it."

"Is that what you want me to do?"

She looked toward the place from which she had fallen. "He saw me fall and he left me to die."

He slowly stood up.

"Where are you going?"

He repositioned himself behind her and grasped

her shoulders to ease the stiffness. "Can you feel your arms? How long were you waiting for him?"

"I don't know. I think it all happened about half past four."

God, she'd been there for nearly three hours.

"How far away is . . ." He stopped.

"At most a quarter hour by carriage. And no, allow me to assure you there is no possible reason for his delay." Her voice rose. "You see, I've had a quiet afternoon to reflect on every possible impediment. And there is only one reason you are here instead of Lawrence."

"Lawrence?"

"My husband. The Earl of Paxton."

"You're a *countess*?" The moment he said it, he regretted it. Oh, not the words, the tone. He braced for the worst.

She said not a word. Instead she bowed her head.

No. Oh, not tears. Anything but tears. Well, the day was all shot to hell as it was. He plucked a handkerchief from his discarded coat nearby and came around to face her, on his haunches.

She dabbed at the caked gray clay on her face. "I am not crying."

"Of course not. There's a bit of, um, chalk in your hair."

She shook her head and a spray of dust flew all about.

He bit back a smile. It was unkind to find humor in any part of this unfortunate lady's circumstances. "All right. Here is what I propose," he continued. "Let us get you to the magistrate of the parish. He will sort this out and mete out the justice your delightful husband deserves. No one is above the laws of the land, no matter what his station."

"He *is* the magistrate."

"Then I shall take you to the neighboring parish. Surely—"

"Stop, I beg you," she interrupted dryly. "Lawrence has ties to every man of importance in all of Cornwall. They ride and hunt together, dine together, drink to excess together . . . " She flailed an arm in frustration.

"But—" He should know better than to press the point. "All right. What do you suggest?"

"You'd be willing to help me?"

"Why, you cut me to the quick, madam. Have I not proven myself a prince among men?"

"Um, well . . . yes. *And no.*"

"Explain, if you please."

"You did come through in the heat of the moment. But . . . if you'll pardon me, you have a look about you that speaks the opposite of everything you say. And . . ."

"Yes?"

"Well, I don't trust handsome gentlemen any longer."

"Flattery will get you everywhere, madam."

She hesitated. "So, you'll help me, then? Really?"

"Alexander Barclay—your servant." That ringing in his head, which always preceded regret, sounded in his ears. "So . . . what precisely did you have in mind?"

"Do you have a pistol?" She studied him with her big, round blue eyes and a smile that made him nervous. "Or, perhaps, a lovely little dagger?"

Chapter 2

It was beyond maddening that this overly hand-some gentleman with harshly hewn features had managed to keep any and all lethal objects out of her reach. Actually, it hadn't been all that difficult. The trial of hanging on the cliff for hours, and now riding pillion on his skittish, ill-tempered stallion, had left her near to dead as they made their way toward Penzance, twenty miles southwest.

At first, he'd been reluctant to take her with him, but then he'd seemed even more reluctant to leave her to her own ideas. To his credit, he'd grumbled a lot less than his horse when she'd insisted on bring-ing her dog, who trotted behind them.

"So where exactly is this new residence of yours?" she mumbled, her head jostling against his back. She prayed she would not see anyone she knew just yet. She needed time to think. Not that she and Lawrence frequented the seaside town very often; it was just a little too far afield of the Paxton estate and they typically visited the burgeoning port of Falmouth since it was much closer.

"The Mount," he replied casually, turning his head sideways.

She sat up, and stared at his strong profile, with the stubborn chin, long, straight nose, and well-defined lips. "The Mount? You mean St. Michael's Mount?" The ends of his dark chestnut hair flirted with his collar and shimmered many shades of brown as the last rays of light flooded the sky.

"Yes."

"So you've inherited one of the cottages at the base of the fortress?" He'd already told her he was traveling to his never-before-seen new residence.

"It's larger. But a mostly rotting ruin as I was given to understand."

A cool trickle of certainty pooled at the base of her spine. She closed her eyes. Lord, he was the dashing new duke, of course. The one all her neighbors had been yammering about for the last few days. The one all the trade people in the villages were hoping would deign to visit and revive the once magnificent castle gracing the projection of granite in Mount's Bay. He was also expected to marry one of the chomping-at-the-marital-bit noble daughters in the neighborhood and bring other gentlemen for those young ladies who failed to engage his notice. It was whispered he was half French, but his background and former life prior to becoming a duke was as mysterious as the reason he had agreed to help her.

"Have no fear that anyone shall recognize you," he continued. "Thanks to the charming effect of a relation, I am certain any former servants have given notice. My great-aunt has a, um, dislike of this country. Most likely only three or four of her stalwart favorite servants from France or Town are down and in residence now. But . . ."

"I'm listening, Your Grace."

His back stiffened before he relaxed again. "Well, thank God you have brains. You'll need them if you stay longer than a day or two. A large party of guests from London will descend by the end of the month. So you will have to concoct a plausible reason to be there. My great aunt will provide the first test I assure you."

"Why are you helping me?" she suddenly asked.

"Do I have a choice?"

"You know you do."

He paused. "Perhaps it's because I might know what it's like to have nowhere to turn. And sometimes, just sometimes, you are given a second chance." He cleared his throat. "Look, I might not be a long-lasting second chance, but you look the sort who will figure out what to do with a minimum of time and input from me."

"That's what I like about you," she muttered. "All gallantry, without a hint of charm."

He halted his horse and gathered the reins in one hand to turn fully to look at her. His lovely chocolate brown eyes met hers. "Well, at least it can be said I kept a weapon away from you."

"I shall pay you for your help," she said quickly. Roxanne tugged on the ruby and diamond ring Lawrence had given her on their wedding day.

"It's not very big, is it?" He examined the dusty ring closely. "I'm not sure it's enough to repay me."

She struggled to smile. "I know, but I don't want it. And you might need it if any of the neighboring mothers have their way."

"So why did he leave you to die?"

She liked the way he changed subjects as fast as she changed emotions. "I don't know."

"Does he want to marry someone else?"

"How would I know?" She was just grateful he believed Lawrence had tried to kill her. Many true blue-blooded aristocrats would never take her side. "I've always thought he cared about his gardens more than anything or anyone else."

"Your husband prefers shrubbery over females?" His raised eyebrows gave away his disbelief.

"He prides himself on the many flowers he's cultivated on the vast estate. Spends hours in the gardens."

"Now then, let me dismount," he said when she didn't continue. "My legs are stiff and I want to walk a bit."

She accommodated his nonsensical request and moved forward into the still warm saddle. In one swoop, he handed up Eddie, who was panting, and then he took up the reins and led the horse forward.

She heard him mutter something in French about women, and relatives, and dogs. Then again, her knowledge of the Gallic language was so poor he could have been talking about puddles and the way his stallion stomped on his foot in an effort to avoid the muddy dip just then.

"Hmmm. I'd wager it has to do with money," he said after a moment.

"Do you want the ring or not?"

He glanced behind him and then after a pause, grasped it. "All right. I might just put it to good use later."

"Later?"

"To scare off those mothers and daughters expecting a clutch of jewels worn by Marie Antoinette," he said, laughing. His bronzed skin set off his white teeth and dazzling smile to perfection.

"I promise I will truly repay you for helping me,"

she reiterated, trying not to stare at his startling dimples. He was a Frenchified snake charmer in London fashions, this one was.

"Yes, well, I shall charge quite a bit for your care and feeding. With interest. I'm more than a little dipped in funds right now."

"And I shall pay it."

"I shall not ask how."

"So that means you'll agree to hide me on St. Michael's Mount for as long as I choose?"

He shook his head. "I must be losing my mind."

There was just something about her that made him agree to her ridiculous request. Then again, he was so mired in muck at this point, it was hard to see how one squawking firebrand of femininity in the middle of nowhere could make his life more complicated than it already was.

He was a good assessor of humanity. And she was either one of the best liars he'd ever encountered, or everything she said was true. The only thing that was off was her accent. She didn't sound like a countess, or at least any countess he knew. And he knew quite a few. French, English, Russian, they all sounded very much the same—and it wasn't at all like this tall, thin, scrappy woman who didn't wither at his blunt assessments. The countesses he knew spoke of the minute vagaries of the weather, the fashions of the moment, entertainments, and gossip. Mostly the latter. And in the bedroom, their words were all the same too: "more" and "again."

"So tell me a bit about this Paxton fellow," he said. "How long have you been married?"

"Eight years."

"How did it come about?"

"Oh, I knew of him most of my life. I've always lived here, or north of here, near Redruth." She paused. "But Lawrence didn't know me until eight and a quarter years ago."

"I see." He didn't at all, but knew better than to risk a question at that moment.

"My father was the richest copper and tin miner in the south of England, Your Grace."

"You can stop that. I've had nothing but bad luck since assuming the title—and I think we can dispense with the formalities, considering."

"Well, after an extraordinary string of bad financial luck over the years, Lawrence called on my father and asked for my hand along with a large dowry."

"So your father chose the old-fashioned method of disposing of females and sold you."

"No, he did not sell me," she enunciated each word sourly. "He knew that I was just like every stupid girl in all of Creation—dreaming of a fairy tale prince or earl who would fall head over ears in love with me and drag me off to his castle. And Lawrence was the most desirable gentleman in Cornwall."

"Except for that tiny propensity of his to murder a wife," Alex said in a dry tone.

"And I was in love with him." She stopped. "Or at least I thought I was." She paused. "It wasn't until later . . . Until he forbade me to associate with all the people I had known before our marriage that the romantic façade dropped away. Toward the end, I wasn't even allowed to see my father, except on Christmas and . . . Oh, this is truly the stupidest story ever. I had a happy life. It was not gothic in the least. I refuse to complain. Except for the part where he left me to die."

"Dare I ask you to tell me more about this so-called happy life?"

"I will answer if you promise to tell me your entire life story after."

"Well, so far it seems as if you've been living your husband's life story, not your own."

He could see her fight to hold back tears from entering her eyes.

"I rather think you're right," she finally admitted. "You're the first person who ever explained it exactly as it was."

"Never doubt me."

She laughed awkwardly. "Are you always so cocksure about everything?"

His lips twisted into a devious smile.

The only luck of the entire miserable day had been with the tides. They crossed the exposed shingle path at low tide from Penzance to the Mount with only a sliver of moonlight guiding their way. Clumps of slick seaweed glistened against the ridges of wet sand.

She roused herself during the crossing. "So, what is the plan?"

"Plan?"

"Where will I hide . . . or should I take another name?"

"Look, plans rarely work. Don't you know that by now? Life never goes according to any grand scheme. Don't count on anyone or anything, even me. You of all people should know that by now."

"Hmmm. I didn't take you for a philosopher," she replied. "Well as you've no opinion, I'd like to hide in your turret. Seems like the perfect spot for a raving lunatic, which I'm sure to become soon enough, no?"

He made a long-suffering sigh. "I think it will go over better if you assume the role of one of my long-lost relations."

"Long-lost . . . ?"

"Yes, you know, the ones that always appear when someone inherits. Like Harriet, the granddaughter of Mildred, the third cousin four times removed."

"You have a cousin named Harriet?"

"No, of course not."

"You don't have to be so grumpy."

"I'm never grumpy," he said annoyed.

"I don't think that would work," she replied. "Someone like that sounds very young and dependent."

"Right. I keep forgetting you're a frumpy, old, independent countess under all that dirt."

She refused to respond.

"What is your age?"

"I think I'm older than you," she said quietly, "so that is an impertinent question. And it's your turn to spill your story."

"All right," he said with false amiability. "I'm two and thirty. A mutt of sorts, and on the outs with the Prince Regent."

In her dirty state she felt far more than two years older than he.

"I've been given one month to saddle myself with a young, fertile, rich, aristocratic bride of someone else's choosing before I've a shred of a chance of returning to London, where I belong, instead of moldering away in a rotter of a sea castle, which Prinny wants rebuilt. Oh, and my entire fortune is missing, and the one gentleman I consider a true friend has gone astray, too."

"Tatiana," she replied after a long pause.

"Tatiana?"

"If I'm going to pretend to be one of your relations, I'd prefer to be Tatiana instead of Harriet."

"You sound more like a Harriet," he drawled. "And thank you."

"For what?"

"For not battering me with a thousand questions."

"You're welcome."

In the end, they settled on the octagonal-shaped dairy parlor of the Mount. Parlor was a grandiose term for what had probably once been a pristine milking barn for the cows of the estate. Only two cows stood in the many stalls. They had agreed it would not do for her to arrive on the back of his horse that first evening and so she would spend the night on a makeshift pallet of old straw while he made his way to the castle.

After arranging a sleeping place, she sat on one of the milking stools, her small dog in her arms, and tried to battle back a wave of sadness that threatened to break over her in the wash of the light of a single lantern.

Alone. This was how it felt to be totally and completely alone—cut off from all she had ever known. God, she realized she had absolutely no one to whom she could turn. She had been swimming against a tide of ill-will swelling from the small, tight-knit group of aristocrats' daughters and wives for the last eight years. Everyone knew her dog was her best friend. Worse, she had isolated herself from her father's acquaintances to appease her husband. And now she was at the mercy of a gentleman and stranger who could change his mind at any given moment.

He returned an hour later with a jug of water, bread, cold meats, and strong, hot tea laced with honey. "You do realize how hard it is to walk out of a castle with a midnight picnic without a thousand questions?" He dragged another stool to sit across from her.

He probably had no idea how important it was to her for him to keep up this sort of banter. She was on the edge of losing her wits entirely. She grasped the tea, the shadows hiding the small tremor of her hand. Time had finally allowed the great weight of the day's events to rest on her mind. She drained the tea.

"It's as I thought. In the past fortnight since she took up residence, Mémé has given notice to all the old servants. So there are only four: her tiresome French cook, her personal maid, a new housekeeper from London who will not last if I have the right of it, and a Cossack footman who will."

Roxanne mustered the mask of a sane person. "And who is Mémé?"

He nudged the cold meats and bread closer to her. "A maiden great aunt. She's one of those hanger-on relations I told you about. The ones who refuse to disappear into the shadows of your life. Although, I suppose you could say she has her uses. Have no fear. She is blind as a bat. But she has somewhat perfected the art of interrogation."

She had the oddest sensation he was watching her carefully as he rambled. She broke off a chunk of bread and gave it to Eddie who swallowed it almost whole. She forced herself to eat a few bites of meat and a little bread despite the fact that her appetite had completely deserted her. She quickly gave Eddie the last of the meat.

The duke stood up suddenly. "There's a length of toweling along with the water. Tomorrow you can concoct an amazing story to coincide with your dusty appearance."

She shook her head dutifully but could not meet his eyes.

He continued quietly, "He's not worth it, you know."

Her gaze flew to his.

"It's not about that louse," she said boldly. She didn't trust herself to continue. But when he refused to speak, she felt forced to fill the awkward silence. "Look, this is about the time of night I usually walk through the rooms of the house . . . checking that everything is as it should be, taking Eddie out one last time, looking at the stars, and, and . . ."

"Yes?"

"And thinking about the next day," she slowed to a stop. She would never tell him that she had also spent those last quiet moments of the evening reflecting on what she could do to improve her husband's variable moods and the feeling that she was becoming less and less like the girl she had once been. She had tried for so long to ignore that her husband had slowly undermined her vibrant, confident outlook on life. Each week, each month, indeed, each year he had chipped away at her dignity until she had sometimes begun to doubt her actual self-worth. That part had not happened often, only in the wee hours of the night when sadness reared its gray head.

It was all ridiculous. Everyone had doubts. No one could be happy all the time. And she had accepted her lot in life. But even she would never have anticipated today's awful events.

"Look, it's all going to work itself out," he said.

"Really?" she said with more emotion. "You don't

have to placate me with false promises. They don't ring true, especially sitting here in a dairy. "

"Well, you've got one thing in your favor."

"And what is that?"

"You've suggested you've got the wherewithal to make your own way and that's half the battle. Although how you've managed to keep it out of your husband's pockets . . ."

She should know better than to trust this elegant stranger, with his warm brown eyes, disquieting good looks, and the aristocratic tilt to his head. She was a fool—an old fool. "My father never trusted my husband. But, he wanted the best for me, and so he agreed to the immense dowry." She paused and continued quietly, "Lawrence always expected me to inherit a vast sum when my father died since I was his only child. Yet my father managed to hide the majority of his wealth."

The duke raised his eyebrows. "And you know where it is."

She looked away.

"No. That's right. You shouldn't tell me. Shouldn't tell anyone." He smiled with just a hint of wickedness. "But why not just take the blunt and pack yourself off. Begin a new life, assume a new name, *Tatiana*?"

"I am not leaving Cornwall until I find out why he did it."

"Fair enough. But just remember there are to be no duels, no scandals, and absolutely no daggers. The Prince Regent would have my head on a platter. Besides, my liver will suffer."

"You really are French, aren't you?"

Chapter 3

Alexander Barclay, the ninth Duke of Kress had not done Mémé justice in his description the last evening. At least that is what Roxanne decided within precisely one minute of meeting the elderly Comtesse de Chatelier.

As Roxanne faced the beautiful older woman in the grand salon of the Mount, it was hard to account if the countess possessed fifty or seventy years in her dish. Her jet black hair, dyed without a trace of gray, was pulled back so tightly in an elaborate coiffure that not a wrinkle could be seen on the porcelain complexion of her forehead. Only her eyes, blue as Roxanne's own, were odd, as they were fixated on a distant point above Roxanne's shoulder when she addressed her.

"I see," the comtesse said with immense doubt dripping from each word. "You are Mildred's great-granddaughter?"

"Yes."

"*Et bien, dites donc.* And who is this Mildred? I've never heard of a Mildred *dans la famille.*" She turned her vacant eyes toward the duke.

"Of course not, Mémé. You only remember your

side of the family. My father had a step grandmother. She was great grandfather Nicholas's second wife." A glint of amusement sparked from his deep brown eyes.

"No. I most certainly kept account of all the relations and even know the relations of all our friends." The comtesse elegantly pleated her gloved hands in her lap. "Well, are there any more of the famous Mildred and Nicky's great-grandchildren to contend with? Or are you the only one, child?"

Roxanne cleared her throat. "Madam, I am not a child. And no, there are no others. They all, um, died in a terrible, terrible carriage accident this past spring." She should have prepared better. She definitely shouldn't have used the same lie again if Mémé's sour expression was any indication.

Silence invaded the room like an army in wait.

"Such a coincidence," the comtesse said acidly.

Roxanne swung her gaze to Alex, who rolled his eyes skyward.

"Coincidence?" Roxanne mumbled.

"Yes, that Alexander's uncle, the eighth duke, and his entire family perished in a *terrible, terrible* carriage accident this past spring as well. And your own carriage broke an axle and sent you flying, too. Who knew carriages were so flimsy on this awful island?"

"Island, ma'am?"

"England," Alex murmured, a small smile playing about one corner of his lips. He obviously enjoyed watching the raking as long as he was not over the coals.

The older lady was not going to win this game, Roxanne thought. "Actually, I think it is a testament to the horrid condition of the roads and toll ways in our great country. I do hope our newly elevated relation," Roxanne looked toward the duke, "will take it upon himself to deplore and condemn the rutted, and ofttimes muddy roads of England in the House of Lords at the very next opportunity."

Alex stopped smiling.

"You have many opinions for someone who has arrived without invitation." Mémé turned to her great-nephew. "Well, as long as you are not passing her off in an effort to force another one of those loathsome creatures on me again."

Roxanne stifled a cough.

The duke laughed and his brown eyes looked in Roxanne's direction. "Companions. She doesn't care for them. Lord only knows why."

"Companions are for doddering old women who talk only of knitting shawls and *la vieillesse*."

"Mémé," the duke stepped in, "give over. Harriet, the housekeeper shall show you to your room and shall send up a bath."

"Harriet?" Mémé said. "I thought her name was Tatiana."

"It's Tatiana Harriet," Roxanne quickly smoothed over. "Actually, my family always called me Taty."

"But her pet name is Hettie." The duke obviously couldn't resist the game.

"And your dog?"

"Is Eddie." She instantly regretted giving her dog's real name. Then again, the interview had gone so poorly, at least she would not get stuck in one more lie.

"I like dogs. He may stay outside," the comtesse stated contrarily. "How long are we to have the pleasure of your company, then?"

The Comtesse de Chatelier changed subjects almost as quickly as her lofty great-nephew.

"My dearest *cousin* has been so kind to invite me for as long as I like." She did not add that Eddie would *not* sleep outside.

She glanced at Alex who winked. It appeared she had passed the test.

"We shall see," the comtesse said, her aquiline nose high. "As soon as you attend to your toilette, I shall give you *un petit tour* of the interior rooms that have not fallen to ruin. Shall we start with the armory? The former monks appeared to be much more bloodthirsty than most religious I know."

The duke shrugged his shoulders in a fashion only a Frenchman could manage. It should have looked silly. But it did not. Roxanne was certain his constant casual disinterest was merely a veneer for a force of character he took great pains to hide.

The question was, why did he try to conceal it?

God only knew why he was allowing another willful female into his domain. Surely he was destined for sainthood for taking on Mémé, although he'd never really had a choice in that corner. His French great-aunt had kept track of his whereabouts better than the three-legged hunting dog of his youth. And the moment good fortune had struck by way of the dukedom? Why, Mémé had installed herself at St. Michael's Mount without even a by-your-leave. Actually, he had thought she would do very well there, tucked away in the south of England never to be seen or heard, while, he, the proud ninth Duke of Kress, took London by storm as he had always wished to do. Bloody hell, he despised the seaside.

But then, his plans never came to pass. *Ever.* Not once in his entire godforsaken life had luck stuck by him longer than a day or two. And after, invariably, disaster struck twice as hard.

It was the reason he worried about allowing Roxanne, the probable Countess of Paxton, into his ruin of a castle. He had no reason to doubt her, yet he would rather avoid any part of her domestic debacle.

But there was something about her. After she had washed away the gray clay dust, she was actually quite pretty. Her glossy hair had gleamed many shades of gold in the stream of light from the bank of windows. And the rare poetry of her features—her fair complexion and vibrant blue eyes, especially—charmed him. Oh, hell, it had nothing to do with her appearance—he'd had dozens of simpering blue-eyed, blond females hang on his every ridiculous utterance.

He knew what it was about her. Her courage. Her relative cool-headedness despite her ordeal. Every other female he knew would have at least had a fit of the vapors or clung to him like a flea on a dog. She had pluck, this one. That small, shriveled chivalrous part of him wanted to help her exact justice; but that larger part of him, that wiser and older survivor by-the-skin-of-his-teeth, told him to keep her at arm's distance. Roxanne had the blunt to take care of herself and would be departing the Mount within a week, if he had to place a bet on the outcome.

Alex walked around the perimeter of the ancient castle lost in thought. While the base of the stone structure appeared sound enough to withstand the end of the world, it was only the uppermost tiers that needed repair. That said, there was one side, the southeastern exposure, which had suffered the worst under the constant assault of the elements. He had not the slightest idea how long it would take to repair the great pile, nor did he want to become involved for he was determined to leave the horrible clean air of the country for the lovely dank stink of Town as soon as humanly possible. He would hire an overseer, and leave him to the task of rebuilding this haunting vision from his childhood.

In the meantime, he would entertain a house party full of noble milk-and-water misses and their parents before being forced to single out the most docile one to marry, all to appease His Majesty so he could return to his beloved life in London. And leave his future duchess to entertain herself in the wilds of Cornwall.

As he climbed up a small grassy hill on the western slope of the estate, a young man suddenly appeared at his side, and fell into step with him without a word.

Alex stopped to face him. "And who may you be?"

"John Goodsmith, Your Grace."

"And what are you doing here?"

"Introducing myself."

The young man could not be more than seven and ten, although it was hard to tell given the state of his ragged clothing. "I see. And do you live in one of the cottages below?"

"No, sir. I'm a bit of a hermit. We're standing on my dwelling."

Alex looked down and could see nothing more than the small hill of grass. He scratched his jaw.

"Would you like to see it, sir?" The boy's eyes crinkled with enthusiasm, but Alex could also see a tinge of anxiousness, too.

Alex walked down the small slope and came 'round the front to spy a small door built of ancient wooden planks.

"How long have you lived here, John Goodsmith?"

"I was born here, sir. My father passed on five years now. We always kept the chickens well enough for the residents of the castle, and earned our keep that way."

The boy had a noble slope to his brow and nose, and a pleasant enough countenance. "And you're asking my permission to carry on, is that it?" Alex wondered how many other ragtag assortment of personages he was going to have to take on.

"Yes, Your Grace."

"I thought my great-aunt had dismissed all the servants."

The boy hung his head until all Alex could see was his long deep chestnut hair.

"I'm not really a servant, Your Grace. My family has lived here for as long as the Mount has existed, I think. My father said our relations watched the Archangel Michael appear from the heavens above and throw down a bolt of lightning to make the granite rise from the sea."

"So she couldn't find you, is that what you're saying?"

"Yes, sir."

He sighed. The boy was educated, which was odd. His cultivated voice gave him away. "Well, as long as you tend the chickens well, as I'm sure you will, who am I to take the home away from over a thousand years of Goodsmiths?"

The boy's smile and dimples lit up his face. "So I may stay?"

"Just keep out of sight of the comtesse, and keep her cook happy. Best prepare for the onslaught, too."

"Sir?" The boy pushed his locks away from his face.

"Two score of house guests. Arriving within ten days." Candover's express had been very clear on those two points. The new, earlier arrival date was clearly a testament to Prinny's ire.

Well, at least Alex had a hideout if the going got rough. That young hermit's earthen hut was big enough for two. And he would bet there would be books inside, if a reprieve from females was required.

The armory proved vastly entertaining. Swords, pikes and chain, mixed with pistols and shot, warmed Roxanne's heart. And the comtesse knew all the names and uses of each despite her blindness. She also had the uncanny ability to sail about the rooms of the castle with merely the slightest touch of her long fingers resting on the top of Roxanne's hand.

If the ninth Duke of Kress thought he could keep a weapon out of Roxanne's grasp now, well, he was mistaken. It wasn't so much that she wanted to kill her odious, handsome husband, as much as she wanted to be prepared if she ever faced him. All right, perhaps she just wanted to scare him. A little. Or perhaps quite a lot. Tears sprang into her eyes and she quickly wiped them away with her free hand. She was being completely ridiculous.

"Are you crying?" the comtesse demanded.

Before she could stop herself, Roxanne blurted, "Are you truly blind?"

"Of course. But I have a highly developed sense of smell."

"You can smell tears?"

"Of course I can. They smell of the sea, and a little bit of the earth—of copper."

For someone as practical as Roxanne, this made absolutely no sense whatsoever.

"And why the tears, mademoiselle?"

Words failed her when she needed them most. "I . . . I don't know."

"Ah, those are the best sort of tears," the comtesse insisted.

"There are different sorts?"

"Of course. Tears of joy. Boring. No one should cry with joy. One should shout with it. Tears of pain and suffering. Justifiable, but not very courageous, *non*? Tears of remembering the past. Waste of time. Ah, but tears without reason? Usually a sign that things are about to change . . . for the better."

"And tears of anger?"

"Only females do that sort of nonsense."

"Right," Roxanne muttered.

"Alexandre has never shed a tear in his entire life." His great-aunt always used the French version of the duke's Christian name.

"You spent much time together?" Roxanne knew the answer already, but needed to make conversation if she was to find what she wanted.

"Yes, of course. Although I'm certain Alexandre would give a different version."

Roxanne gave a sidelong glance toward the comtesse.

"Surely you know the story?" The older woman smoothed one side of her hair in a reflexive gesture. "Our entire family lived on Mont-Saint-Michel on the coast of France. Before the revolution, of course."

Roxanne went still. "Of course," she echoed.

"Everyone knows this small Mount is a replica of the much grander Mont-Saint-Michel." The comtesse's eyes glazed over with memories. "Yes, Alexandre's parents' marriage was considered the most brilliant match ever unplanned in both countries."

"How did his parents meet?" She quickly tacked on, "I never heard that part."

The comtesse's gaze softened. "My niece was so beautiful. Her hair—*cheveux marron*—chestnut, *non*? Her eyes a lovely brown. No one appreciates the beauty of brown eyes, do they? Alexandre's English father did, however. He came to see Mont-Saint-Michel. He said he wanted to see with his own eyes if it was very like the Mount here—where he had been raised with his cousins and the former Duke of Kress."

"And they fell in love," Roxanne coaxed the story forward.

"As only young fools will do. Ah, it was a beautiful wedding, even more lovely than King Louis's, I daresay. And they choose to reside at Mont-Saint-Michel, because, of course, even Alexandre's father could see it was the more important of the two landmarks."

"Of course," Roxanne murmured again, hoping that the comtesse would continue the story.

"But all stories must have their darkest moments, and ours came during the revolution's Reign of Terror, when aristocrats were persecuted by frenzied commoners wielding torches and pitchforks." The comtesse looked away. "While all of us refused to leave le Mont, Alexandre's father had at least the presence of mind to suggest that I take Alexandre away along with his younger brother, William, and the precious family jewels. We escaped the very night the castle was besieged. Our last sight was from a fishing boat. Le Mont was in flames and all those within its hallowed walls—all those we loved—perished. I think that was when Alexandre finally learned the truth about life."

"Yes?"

"That it is better not to form deep attachments to anyone or anything for it can all be taken away in an instant."

"But you don't really believe that, do you?"

"Of course not. That is his belief not mine. But I was not a boy of fifteen when everything was taken from me. I was, ahem, a woman of a certain age. I already knew life was about change. But, of course, you already know this, too."

Roxanne swallowed back the emotion filling her throat—all for the boy of fifteen who had lost everything. "Of course," she whispered.

"But don't think for a moment that he was not up for the challenge. When Alex and William's rich English relatives refused to have anything to do with their 'froggish distant relations,' Alexandre sold the jewels. Two years later, when the money became thin, he sent me and William to England, while he stayed behind to support us by joining the Hussars. He even arranged to send William to Eton's spartan colleger program."

Roxanne swallowed. She had had no idea he had suffered so much.

"What color are your eyes, my dear?"

"Blue."

"Pity." The Comtesse de Chatelier sighed.

Roxanne straightened. "Yours are blue, too."

"So everyone tries to convince me. Well, you obviously take after Alexandre's father's side of the family. Almost all Barclay eyes are blue. Alexandre inherited that deep velvety chocolate from his mother."

Roxanne shook her head. The comtesse had the oddest habit of turning the conversation whenever it became too serious.

Roxanne tried to open a nearby glass case, but a small creak had the comtesse whirling about. Roxanne froze.

"The housekeeper tells me you arrived without a valise."

"Yes, ma'am."

"Lost in the *carriage wreck*, too?" Those owlish eyes of the comtesse might not see anything, but they *knew* everything.

"Yes." Roxanne quickly palmed a small, intricate chisel and stuck it into the side of her boot.

"Celine, my maid, suggested we are almost of the same size, even if you are rather too tall. I shall have her add a ruffle to several of my cast-offs, then."

"I cannot accept such generosity, Mémé."

"I detest informality. You may not call me Mémé. But, I suppose, since we are in some thin fashion related, you may call me Antoinette."

"I would be honored to do so."

The older lady harrumphed.

It wasn't until the evening meal that Roxanne learned that the comtesse's true given name was Jacqueline.

It was three days before a convoy of servants arrived from town along with Jack Farquhar, his audacious valet. Jack and Mémé should not have gotten on so well, for Alex's valet was as English as a crumpet, except that due to some peculiar, unexplainable reason their various quirks of nature seemed to mesh in the oddest, most perfect fashion.

Alex would have been more grateful to see the

man if Jack wasn't the reason he was stuck in the wilds of nowhere to begin with. At least the valet brought news from Town even if none of it was good.

Apparently, small mobs of peasants were routinely shouting obscenities in front of the Prince Regent's Carlton House. And someone had had the audacity to throw a rotten piece of fruit at His Majesty in the royal theater. The newspapers decried daily the excesses of the royal class; and Prinny was as furious as ever at all the dukes present during the infamous evening of debauchery.

And still worse, Alex's one true friend, Roman Montagu, the Duke of Norwich was still missing. All of Jack's efforts to track him down were for naught. Alex tried not to think of it. Roman, the first gentleman to befriend him when Alex had arrived from France all those years ago, might very well be dead in a ditch, or drowned, or . . . Alex halted the painful train of thought with ruthless efficiency borne of years of experience.

Silently, Jack handed the local newspaper to Alex, and settled to the task of unpacking all the trunks that had arrived. Alex scanned the contents of the news sheet and sighed.

Of course there was mention of the Countess of Paxton gone missing, even her dog. Well, at least she was who she said she was. The column made no mention of her husband being with her when she fell from the cliff. Instead, he was quoted as suggesting his wife had been inconsolable since the disappearance of her beloved dog. While it stopped short of the notion of suicide, which would have gravely tainted the entire family, it was noted that only a blue sodden hat had been found on the rocky beachhead. A moderate reward was offered for the recovery of anything relating to the Countess of Paxton.

He exhaled.

Alex had avoided spending very much time with Roxanne the last three days, except during the afternoon and evening meals. She made him nervous with her steadfast gaze and her mind, which obviously churned with a host of very bad ideas. And he had far too many unpleasant tasks to face, such as interviewing the two foremen Jack had brought from London.

Oh, what the hell. He knew he had just been putting off contending with her.

Alex rocked to his feet and stalked into the huge library, where the housekeeper had directed him. The room was inspiring even if it did make his gut tighten in remembrance of another such room, far larger. The one in which he had spent so many hours as he grew of age in France.

He spotted Roxanne's even profile leaning over an enormous atlas covering a large portion of the main reading desk. A single dark blond curl had escaped from its pins and now rested on her cheek.

He placed the local newspaper over a map of Scotland. "Planning your departure already?"

"Yes, now that you ask."

"Well, it appears your dear husband is ahead of you on that score."

Her startled blue eyes swung up to meet his gaze. And not for the first time, he was pleasantly surprised by her appearance. She was tall, and spare to be sure. Her large eyes dominated her oval, determined visage. A long, straight nose sloped to lips with a prominent bow shape. And a single freckle rested an inch below the outer corner of her left eye. The aspects of her open countenance somehow came together to make for a fascinating face.

"Whatever do you mean?"

"Your funeral is set for a week from today."

She snatched the newspaper and quickly scanned the page. "The devil. The absolute wretch of a man. And what will he bury?"

"It's on page two. I think he means to bury your hat, unless one of the fishermen, who he has implored to search for your remains, can find you."

"My hat? Oh, that is rich. Well, I am going to witness this. I shall scare the living daylights out of him."

"Really? Is that how you want to play it, Roxanne?"

She sank into the embroidered cushion of the stool underneath her. "No. Of course not. But I will attend. I want to see who is there and I must hear what he dares to say."

"I have a better idea," he suggested. "I shall go instead. I've managed to avoid all the visits of the local peerage and gentry this week, but I might as well give over, make my bow, and allow the others to scrape and then depart at my leisure. And think how much your husband will wonder why I made the effort to pay my respects to a woman with whom I was unacquainted."

"You do not know him. He will decide you came as a sign of respect to offer condolence to a fellow nobleman."

"Well, I should like to see the fellow. Say a few words. Assess his performance, and look for weakness. And perhaps something a little more."

"A little more?" Her expression perked up. "I have an idea."

"I'm sure you do."

Chapter 4

～～～∽∞～～～

The morning of the Countess of Paxton's funeral was as blue and cloudless as the day she had died. At least that was what her husband had to say as tears poured in unrelenting rivulets down his ashen cheeks. He told everyone who would listen—and that was all eighty mourners—gathered at the cemetery overlooking St. Ives, that he would never be able to be happy again on a sunny day. Amazingly, not one of them laughed.

Alex had to give Roxanne credit. Her husband was every bit as good an actor as she had insisted. And he cut as dashing a figure as she had claimed, too. Dark hair, light eyes, muscular of frame, and not one, but three ostentatious white orchids attached to his lapel. Roxanne had not been funning him when she'd suggested the man had a partiality to flowers.

Alex had not failed to notice that more than half of the mourners were young females of the neighboring families. They were rather like sleek black buzzards circling for the kill. The only problem was that half the time these same birds of prey were looking in his direction too, curiosity and interest lacing their brows.

Alex had taken care to stand far back from the proceedings. He was only close enough to hear the earl's words.

All of it unfolded with the utmost decorum. Everything and everyone was proper in all respects.

Except for one tiny thing. One tiny, little detail.

He spied the edge of a granite headstone propped against a tree far from the gathering crowd. He slowly sauntered over to take a gander as the vicar began the recitation of the final words.

Alex knew little about funerals. In fact, he avoided them on every occasion. But he did know that it would take quite a while for a stone carver to produce the gaudy, flowery wording on this monument to Roxanne's life. The Earl of Paxton had obviously not spared a day before ordering this travesty of clichés.

Roxanne Vanderhaven née Newton
Countess of Paxton
1784 – 1818
Beloved wife of the
Sixth Earl of Paxton
Taken all too soon from
his grand lordship's side,
leaving him broken-hearted.
She died a noble, courageous
death and she will
be missed by all who knew her.
Forever may she
rest in peace.

A shadow appeared at his side, and Alex supposed he had known all along what would happen. He glanced sideways only to find Roxanne Tatiana

Harriet, standing next to him glaring at the headstone. Oh, no one else would guess it was she, for she looked like a he. Like a thin man, who dug graves at the cemetery. Her hair was completely covered by a large woolen cap, and her dingy pantaloons were belted too high, the frayed hems an inch too short.

"Oh, I'll rest in peace, all right," she whispered furiously, one side of her false moustache slightly unglued. It looked very like the one his damned valet sported on occasion. "I'll rest in peace so loudly, he will be *happy* to see the sun shine again!"

"I'll not ask where you managed to find that fetching ensemble," he replied. He paused before continuing. "I knew I could count on you to keep to our bargain."

"What bargain?"

"You know, the one where you stay on the Mount and I go to the funeral."

"That was but a Faustian bargain—a suggestion I chose to ignore. A person should be allowed to come to their own funeral if they can."

"Absolutely," he said, to diffuse her.

"Well," she said, running out of steam. "Now what?"

"You were the one who said you had an idea."

"I do," she said lightly. "But that comes later. Uh-oh."

"What?"

"They're coming to get you," Roxanne said cheerfully.

"Who?"

"The mothers."

"Pardon?"

"And the daughters. Looks like the widows are going to make a play for you too. Bye-bye."

Alex gave himself over to the process. The process of being plucked over by a group of hens and chicks. The former clucked, and the latter preened. Then the roosters strutted by to take stock of the proceedings. The last of them was the Earl of Paxton, who was careful not to remove the traces of glistening tears on his pretty face.

"Your Grace, I presume," the earl said, with a proper amount of sadness radiating from a small smile. "You do me a great honor in coming today. My dear, dear Roxanne would be in awe that you graced us with your presence. I am only sorry it had to be on this saddest of days that we finally meet."

"I always liked the name Roxanne," Alex said. "Almost as much as Tatiana. Although I think Harriet would suit a countess better, don't you?"

That silenced the crowd. All the better for them to think him destined for an asylum. It might thin the ranks of the matrimonially inclined.

"Tell me about your dear countess, sir. Was she a docile sort or a hoyden?"

The Earl of Paxton pursed his mouth. He recovered nicely. "Indeed. She was the best of wives. Kindhearted, beautiful, always inclined to think of others before herself. A perfect countess. All the other wives and daughters of our acquaintances cherished her friendship."

Not a single sound of agreement echoed. One lady coughed into her lace handkerchief.

Alex smiled. "I was given to understand that she was an excellent boot polisher."

"The best . . ." the earl said before halting abruptly and standing back on his heels. "I can't imagine who would have told you that."

"Why, your footman, my dear man. When I came to call."

"You came to call?"

"Yes."

"Really?"

"Yes, I came to make your acquaintance and to extend an invitation to attend a supper and dance Thursday next. Of course, I did not leave the invitation when the footman informed me that your wife had disappeared and was presumed dead. I knew you would be in mourning."

Desire warred with correct decorum on the earl's face. Desire won out. Of course.

"Well, I certainly cannot have you thinking that we would not offer you a warm welcome in Cornwall, Your Grace. I will, of course, attend. But I shall not dance."

"Not even a quadrille?"

The earl blinked. "Well, certainly not a waltz."

Another gentleman, whose corset did not quite meet the challenge of his substantial girth, cleared his throat. "Paxton, we shall release you from your engagement to dine with our family Thursday." The pretty face of a young lady beside the man appeared crestfallen.

"Nonsense," the duke replied before allowing Paxton to attempt any sort of diplomacy. "I invite you and your family as well, sir. Indeed, I am sorry I cannot invite you all, but there will be other entertainments this summer, of that I promise." That he might not attend them was something he did not feel he had to impart.

A flurry of happy noises erupted all about.

"But I am interrupting a solemn occasion. Please, I beg of you to continue. Now is not the time for us to discuss parties, and soirees, and summer balls." He scanned the crowd and could not find a single person whose countenance agreed with his sentiments. All of them wanted to talk about parties, and soirees, and summer balls.

Except one.

A thin, older, less formally garbed fellow had wandered to the gravesite and was staring at the coffin that lay therein. His long salt-and-pepper hair was tied into a queue, and his matching moustache was drawn high on the ends.

Alex wondered who he was but decided against drawing attention to him. He was sure, if Roxanne was still skulking about the tree trunks as he suspected, that she would tell him later.

"Well, I suppose it is time," the earl said with a deep sigh. "Will you do me the great honor of tossing the first bit of sod on my dearest wife's coffin?"

Alex looked down at the proffered hand shovel and pail of earth. He had the strongest desire to throw the bucket of dirt in Paxton's face. "Oh, no, no. I can never accept such a privilege. Is it not a husband's right to throw dirt on the coffin of the wife who served him dutifully for eight long years? Polishing his boots, laying out his journals, pouring his wine, and the like? That is what all good wives do, yes? Not that I would know the slightest thing about the duties of a wife. But you must honor her with this mud first, before the rest of your friends and neighbors."

The good earl paled. "I, uh, appreciate your good understanding of the matter. Thank you." As if on cue, Roxanne's husband allowed a fresh wave of waterworks to trickle down his face.

Perfect.

The assembled crowd offered murmurs of encouragement. And Lawrence Vanderhaven, the handsome Earl of Paxton, drew in an unsteady breath before he strode to the open grave at the same moment the gray-haired man sauntered away. Paxton stuck the shovel into the pail and sprinkled a large amount of earth onto the plain coffin.

A few handkerchiefs unfurled in the slight breeze but it was mostly for show, the duke guessed. Whoever said people from Town were more callous than countryfolk had obviously never been to this corner of Christendom. Tin should never try to mix with gold—even tarnished fool's gold such as all those before him. She had probably been considered lower than a governess, that poor creature who was neither of the servant class nor of the upper class.

The great show continued, each person grasping at the chance to put a few more inches of sod on Roxanne's false pyre. Whoever had thought of this grim custom was surely half devil.

A chill raised the hair on his arms. And then he heard it. The one thing that could bring a smile at this moment.

A dog barking.

A very particular dog with a very particular sort of bark that melted into an earsplitting high whine. Eddie darted into view, a blur of white and black that weaved in and among the fake mourners until he reached the edge of the grave. He put on quite the show and howled like a lost soul at midnight.

It was almost as good as the show that ensued by the Earl of Paxton.

"Good lord, 'tis Edward. Come here, dog. Where have you been? Oh, I've been searching, and searching."

The canine evaded all the different assortment of arms attempting to capture him. He bounced and leapt and almost turned a cartwheel in the air. And each time the earl approached, he growled.

Alex would bet his last farthing that Roxanne was enjoying it all, but he could not spot her.

And then, in one last display of familial disloyalty, Eddie took a huge leap and landed in Alex's arms whether he liked it or not. That was obviously his reward for secretly feeding the hound the French cook's overly rich delicacies. He immediately placed the mutt on the ground.

"Oh, do hold on to his scruff, Your Grace," the earl implored. "I do beg your pardon. I hope he did not ruin your coat."

"Of course not," Alex said, trying to nudge the dog aside.

"Edward," the earl said in an I-am-not-to-be-disobeyed voice. "Come here now."

The dog practically climbed up Alex's leg.

"You must be one of those sorts of people who dogs naturally like and obey."

Alex rolled his eyes. "You think?"

"Will you not give him to me? He is my only link to my dearest, most beloved wife."

"I think you already used those words on the headstone. Repetition is tedious."

The earl squeezed out another tear and held out his arms for the dog. "I am in mourning, Your Grace."

"But, he doesn't like you." It was one of the perquisites of being at the top of the food chain of nobility—the advantage of speaking your mind. Plainly. Bluntly. Loudly.

A few murmurs rose from the breathless audience now surrounding them.

"How about if I keep him for you," Alex said, trying to sound more kindly than he felt. "Until Edward is through his own mourning period at least."

Roxanne felt surely as cold as her hat residing under six feet of sod in the St. Ives cemetery.

St. Ives cemetery . . . Not the family chapel at Paxton Hall. It was the final insult. He had so disliked the tin under her fingernails that he had not arranged for her hat to be entombed with generations of Paxtons under the stone floor of the hall's private chapel. Nor had he chosen the cemetery near Redruth, where she had lived with her father. Obviously her husband had not wanted his name associated with her father's home. And so Lawrence had planted her in a town neither of them visited overmuch. Oh, she knew she was being ridiculous to care.

In truth, all this absurd rumination was just an excuse to avoid going downstairs. As soon as she had ridden hell for leather back to the Mount, she had locked herself in the chamber she had been assigned. This, despite the fact that the Comtesse de Chatelier had asked for her presence in the grand salon.

The houseguests from town were trickling in at an alarming rate. Roxanne could hear the soft-spoken curses of each of the guests' servants as they carted up the endless series of trunks and possessions along the treacherous winding path to the castle, for no carriage could make the trip.

Roxanne glanced down at the list of names the personal maid of the comtesse had drawn up for her. Names, an impossibly long list of names, along with a few descriptions of some.

There were so many lofty people on the list that she grew almost faint. There were three dukes, one duchess, and half a dozen lords and their ladies. But the largest contingent was the names of all the eligible daughters and sisters. She almost felt sorry for him.

Almost.

She refused to pay any attention to the tiny voice that said she did not feel sorry for him at all. She was feeling something entirely else. What it was, she could not say. Oh, perhaps she had a warm spot for him.

How could she not? He had saved her. He had put her up; and perhaps most lovely of all, he had said just the right things to her arse of a husband at the funeral for her blue fanned-lace bonnet.

She felt her hands meld into fists, her nails biting into her tender palms. She was not going to feel anything more than admiration for him.

She knew very well where the other could lead. She was not going to make a fool of herself twice over. She would feel gratitude toward him. But that was where she would draw the line.

And besides, there were plenty of reasons why she could never feel anything more than appreciation toward him . . .

1. She was too old for him. Indeed, she was older than him by two years.
2. He was a duke—a dyed-in-the-wool, outrageously virile, classically handsome *duke*.
3. She was a tin miner's daughter.
4. He was under orders to marry a nobleman's daughter with impeccable lineage and great fortune.

5. She would never give up her fortune.
6. Oh, yes. The most important thing: She was legally dead. Or married. Or, perhaps, both. Yes, she was both.
7. He liked Town, she, the country (not that she'd ever been to London. Why, she'd never been north of Falmouth.)
8. Most importantly, she would see to her own happiness, thank you very much. And not entrust it to someone who was most likely a secretly tortured soul unable to give his heart to anyone—even if he did seem to like her dog.
9. And, she was . . . utterly ridiculous. She was after all, above all, #6, which discounted everything else on this blasted—

A knock sounded at the door. She stumbled to her feet from her hiding perch near the window.

It was he.

"You know, you could show just a little appreciation by at least attending to my great-aunt's request. I understand your inability to obey any gentleman, at this point—especially after that nauseating display by your darling husband. But really, is it too much to ask you to meet the hordes who seek my hand in marriage? I mean, if I can do it, surely you can, too." His brown eyes sparkled with wit.

She tried not to notice it. "Did you bring back my dog?"

"What? You didn't stay for the grand finale?"

"I dared not."

"Well, you owe me a new coat."

She raised an inquiring brow.

"Edward is partial to buttons."

"Really?"

"Yes. And Weston's finest worsted wool. He at least had the propriety to stop at the buttons of my pantaloons, but it was a near thing."

"My dog prefers to be addressed as Eddie."

"That was made clear in your husband's presence."

"Did he bite him?"

"No. But it was obvious each wanted to tear the other's throat out."

"Good. Well, I thank you for bringing him back to me."

"I know how to play my part. It's just too bad you refuse to play yours."

"And that would be?"

"That of my mysterious step great-grandmother's great-grandchild. My cousin many times removed. That hanger-on relation who will help me keep the more impertinent misses at bay."

"So that you have enough time to make your own choice."

"Precisely. Before one of them takes things into her own devices and makes it for me."

"All right. I can do that for you."

"Thank you." He extended his forearm toward her, and she had no choice but to place her arm along the top of it. The fabric of his fine coat was warm to her bare cold arm.

Without another word, they descended the two long staircases toward the salon.

She could do this. No one would know her here. She could pretend to be the impoverished noble relation instead of the rich tin miner's dead daughter. She could fawn.

Well, perhaps not the last part.

She could do this for the man who had most probably scared her husband out of at least one good night's sleep.

Just before they rounded the last corner toward the two French doors guarded by the hulking Cossack, he pulled her to a stop.

"Be careful of Candover," he murmured.

"The duke?"

"Yes."

"Why do I need to be careful of him?"

"And also of Vere Sturbridge, the Duke of Barry."

"He's the Lord Lieutenant in Wellington's army, correct?"

"You've studied the list I see," he said. "And, stay away completely from Edward Godwin, the Duke of Sussex."

"And why is that?"

"I don't know. I just don't think it would be a good idea to spend any amount of time with him. He has a reputation for wearing ladies' jewelry."

"I beg your pardon?!"

"And he has a certain look about him." He paused.

"And what look is that?"

"That wolfish, I-like-all-females look."

"Ah, I see. You mean kind of like the same look you sport?"

"Precisely."

Chapter 5

"**C**andover," Alex said with the slightest of bows, carefully conducted to show neither deference nor offense. The other duke's icy expression, just short of glacial, suggested that forgiveness for instigating the debacle in London was not in Alex's near future.

Candover glanced about the opulent salon, which had been quickly turned out for the august gathering. The upper echelon of London aristocracy graced the room in studied poses. Alex nudged Roxanne Vanderhaven toward Candover. "I should like to present to you my third cousin four times removed, Tatiana Harriet Barclay. Taty, James Fitzroy, the Duke of Candover."

Roxanne curtseyed very prettily in a made-over pale blue walking gown, Alex noticed. She appeared far more slender in the fine silk. And the delicate bones of her face accentuated her natural elegance.

"Your Grace," she said in a cultured, well-modulated voice, "I am honored to meet you."

Candover fondled his gold looking glass and raised it to his eye to peer down at her from his great height. "Delighted," he said, without an ounce of delight in his tone.

"I didn't know your eyesight was failing," Isabelle Tremont said to Candover, with a warm laugh. She stepped around the cool-eyed duke and curtsied in front of Roxanne. "I am the Duchess of March, but please, you must call me Isabelle. Allow me to escort you about, and introduce you to everyone here. There are far too many of us for you to remember all at once, while many of us have the advantage of knowing each other since we were in leading strings." Isabelle paused. "Except for Candover, of course. I cannot imagine him ever in leading strings."

A lady who looked remarkably like a shorter version of the Duke of Candover in a gown laughed. "Isabelle, you're altogether right. Mother always said my brother had such a tantrum the first time they were attached that the governess resigned her post on the spot."

"I'm certain Miss Barclay has very little interest in such things, Faith," the duke replied with a long-suffering sigh.

"Oh, I'm certain she does," another lady said who also looked like Candover. The same prominent nose, dark hair, dark flashing eyes. She, just like her sister, had *character*—that dreadful term that bespoke of little beauty but high intelligence. She continued, "I am Hope, by the way. And those," she nodded toward two other young ladies who obviously had the same parents, "are our other two sisters, Charity and Chastity. Our middle sister, Verity, is . . ."—she paused uneasily, when Candover made an impatient sound—"detained at the estate."

The two youngest sisters curtsied.

Roxanne gained her ease with all the ladies. Very much so—if her smile was any indicator.

Alex had always liked the lovely Duchess of March, but he did not particularly like what she said next.

"You must also meet Sussex."

The charismatic second Duke of Sussex, Edward Godwin, crossed to the mantel and grasped Roxanne's hand to brush his lips against the back of her palm. Alex could see the man looking sideways up into Roxanne's face with a devilish grin.

"Delighted to make your acquaintance, Miss Barclay. I do hope I am not being presumptuous in asking if you would do me the honor of a tour of the Mount before someone else stakes a claim?"

Roxanne's smile widened, and Kress sighed inwardly. *Blast the charmer.* He had the same effect on every damned female—milkmaid and duchess alike. And the opposite effect on every man in possession of a sister, lover, or a wife. Kress had always liked him, until he watched the Englishman's eyes rake down Roxanne's form.

"Of course, Your Grace," she simpered.

Where was the female whom he had had to coax from her room a mere quarter of an hour ago?

"And"—Isabelle marched onward, as if she knew not to give Sussex too much more time to bedazzle and coo—"then, of course, there is Vere Sturbridge, the Duke of Barry. Barry? Miss Barclay."

The other duke's cockade-styled hat was tucked in the crook of one elbow as he bowed over her hand. The harsh, spare dark green of his military uniform left Alex ill at ease. He had seen too many of them during the war. The 95th Rifle Regiment had always been pointing weapons toward, not away, from him.

For some peculiar reason, the other man must have sensed the French dirt under Alex's nails for he was more aloof with him than he was with the other dukes.

Kress wondered who Barry had shot the night of Candover's botched bachelor evening. He'd been unable to discover more details since he had been the first to be booted from Carleton House the morning after. The English officer and duke was far too serious, and far too silent, since the event. However, this did not seem to bother the females overmuch in the salon. Each of them looked at the lord lieutenant's even features with something akin to reverence in their silly countenances.

"Miss Barclay," the Duke of Barry said quietly.

"Your Grace," Roxanne replied a little breathlessly.

"Now then, everyone," Kress inserted before she could say another word. "We can't have all of you standing about while Tatiana makes her curtsies. It will take all night. I say, Isabelle, won't you be so kind as to oversee the tea tray while Taty meets the other guests?"

With that, a small horde of females in the salon gathered about Roxanne to quickly do their duty before concentrating on the main task of prioritizing their efforts to snag one of the four dukes in the room. Their parents followed suit.

Of course there were far too many young ladies present. Alex's gaze bounced to Lady Pamela Hopkins who he had heard was a hardened gambler in a dainty package. At least her fortune was such that it would take at least a decade for her to run through it. Then there was Lady Katherine Leigh, who apparently liked horses more than gentlemen. Her red-haired sister, Lady Judith Leigh, was all giggles and no conversation, according to his great-aunt. Lady Susan Moore was very pretty, just like a doll. She would do if it were not for the lisp, which he understood she affected on purpose in the odd style of the last century.

The only real danger in the salon was in the form of Lady Christine Saveron. There appeared not to be a single defect in her form or in her manner. And his great aunt had spent no less than a quarter of an hour privately detailing all the reasons she was perfect for him, including her parents who appeared equally refined and gracious. Indeed, her mother was French, and her father, English. Mémé had already besieged him with a seating chart that foisted the girl on him at almost every occasion.

Candover sidled up beside him, still fingering his looking glass. "Your third cousin, four times removed, eh?"

"Yes. Great-grandmother Mildred's great-granddaughter."

Candover removed a handkerchief and rubbed his looking glass. "Just assure me she is not your *great* mistress."

"I take offense at your suggestion," Alex replied. "I should call you out. I should—" He made a half-hearted motion to remove a glove in the age-old tradition of slapping it on another gentleman's face.

Candover put a hand on his arm to stop him. "Oh, give over. Look, she shouldn't be here. There should be no distractions from our primary purpose. She's not high enough in the instep nor are her pockets deep enough—even if she is the most intriguing lady present."

"You were much more entertaining in London."

"And you were far less. Now, see here. Just do

your duty, and choose one of these rich chits as soon as decently possible."

"Easy for you to say," Alex said, under his breath, "since Prinny let you off the hook to mourn your furious fiancée."

Candover's face turned to granite, but he refused to rise to the bait. "Look at Sussex and Barry. They know their duty."

Sure enough, the two other dukes had allowed the buzzing horde of young ladies and their smiling parents to besiege them.

And Roxanne? She was near the tea tray with Mémé and Isabelle, who Kress caught staring intently at Candover.

Hmmm. He had always wondered about Isabelle. She was the only female who was a duchess in her own right. The unusual Letters Patent granting the duchy allowed for a female to inherit the title should the Duke of March have no male heirs. And Isabelle had had no siblings. She also had no eyes for anyone except Candover. He glanced at the infamously cool duke and wondered if the man realized the state of affairs. It was worth a test.

"You're absolutely right," Alex murmured. "I know I can confide in you, Candover, since we're both on the same wrong side of the Prince Regent's graces. I've actually been thinking the matter over quite a bit. Do you think the Duchess of March would have me? It would be killing two birds with one stone, don't you think?"

Candover nearly scorched him with a disdainful glare. "I should have guessed you'd try to nick a cradle."

"Oh, come, come. She's of age, is she not?"

"Isabelle was seven and ten last summer."

"Yes, but now it's *this* summer and she is eighteen, no?"

"She is far too young. Look elsewhere. You are old enough to be her—"

"Brother?" Alex threw back his head and laughed. He wondered how long it would be before Candover owned up to his sensibilities. It might just take an ice age.

"I was going to say *father*. And stay away from my sisters."

"I thought it was a well-established fact that you would happily part with any one of your sisters along with a fifty-thousand-pound dowry."

"Any man capable of orchestrating the sort of debacle you did to ruin my marriage cannot be considered suitable in any form for one of my sisters."

"Says the man who swam with swans in the Serpentine."

Annoyance radiated through the other man's stature.

"Oh, come now. No need to be so thin-skinned. I must have been bobbing along with you if the state of my boots the next morning was any indication. Must have been utterly delightful," Alex said with a hint of a smile. "And one day, you might just thank me."

"In your dreams, Kress."

"No. In yours. Oh, and by the by?"

"Yes, you imbecile?"

"Stay away from Harriet."

"You mean Tatiana."

"Yes, Tatiana Harriet," Kress said, examining his fingernails. "I will not approve the suit of any man who has a well-established partiality for frolicking with fowl."

Well, that had gone spectacularly well, Kress

thought as he strode across the room toward the tea tray.

Tea. The beverage designed for negotiating the treacherous course of females with marriage on their minds. The only safe place in the entire castle was here with Isabelle, Roxanne, and Mémé. These were the only three females who would not have him trussed like a pheasant in church before the archbishop, who was to arrive very soon too, since he was equally in disfavor in Town.

"It's too bad, you and Candover don't get on," Isabelle said sweetly.

"I get on very well with him," Alex ground out.

"He's very handsome," Roxanne remarked to Isabelle.

"Handsome as long as you are partial to boorish gentlemen as lifeless as a fishmonger's day-old cod," Kress continued.

"There is that," Isabelle conceded. "But he is a very good man. You just don't know him well."

Kress laughed. "Yes, I must agree. Someone who leaves his future wife cooling her heels at the altar could be considered the best of men."

Isabelle smiled. "It was your fault."

"Forgive me for saying it," Alex said to the duchess, "but you don't seem all that put out about the state of affairs."

"Actually, I enjoy watching gentlemen receive their comeuppance. Don't you, Taty?"

"Always. Well, now that that is settled, would you care for some tea, cousin?" Roxanne asked with a sly smile.

"No," Alex replied.

"You know," Roxanne murmured, forcing a dish of lukewarm tea into his hands, "if you just play up to a person's vanity, you might have far more success."

"Are you speaking about Kress's chances with the eligible ladies or with Candover?" Isabelle giggled.

"I refuse to toady," Alex stated. "Flattery, of course, but no toadying."

It had not been as bad as Roxanne had expected once she had gotten over the fear that someone might recognize her. The ordeal had lasted one hour, and she had kept her wits about her enough to match almost all the names and faces of the four and twenty houseguests.

Dinner had been far more interesting. She'd been placed in the potter's field position at table, between the mother of the girl who lisped and another mother, possibly of the girl who only liked to talk about horses' lineages. There were too many females to even out the numbers. On the bright side, she had an excellent view of the Duke of Sussex, who was seated opposite her.

"My dear," the large lady on one side said, "I do believe my grandmother was the best of friends with your great-grandmother Mildred."

"Was she?" Roxanne managed without choking on the asparagus spear. "Do tell."

"I remember her saying that Mildred Barclay's fondest wish was to unite our two families one day."

"Really?"

The older woman sighed. "They would both be so happy if they could only see my daughter and Kress here tonight."

"In raptures," Roxanne agreed. She really wished she had more control of that fiendish side of her that made its appearance at the worst of times. "And it is so convenient, really."

The lady looked at her expectantly.

Roxanne smiled. "That both your daughter and Kress adore horses above anything else. My cousin has the most wonderful stallion stabled here—smoothest of gaits, even temper, except when he encounters water, if you can imagine. You must tell your daughter to ask Kress to show her the animal."

"Oh, thank you, my dear," the overly eager mother replied. "I shall do precisely that. Perhaps he will give her the horse as a wedding gift."

There was nothing like a mother on the make, unless of course you had a second like-minded mother on the other side of you.

"Well, the duke asked my Susan to stroll the portrait gallery with him after supper," the other lady said—she of the odd French accent and the ostrich feather in her headpiece, which swung triumphantly.

"He asked all the ladies to do that," the other mother replied tartly.

"Perhaps, but he asked Susan *first*," she purred.

At that moment Roxanne's attention, which had been bouncing between the pair of clucking hens, was snagged by the visage of the Duke of Sussex who was grinning at her. Well, at least one person was enjoying the show.

He winked at her. His eyes were so very green against his sun-bronzed complexion, and his hair was like a lion's mane of rich golden hues.

She brought her napkin to her lips to hide her smile.

"I say, Miss Barclay, would you be so kind as to inform what we are all to do after gazing at the generations of your family in the gallery? Do say there is more than a show of dearly departed Kresses to entertain us."

"I understand, Your Grace, that there is to be cards."

"What? No dancing?"

"Not tonight. No musicians have been engaged as of yet."

"Pity," Sussex replied. "I, for one, prefer dancing to cards."

"I do, too," she whispered, biting her lips not to return his grin.

"Well, then it is settled."

"What is settled?"

"I claim the first dance on your card, wherever and whenever your cousin plans the first soirée."

She should know better than to be charmed by this obvious dandy. But she could not help herself. "Delighted, Your Grace." She was obviously fated to make bad choices in all her partners.

Surprisingly, the two mothers had not a single thing to say on the subject of dancing.

An hour later, as the guests strolled into the card-room, Kress had plenty to say on the subject to her. Who knew dukes had such excellent hearing?

The next morning, Roxanne could not manage the idea of facing the hordes again so soon. Her head reeled at the prospect of the mindless, idle chatter. And so, after a tray was delivered to her chamber, which had finally been emptied of a decade's worth of dust due to her own handiwork, she escaped to explore the upper reaches of the castle, where she hoped to ponder her predicament in peace.

There was so much to consider. First, she had to mull over the best fashion to unearth the fortune her intelligent father had secreted for her. This would not be easy to accomplish all alone. Second, she had to figure out how and when she would go away to live out the rest of her life, in the village in Scotland where her ancestors had lived. And lastly, she had to determine exactly how far she was willing to go to risk exposure all in the name of petty, useless, but delicious revenge.

Oh, she knew she was never going to have complete satisfaction. And she wouldn't risk discovery since then she would become the infamous tin miner countess whose husband had loathed her so much that he had tried to murder her. But there had to be a reason he had done it.

Perhaps it would not have happened if she had had a child. She would have liked a child . . . She would have *loved* a child with all the devotion she was capable of giving. But then, Lawrence had never shown any strong desire for an heir. He had adored his younger brother before the latter died, and he equally adored his nephew, who was his heir. The two gentlemen—the older and the younger—were of one mind. Theodore Vanderhaven loved horticulture every bit as much as his doting uncle. Their only difference concerned their sub interests. Lawrence preferred flowering plants and bulbs second to his lawn, while Theo preferred shrubbery and trees. Even now, his nephew was in Ireland, searching for rare shrubs.

As she crossed a vast expanse of fraying carpet covering an endless series of long passages, Roxanne stumbled upon a curving staircase and heard male voices in the distance. She advanced to the next story and turned a corner only to find a treacherous break in the castle wall and flooring.

Two men and a younger one in ragged clothing were deep in conversation.

"I'm telling you that it can't be done," said the older tradesman, he of the bulging belly.

"And I'm saying it can," the middle-aged thinner man insisted. "Provided similar stone can be found. What do you say, young man?"

"There is a stone quarry northwest of here, in a place called the Lizard. You'll find stone very like this there." He could not have been more than eight and ten. His clothes spoke of humble origins, but his face spoke of something more. The two older men looked at him with doubt.

The younger one suddenly turned to find her before she could back away in her quest for privacy.

He tugged on his dark forelock. "Ma'am."

The other two London tradesmen instantly removed their hats and bowed while echoing the greeting.

"So sorry to interrupt," she said in the cramped hallway. "I should—" she started to turn away from the group.

"Pardon me, ma'am," the thin tradesman begged.

She slowly turned back 'round. "Yes?"

"Would you happen to know about stone quarries in the area?"

She tried to bite her tongue. Really she did. But it was that innate desire to please that always reared its ugly head at the wrong moment, as well as the fact that she knew the county better than almost anyone. It was where she'd lived all of her life. "Um, well, you see . . . I'm not really from this neighborhood. But, I do believe that His Grace mentioned during the tour here that there are two excellent stone quarries. The first is in the Lizard as was just mentioned, and the second—"

"Was almost three miles farther north," a familiar voice said behind her.

She whirled around only to find Alexander Barclay looking at her, with an arched brow.

"It is excellent to know that you paid such careful attention to my ramblings, cousin," he continued.

"How could I not?" She tried not to laugh.

The three men behind her hemmed and hawed.

"Good day, Mr. Wooling, Mr. Townson." Kress nodded.

The tradesmen bowed deeply.

Kress studied the ruined, unstable hallway. "Please tell me you are not relying on my dearest cousin, who knows nothing about rebuilding castles, to find materials?"

The larger of the two gathered up his nerve. "But you told us you, uh, you, uh . . ."

"Yes?" he insisted.

"Pardon me, Your Grace, but you said you didn't give a fig about how or where we found the stone, or how we were to go about it."

Roxanne bit her lower lip to keep from smiling.

"You're correct, Wooling. But you're leaving out the most important part. I want to see your plans, your estimates, and in a timely fashion. Indeed, the Prince Regent insists upon it. I had hoped," he paused for effect, "that this would be a test—or bid—between the two of you to see how you each *independently* would suggest a plan to restore this pile of rubble." He looked at her from his heavy-lidded eyes. "Come along, my dear. Mémé insists you join the ladies on some sort of wild mushroom gathering expedition. Lord only knows how she thinks she'll find mushrooms in her condition."

The two men nearly fell to their knees in an effort

to get back into the duke's good graces. He tolerated their jumble of apologies for only so long before he escorted her out of their hearing.

"There is no other stone quarry within three miles of the one on the Lizard."

"And how was I to know that?" he replied indignantly.

"Well, then why did you say there was?"

"Because you told them I knew of two stone quarries. I didn't want to make a liar out of you."

She inhaled. "So you lied instead."

"Precisely. And why do I not hear you thanking me?"

"I'm supposed to thank you for misleading those two men?"

"Not at all. Everyone should be thanking me. That young man, John Goodsmith, is the only person they will need to turn to for help. I just ensured that they would."

She paused. "Wild mushroom hunting?"

"Something like that," he murmured, looking down at her from his greater height. "Or perhaps something else."

Suddenly, Roxanne Vanderhaven, the not-so-deceased wife of the Earl of Paxton, felt as if most of the air had left the narrow passageway. He was standing far too close to her, and she was not backing away. His voice was far too rough and tumble, and his eyes were intoxicating in the way of fine wine.

The thought reminded her of Lawrence and the pride he took in his wine cellar—the one she had organized for him using his vast stores of smuggled goods.

She stepped back.

"Coward," he whispered.

"Devil," she hissed.

He laughed, his eyes crinkling in the corners. "You are ruining the moment."

"What moment?"

"The moment when I was going to find out what sort of courage you really had."

"Courage?" She widened her eyes in astonishment. "Courage? Why, that's the most ridiculous thing I've ever heard. What has this to do with courage? You were about to take liberties."

He stepped closer. "Liberties? I've never heard it called that before. Only an Englishwoman would call it *liberties*." He made a funny face when he said the word. "Sounds almost revolutionary."

"And only a Frenchman would suggest a kiss was courageous."

"So you think I was about to kiss you?" He said it with such innocence on his face that now she was the one who felt like a fool.

Perhaps he hadn't meant to kiss her at all.

"Not that I think it would be a bad idea," he continued dispassionately. "Not a bad idea at all. While I'll not risk stealing a kiss from any of the simpering virgins setting their sights on me here, you are different. And both of us know nothing can come of it. But I think it's obvious that there is a certain attraction between us and—"

"So you admit you like me," she interrupted.

"Of course, who could not admire an irregular woman such as you?"

"So I'm irregular? Sounds singularly unattractive. Like a grammatical problem actually."

"Not at all. Your face is a symphony of features

blended to perfection, and your manner? Nothing but pluck mixed with verve."

"I've never liked compliments."

He laughed. "Of course you don't."

She tucked a loose curl behind her ear. "Well, I'm married."

"No," he said slowly. "You're dead."

"And that makes it better?" she blustered and then changed course. "You know, perhaps I like Sussex more."

"*Impossible.*" The slight French accent made her all the more nervous.

Ah, but there was a spark of worry in his eyes, she was certain.

"He at least had the decency to ask me to dance before he might try to kiss me."

"So you will kiss a man who you dance with but not the man who saved you, and also took the trouble to attend your funeral? Not to mention housing and clothing you without anything more than an ugly ring in return?"

"Exactly," she retorted.

"Then I claim the second dance."

"You haven't even named the date of a soirée."

"But, of course, I did. If you hadn't left your funeral early . . . It's June twenty-sixth, at the ungodly early hour of seven o'clock for those we must feed, nine o'clock for those we must water."

"Well, perhaps I will be too hot from dancing the first with Sussex."

"Then, perhaps I should warn you that your husband has invited himself, so you might want to reconsider dancing altogether."

She suddenly felt deflated.

The duke paused, and then tilted up her chin to examine her face.

"You're not going to cry are you?"

"Absolutely not. I'm not the sort who cries about being an idiot for marrying a man who tried to kill me."

Alex had the most unnerving way of looking at her. She had not a clue what he was thinking, and she very much feared he knew precisely every last thought in her head. She lifted her chin.

"You're not going to attend the ball," he said slowly.

"That's not what I was thinking."

"Really?"

"Really."

"Then what, pray tell, were you thinking?"

She was so glad females had much quicker brains than men. "That you should be forewarned about my dear husband's unusual diet."

His brows drew together, and a funny wrinkle appeared between them. "I beg your pardon?"

"He only eats things with eyes."

"And dare I ask why he would do that?" Faint amusement teased the corners of his mouth.

"He loves plants so well, he always said he could never kill fruits and vegetables and grains, only animals."

"What about potatoes? Potatoes have eyes."

She rolled her own.

"Delightful," he said dryly. "Well, then I shall terrify him with bloody raspberries and carrots, and maybe even fresh-cut asparagus, but not a hint of meat, fish, or fowl. I shall tell everyone that evening that I do not eat anything containing a heart except artichokes. It shall also have the added benefit of making the neighboring families think twice before accepting any future invitations."

She felt an enormous grin overtaking her. "It would be delicious to see the expression on his face during dinner."

"Look . . ." He exhaled roughly. "Much as it would entertain us both, I must ask you not to go about spying. I think Candover and the Prince Regent himself would publicly execute me on the spot if even a breath of scandal emits from the Mount."

"Well then, why are you helping me?"

"Lord only knows."

Chapter 6

S he had the worst sense of déjà vu.

When Roxanne had been two and ten, during the era when the former Earl of Paxton had resided at the estate that would one day become her home, she had shimmied up a tree and spied on the guests of a summer ball. Mesmerized by the shimmering ball gowns of every hue and design, she had clung to a branch in the shadows and watched the couples dance. Never had she seen so many beeswax candles dripping and glowing from chandeliers, wall sconces, and candelabras.

It had been simply intoxicating. She had envisioned herself perfumed, and bedecked in finery, with a dance card overflowing with lords' names on her wrist, all whilst smiling behind the back of a Chinese silk fan with a handsome gentleman before her. And he was smiling back at her, drowning in all the witticisms she would utter.

Her vivid imagination had never served her well in her childhood.

Now she was two decades older and wiser. But she was back in the shadows all over again. The only difference was that she was not up in a tree, but behind it; and it was St. Michael's Mount, not Paxton Hall. At least she had no interest in trading barbs with any of the gentlemen she spied through the windows.

She had enough of that every time she saw the Duke of Kress, whether she liked it or not. And she rather feared she liked it too much.

But right now she was far more interested in how she could scare her husband into an early grave. The skunk was sweating all over a petite dark-haired young lady Roxanne knew from their neighborhood. Miss Lillian Tillworth, possessor of a very modest dowry, was just out of the schoolroom. Barely.

And they were waltzing.

Anger had finally gotten the better of her self-pity. Why? Why had he left her to die such a horrid death? Alex might think it had to do with her fortune. But Lawrence had no way of ever finding it, nor was he even certain of its existence. And here he was falling all over the charms of a dainty miss without a fortune. Had she been a nagging wife? Or was the stink of trade on her person just too odious for her high and mighty husband?

Lawrence's black hair was drawn up in a fashionable queue, and he was wearing his finest blue coat; his lapel bore one of his ridiculous concoctions of feminine flowers. And for the first time since she had laid eyes on him, his striking face did not register as handsome at all.

What she felt was anger, yes. That was the pain she felt in her sternum. It had to be. She absently rubbed the chisel she had hidden in the deep pocket of Mémé's cast-off aubergine lace ball gown that had been lengthened for her.

She had until tomorrow morning to come up

with a plausible excuse for not having attended the ball. Mémé would not settle for a simple reason. Until then—

A shadow fell across her in the moonlight. She edged farther around the base of the large oak.

"Miss Barclay?" The deep voice was not one she recognized. "It is only I, Barry."

She exhaled in a rush and turned toward him.

"Oh, Your Grace." She curtsied slightly.

"I see you are not over fond of entertainments," he said. "Nor am I."

She spoke too quickly. "Actually, I love balls, but it was too hot inside."

He laughed. "Finally."

"Finally, what?"

"A lady who is not afraid to disagree with me."

"Has it been that awful this past week?"

"Worse than you can imagine."

She smiled. "Well, if it shall please you, let us discuss all the things that I might like that you do not. You have nothing to fear from me. I'm not in search of a husband."

"And why is that? I thought all unattached females were in want of a husband."

As usual, she had managed to lead a gentleman to the very topic she least wanted to discuss.

"Well, you see, Your Grace—"

"Vere. I sense we are to become great friends."

"All right, then, Vere." *Think quickly—very, very quickly.* "I am too old and set in my ways. For example, I cannot be persuaded to loath entertainments and most gentlemen prefer just about anything to dancing. Except, of course, the Duke of Sussex."

"Ah, so Sussex has the edge on the rest of us."

The man had a way of speaking that sent a shiver

up her spine. It wasn't of fear. It was just the opposite. His voice was like her father's preferred whiskey, drizzling over ice. It was deep and mysterious, just like his true character she sensed under his careful, cool façade. "No, not at all." *Must change the subject.* "So—other ideas we might disagree on . . . What food do you like least?"

"Biscuits," he replied immediately. "I think most in the militia would agree that a steady diet of hard biscuits is tiresome."

"Hmmm. Well, I adore biscuits. Chocolate ones, and sugar ones. Even hardened ones."

"I see," he said finally, allowing a crack of a smile in the moonlight.

"There," she said sweetly. "That proves my point."

"And what point is that?"

"We can only ever be friends."

"But, I'll allow, chocolate and sugar biscuits are perfectly acceptable. You see, Miss Barclay, I am capable of compromise."

"Alas, but I am not. I will only truly adore a man who loves to dance, and who *craves* all biscuits."

A full smile overspread the Duke of Barry's face, transforming the harsh, hollow angles into a thing of mesmerizing splendor in the night.

"You should smile more often," she said without thinking.

He chuckled. "Care to dance, Miss Barclay?"

"No"—another male voice, far more familiar, interrupted her answer—"she does not care to dance."

"Kress," the Duke of Barry said with surprise.

"Barry," he replied curtly. "What are you doing here? I cannot allow you to cavort in private with my cousin. Are there not plenty of other chits inside, all panting after the chance for a dance with you?"

"I've danced with half of them," the Duke of Barry said. "And I needed a respite. Miss Barclay and I *both agree*"—he looked at her and winked—"that it is too hot inside."

"No, it's that you loath all entertainments. Candover warned me about you," Kress replied.

"And what are you doing out here . . . deserting your post, are you?"

"Not at all. It's like an inferno in there."

Roxanne stifled a giggle. Both gentlemen looked at her.

And then, to add to the absurd conversation, a feminine voice with an awful lisp called out from the balustrade. "Your Gwace? Oh, yoo-hoo, is the Duke of Bawwyy in the gawden? The minuet is fowming."

Kress's smile widened. "Your future calls, Bawwy."

The Duke of Barry exhaled in annoyance. "As does yours, Kwess."

"Go on," Kress purred.

Barry departed with such reluctance that his ramrod straight posture sagged for the slightest moment.

Kress watched him leave and slowly turned to face her.

Again, she felt as if he was too close to her. And yet . . . she wanted him closer. *Sort of*. Another part of her wanted to push him away. She was tiring of the game and it was putting her off her main purpose.

Distance. What she needed was distance. "You were right."

"Of course I was right." Confusion darted across his face. "About what, precisely?"

"That I shouldn't be here. Spying. I shall see you

tomorrow. I'm going to take a roundabout way back to the servants' entrance."

Before he could reply, she turned and walked quickly away from the castle, running headlong into the darkness. She skipped down the three little stone steps to the lower lawn and then continued on, a gurgle of emotion, something like laughter and sadness, rushed past her throat.

She knew not if he followed her, but she darted to the left and continued toward the one place she doubted anyone would find her.

She'd discovered a small pool behind some of the very tall sea grasses on the southern portion of the outcropping. Carved into ancient granite, the pool appeared as if a giant had punched the rock and placed moss about the edges in remorse.

Roxanne tossed off her borrowed slippers, now surely grass-stained, and rolled off the fine white silk stockings. She sat on the cast-off items to protect the back of the ball gown, and dangled her feet in the cool water.

Heaven. This was heaven. She wished she could stay here all night and pretend that none of the last few weeks had ever happened. Instead, she drowned in memories of the past, when she knew who she was and where she belonged.

There was a little pond on the Paxton estate and she had sometimes gone there late in the evening with Eddie—during those overwarm summer nights when her husband had consumed too much from the wine cellar, and then snored in his leather chair in the study. She had dared to do what she had done as a girl near the small lake on her father's property. She'd shed her gown *and* her undergarments, and dove into the water stark naked all to recapture the joy of her girlhood.

But now, she did not dare. She was too old for that sort of nonsense.

"Why am I guessing you prefer swimming to dancing?" A male voice came from behind her.

She didn't need to turn her head. "I'll tell you why I like swimming if you tell me why you always like to sneak up behind me."

"I suppose it's a reflex from a former life," he said quietly.

"I suppose you will refuse to explain?"

"Correct."

"Well, then I shall say the same. Swimming is a reflex from a former life, too."

"Fair enough," he murmured. "Everyone is allowed their secrets."

In her heart, she *had* known that he would find her. And she had a very good idea of what might happen. There was a small part of her that wanted this—wanted to prove that she was not too old, not so unappealing that someone would leave her to die on a cliff. Could she still be the same girl she had been when she was much younger and life had held so much promise?

There would be no harm and certainly no future in it. But at least there would be something other than the pain of the past—even if it meant more pain in the future. And most importantly, it would hurt no one other than herself. She heard rustling just behind her and then her throat clogged and she could not manage a single witty comment.

Alexander Barclay sat down beside her, his elegant black velvet footwear gone, his fashionable stockings below his black satin knee breeches drawn off as well. He dangled his lower legs in the water beside her.

For once not a single word was spoken between them.

Time drifted. And for the first time since her father had died, she felt the simple pleasure of sharing silence with someone, without the discomfort of feeling the need to fill it with nonsense, which it seemed she was only capable of uttering to this gentleman.

A few minutes later, she felt the warmth of his palm cover her hand, resting on the moss between them.

She turned to stare at him, only the sliver of moonlight guiding her vision. His brown eyes were black in the evening shade, his skin shadowed white.

She inhaled and leaned toward him. "Kiss me," she whispered.

"I thought—"

"Stop talking," she interrupted softly.

Suddenly, strong arms drew her across his lap, and she didn't care that the hem of the gown was getting wet.

He drew her into the crook of his arm, and tucked her tight against his chest. He stared down at her and brushed a lock of her hair from her cheek. "You know," he whispered, "this is the best idea you've had so far." His expression defied his words.

She wrapped her free arm around his neck and tugged him down to her. "Well, do you want to kiss me or not?"

It was the first time in her life that she had instigated a kiss. She strained to get closer to him. His scent was vibrant—of man, of ardor, of clean sweat, and old-world elegance. He searched her eyes for a long moment before he bent toward her.

His mouth caressed hers, nudging, nibbling, and finally urging her lips to part. She could barely breathe with the insanity of it. She shivered involuntarily at his slow, deep kiss—and he pulled her ever closer to his body until there was no space dividing them.

His tongue played at the seam of her lips and then beyond, finally intertwining with her own. All this while he caressed the nape of her neck, and teased the curls there before he cradled her head in his hand.

Great waves of emotion flooded her, leaving her numb with shock. But she would not shrink away from the intimacy of it. She was parched, but now filled with desire, and something else she could not name. It all felt so wonderful, and yet . . . wicked and wrong.

But wicked was better than where her proper, virtuous life had led her until a fortnight ago.

His mouth eased from hers. "Mmmmmm . . ." he murmured. "You taste divine. Like—"

"No ridiculous compliments," she whispered raggedly.

She felt his mouth curve into a smile as he dragged his lips along the column of her neck. Her heart was hammering and she could feel the blood pounding in her veins.

He tenderly kissed the wild pulse point on her neck. "Thank you for making this seduction so easy."

"I rather think it is me who is doing the seducing. The older taking advantage of the—"

His hand dipped inside her gown's bodice and cupped her breast, and she could not have continued if her life had depended upon it. Her small breasts had always been her greatest embarrassment.

"You were saying?" Without preamble, he pushed her breast past the edge of her gown, exposing the nipple. He leaned in and took the whole of it into his mouth; his tongue swirling the suddenly ruched tip.

Oh God. What was he doing? Worse, what was she doing?

Or what should she not be doing? She didn't want to have to think. She just wanted to do. To experience. To live. Was it wrong? For her entire life she had always taken the high road, taken the correct, moral road. She was the patron saint of always doing the proper thing.

"Why do I suddenly get the feeling that I'm the only one enjoying this?" Alex nipped the bud of her breast and then examined her face with his hooded eyes.

"What would you do if I agreed?" she asked, her voice uneven.

"I'd know that I'm going about this all wrong."

She exhaled with a shaky laugh.

"Let's start again from the top." Despite the humor in his words, his dark eyes were still studying her, gauging her. "Look, it's all right if we just don't remove all our clothes, right?"

She looked at him, and finally laughed, relaxing her nerves. "How many have fallen for that ruse?"

"You'd be surprised."

She pushed slightly away, regret obvious in her action.

"Oh, no, you don't," he said, gently pulling her back. "This was all your idea, remember?"

"Yes. The best bad idea I've had so far. I remember," she mumbled.

He laughed. "It isn't so bad after all. All in all I would say it was an excellent idea."

"You would say that. You're French."

"Half. The English part of me will be begging your forgiveness tomorrow for taking advantage of your suggestion tonight. It might even include a sorrowful yet dutiful proposal of marriage."

"Which you will offer only because you know I will refuse since *I am already married.*" The last she said with exasperation.

"Look . . . just stay," he growled. "You can hit me, blame me, whatever you like, but I don't want to let you go."

"It's hard to resist an offer like that," she said, biting back a smile. It felt so right . . . to be able to speak her mind. Not to hold back. Not to put on airs or walk on eggshells. No matter what she said to this man, he never became angry or sullen, or disagreeable. And he didn't lie to her. At least she hoped he did not. More to the point, he spoke to her as an equal.

And now he was as good as his words and changed tactics. He leaned in and kissed her. Not the earlier gentle, slow kisses. These were primal, male, I've-got-you-and-you-won't-say-no arrogant kisses. He nipped at her upper lip and demanded entrance. And when she capitulated, he ransacked her emotions with that hellish tongue that made her want more. His hand held the back of her head in place and she could do naught but keep her balance during the onslaught. This was not the kiss of a gentleman. It was the kiss of someone who knew all about pleasure, and was used to getting his way, since no woman in her right mind would ever deny him.

And she was definitely in her right mind.

His gaze drifted to her exposed breast. "Such beauty, such—No, I won't say . . ."

If she didn't know better, he almost seemed three sheets to the wind.

"I'll just show . . ."

The tip of her breast was so tight it ached. As if he could read her mind, he again drifted down and soothed her tender flesh with his mouth. She could have shouted for the pleasure coursing through her, all emanating from that one delicate point on her body. His tongue teased her, licked her, and gently nipped her, causing violent sensations unlike any she had ever known.

And that was just the beginning, for he would not stop until he duplicated every lush movement upon her other breast. All the while his hands massaged her back, the curve of her waist, her head, and finally, his fingers traced the contours of her face.

She felt revered. No, desired.

He paused, drew his face to hers, and closed his eyes before resting his forehead to hers. "*Cherie* . . ."

"No, don't say anything," she stopped him. "Just kiss me one last time and then we must end this foolishness. We must go back . . ."

For once he did not argue with her, or even try to find humor in her words. He simply kissed her with barely reined-in lust. He held back nothing. It was as if she was an exotic flavor to savor, and he was starving. Then again, what did she know of gentlemen and kissing? Other than Lawrence's kisses, which in comparison had been very few and very limpid, she was singularly lacking in sensual sophistication. Through sheer desperation, she refused to drown in Kress's dark embrace.

And just like all good things in life, it came to an end. Little did she know that this little slice of insanity was just the prelude to the evening from hell.

* * *

She just had not had enough time to learn all the nooks and crannies of this jumbled pile. The servant's side entrance, which she used to try to escape to her chamber high in the castle, did not lead to stairs above the main floor—the same level as the ballroom.

Her hem was sodden, her coiffure surely a wreck, but more important than all of that, she would never dare attempt the main stair for fear of running into Lawrence. Or the comtesse. Or anyone for that matter.

She peeked around a column in the hall, only to watch as the ballroom doors opened outward. Lord, someone would see her. Roxanne had but a moment to dash into the nearest chamber, a small, inelegant room the comtesse used to escape from the houseguests when she chose. It featured a single sofa facing the door, and two uncomfortable chairs that promised short visits by all those unfortunate enough to attempt to sit in them.

In the off chance she would be found, Roxanne ducked behind the light blue velvet sofa. And, of course, a moment later she heard the door scrape open and the murmurs and music from the ballroom became louder before the door reshut with a click.

She could barely breathe. Was it Alexander? She dared not take a peek. She had only a moment of suspense before the smooth voice of her husband reached her ears.

"Oh, my dear Miss Tillworth . . . My dear, dear, dearest . . ."

Repetition had always been Lawrence's strong suit, Roxanne thought with ill-timed humor lacing the overall horror.

"My lord," the soft voice of their neighbor's

daughter, the one who used to wear unpinned plaits not so very long ago, replied with uncertainty. "I don't think Mama or Papa would approve of us leaving the ballroom," she cooed.

"Oh, but when one is in mourning, there are times when the need for solitude overcomes me," he replied sadly. "And you, my dainty flower, have been the only one who has brought me any measure of relief from my sadness."

Dainty flower? Roxanne wasn't sure if she felt more like gagging or crying. She could never be called a dainty flower. More like a stalk of sea grass.

"Perhaps I should leave you, then." The girl hesitated. "To your solitude, I mean."

"Oh, no, no, no, no, no, my dear."

Since when had Lawrence acquired a stutter?

"Sometimes solitude can only be gained by being with someone else," her eel of a husband insisted.

"I don't understand," Miss Tillworth said, a single plume of intelligence shafting the air.

"Of course, you don't," Lawrence replied. "You are too young and fragile to comprehend the mind of a man who has suffered so long."

"But the countess only died two or three weeks ago."

Roxanne sort of liked Miss Tillworth.

"But it seems an eternity," Lawrence purred. He changed tactics. "And you are the balm that soothes. Your sweetness, your gentility, your—"

Miss Tillworth's voice interrupted. "Mama said I was only to allow a gentleman to kiss my hand. And only gloved. A gentleman may only kiss my cheek if he declares himself."

Roxanne liked Miss Tillworth's mother even more.

"Forgive me, I find it hard to restrain myself in your delicate presence, my loveliest Lillian."

"And Papa said there must be a year of mourning at the very least—lest there be talk, which would taint my reputation and ultimately our respectability if we were ever to marry."

Miss Tillworth's father's cool assessment was like a bucket of seawater thrown in Roxanne's face. Good God. They had already spoken of marriage? Roxanne glanced down at the flounce on her gown and realized it might be in sight if one of the pair looked over the sofa's arm. She jerked it closer.

"What was that?" Miss Tillworth's voice became decidedly less genteel.

"Pardon?" Lawrence asked forlornly.

"That sound."

"Perhaps it's my belly. Can't stop it from growling. Did you not notice that our host served only tiny, innocent vegetables and fruits? It was a crime, I tell you."

"It wasn't your intestines, my lord."

"Well, I couldn't eat a bite. And now, I'm starving."

"It sounded more like a mouse. I don't like mice. They can run up a petticoat," Miss Tillworth babbled. "It happened to me," she squeaked. "Just last week."

"My dear, calm yourself. Here, tuck your slippers into my lap," said the older man to the young girl. "Everyone has fears."

"But you probably don't," Miss Tillworth said, voice shaking.

She had obviously been tutored in the art of flattery even if she did exhibit good sense in fighting off a lecherous widower.

"Well, I am not afraid of anything except . . ."

Oh, he'll be afraid of more than one thing by the time I leave if there is anything right in this world, Roxanne thought.

"Except . . ." he repeated, "moles."

"Pardon me?" Miss Tillworth asked.

Roxanne bit her knee to keep from making a sound. She could not believe how idiotic her husband was, how blind she had been, and how far-sighted her beloved father had proved to be.

His voice betrayed his defensive posture. "It's not unusual. No one wants vile, sightless underground creatures tearing up years of labor and perfection. And then there are also locusts to worry about, and—"

The sound of the door scraping open interrupted Lawrence. Roxanne heard the couple jump to their feet awkwardly. She prayed it was someone who would save her from her predicament.

"Your Grace," her husband exhaled.

"Paxton," Alex replied. "And?"

"Miss Lillian Tillworth," the girl replied.

"Miss Tillworth?" Alex repeated. "Oh, I'm sorry, I thought you were Paxton's *daughter.*"

"No, not at all, Your Grace. I'm—"

"Well, Miss Tillworth, do you think you should be alone with this gentleman? Your parents might . . . Or worse, all of society here might . . ." He let the words drift.

"We were only discussing, um, *moles,* Your Grace," the girl said, her awe apparent.

"Moles?" He was very good at ducal hauteur and disinterest mixed with distaste.

"Devious devils that can destroy a lifetime's work," Lawrence replied with fervor.

"The same could be said of a gentleman alone with a young lady," Alex retorted.

Roxanne Vanderhaven, the not very deceased wife of the Earl of Paxton heard her dog bark, which made her smile. Maybe Alex had let Eddie loose, and her dog would give Lawrence a quick, viscious bite just below the ankle, where the flesh was most tender. At least then her husband would leave alive instead of suffering a heart seizure. Yes, she had spent the last quarter hour tempted beyond measure to rise from the dead to torture and terrify the living.

Where in hell was she? Alex restrained the silly mutt in his arms. He'd entered the castle's side entrance a minute after her, only to find a sprawl of guests crowding through the main salon's doors to the grand hall. He was afraid Roxanne hadn't been able to escape unnoticed. Then, he'd found Eddie standing in front of the closed door, his head cocked to one side and his tail wagging.

Well, if she wasn't in here, at least he would accomplish the one and only task he'd planned for this entire, ridiculous evening.

It had not been often that he had had the means to see through a brilliant idea in the past. But here and now, this was a true chef d'oeuvre that could not be denied. And a prank like this was just the sort he favored most.

He'd involved his valet in part of the scheme—the construction of the tiny lead canister now dangling from Eddie's collar. But the rest of the plan was all Alex's own. It harked back to his dark days as a courier in the French Hussars.

Both Paxton and Miss Tillworth had been silenced with his last comment. The girl looked like she'd give her eye teeth to be anywhere but in this chamber. At that same moment, Alex spied a hint of ruffled aubergine silk gown at the back corner of the ugly blue sofa.

He smiled.

"Your Grace, my lord," Miss Tillworth said with the correct amount of color cresting her cheeks. "If you will excuse me, I must find my mother. And, um, thank you for your advice, Your Grace. You are entirely correct, of course."

"I always am," Alex replied. "And your extreme good sense shows by following my suggestions, like every other female I know, save one." He could swear he heard a sigh coming from the vicinity of the sofa.

"Miss Tillman," the earl inserted, "do be a dear and remind your parents that the barouche shall await all of us at half twelve."

The soft click of the door behind her signaled the privacy Alex had desired.

"Kress, it is not as it appears—"

"Oh, I'm sorry. I did not realize I'd given you leave to address me so informally. An invitation to a soirée does not naturally confer . . ." Alex let his words drift in the stifling air in the room.

"Pardon me, Your Grace. I did not mean to cause—"

"None taken," he interrupted. "None at all. In fact, I'd intended for us to become friends. Great friends. Are we not two of the most important gentlemen of distinction in Cornwall?"

The most divine look of confusion crossed the other man's face. "Uh, yes, and of course, Helston, who is on an extended sailing voyage," the earl replied, ill at ease.

"Well, then." Alex slapped the idiot on his back,

almost sending him flying. Eddie growled under his arm. "Good dog," Alex said under his breath.

"I do not mean to take up any more of your time, Your, um," the earl said, stopping just short of attempting an incorrect title.

"Not at all, Paxton. Do have a seat. I long for a good coze. Like two old biddies at their embroidery. Lovely posies, by the way."

The man actually preened. "Thank you. I was hoping they would bloom this very morning so I could display them for you tonight. You have an interest in horticulture?"

"Not at all," Alex replied, petting the dog. "What's that sound?" He cocked his head.

The earl's face grew flushed to the roots of his black hair. "A mouse?"

"I'd say it came from your intestines. I should know. The French are experts in digestion. Your condition isn't surprising, really."

"Surprising?"

"Well, everyone noticed you did not eat the dinner my great-aunt's chef prepared so carefully in your honor since I understood you prefer plants to anything. It was a great insult actually."

"I—I did not mean to imply—"

"Forget it, Paxton. You're probably experiencing a *crise de foie*—a crisis of the liver. I'll arrange for your dinner to be packed in a basket. You can write a long note detailing your appreciation to my great-aunt at your leisure."

The earl's eyes bounced from object to object in the room, too uncomfortable to rest on his face. Alex sighed. The man was too stupid to even play the game.

"I've been pondering your obvious grief from the death of the countess."

"She was the best of wives," Paxton said with the clear-eyed, innocent gaze of an inveterate liar.

Eddie yowled.

The earl continued as if the dog had not made a sound. "I do miss her most dreadfully."

Miss her boot polishing, thought Alex sourly upon examining the state of the earl's footwear. "And so . . ."

"Yes?"

"Well, I thought you might like a token to remem—"

"What sort of—"

"I don't like to be interrupted, Paxton," Alex said interrupting the other man.

"Of course, Your Grace."

"You may call me Peter."

"But I thought your name was . . ." The earl stopped abruptly. "Of course, Peter."

"So I thought you might like a token," Alex recommenced, glancing down at the dog in his arms.

Paxton had the most amusing expression of confusion mixed with horror in his countenance—as if he knew what the dog would do to the wilting concoction on his lapel if the earl dared to touch a single hair on Eddie.

"Oh, no, you misunderstand," Alex continued. "I could not bear to part with the dog at present. Did you know he likes to sleep under the covers? How he doesn't suffocate under all those bedclothes, I'll never know."

"You allow him in your bed?" The earl's eyebrows were close to his hairline.

"Not at all. He sleeps with Mémé—my great-aunt. You must ask her to tell you all about it," he continued. "Ah, but you have led me off course. I thought you might like his collar as a token. Perhaps you might like to place it on the hat's grave." Alex unbuckled the dog's collar and handed it to the earl, who accepted it with two pinched fingers, as if it was contaminated with lice.

This would never do, thought Alex. The man would likely throw the thing away without a second glance. "Interesting tin ornament on the collar. I, of course, would never pry, but we have all of us been wondering what it signifies."

Paxton darted his eyes to the article. "Oh, um, *that*. It's merely a bit of tin," he muttered a little too loudly as his eyes grew round with excitement. "You know my beloved wife's father once held the largest string of tin and copper mines in the area near Redruth."

"And now?"

"He sold it all, within the last year of his life."

"Why, you must be a very rich man, then, Paxton, albeit hugely tarnished by your association with trade. I don't know how you tolerated it to begin with. Tell me, was it worth it?"

He should be outraged. He should be honorable. He should be blustering. Paxton was not. He was, instead, captivated by the item on the collar, which he had *finally* divined was a container of sorts.

"Pardon me, um . . . I'm afraid the sight of a token from my wife's pet has, indeed, undone me. Will you excuse me if I take my leave of you now? I find I must return home if only to spare others my grief."

"One can only keep one's mourning in hiding for so long, Paxton. I fully understand your predicament. I shall tell my great-aunt that she must call on you, to better her acquaintance with the only other gentleman of worth in Cornwall. I'm certain she would enjoy sampling offerings from your gardens as well."

His face became gray. "You are too kind," he croaked. But Paxton was already off the couch and backing away toward the door, as if Alex was the Prince Regent himself.

With his departure, Alex crossed the room, locked the door, and pocketed the key—eliminating all chance of escape.

When he turned to face her, she was brushing the wrinkles from the tight-fitting gown before she spoke. "And just what was that bit about Eddie's collar?"

"A way to further your objective."

"My objective?"

"To make your husband realize that an asylum is a place he should very soon desire to make his residence above all things."

"And what is in this famous canister?"

"Just a scrap of paper."

"A scrap of paper."

"Yes. A rude map of Paxton's estate with quite a lot of Xs in certain spots."

She bit her lips to keep from smiling, but the crinkles near her lovely eyes gave her away. "You took the trouble to go to Paxton Hall?"

"Um, no," he lied as he took a step closer to her.

"Really?"

"I have no time for such nonsense." He closed the gap between them. "Sent someone else," he said, voice lower.

Her expression confirmed she didn't believe a word he said. "I see. And the Xs . . ."

"Are in the gardens, I suppose. You did say Paxton is particularly partial to his smelly roses."

Alex drew her close and nudged with his nose a curl next to her ear.

"And irises," she whispered.

"And his ancient, deep-rooted flowering bushes—impossible to replace." He kissed a pulse point on her temple.

"Um, do you know where I could find a dozen or so hungry moles?" Her eyes sparkled.

"You are the least romantic creature I've ever encountered," he whispered.

She giggled in that fashion he was beginning to relish. A deep throaty sound that made him happy—a most curious sensation he'd almost forgotten.

Chapter 7

For some ungodly reason, the next morning Alex awoke with the chickens, something he had not done since his boyhood and his stint serving Napoleon, which he was loath to remember.

He realized why he was awake when he felt warm quivering along his gut.

Her bloody dog was in his bed again, dreaming about chasing rabbits or Paxton, no doubt. The canine, he had learned, was as fickle in his choice of sleeping partners as a Hyde Park light-skirt, and snored just as loudly. In fact, Eddie made the rounds most nights, worming his way under Mémé's bedclothes, or his own whenever the dog skulked away from Roxanne's distant chamber. Alex rolled onto his back and the entire massive bed heaved and creaked. This was Eddie's reveille, and the mutt tunneled his way up from the darkness and licked Alex's face, leaving traces of decidedly pungent dog breath.

In dawn's early chill, Alex gave up any pretense of trying to sleep and hurriedly dressed without calling for his valet. The dog danced about on his legs until Alex ordered him to stop. Eddie dropped his front paws to the floor and tilted his funny white head with the one large black spot eye.

A quarter hour later found Alex walking the perimeter of St. Michael's Mount, an uncertain peace settling over him. Eddie trotted ahead of him into the western shadow of the Mount. Instinctively, Alex glanced up. Several workmen were already laying new stone work to repair the crumbling edifice of the turret. A small plume of an unknown emotion bloomed in his chest.

He'd approved the plans of Mr. Townson in the end, and had sent the pessimistic, more experienced Mr. Wooling on his way. It had pleased his young chicken keeper, John Goodsmith, to no end. The thought brought a smile to Alex's face.

It had also pleased Roxanne Vanderhaven. He refused to consider why that mattered to him.

The Prince Regent had ordered him out of London, and demanded he rebuild and fortify the duchy's ancient fortress that had probably seen more sieges as England's southernmost outpost than any other castle. He was only following a royal directive, something he knew how to do when it suited him. If in the end he could not bring himself to satisfy the king's other order, that of marrying one of the aristos the prince had hand selected, he might as well attempt to curry the favor of the future king by rebuilding the fortress. Yes, those were all the arguments he used instead of admitting the obvious.

The Mount was seducing him with its familiar beauty, which jogged long-dormant memories of happiness of a long time ago. He didn't want to remember. He wanted only reminders that nothing ever stayed the same. It was better to count on very little than to be disappointed.

The sun slowly ascended the rose-colored sky and Alex was rooted to the spot, his temples pounding in remembrance. He turned away only to find the young hermit standing not twenty yards from him, leaning against a large oak.

The boy was too well-mannered to speak before spoken to. "Well, John, what say you of Mr. Townson's work so far?"

"He chose wisely at the quarry, sir."

"And?"

"And what, sir?"

"The form of the turret. It looks off. It appears slightly different."

"Not to me, Your Grace," the young man said gently.

It was what Alex liked most about John. He was unafraid to voice his opinion. "It is not too small?"

"Not from my memory," John halted. "And not upon close inspection of the painting in the gallery."

"Hmmmm. I suppose I am remembering Mont-Saint-Michel."

"Would you tell me about it, Your Grace?"

Alex looked into the depths of John's brown eyes and wondered if he himself had ever been that innocent. Without thinking, he poured out what he had not dared to speak of the last two decades. "My family in France always said this smaller castle was similar to our greater masterpiece. Just as the Archangel Michael appeared here, he appeared earlier on the larger outcropping of granite off of the Normandy coast and ordered a French bishop to build a church there." Alex looked at John, who did not smile. The young man was as silent as a statue. Waiting . . .

"I merely thought of Mont-Saint-Michel as my

home. The most wonderful, mystical place in the center of the universe."

The words hung in the early morning mist.

"Now it's a prison," Alex continued slowly, forcing the flames out of his mind as he was adept at doing. "My family and all the monks were," he inhaled slowly and softened the truth, "forced out. Valuables were sacked, and now the chambers are cells holding opponents of the republican regime. It was and is an epic waste."

John Goodsmith turned his gaze to the turret. "Father always said you can try and change the past and get nowhere or you can try to shape the future. But at all times we must embrace the present moment."

Alex finally laughed, glad to relieve the tension that had built in his chest. "Your father was a very intelligent man." Without thought, Alex tousled John's fine dark hair and swung his arm about the younger's thinner shoulders to urge them both along the path toward the castle. There was something about being with this young, wise man that did him good and gave him ease. "Come on, then. Tell me more about Mr. Townson's bloody ideas. I suppose we could go up there and I can worry the man into a faster pace if only to get the hell out of here all the sooner."

John's face dimmed. "Well, sir, may I tell you about the idea I had for the—"

They ground to a halt as a flurry of females emerged from the castle's entrance. What on earth . . .

Lord, every last marriageable female had set their sights on him. Only a small group strolled in the rear: Roxanne, her arm linked with Isabelle, and the four plain sisters of Candover chatted gaily beside them. But the others . . .

The horse-lover, Lady Katherine Leigh, held the lead narrowly to Lady Pamela Hopkins, whose lips were thin with exertion to keep pace with the former. Lady Judith Leigh trotted as stately as she could with the dainty Lady Susan Moore and her widowed mother. Only Lady Christine Saveron contained herself despite the frequent tugging by her younger sister Lydia.

If this did not prove that thirteen was, indeed, an unlucky number then nothing ever would. He would never have dreamed that he would one day want to run from females.

"I suppose I should see to the chickens, Your Grace."

"Oh no, you don't," he said grimly. "At least not alone, you won't."

"What?"

A tumble of trouble rolled to a stop, breathless. "Your Grace," Lady Katherine Leigh said, her cheeks pink with excitement. "I do beg your pardon, but I adore early morning strolls and I chanced to see you from my chamber's window." She breathed deeply to exhibit her delight but before she could go on, Lady Pamela Hopkins stepped into the breach.

"I thought you preferred riding, Katherine."

"Riding, strolling . . . I am very flexible in my tastes, as well you know, Pamela. Actually, I thought you preferred cards to taking the air."

There was nothing worse than a cat fight, Alex thought. He had to escape the hissing and spitting. "I'm delighted you're all here," he said with a straight face. "But this is the time of morning when

I tour the estate. I would not want to bore you with construction plans and inspecting animals."

Thirteen pairs of eyes blinked at once.

"Wittle animals, Yow Gwace?" The very blond, blue-eyed Lady Susan Moore sported a puzzled doll-like expression with her tiny mouth.

"Little, big—I adore them all," Lady Katherine said with glee.

Out of the corner of his eye, he saw the traitorous bed-hog, Eddie, slink from his side to Roxanne's grinning form in the rear.

"Come along, then," Alex said with resignation. "Mr. Goodsmith and I were about to tour the henhouse."

Lady Judith Leigh giggled, her bright red corkscrew curls bouncing.

Roxanne turned to Isabelle. "My cousin is very fond of collecting eggs. Did you know that? He says it's good for the soul if only to remind oneself of the godliness of common chores."

What in hell?

"That's funny," Isabelle said laughing. "I overheard my undercook complain of our hens pecking her to death. I guess southern hens are more docile."

Candover's four sisters came forward in unison, their faces so alike yet slightly different in one small aspect or another. Only their dark brown hair was the same shade and the same style—severely parted in the center with loose wings covering their ears and sloping high on top of their heads. Hope looked at John with a kind smile. "My brother would never allow us near the henhouse. I should very much like to learn more."

"As would I," insisted Charity, her brown eyes shining.

"Well, I would prefer it more than they would," Pamela insisted petulantly.

Lord, deliver me from this insanity, Alex thought.

John was already dubiously leading the bevy of colorful ladies toward the protected small fenced area on the sunny lower portion of the island.

Alex attempted to make his way to Roxanne and Isabelle's sides without any success. And then he looked down to find Christine's lovely face looking up at him. Thank God for her. She was not only beautiful, and refined, but she knew when to keep silent or speak of sensible things. As a bonus, her sister Lydia never spoke at all. Not one word.

"If you like, Your Grace, I shall find a way for all of us to leave you to your morning tasks. I only joined them in an effort to help you if I could. I realize how burdensome all of this must be for you."

"How kind you are," he said, taken aback at her honesty and goodness. "Do your best, but I think, sadly, you are outnumbered."

She beamed radiantly. "We shall see."

"I should be greatly in your debt if you succeed." He employed the smile that frequently caused a lady to do things she should not.

He had forgotten the comforting sounds of a chicken house. Clucks emanated from the coop as they drew close to the square wooden structure complete with a cupola. John cleared the fence and lifted open the pop hole before he scattered a great amount of feed in the yard. It pleased Alex to see how well maintained John kept the area.

A multitude of birds all shapes, sizes, and colors poked through the pop hole, delighted to find a new day, and breakfast. John chuckled and called a few by name.

"Oh, what a pretty cockerel," murmured Lady Christine Saveron.

"The fawn-speckled one?"

"Yes," she murmured.

"Why, that's a Hamburg, if I remember correctly. It's a hen, actually. See, there are no spurs." He was shocked that he remembered these facts.

"And the white one, Your Grace?" Christine cooed.

"A Marans."

"Actually, that is not a Marans," Roxanne inserted as she sidled up arm-in-arm with Isabelle.

Alex slowly turned his head. "Really? I beg to differ with you. The Marans is a French breed I know very well."

"Well, that is not a Marans," Roxanne continued, overconfident.

Isabelle giggled. "Do we really care what breed it is? I only want to know if its eggs are better than the others."

"Of course, all of the Duke of Kress's hens lay the most perfect eggs," declared Christine Saveron.

"Of course," Roxanne said with a grin. "He orders them by threat of the carving knife."

"Can we not visit the stable now?" Katherine pouted slightly. "What importance are birds when we have horses to ride?" Her sister's red corkscrew curls bounced in agreement as she giggled.

"I, for one, would like to know all the specifics of the hens." Charity's spectacles glittered in the sunlight.

"Oh, me too," Faith jumped in along with the other Candover sisters.

Lady Pamela Hopkins appeared bored to tears. Alex could not help but laugh for that lady was only excited when spades, hearts, diamonds, or clubs were in evidence.

Alex tried to regain his sanity. He had never thought he would find himself standing next to thirty-odd hens and almost half as many females at six o'clock in the morning. For the first time in his life, chickens held far more appeal.

"It's a *Sussex*," Roxanne stated with a huge smile.

The hair on the back of his head prickled. "What did you say?"

"I said that hen is a Sussex not a Marans."

"There is no such bird," Alex said, trying to sound casual in his remark.

"If you had been raised in Cornwall, you would know that that hen is a *Sussex*. She will lay over two hundred dark cream-colored eggs a year, and is also a good table bird. She is the most common hen in the area."

"You dare to question, His Grace?" Lady Christine Saveron asked softly while picking a feather from her gown. "I thought you were as much a stranger to Cornwall as the rest of us, Miss Barclay."

Roxanne ignored her. "Would you care to wager, *cousin*?" She tilted her head slyly. Only a small tic on the inner corner of her left eye gave away her ill-ease.

"I will wager anything you like," he murmured, *"my dearest, darling cousin."*

"All right. If that hen is a Sussex, then you must clean the henhouse while John takes a dish of tea with me."

"And if I am correct?"

"Then I suppose I shall be cleaning the henhouse instead of you. Must give the appearance of fair play, don't you think?"

Her smile was just a little too big. He wasn't sure what she was out to prove, but he'd be damned if there was a chicken named Sussex, unless it was the smug peacock Alex used to consider a friend until the other duke had shown interest where he should not.

Inviting her to dance, indeed.

He knew he was being a bloody nodcock, and he was even more annoyed that she knew just how to get under his feathers, er, skin.

Yes, that interlude by the pool was now etched in his memory. He'd spent hours remembering her slender form and warm kisses. Why, he was dying to get her alone again and—

"Who cares about chickens," Lady Katherine Leigh moaned.

"It's very hot today, don't you think?" Hope turned to her sister, Faith.

"I'm starving," muttered Pamela Hopkins.

Christine whirled her blond head toward the others. "What a lovely idea, Pamela. Shall we not all return to the Mount for breakfast?"

"Haven't you forgotten something?" Roxanne spoke to Christine, while keeping her steadfast gaze on Alex.

"Really? I can't imagine what you mean," Christine replied politely, yet with the tiniest edge.

Roxanne entered the fenced enclosure and picked up a wire egg basket as she headed toward the hen-house where John had disappeared as soon as the caterwauling had begun. "The eggs."

"The *commoner* shall collect them for us," Christine Saveron, daughter of the Earl of Dalton, replied.

Roxanne paused in mid-step, then straightened her spine and kept walking. Alex had the troubling notion that Roxanne misunderstood and thought Christine was referring to her, not John Goodsmith.

Christine tugged on his sleeve. "We shall take our leave of you, then, sir." She lowered her voice, "As I promised."

"You are a treasure," he whispered down to her pretty face.

She managed to cajole the other ladies to join her, with the exception of Isabelle who lingered behind. An earl's daughter knew better than to cross a female above her own station.

"I've never seen you wager with a lady," Isabelle murmured to Alex.

"She is not a lady," he retorted. "She's my cousin."

"Careful, Alex." Isabelle's warm laugh tumbled from her pretty lips.

"About what?"

"Your sensibilities are showing."

"Lady Christine Saveron is, indeed, a treasure."

"I was speaking of Tatiana."

"Don't be ridiculous," Alex said, loosening his collar which had grown hot during the last quarter hour.

"There's no reason you cannot choose her, you know," Isabelle said gently.

"Whatever are you talking about," he said without much hope at ending the conversation. Isabelle was as dogged in her pursuit of a subject as Roxanne.

"She is what again? Your third cousin four times removed? Or is she your fourth cousin three times removed?"

He stared at Isabelle, and her pretty visage infuriated him. "My dear, I suggest you drop this absurd topic. And no, I will not *ever* marry my cousin."

"That is a good thing," a low, feminine voice answered.

He started and looked up to find Roxanne before him extending her arm, on which a basket of eggs resided.

"For you see," Roxanne said sweetly, turning her head toward Isabelle. "I will not have him. I would not take him if he was the last—"

"Another reason I would not have her. I will not marry a woman who loves a cliché." Alex took the egg basket she offered.

"I was about to say, if you were the last old hen in the henhouse."

"You could at least admit I'd be a cockerel."

"I think not—since it's painfully obvious you have not the slightest idea how to rule a gaggle of females."

He sighed and shook his head when Isabelle laughed.

"I'm sorry, Kress," Isabelle said, wiping her hand under her eyes.

"Whatever for?"

"For suggesting you and Tatiana might consider tying yourselves to each other. It would be bicker, bicker, bicker all day long."

"For once we see eye to eye, my dear," he murmured and offered his arm to the petite duchess.

"Says the man who detests clichés," Roxanne muttered.

John Goodsmith was making his way to the threesome.

"Ah, the answer to our wager." Roxanne smoothed a blond curl behind her ear. "John, is that not a Sussex hen over there by the water trough?"

The young man studied the bird in question. "Of course, ma'am. Her name is Roxanne."

Alex threw back his head and laughed.

The chicken debacle, as Roxanne liked to think of it, forced her to turn her mind to her absurd circumstances. She'd dabbled with these aristocrats, she'd tried to help Alex on several occasions, he had helped her, but now it was time to address her future, which her fortune would amply provide. Yet, she was having the most difficult time accomplishing anything of importance.

As someone who was conscientiously trying to avoid the gentlemen here, while every other female residing within many miles of the Mount was attempting to corner them, the entire state of affairs had become something of a farce to Roxanne. It also proved a theory she had always held dear, that attraction bloomed in the face of indifference, especially if one was truly uninterested versus pretending to be indifferent, the latter being a strategy many females attempted and failed. Gentlemen appeared to have a better nose for matrimonial intentions than hounds on the hunt.

Two times during the last two days she had tried to leave the Mount, cross to Penzance, and secure a horse to secretly go to the site where her father had told her he had hidden his fortune. She had never dared set foot near the place of her childhood since that awful day on his deathbed when he had whispered to her what he had done and sworn her to secrecy. By then she had known why he had done it.

Eight years had taught her that her handsome husband was apt at completely draining an entire fortune in the most cavalier manner. Oh, he wasn't a gambler, merely a man who liked to spend. He enjoyed luxury, and opulence, and doted on his horticultural projects. Lawrence had relished refurbishing his estate, along with acquiring an exorbitantly expensive fine art collection, a majestic townhouse in London, new horses, and new carriages of every sort every year and so forth and so on. Eight years of his indifference toward her had taught Roxanne that her father had been correct.

So, she had kept her word and never revealed to Lawrence her father's last gift. In some deep inner recess of her soul she had refused to examine, she had probably known Lawrence would ultimately let her down one day.

And that day had come.

Now it was just a matter of getting a few last affairs settled before she would start a new life far, far away from everything she had once loved and lost.

But the Duke of Sussex was proving to be the proverbial fly in the ointment. On the two occasions she had set out to skulk about the area her father had named, he had come after her.

It was as if he was watching her movements. She felt rather like the mouse being watched by the cat, who was being watched by a pack of wild female dogs. It had taken a while to notice it.

The first time, when she had set off from the castle after the unfortunate henhouse incident to cross the wet sand to Penzance, he had intercepted her on the descent to the beach. She had been forced to come up with the vague excuse of wanting to pick flowers and he had insisted on helping her.

Not that she had really minded it. He was an extraordinarily handsome, charming gentleman, who went out of his way to smile at her on every occasion.

Oh, it was beyond ridiculous.

He was flirting with her and she could not help but flirt back.

And now, here in the dead of the very next night, along the very same stone path, Sussex fell into step alongside her yet again.

"You are not going to tell me you are out here picking flowers again, are you?" He offered his arm as she negotiated the steep decline.

His touch and his warm baritone voice made her almost leap out of her skin. "Your Grace," she murmured. "I didn't see you."

"Of course not. I didn't want you to," he said quietly. He cleared his throat and continued louder, "Hey, why are we whispering?"

"I don't know, Your Grace," she replied with a forced laugh. Roxanne wasn't at all sure what she should do, and so she continued down the treacherous path, her hand on the rusted iron railing. "I thought everyone had retired for the evening."

"Yes, they were for Bedfordshire, except for me, of course. Can't get used to these terrifying country hours. Who goes to bed at ten o'clock? Why, that's when the best part of the day begins in Town."

"Really?"

"What? Don't tell me you've never been?"

She dared not lie in case he questioned her. "No, I've not had the pleasure."

He made a disgusted sound. "Your cousin is more draconian than I thought. He has not provided you with a season?"

She could not help but laugh. "A season? You

must be joking. That is for young ladies of marriageable age, not spinsters."

"You always do that."

"I beg your pardon?" They were nearing the bottom of the steps and she could not figure out where to go next since Sussex had ruined her plans.

"You always insist you have no interest in dabbling in the high stakes game of finding a spouse. You know, the single-minded devotion of every female in Christendom."

"Perhaps I have reason," she murmured. Where to go? The small dock and tiny port was deserted. And there was not one candle burning in any of the rustic cottages dotting the base of the Mount. She stopped in the evening shade of a tree next to the cobblestone lane and faced him. His sculptured face stared back at her without a hint of his usual carefree smile. This was not a good sign.

"Care to tell me the reason or perhaps where we are going?" he murmured softly.

"Not at present."

"Good," he said, finally breaking into his goodhumored grin. "I like surprises."

This was his favored diversion. The game of flirtation, an amusing activity, thank the Lord, she apparently knew how to engage in when there was not anything to lose. "I've suspected that you do."

All at once he was very close to her and she had the unnerving feeling that he was about to kiss her.

The irony of it made her giggle. As a rich tin miner's daughter, nobles had never taken any interest. As an impoverished distant relation to a duke, it was another story. "Oh . . . I'm so sorry," she said quickly.

"For what?" he murmured.

"You want to kiss me and it was rude to laugh."

He shook his head, but she could see the white-ness of his grin. "You are singularly refreshing." He took a small step closer to her and she took a small step back.

She couldn't find a word to say in response.

He stared at her for a long moment, his smile fading. "You have me behaving in the oddest fash-ion," he whispered. "Usually, I don't bother asking a lady if I may kiss her."

"That's because you know they all want you to kiss them," she replied.

"But with you . . . I'm not at all sure." He brushed her cheek with one hand. "May I kiss you, then?"

She looked away. "No," she answered quietly.

"Do you love another? Do you love—"

"No," she replied quickly. "I don't love him. Or rather, I don't love anyone." What was wrong with her? Why had she said—

"Him?" Sussex's eyebrows rose. "Hmmm. I would wager that 'him' is—"

She interrupted. "What I told you was true. I'm not inclined toward marriage. The only 'him' I love is my *dog*. I'm so sorry if I misled you in any way." She slowed to a close, unsure if she had hurt his sensibilities.

He smiled finally. "No, you really needn't go on. Have a care. Rejection is new to me, my dear. And to be bested by a tiny beast no less." His expression turned serious as he stroked her cheek again. "It's too cool to be outside without a shawl. May I escort you inside? You must allow me at least one chival-rous act, my dear."

Well, there was no question that she would not be able to go on her exploration tonight. It would just have to wait. But come hell or high water, she was going to try again.

Tomorrow.

Chapter 8

The tides ruled all activity on the Mount, as it had from the moment it had risen from the sea. When the shingle path was exposed during low tide, it was the easiest way the occupants of St. Michael's Mount could make their way to the mainland. Oh, of course, there was always a boat that could be engaged during high tide, but that required servants to help row. And servants were in short supply at the castle, thanks to his great-aunt.

None of this made the slightest difference to Candover, who Alex delighted in painting a prig whenever possible. It was for that reason alone that Alex had privately declined the aid of the Cossack footman when Candover had insisted on forming a party to visit Penzance three days after the ball.

If the truth were told, all the gentlemen were so weary of being imprisoned and surrounded by a herd of ladies, that they would have latched on to any idea involving a respite from the formal mating process, which had included tedious conversation, false laughter and compliments, tepid spirits, gargantuan dinners, ridiculous card games and charades (of all things), endless tours to nowhere, and gallons of tea. At least the female herd had been culled by one. The most tedious young lady, the one who loved horses, had been confined to her room, after her attempt to ride Bacchus without Alex's leave. For some odd reason she had decided to race his stallion on the tidal flats. It was a near thing the foolish girl hadn't broken her neck in the fall.

Only one of the ladies had not driven Alex to the brink so far. Lady Christine Saveron. He studied her a few feet away from him in the boat.

"Come now, Candover," Alex finally uttered, rowing the first boat crammed with three gentlemen and four ladies. "Care to lend a hand? This was your idea, was it not?"

The other duke regarded him with his usual cool disdain. "Thank you, but no."

Isabelle and Candover's eldest sister, Faith, both laughed. Roxanne looked at him, in a way that proved she knew very well his game of needling Candover, but refused to encourage him.

Christine smiled too, but in her typical pleasing fashion offered something more. "Your Grace, I would be most happy to come to your aid. My brothers and I always loved to form little rowing and swimming races on our lake in Surrey."

"Finally, someone who is willing to take on a share of this infernal rowing," Alex replied with a grin.

Her eyes widened slightly, as if she was just the tiniest bit surprised to have her offer accepted. A moment later, Lady Christine Saveron, with her sea green eyes, lovely smile, and light brown hair reseated herself next to him and accepted one oar with her gloved hands. "I always take pleasure in helping, sir."

A small cough from Roxanne punctuated Christine's remark, and Alex smiled. He knew Roxanne did not like her, and it made him want to laugh, just like an adolescent. Which was absurd. But there was something about Roxanne that always spurred his good humor.

They settled into a rhythm after a false start, Alex adjusting his stroke to Christine's awkward, weaker one. She had been wearing down his natural bachelor defenses all week.

He glanced at the cool beauty of the lady beside him, who had exhibited not one serious imperfection of nature, character, elegance, or form. She was kind, she was young but not too young to be tediously silly, she was gracious, and she tried to please at every opportunity.

The problem was . . . she had not one flaw he could detect.

It was entirely too suspicious. No woman or man was without fault. She was also the exact opposite of Roxanne.

Alex turned his gaze toward his false cousin, who trailed her hand in the water. Barry, despite his usual rigid manner, was sitting beside her, mesmerized. It had gone thusly all week with both Barry and Sussex. And Roxanne? Why, she appeared completely unflustered by the attention of not one but *two* dukes.

Not that anything would ever come of her acquaintance with Barry or Sussex. But the thought that she might be interested in either one if she was not already married was nonetheless irritating. Like an itch in the middle of one's back that could not be reached. And worst of all, he had no earthly idea what she was thinking.

Hang it all. Roxanne's mind was none of his concern. Nor was the mind of any female for that matter. None of it mattered in the grand scheme of life.

Life was merely a rootless existence with the occasional brush of a mirage of happiness promising refuge. And one could never for a moment count on another being. Indeed, searching for lasting happiness only promised future unhappiness. Fiercely solitary, he refused to rely on the chimera of anything or anyone being everlasting in his life. It was an illusion worse than any enemy he'd faced during his years as a young Hussar.

He glanced at Lady Christine Saveron, whose brow now had a fine gleam of exertion below the brim of her modest hat.

He was going to have to offer for her. There was but two weeks left of the house party. Two weeks of relative freedom.

But that was also an illusion. Prinny's scribe had sent couriers with letters for each of the dukes every other day, demanding reports, insisting on declarations to feed the growing, furious masses in Town. Indeed, the price for becoming a duke was high: complete loss of independence and anonymity.

St. Michael's Mount appeared smaller and smaller as he rowed away from it. He forced back the bittersweet remembrances of his youth at Mont-Saint-Michel. He would never live here after he married. Depending on his future wife's true nature, she might never live here either, or the reverse. She might live here permanently. The latter seemed more appealing, yet neither option seemed very important.

"Christine," a feminine voice roused Alex from his thoughts. "Please allow me to take your place. I long for a bit of exertion." Roxanne's words were kindly spoken, but the expression on her face was odd.

Barry rushed to her aid. "Miss Barclay, you must allow me. I shall spell Lady Christine."

"My dear," Alex insisted to Christine, "I should not have allowed you to row so long. It is too taxing."

"Indeed," said Roxanne smiling.

"Do take Barry's place," Alex insisted to the lady beside him.

"No, I said I would—" Roxanne began.

"No, I insist," Barry interrupted as Christine Saveron rose.

The combination of three people rising at the same awkward moment, all on the port side, caused the small vessel to precariously list.

Isabelle and Faith squawked, and held on for dear life. Christine Saveron lost her balance, and Barry didn't even try to maintain his own, given that it was a lost cause. Only Roxanne did the proper thing. She threw herself starboard and ducked down. Two splashes erupted white in the deep blue.

In the next instant Candover's eyes met Alex's and he nodded toward the flailing couple. Candover obviously expected him to go in after Lady Christine. But she was an expert swimmer. Had she not just mentioned it? And surely Barry could maintain his own, being a former naval officer.

Alex swiveled his head to see Roxanne's lips curve into the smallest smile.

"Oh, my dear Christine, do grab the end of this," Isabelle cried, extending her parasol. She was the only sensible person among them.

"Or swim to my arms," Faith insisted, proving to be the second sensible person.

Roxanne's smile grew just the tiniest bit before

Alex turned his attention to the daughter of the Earl of Dalton, struggling to keep her head above water.

Alex sighed, and peeled off his coat. He was hot anyway, and watching Roxanne's reaction was only making him hotter. "Come on, Barry. Help her," Alex called out, but the duke appeared dazed and barely able to save himself.

The boat shifted, and before he could say a word, another splash blossomed in the sea. Good God, Roxanne was determined to undermine his nonexistent gallant nature. He wasn't sure if he wanted to strangle her yet again or laugh.

Despite the weight of her sodden gown, Roxanne easily reached the drowning couple and grabbed the scruffs of Barry and Christine Saveron. Awkwardly, she tugged them both to the side of the boat. Isabelle grasped Christine's hands, while Candover dragged Barry starboard.

"Do help Tatiana, Kress," chirped Isabelle.

"No, you help her. I'll take Lady Christine." Christine Saveron, the best little liar he'd yet to encounter. *Family swimming races, my foot.* Why Barry looked half drowned remained to be determined.

The second boat from the Mount finally caught up to them, and the ensuing babbles of concern added fuel to the chaos.

With much effort, and several inelegant, coarse shrieks by Lady Christine, Kress managed to haul her back into the boat, her every movement making it more difficult. Barry remained the stoic military officer that he was and received a vast measure of female concern when a large lump was discovered on his forehead, the result of falling on one of the oars. At least it explained his trouble swimming.

Tatiana Harriet Barclay, also known as the Countess of Paxton in a former life, and Roxanne the tin miner's daughter in another, managed quite well all by herself.

Of course.

Her full-blown, self-satisfied expression was seen by no one except Alex.

That was because everyone was drawn to the vulgar display by Lady Christine Saveron once she spat out seawater and continued her histrionics.

"Why anyone would allow a lady to row this stupid boat is beyond me," she gurgled. "I should not have to put up with these ridiculous sorts of trials. Ladies do not row. Where is my mother?"

"Yoo-hoo, dearest. Your father and I are over 'ere," exclaimed Christine's mother, with less of her French accent in evidence. Actually, the mother now sounded a trifle cockneyfied if anything.

Alex glanced again to Roxanne and finally could not stifle his laughter any longer.

Roxanne joined in despite the silent dismay of everyone around them, save Christine Saveron whose screeches were more deafening than those of the gulls swooping above the entire farcical scene.

It was the first time in ages that she felt like her old self. Of course, the feeling would fade after a short while, but she reveled in it while she could. Roxanne felt happy, mischievous, while surrounded by a large group of characters endowed with varying temperaments.

Soon after, only half the people remained. The other half had immediately rowed back to the Mount after their arrival at Penzance. It was no surprise to anyone that Lady Christine and her parents, along with the Duke of Barry and two cooing ladies, were among the deserters. Happiness suffused her every thought as she walked along the seawall with Isabelle and the Duke of Candover. She didn't even mind that her damp, salt-encrusted yellow gown was sticking uncomfortably to her skin.

For some absurd reason, she felt *included*. At her ease. The last time she had felt thusly had been before her ill-fated marriage.

Those earlier years were her fondest memories. Mornings had been spent with a succession of tutors arranged throughout her life. Afternoons flew by with the most intelligent and amusing man she'd ever known, her father, who had only protested her presence in his bustling business affairs the first couple of years. She knew he secretly adored her interest in tin and copper mining, and loved her with every chamber of his heart. He was the most enlightened of fathers with the strongest capacity to love. However, this same heart had not been strong enough to support his life much past his fifth decade.

But while he had lived, and before she had become a proper countess, Roxanne had found herself surrounded by her own kind. Common folk of little money but of much worth and good character, who liked her or respected her, at the very least, if they did not love her like her father.

The Cornish nobles had always exhibited restrained disgust for her due to her low birth. But flanked now by these two aristocrats of the highest birth, she felt accepted. She wondered if they would still treat her as an equal if they knew her true roots. It saddened her to have to question it.

She also knew that many of the other peers on the Mount privately questioned her relationship to the Barclay family. An impoverished third cousin, four times removed, indeed.

Isabelle nudged her elbow. "Are you sure you're all right?"

"Of course. Actually the water cooled me off nicely." Roxanne was grateful that the seawater had also lowered the brim of her bonnet, which allowed her the measure of anonymity she desired.

"That was a brave thing you did," Candover admitted gruffly on the other side of her.

"Not really. It was obvious they weren't going to be able to get back into the boat without help."

"Which was the correct thing for her to do since she caused them to lose their balance in the first place," Alexander said, coming up behind her.

Why was he forever popping into view and surprising her? Was it one of those strange French customs like calling someone a cauliflower as an endearment? Actually she sort of liked the way he came up behind her for some perverse reason that was most likely very childish.

Alexander Barclay walked around them and turned to face her.

"Don't make an idiot of yourself, Kress," Candover ground out.

"He can't seem to help it," Isabelle quipped.

"Do you deny it?" Alex asked her with a hint of a smile.

Roxanne giggled. "Of course not."

Isabelle's eyes rounded in disbelief. "Whyever would you do such a thing?" She paused before rushing on. "Please tell me Barry wasn't trying to take liberties?"

"He's been trying since he got here," Alexander Barclay answered for her.

"He most certainly has not," Roxanne corrected.

Candover's eyes grew darker. "Well, has he or not?"

"Who?" Roxanne laughed and looked at Isabelle.

"What do you mean *who*? Barry of course. Unless . . ." Candover turned his acidic gaze to Kress. "Oh, God."

"I rather think she means Sussex," Alex retorted with an odd sort of expression, a little sour and a little amused. "The man of a thousand smiles. The one who tries to take liberties with any female he can. Why, the night of the bachelor—"

"Kress, I would rather you didn't sully the ears of the ladies."

"Tatiana and I don't mind at all," Isabelle chirped.

"He only tried once," Roxanne admitted. "Last night."

"What!" all three of them echoed, without a single more dignified "I beg your pardon."

"I think it was because I bested him at billiards. Thrice in two days. One would think Sussex would have been put out and all, but he appeared quite the opposite. I must say, I do like a man who doesn't mind it when a woman trounces him." Roxanne looked pointedly at Alex. While she had never bested him at anything, she had the strangest desire to do so.

"I warned you to stay away from him," Kress said, a little darker than usual.

"You said the same thing about Barry and Candover."

Candover made an annoyed sound.

"You were not supposed to tell anyone I said that," Alex ground out.

"Well, you were not supposed to tell anyone I caused Barry and Christine to tumble overboard."

"And I suppose you now think we're even."

The Duke of Candover was rocking on his heels, looking at the sky for deliverance from this madness. Isabelle was looking, beneath lowered lashes, at the duke.

"Excuse us for a moment, will you?" Roxanne murmured.

Not waiting for permission, Alex took her arm and they walked to the end of the lane to stop and stare at one another.

Roxanne fidgeted her fingers. "Now that you've asked . . . Yes, I do consider us even, actually."

"And why is that?"

"Because I saved you from marrying a liar, and a shrew. And that is just as good as you saving me on that cliff."

"Just tell me one thing."

"Yes?"

"Did Sussex really try to kiss you last night?"

"And why would you care if he did? You were touring the portrait gallery with Lady *Pristine*. Again."

"Jealousy is such an ugly trait," he said, a smile teasing the corner of his lips.

"You're absolutely right. Which is the reason I cannot fathom why you would care a whit about what Sussex and I did."

The duke adjusted his neckcloth as if he were trying to loosen it. "I just don't like the idea of Sussex pawing a married lady."

"Oh, I understand. It's all right for you to have kissed me three nights ago, and then pretend that nothing happened between us, but it's not all right for Sussex to try to kiss me, and then deepen our friendship by alternating between complimenting and teasing me this morning."

"You told me you didn't like compliments."

"And you still haven't said thank you for dunking that stupid, lying girl."

Both their hackles were up now. And then suddenly, he visably deflated, like a hot air balloon. "I cannot believe you're doing this."

"What?"

"Getting me angry."

"Pardon? You never get annoyed? I've seen you with Candover, don't forget."

"He's a man. I never get angry with a lady."

"And why is that? Are we not important enough to merit a good fight? Oh, you know how to charm"— she shrugged her shoulders—"but then once you've had your kiss, you become as cold as vichyssoise and bored to pieces. So you then ignore, and avoid the lady, and forget all about her. I'm guessing you're already regretting that you said I could stay at the Mount as long as I want."

"Thank God."

"Pardon me?"

"Until now you've been acting too much like a man. Clear-sighted, practical, fearless. You were scaring me by changing the natural order between men and women. But now I realize, you just managed to hide your insanity quite well."

"Insanity?"

"Yes, the part when females imagine all sorts of ridiculous machinations of the male mind. I assure you that nothing of the sort passed through my head."

"Really?"

"Yes, really."

"So you contemplate the possibility of a deep, lasting commitment each time you kiss a woman?" She looked down and noticed a fine mist of salt dusting her skin. "Not that I have the slightest interest in pursuing a deep, lasting commitment, you understand."

"I think I may have to strangle you now," he ground out. "And for the record, you do not bore me to pieces. *Au contraire.* You infuriate me like no other."

"Thank God for that," she replied wickedly.

Gentlemen, Roxanne thought, you can't live with them, and you never, ever should—especially when they were incapable of love. And she was beginning to think all of them were, which was perfectly fine since she was in no position to ever marry again.

It was unfortunate, to be sure, that she really did owe this particular specimen. And she knew very well that dunking one silly, spoiled girl did not erase her debt at all.

Well, even if he wasn't his usual unruffled self, she wasn't going to lose the opportunity to help him whether he liked it or not.

His eyes had become glassy. Or maybe he was just trying to be polite by acting as if he was listening when in fact he was concentrating on doing everything to ignore the words flying from her mouth. Yes . . . it was surely the latter.

"Look, you asked me to help you," she finally continued. "And I'm doing it by narrowing the field. By now you should have realized that there are only three females here of any worth, and one of them is out of the running."

He shut his eyes and inhaled, shaking his head.

"Isabelle is in love with Candover, of course. So that leaves Faith or Hope. Charity and Chastity are too young. All the others are not to be endured."

"Faith and Hope," he repeated quietly. *Dangerously*.

"Yes. They are both wonderfully adventurous, highly intelligent, and have been raised to become duchesses from the moment of their birth." She knew enough from debating with her father that this was the moment for her to stay quiet and for her excellent advice to sink in.

"So," Alex said, finally opening his eyes, "you think I would do very well waking up and staring at an image of Candover every morning for the rest of my life?"

"I don't know what you're talking about. Faith has the most extraordinary eyes and kind heart, and Hope has such infectious good humor."

"You can forget it. I will never marry either of them. While I refuse to disparage either of your new friends, suffice it to say, I will not marry into Candover's family for that would mean seeing his image in far too many faces on far too many occasions for the rest of my life. It would be insupportable."

"You know, I'd hoped you were more intelligent than other gentlemen who are notoriously shallow. Don't you know that looks fade? And the most beautiful lady can become ugly in one's eyes if their character is flawed, and the reverse is true, too. Just because these marvelous ladies might have foreheads a little too prominent, noses somewhat pronounced, and they might occasionally wear spectacles does not lessen them in any way. Their cheerful nature and intelligent conversation guarantee your future happiness."

"Just remember, you described them—not me."

She sighed. "So which one will you choose?"

"I'm not going to tell you, if only to protect the future mother of my heir—if your display this morning was an example of what you are capable of."

"You asked me to help you ward off any ineligibles so you could make up your own mind."

"And I just told you I've made up my mind."

She was highly annoyed that she had not a shred of her usual intuition to imagine who he might be contemplating taking as a wife.

"Now, do be a good girl, and go with Candover to choose new hats, while I escort Isabelle to the draper."

Roxanne felt heat rise to her neck. "I see."

"No, you don't see at all. Now off with you. And do try to stay out of trouble, will you?"

She pursed her lips and then forced herself to relax and speak slowly. "Of course. Whatever you say." She smiled and mimicked Lady Christine Saveron, "I *always* take pleasure in helping."

He looked at her dubiously and then steered her back to the other couple who appeared anything but comfortable. Isabelle was trying to force a smile to Candover's stiff face, and Candover was trying not to stare at the pretty, young duchess.

"Your Grace," Roxanne said to Candover, "I do believe the footman mentioned there were hats to be found at the top of this street. Shall we not look together since you lost yours in the melee and mine is but a lost cause?" An understatement if ever there was one. Now there were two bonnets that needed to be replaced, her pretty blue one buried at St. Ives and this ruined confection of Mémé's. She would repay Alex as soon as she recovered her father's gold guineas.

The couples switched partners, and made their way to different spots in the village. After quickly choosing a simple straw hat with a wide brim, Roxanne excused herself from the duke with a flimsy reason. Candover was sure to take an age to make a selection for he was fussier about his appearance than any woman she knew.

Roxanne was still on a mission to find her father's fortune. And Lord knew that when she was on a mission, nothing could stop her.

It was a simple enough matter. Her only fear was that someone with whom she was acquainted in her former life might chance to see her.

First, she went to the livery stable in Penzance, where most of the guests of the Mount had arranged to keep their carriages and horses that could not be accommodated in the smallish mews on the island. She informed the stable boy that she required one of the Mount's horses. She had been prepared for the ride and had chosen the most durable of the morning gowns, the yellow one with the wide hemline. She draped herself to the best of her ability in the sidesaddle.

In the end, Roxanne changed her mind. Instead of continuing northward, she eventually made her way to the isolated cemetery in St. Ives. It had been a toss-up really. She had a difficult time deciding whether she should use these precious moments of freedom to prepare for her ultimate escape from eight years of humiliation, or for revenge.

In the brilliant sunlight, she deduced she had all the time in the world to go away but not much time to send one last message to Lawrence.

The graveyard was empty of anyone mourning

the lost souls, for no one stood before any grave. Those who strolled the high path above the cemetery were there to take in the air and the beauty of the seaside landscape.

Roxanne located her tombstone and fished from Mémé's borrowed reticule the small chisel she had taken from the armory as well as a mallet she had found among the tools of the workmen beginning the reconstruction of the turret. Kneeling in the turned sod, which was already losing signs of its recent disturbance, she faced the words on the stone. A sudden ball of hurt arose in her ribs—a hurt that she had thought had dimmed just the merest bit. It annoyed her that she couldn't stop the emotion welling inside.

She easily handled the tools of her youth. Everyone familiar with mines knew how to chisel. She had just never thought her talent would ever be put to use again.

She stared at the words and tried to regulate her breathing. Anger raced in her veins before a tinge of humor slowed the speed.

Beloved, indeed. She struck through several key words and chiseled a few new ones, leaving a much more interesting version of the original headstone.

Roxanne Vanderhaven née Newton
Countess of Paxton
1784 – 1818 *The not so*
Beloved wife of the
Sixth Earl of Paxton
Taken all too soon from
his grand lordship's side,
leaving him broken-~~hearted.~~

She died a noble, courageous
death and she will *not*
be missed by all who knew her.
Forever may ~~she~~ *her hat*
rest in peace.

In the beginning, she had been nervous as she furtively attacked the stone. By the end, though, she flouted her movements and gave herself over to the giddy madness of the moment. However, she would never admit to cackling like an insane witch.

"You know . . ."

Roxanne jumped to her feet, the mallet and chisel flying behind her. She knew that voice.

When, oh, when was she going to remember to be on the lookout for this handsome devil who apparently loved skulking about more than anything else?

Chapter 9

"I was wrong about you earlier," Kress said, a grin marring his attempt at a disinterested expression.

"Of course you were," Roxanne said, failing miserably at composing herself. She prayed he had not heard her mad laughter.

"You are not insane at all."

"Of course not," she replied, a little out of breath.

"That was a compliment, by the way."

"Thank you."

"I thought you said you didn't like compliments."

"False compliments. You know, like your eyes are the color of the sea at sunrise. That sort of nonsense." She quickly gathered the tools that had shot out of her hands upon his approach.

"Right. Well, is your work finished here?" He was staring at the headstone, amusement coloring his dark features.

A curious feeling of pride wound through her. "I think so. Wouldn't want to overdo and draw too much attention."

He quirked his brows. "Oh no, this is hardly noticeable at all." He coughed. "One has to be at least two hundred yards away before noticing stone fragments in every direction."

He offered his arm and she placed hers on top of his, as gracefully as she could, which was not very graceful, considering she had stone dust covering her arms, and tools clanging in Mémé's reticule.

She forced herself to continue talking. "You followed me here?"

"No, I just have an odd fascination for cemeteries," he said as innocently as a pickpocket in front of a judge.

"You followed me, yet you didn't stop me. Why is that?"

"You were having too much fun."

She pursed her lips to keep from smiling. "I don't care for the idea of you thinking you have the right to follow me."

He guided her through the irregular maze of headstones toward the upper path. "Yes, well, you have a history of not doing what you are supposed to do."

"Are you always going to bring up the funeral?"

"No, I'm bringing up your more recent effort concerning Lady Christine."

"You are going to have to learn to forgive and forget. It is the Christian thing to do."

"Are you always this much trouble?"

She smothered a smile. "Yes."

"Fair enough. Then I shall always follow you."

"Well, as long as it does not involve any more kissing," she replied tartly. "But then, we've already discussed that issue."

He stumbled over a tuft of grass. "I beg your pardon?" His voice was strained and she liked that.

"You know," Roxanne continued, "*you* might not

be taking this marriage business seriously, but I am."

"Are we talking about my future marriage or your past one?"

"I've said we're even, and you've made it perfectly clear that you would now prefer to make your own mistakes. I only ask that you allow me to make a muddle of my own future too."

"But you are already married."

"Yes, but as you have pointed out on numerous occasions when it suited your purpose, I am also dead." She nodded toward the cemetery.

"Oh, so now you are going to find a new husband?" His voice sounded the merest bit odd before he chuckled. "One would think your experience with the first one would put you off entirely from the notion."

"I didn't say I wanted to marry again. But theoretically, just because you refuse to open your heart to the possibility of love, doesn't mean I would do the same."

"I was wrong."

"Again?"

"Yes. You are just like every romantically minded female. You are mad."

"Do try to make up your mind." She inadvertently dropped the heavy reticule, and the chisel fell out. "Do you want to know what I think about you?"

"No," he said and ungallantly continued on without her as she stopped to retrieve her affairs.

She scampered after him, his ground-eating strides equaling two of hers. "I think you're . . ."

He had clamped his hands over his ears like an infant and began humming the French national anthem.

She swirled in front of him to block his path. He

took one giant step to the right and she mirrored his action. She jerked one of his hands from his ear. It was a good thing that the path was now deserted.

"I think you're afraid to love," she stated.

"Love? Afraid to love?" He sighed, lowering his lids in a fine display of cool, male boredom. "Well, at least I will give you this . . . you're bold enough to say the one thing every female I know is secretly thinking or plotting to cure."

"Why would I ever hide anything from you? You're as harmless as a goat to me."

He narrowed his eyes.

"We've no expectations from each other, and soon we'll part. By the way, you have an excellent talent."

"Talent for what?"

"For dodging questions and subjects at hand quite nicely," she replied.

"I'm not dodging anything," he continued. "You want to talk about love?"

"Yes."

"You have imagined that I am afraid to love."

"I've not imagined a thing. You *are* afraid to love. It's quite obvious."

"The only thing that's obvious is that you've made the mistake of listening to Mémé, who has made the mistake of conveying to you her favorite thoughts on her favorite subject . . . me. You think I have not heard her dance around maudlin sentiments a thousand times before?"

She tried to interrupt him without success. He plowed through her stuttering. "She always paints the same melodramatic picture. A sensitive, carefree boy, who watched his parents, and almost his entire family, perish in the flames surrounding Mont-Saint-Michel. Then she hints very badly that this boy—i.e., me—stoically wallowed in grief, which haunts me still, making me irreparably damaged. Of course, my younger brother was spared this tragic affliction as he was too young to fully understand his loss."

She fidgeted her hands as they continued walking in the heat of the afternoon. "You never speak of your brother."

"Are you going to suggest that I'm incapable of an attachment to my brother, too?" He made an inelegant sound. "I would have thought you knew gentlemen don't gush." He intently stared at her. "Of course I'm partial to my brother. He is a brilliant fellow, married to a charming heiress, and he's making his mark in life by creating a new sort of financial institution that will help others and lead to a fine fortune of his own. He has the particular notion that it isn't proper to feed off of one's wife. Imagine." He pulled her around the huge trunk of a chestnut tree as an old man with a bunch of flowers clutched in his bony hands drew close.

Alex gripped her shoulders. "You can do me one favor, though. Can you explain why females are so entranced by the notion of a tortured man? Why does this make him beautiful? Why does this make a lady instantly want to nurture, and even admire him? And worse yet, fall in love with him and imagine he will fall in love with her if she is only allowed access to his heart, which the woman believes she alone can mend?"

"You think all females who learn your history think these things, do you? I assure you most of them just want your title." Roxanne could not keep the pretense of a smile on her face.

"Perhaps that is true now that I've the duchy, but that was not the case before this summer."

"Boasting is not attractive. You do not need to remind me of your prowess with the feminine sex."

"You think I'm boasting?" His face colored with emotion and it was easy to see the trouble he had keeping a jumble of responses from his lips. "Hell and damn, I don't know how you do it."

"Do what?"

"Put me on the defensive. Most ridiculous. I've never felt the need to defend myself."

"It only shows that I am right." She rearranged the folds of her damp gown.

"You know the only reason I tolerate these idiotic conversations is that I know which camp you're in."

"Ah, so you place females who want to marry you in an enemy camp and those who do not in a different camp, an ally camp, so to speak?"

His chocolate brown eyes searched hers. "Precisely."

"Well." She inhaled. "You do realize, I hope, that there's nothing wrong with wanting to nurture someone. And you yourself are an excellent caregiver. I am living proof of it. But I still say you are afraid to love. And I assure you that to have a satisfying marriage, there needs to be love."

"And what if I tell you I'm not afraid of love at all. I just don't need it or want it, and it's never been part of the marriage equation, especially when I have the Prince Regent breathing down my neck as well as his faithful watchdog, Candover." Sunlight, filtering through the branches of the chestnut tree, lit his handsome face.

"Sometimes one doesn't know what one needs." She caught her lip between her teeth to keep from smiling. "And you're still defending your position, by the way—something you just told me you don't do."

His warm, large hands gently cupped her face. "And you do not know how to quit when you're ahead."

She could see the depths of his brown eyes, and she didn't want to melt like every stupid female before her. He didn't need saving and he certainly wasn't interested in a deep, passionate love, not that she had any interest in it herself at this point in her ridiculous life. But she at least knew that the only true chance at happiness involved leading a good life, service to others, and giving and receiving love, even if it was not romantic love.

His face was too close to hers when she finally continued. "There's only one thing we agree on, then."

"Dare I hope it is a bit of innocent nurturing at this moment?"

His whispered nonsense warmed her insides. "Call it anything you like. I have no designs on you, as you pointed out. And who am I to enlighten you?"

"Exactly so," he breathed. In the next instant, his lips descended to meet hers.

All the fight went out of her. She tried to remember that wonderful list of all the reasons she should not be doing this. She was almost coherent enough to recall all the things he had just uttered.

But she just could not deny herself. And perhaps, she finally admitted to herself, she was the one who needed coddling, even if it was of short duration. As long as she could keep her sensibilities at bay, and not read anything into his actions, she would be safe. She could lock away these few impassioned occasions and take out the remembrance of them during the many bone-chilling winter nights she would spend in some tiny hamlet far, far north of here.

His lips were slightly salty, and yet beyond he tasted of warm, delicious spirits. He gently bit her lower lip and groaned. His hands protected her back from the bark of the tree trunk as he leaned into her body. For the first time ever, she felt petite, breakable. It was the overwhelming strength with which he held her close that left her dazed, so unlike the perfunctory sensibilities she had felt in Lawrence's limpid embrace.

He made no effort to hide his body's desire to take her. He was hard where she was soft, and they fit together as snugly as two puzzle pieces in the game of life. He refused to let her come up for air; his breath fanned her cheeks as he rolled his head to the other side, tasting every inch of her.

Oh, he kissed so expertly he made her feel like she was the only woman he would ever want. His lips trailed to her ear.

And then one silly romantic word he had never dared to utter to her before brought her back to her senses . . .

"Darling . . ." he murmured slyly, a slight French accent marring his speech.

Oh, she was being played like the ten leagues of females who had found beauty in his tragedy and tried to mend his heart, which did not need mending. Roxanne pulled away suddenly. She would not be like those other females. She had more important things to do, and she would not let a half-French nobleman seduce her and tug at her heartstrings.

"Well," she said as she pulled a handkerchief from her pocket and dabbed at her lips. She hoped he didn't notice her shaky breath. "That was lovely.

But I think that is your allotment of nurturing today. There are others to tend to, you see."

He pursed his lips in frustration. "If you dare utter his name, I shall . . ." He trailed off, uncertainty crossing his features.

She leaned close to his ear and chanted, "Sussex, Sussex, Sussexxxxxxx." And then she forced a smile she did not feel, and turned away to dash toward the horses. She did not want him to see how much he affected her.

The last thing he saw before she ran were those blue, blue eyes of hers sparkling in merriment. He didn't try to catch her. Instead he turned his face to the wind and ignored her escape. She had a penchant for running away from him. It was a first among the ladies he had known.

She was paving the descent to madness. It was that voice of hers. No, it was a combination of things. It was her throaty voice and laugh. It was the taste of her, and her unusual physique. She was tall, yet small of frame, and had none of the soft padding he preferred in his bed partners. He sighed and finally admitted the truth of it. He was attracted to her because of the absurdities she wasn't afraid to utter during any and all occasions. She would not kowtow; she would not flirt. She was two parts utterly female to two parts friend and, one last part, enchanting, annoying witch.

He also found it vastly confounding that she alternated between taking seduction into her own hands and allowing him to take the lead. It was reducing him to infantile-like behavior whenever Sussex or Barry's name came into play. It was absurd. He had thought the two gentlemen decent enough sorts when they had caroused London's dens together. Nothing had changed since then. He would just have to regain control of his thoughts and immediately stop acting like a fool.

He stalked to the place Roxanne had retrieved the gelding and ridden off. She was out of sight now. Alex went after his own horse, who was munching on a patch of withered grass nearby. Bacchus turned his magnificent head and gave him a baleful stare as Alex threw his leg over the stallion's back. His horse looked like he wanted to nip him for being forced away from his shady respite.

Blast it all. He could not stop thinking about Roxanne. So much for his new resolve. And now he was reduced to lying to her. He had never had to do such a thing. He had absolutely no idea who he was going to ask to marry. The lead mare was Isabelle, of course. Beautiful, amusing, intelligent Isabelle—a very rich duchess in her own right.

There were only two problems. First, of course, Isabelle was convinced she was in love with bloody Candover, and second, she was not the sort who would allow him the freedom he required. Isabelle was a true lady who would have to be pampered, and squired about by a husband like the long-suffering sods he saw at events in Town. Yes, if he married the pretty duchess, he feared he would feel guilty, God rest his soul, at the idea of pursuing any of his former solitary late-night pleasures: clubs, gaming, and flying to a ladybird's nest on occasion.

It would be a marriage in a lovely, hellish prison. The alternative was to choose . . . Hell and damn, there were no alternatives . . .

Two hours later in his own study at the Mount, a

host of alternatives were placed before him by the very man Alex wished least to see.

"It's been well over a week. Surely you've narrowed the possibilities." Candover studied the latest express from the Prince Regent. "His Majesty is insisting upon a name. He's gone so far as to promise an important announcement to the public in less than a fortnight. He is being heckled at every entertainment he attends, and has been reduced to staying in his gold-dipped apartments most every day given the unruly crowds."

"He's one to make promises. Has he given up Lady Jersey and Mrs. Fitzherbert? Has he invited Princess Caroline to return to her rightful, wifely place by his side at Carleton House?"

Candover stared at him and replied not.

"Of course he hasn't," Kress retorted for the both of them, while wearing a path on the new Aubusson rug, paid for with the Prince Regent's money. Candover had had the audacity to install himself at Kress's own desk this morning. "And what of Barry and Sussex? Are they not required to give names?"

Candover returned his attention to Prinny's missive and studied it without meeting Alex's eye. "No, they are not. Although that has not stopped Sussex from making his choice."

Alex's blood ran cold in his veins, and a sudden pain bloomed in his chest.

Candover pursed his lips. "It seems you can't take the romantic fool out of a man after all. I tried to tell him—"

"Tried to tell him what?" Alex interrupted in a rush when his mouth finally began to work properly.

"I will tell you," Candover said acidly, "if you will exhibit a bit more patience."

A few seconds drifted by and the tension mounted.

"Look, Kress, this will go easier if you just tell me the truth of it. Is Tatiana Harriet Barclay your cousin or is she not? Honestly, I couldn't give a whit who she is, but His Majesty will not condone a marriage if she is not a true lady. Perhaps he will allow Sussex to have her if she is a penniless third-tier aristo as long as he is the last to trot down the aisle, after all of the rest of us have made spectacular matches. You, however, must go first. And it must be a marriage without a breath of scandal, the most proper of unions. So is it to be Lady Christine, then?"

A feminine, authoritative voice with an old French accent answered before Alex could. *"Mais biensûr, it is Christine."* Mémé swept into the room, along with Alex's intrepid valet, Jack, who delighted in accompanying Mémé whenever he had a free moment.

Alex pointedly looked at the open door and Jack retreated for a moment to close it.

"Well?" Candover asked impatiently.

Alex stared down Candover and Jack. To Mémé he spoke. *"Si tu veut guarder les émerauds du famille, ne dites pas un mot de plus."*

Candover shook his head. "Madame, don't let him intimidate you. I shall give you a lovely set of emeralds from my coffers, should he dare to withhold his newly acquired family jewels. Please speak freely."

"I cannot be bought, young man," Mémé lied and then turned to Alex. "And since when have I given you liberty *de me tutoyer, cheri?*"

Alex was going to strangle all of them before this was through. He felt just the smallest tinge of embarrassment for having addressed his great-aunt in an informal fashion instead of formal address, which showed deference to the one person he respected under all his jaded layers.

"I'll add a ruby necklace, madam, if you can marry him off in the next fortnight," Candover had the audacity to suggest.

Mémé showed the hint of a smile and Alex felt the icy hand of ill ease slide down his neck, rather like a noose. He turned to Jack. "Have we not any news concerning Roman Montagu?"

"I have three Bow Street runners searching for the Duke of Norwich." Alex's valet held out both hands in a gesture that silently implied there was little hope. "They have followed every lead. One report suggested Norwich was last seen in Hyde Park at three o'clock in the morning, another insists he was seen at the dueling ground on Primrose Hill at four o'clock, and the last states the duke was at the docks at quarter to five."

Candover shook his head. "And what has Norwich to do with your impending wedding?" Fury was building on the premier duke's face. He opened his mouth to speak again but Alex cut him off.

"You might not care what happened to Norwich, but I do. He is a friend, something you are not. He happens to be the one person who can help me recover my fortune. He might have won it from me, but I shall win it back. All of England knows I have not a ha'penny to my name unless this is sorted out. And by the by, I certainly don't need you to serve as my governess. I shall do what is necessary on my own timetable." Alex came about the edge of the gilt-framed furniture. "And I will thank you to vacate my desk. *Now*, if you will."

Candover slowly rose from the chair. "Your desk? Take care, Kress. With the amount of coin the prince has spent on you and the Mount, there is a question as to who owns what here."

"Et bien alors," Mémé said, making everyone turn to her. She was standing like a noble Greek statue, straight and tall, her black hair swept back tightly. "I do not want your emeralds, Candover, after all. Or your ruby necklace. I find your manner insupportable. And I will not stand for my family losing anything ever again. Alexandre, tell him to go away."

Alex's heart felt tight in his chest until he suppressed the sensation. "I shall do one better. Jack, you are to go to London and you are not to return until you learn the whereabouts of Roman Montagu, a duke of worth in England. And Candover? I will thank you to stay out of my affairs, and out of my library, for as long as you are a guest here, which will not be much longer. I give you leave to go and remind His Majesty that while I might have provided the means for your botched bachelor evening, I shall only play the whipping boy for as long as it suits."

He felt a thin wrinkled hand slide into his own, and he gripped it as hard as he dared.

And for the first time in many years Alex allowed his heart to swell with deep emotion, something he avoided at all cost in the past. And yet, here, now, it did not feel so terribly dangerous for his soul.

Chapter 10

❧──◯◯──❧

A green stillness always seemed to invade a room before an afternoon storm. And the remains of the day after his confrontation with Candover was no exception. Even the crickets were silent on the Mount.

Alex was certain he heard the first rumble of thunder while he sat at his desk surrounded by architectural renderings of the castle. He examined his pocket watch and realized he had been in the study for nearly four hours.

Entranced by all the possibilities for improvement.

Why, the southern side was crying out for an orangery to brighten the dreary winter months. And the dairy would need to be revitalized if the Mount was to be more self-sufficient. And the dining hall was too drafty. It should be—

A knock sounded at the door, and he finally took notice that there were a great deal of voices on the other side, not thunder.

"Come," he called.

A jumble of personages fell through the door, opened by his Cossack footman, who had effectively blocked the entrance. Maybe his great-aunt did know a thing or three about servants.

He did not need to know the family name of the first lady who entered. She was a new variation on an old theme—the unoriginal Candover theme. She curtsied, a blush overspreading her dark prominent features. "Your Grace," she said as Candover pushed forward from behind her.

"My middle sister, Lady Verity Fitzroy," Candover announced stiffly. "Verity, the Duke of Kress."

Alex rose and bowed to the young woman with the dark brown eyes and dark brown hair. "Delighted you could join us."

Isabelle crowded in between Verity and Candover while Roxanne walked past them to stand by the window in the alcove.

Verity appeared embarrassed as she stole a glance at her stern brother. "Stop glowering, James. I fully understand I'm not supposed to be here. I told you I'm for Derbyshire first thing on the morrow. I just need to speak to . . ." It was obvious the lady needed supporting as Candover's face became darker than a thundercloud.

Alex hastened to fill the awkwardness. "You are more than welcome here, mademoiselle. How may I be of service to you?"

"It's not your affair, Kress," Candover insisted. "My sister is supposed to be at Candover Hall, not cavorting about the countryside, all alone, unattended by—"

"I am most certainly not all alone. I've brought the archbishop." Candover's sister interrupted and then turned and answered Alex. "I should like to be granted a private word with the Duke of Sussex"—

her voice rose to be heard above Candover's annoyed sounds—"and my brother will not allow it."

Alex cleared his throat. "Perhaps I could play the role of intermediary, if it would help."

Candover clenched his hands. "I shall see to my own sister, thank you."

A lovely warm laugh echoed from the doorway. The most ravishing woman Alex had ever seen stood on the threshold. She had bountiful locks of beautiful russet hair piled high in a fashion that made a man want to run his hands through it. And her mouth was sin itself. Pouty, and lush, it was made for kissing. Her catlike green eyes slanted slyly. "I rather think it's the other way around, James Fitzroy. Your dear sisters see to you."

"Mary," Candover breathed. "My God, how came you to be here?" The duke was so blinded by her beauty that for the first time in Alex's memory Candover forgot the formalities of an introduction.

The lady sauntered forward, her slim hips elegantly swaying in a sheer pale green silk gown. *"Enchanté,* Your Grace," she offered her hand to Alex.

Alex's chair, behind him, crashed to the ground as he came around the side of his desk. He took her gloved hand in his and bowed over it. "Your servant, Lady Mary . . . ?"

"Haverty." Her voice was as sultry as her form.

Candover regained his wits first. "I thought you were a McGregor now."

She sighed, and a lovely sadness invaded her eyes for the merest second. "I thought I would be, too. But Laird MacGregor succumbed to a sudden lung fever the day before I arrived for our wedding in the highlands."

"My deepest condolences," Alex said.

"Thank you. While I did not know him—it was an arranged marriage, you see—I admired his family very much, for he was a maternal cousin." She glanced toward Candover. "James, I took the liberty of stopping at Candover Hall on my return journey to London. Your sister invited me to stay. But I must say, James, I am unimpressed with your behavior toward Verity. Why, it is positively medieval. A true gentleman doesn't lock away his sister."

"I did not lock her away. She is there to ponder her . . . her predicament."

All eyes turned to Verity Fitzroy. "I am pondering. And I shall continue to ponder in Derbyshire until I am withered and gray. But I must speak to the Duke of Sussex. James . . . for a quarter of an hour at most."

It was rather like a game of badminton, watching these two siblings do battle.

"I rather think you should be requesting an audience with the Duke of Abshire, if you are to speak to anyone," Candover said dryly, and with a hint of disgust upon mentioning his archrival's name. Everyone knew Candover and Abshire loathed each other, even if no one knew why.

"And I told you I have no interest in speaking to that person."

"I have less than no interest, but that is rather beside the point, don't you think, Verity?"

"Ahem," Lady Mary Haverty interrupted. "James dearest, I would have a word with you, if I may. *In private*."

Isabelle's face fell, but Candover failed to notice it.

"Of course, Mary. As soon as I—"

She dared to interrupt him. "Actually, it's quite

urgent. A message from His Majesty." She pulled a sealed royal dictate from her reticule and tapped it with an elegant fingernail.

Candover narrowed his eyes at his sister and gave up his post with a sigh. Kress did not miss Mary Haverty's pointed glance at Verity Fitzroy before the twosome departed.

"I'll find Sussex," Isabelle said quietly before following the others.

"Thank you, Isabelle," Verity whispered.

"You are cold," Roxanne said behind him. She came forward to offer her shawl to Candover's sister. "Allow me to introduce myself—"

Alex quickly stepped in to do the proper. "May I present my cousin Roxanne, or rather Tatiana Barclay? Tatiana, Lady Verity Fitzroy." Thank God the young lady was too distraught to notice his slip. Roxanne eyed him with a frown as she curtsied and placed her shawl about the young woman's shoulders.

"Look, your hotheaded brother will most likely try to shoot me if I leave you alone with Sussex, but I shall honor your request if you allow Tatiana and I to remain on the other side of the room to give you the privacy you desire."

"Thank you, Your Grace," she said softly. "You are every bit as kind as my four sisters said in their letters. And it is a pleasure to meet you, Miss Barclay. Faith and Hope have mentioned how much they enjoy your friendship and great spirit."

"Is there anything I can arrange for you? Tea perhaps?" Roxanne was everything gracious, to Alex's chagrin. He should be—

"No, thank you. Mary and the Comtesse de Chatelier have already called for a tray to be delivered."

An awkward silence descended, and Alex glanced at Roxanne for help.

"I do believe we are to be great friends. Please call me Tatiana as your sisters do already. Allow me to show you a seat by—"

A quick knock preceded Sussex's entrance. The man looked completely flummoxed. So much so that Alex almost felt sorry for him. Sussex darted a worried glance toward Roxanne and then Verity.

"I was told I was needed here . . . Verity, such a surprise. How do you do, my sweet? How did you manage to escape the dungeon? When we left London, your brother told me he had forced you to—" He stopped and glanced at Alex.

Obviously, there was something afoot that Alex knew nothing about, and he would prefer it remained that way. He had more than enough problems to sort through in the overfilled dish of his life.

"Please, don't let us disturb you. Tatiana and I require a word ourselves," Alex suggested and nodded toward the other side of the chamber. "Over there."

Verity grabbed Sussex's arm before he could answer, and dragged him to the bookcase while Roxanne pulled Alex to the alcove.

"She is quite pretty," Roxanne murmured as they settled in the window seat across from each other.

"The prettiest of all Candover's sisters," he agreed.

"Oh, give over, Alex. You know I'm not speaking of Verity." It was the first time she had used his given name. He took it as permission to do the same.

"Roxanne, why, whatever do you mean?"

"Lady Mary Haverty," she said, her eyes studying him like a half-blind person using a quizzing glass. "She is simply the most beautiful creature ever created. And it is obvious she is not only lovely, but also kindhearted and intelligent. The Lord forgot to add anything distasteful at all, probably in an effort to humble the rest of us mere mortal females."

"I didn't notice," he replied, vastly pleased with his ability to keep a smile from his face.

"Thank you for lying," Roxanne murmured. "You do it quite well—almost as well as my dear husband."

He turned to look at Sussex, whose face had turned as white as the hen with whom he shared his name. Alex nodded toward Sussex and Candover's sister. "What do you figure is afoot?"

The two were huddled together, Verity on tiptoe, urgently whispering something into Sussex's ear.

"I'm not sure, but I'm almost certain I just heard the name 'Amelia' cross her lips. Do you know anyone by that name?"

"No." He returned his gaze to Roxanne, and noticed the beauty of her even profile. A lock of her dark blond hair had escaped her loose chignon and was resting on the side of her long neck. Unconsciously, he reached to touch just the end of it. She swiveled her head and her sapphire blue eyes met his.

"Sorry," she said, and repositioned a pin to tuck the curl back into place.

"I'm not. I—"

Before he could utter another word, Sussex's voice carried across the space. "You must be joking. But she's your . . . sod it. Why on earth would I ever agree to . . ." Sussex halted and followed Verity's gaze, which now rested on Alex and Roxanne. "I beg your pardon," he muttered darkly.

Verity's guilty expression added to the mystery.

Candover's sister cupped her hands and again whispered something in Sussex's ear.

Alex looked away, his gaze retreating to the sill where Roxanne's hand rested on the ledge. Her nails were trimmed short, the white crescents visible. He had not noticed how lovely her hands were. Capable, yet feminine—very like her character.

"Oh dear," Roxanne said. "I do believe he's going down."

Alex swiftly turned his head. In that same instant, Roxanne rushed to the other couple and helped Verity catch Sussex just before his head hit the floor.

Alex made his way to the threesome and fell to his haunches. "Give him some air." He loosened the other man's neckcloth and looked at Verity. "What did you say to him?"

"Pray do not ask, Your Grace," Verity whispered. "He must leave as soon as possible."

"As you wish," he replied a little too quickly.

Roxanne shook her head. "You could be a little less obvious about how this pleases you, Alex."

"You're glad he's going?" Verity's face was innocence itself. "But, I had heard you and Sussex got along famously."

"Really?" Roxanne inserted, a small smile teasing the corner of her lips.

"Look," Alex ignored the question, "the important thing is that I will arrange for my dear friend's affairs to be packed, and his carriage and horses readied by tomorrow."

Verity smiled. "Well, that is a refreshing change. Most dukes I know don't take orders."

"Yes, he's not really like a duke at all," Roxanne said with a grin as Sussex began to flop like a fresh-caught fish. "But I would rethink your ideas concerning his great bond with the Duke of Sussex."

"How very odd," Verity said as Sussex rose to a seated position. "Everyone I know loves Edward."

"When did you meet my dog?" A tiny crease appeared between Roxanne's brows.

"I haven't seen any dog," Verity replied.

"Then how did you know that everyone loves Edward?"

"Stop," Kress ground out. "Edward is Sussex. Edward Godwin, remember?"

"No, I do not remember. How am I to remember everyone's Christian name when I can barely remember their title and family name?" Roxanne moved a flounce of her gown to cover her trim ankle.

"I'm certain I would love your dog, Tatiana. I find pets are such a balm for the strain gentlemen bring to our lives. Don't you agree?"

"No truer words have ever been spoken," Roxanne agreed with a chuckle.

"In that case," Alex inserted, "I shall go and find Tatiana's dog and the tea tray since you both obviously have no use for me here." He regained his feet and helped Sussex to his.

The latter groaned most impressively. "Got to arrange for—"

"Say no more, Sussex. I shall see to it myself. Do be a dear and pour the ladies a spot of tea. I'll find something a bit stronger for you. Something tells me that where you're going you will need it."

Alex crossed the wide expanse of the chamber and exited. His valet fell across the threshold and Alex caught him before he closed the door.

"Eavesdropping, Jack? It's an art form you know.

Thought you would have perfected it by now, *mon vieux*."

"Evidence that this rustication in Cornwall is damaging my skills. Thank the Lord I'm for London. I'm here to inform that I leave tomorrow." His valet's eyes were blank.

"And?"

"And what?"

"What was in that letter from Prinny?"

"You mean the one that unearthly vixen brought with her?"

"Precisely."

"Among other things, there was confirmation that Roman Montagu was, indeed, last seen by the docks."

"Really?"

"Yes," Jack said, examining his manicured fingernails. "And you were there, too."

"I absolutely was not."

"Are you certain?"

Alex closed his eyes and breathed deep. A wisp of a memory threaded his brain. Something about Roman's family, his brother in particular. Or maybe the father? Yes, the former Duke of Norwich. He squeezed his eyes shut harder. "No. I'm not completely certain. I'm *almost* certain."

"A little doubt is absolute doubt," Jack said, mimicking Alex's own favorite quote.

"How convenient," Alex said dryly. "Usually your memory is like a sieve."

"Yes, well, you drum some things in so often I cannot be held accountable."

"Said the purveyor of my ruin."

"It is not my fault." Jack's whiny tone had been perfected over the years.

"No one will ever forget you were the one who brought the poison to the table," Alex drawled.

"Perhaps, but I was not the one to bring it to your lips. All of you managed that very well without me. And locked me in a strong room to boot."

"Reiteration is unoriginal. I choose not to spend the afternoon pecking like two old biddies. Come along then." Alex motioned the way to the main hall.

"But, I should like to be an old biddy." Jack was like a dog with a bone. Half his pleasure in life was reiteration. "In fact, I was looking forward to becoming an old biddy upon your elevation. It was the reward I had been cherishing after all these many years of hard labor under your family's service."

Alex sighed and began to walk to the hall. "Remind me why I hired you away from my brother."

"I was the only one who would take you on for so little pay."

"And?"

"And I grew bored watching your brother moon over his wife. I don't like tending to happy gentlemen. Far too monotonous."

"Right. You never have to worry about boredom and happiness with me."

"Precisely," his jaded valet concurred.

As they turned the corner to enter the grand hall, Alex remembered why he had employed Jack. He was the only man who truly amused him.

Sort of like the way Roxanne amused him, although her voice soothed instead of Jack's high-pitched grate with a side of ingratitude. Suddenly, he decided it was well past time to return the favor to her.

* * *

It was entertaining really. The way ladies were so transparent in their sensibilities. So unlike a gentleman, Alex thought, as he sat across from Roxanne at breakfast the next morning.

The rest of the house party had deserted the room to offer their well wishes to the Duke of Sussex as he departed the Mount, along with the three youngest of Candover's sisters, Verity, Charity, and Chastity. Even though separate carriages waited for them in Penzance, Candover had sent a brigade of chaperones for his sisters' return to Derbyshire.

Just a few moments ago, Roxanne's mouth had tightened just the merest bit when she had learned that Lady Mary Haverty was not returning to London with the rest of the party.

Her reaction delighted Alex.

"So," he said, carefully choosing the choicest morsel of bacon from his rasher, "I thought we might take a small tour today if you are for it."

"A tour?"

"Well, I do realize that if I leave you to your own devices for too long, you are apt to take matters into your own hands if the past is any indication."

"You're very quick."

"What say you to a visit to Paxton Hall?" He rushed on as he saw her about to speak. "You would have to remain hidden, of course."

"Of course," she said gleefully. "If a chance presents itself, I would be grateful if you could nick the miniature likenesses of my mother and father. They're inside the escritoire in the yellow room next to the library."

He shook his head. "Are you trying to give yourself away?"

"Not at all. Lawrence doesn't even know they are there. He hated any reminder of my father."

"Good. I was worried you were going to ask me to ransack the rest of the place while I'm at it."

"No, but I wouldn't mind scaring him the tiniest bit one last time. He's not nearly worried enough." She took a last bite of coddled eggs. "But no. I don't want anything else. Nothing else matters to me. The rest of it is his."

"That your father bought and paid for."

"Yes, but Lawrence chose it all so I don't want it."

"Good girl," he said softly. "And good girls deserve their reward."

"Reward? Care to tell me what you mean?"

"No, but I will show you when we get there." He felt a sly smile slide into place, the one that usually made women hesitant and nervous.

She abruptly stood up, her chair squealing on its hind legs. "Let's go straightaway."

He stood slowly to join her. "Why do I sense an ulterior motive?"

"Well, if we don't disappear now, look at it this way—all the females trying to marry you will return and urge some uninteresting diversion to advance their courtship ritual to fleece you."

"You just don't want Mary Haverty in the same room with me again. Or you want to hurry for the chance to cross to Penzance with Sussex. Which is it?"

She slowly battered her eyelids in the same fashion Mary had done in the breakfast room. "I can't imagine what you mean."

"Do try to curb that. It's most unattractive."

"Not as unattractive as the way you fawned all over her last evening. Do come along. Sussex is at this moment leaving the Mount, depriving me of the last opportunity to dote on him in front of you."

"Well, we cannot have that now, can we?" He liked how the corner of her eyes crinkled when she smiled.

It was not hard to evade the returning group. The two of them merely disappeared out the servants' door and circled to the front as the rest reentered the Mount. Alex and Roxanne traversed the wet shingle path toward Penzance, and despite her halfhearted effort, they never did catch up to Sussex and Candover's three sisters.

Alex arranged for a pair and his closed barouche to be brought 'round from the stables in the village. He would not take any chance at Roxanne being discovered.

She sat across from him in a blue gown of Mémé's that matched her lovely eyes. Her posture correct, and her hands pleated in her lap, she broke the silence after a few moments on the road. "I just thought you should know that I'm making arrangements to leave soon."

"Are you now?"

"Yes."

"And what has happened to your famous desire to learn why your delightful husband left you on the cliff?"

"I've decided to change my thinking."

"Really. How so?"

"No matter what he says, it will not take away the sting. And it might make me feel even worse. Revenge would very likely not be as sweet as I imagined." She looked out of the window and the sunlight lit her face. "And no matter what the reason, I will go forward with a plan to make a new life for myself. I am grown weary of waiting for it to start. Not to mention that I am also tiring of the name Tatiana."

"I told you that you should have chosen Harriet."

"Alex," she said, finally turning to look at him. "My former life was finished when you rescued me. I just couldn't admit it right away. But now that I've had time to reflect, well—my desire for revenge is over."

"It might be over for you, but not for me." He liked the way she said his name.

"You're very kind to suggest—"

"I'm not kind at all, as well you know. Gentlemen are so very simple in our thinking. Primal even. I will not have a lying, murderous clod growing weeds for a neighbor."

She was about to open her mouth to argue with him again when he shoved a book into her lap.

"What's this?"

"A book about dairy cows. Can't make heads or udders over it. Young Goodsmith tells me the Mount used to have three times as many cows. I've neither the time nor the inclination to figure it all out. You must have maintained a dairy of some sort, and I'm certain your husband held no fascination for it save for consuming the beasts on every occasion he could. Would you be so kind as to recommend a good breed for the Mount?"

She raised her brows and sighed. "This is the worst diversionary tactic yet."

She had the most delightful arch to her delicate eyebrow as she flipped through the pages. He moved to sit beside her, taking up all the rest of the room on the bench. "Well, we could pass the time in a more agreeable fashion."

"Are you doing all this because you mean to take advantage of me in the end?" Her attention was snared on the pages of the book.

"You pierce my heart, Roxanne."

She looked up at him. "Better there than somewhere lower. And please stop invading my side of the bench. Besides . . ."

"Yes?" He teased Roxanne by slowly moving closer to her.

"You will find a far more willing participant at the Mount."

"Really?" He gave a shot at appearing as innocent as he was not. "And who would you be suggesting? Not Lady Mary Haverty perchance?"

"Of course. Finally a marriage candidate worthy of your consideration."

"How enlightened of you. I never would have guessed you to be her champion."

"I never lie. And I cannot deny she's young, beautiful, witty, and will keep you on your toes, something you require greatly. Her character remains in question, of course, until you know her better, but I doubt that will matter in the end given her beauty. And Candover's sisters adore her."

He didn't like the turn of the conversation so he grasped one edge of the book in her lap. "So is it to be a South Devon or a Hereford?"

A small smile curved her mouth. "Well, the South Devon is known for its excellent milk, its strength in the yoke, and many years of breeding, while the Hereford provides first-rate beef. But, if you are looking for an excellent all-around breed, I would suggest . . ." She stopped and her smile grew very wide.

"Bloody hell." His head fell into his hands. "Don't tell me. Really, I will never believe—"

"But the *Sussex* does it all. And they have the most placid of tempers despite one or two that might be a tad stubborn at times. You will love the breed."

"No," he said as stubbornly as a Sussex bull. "The last true Sussex left an hour ago and we'll eat the rest of the plucked namesakes tonight."

"It's hard to believe you and Sussex were once great friends."

"Well, I can assure you that our friendship is greater than ever now that he is gone."

"Hmmm, I wonder if there are any Barry breeds. I shall have to—"

"I've taken a decision. I'm purchasing South Devons."

Her smile turned mischievous, and a small feeling of warmth invaded his gut.

Alex leaned forward and kissed her oh-so briefly, so softly on the lips.

"Whyever did you do that?"

"Whyever shouldn't I?" he murmured and then kissed her again.

"I don't know," she said, her expression unreadable.

"You don't know what?"

"I don't know why we're driving past the entrance to Paxton Hall," she said, straightening away from him.

It drove him wild with annoyance that his kiss did not seem to affect her. It had never failed him in the past. Then again he'd never tried so hard to please anyone. It was usually the reverse. Did his kiss mean so little that she remained fully cognizant of everything around them? He was starved to recreate the intimacy of that unbelievable night by the pond. His groin ached at the thought, but he finally mustered an answer. "I asked the driver to give us a tour of the gardens by way of the lane that passes the front of the estate."

"You know quite a bit about Paxton Hall for someone who has never been here."

"If you let me give you a real kiss, I shall tell you more about this overcultivated monstrosity than you know yourself."

"Oh," she cried, pointing to the window. "Look!"

He followed her gaze only to see for the second time in two days an enormous series of man-made holes dotting the manicured, tiered gardens on the south side of Paxton Hall. Three shovels were in evidence as were many large mounds of dirt and flowers, which all lay in higgledy-piggledy fashion, ruining the perfect symmetry that had once been the pride and joy of the plant-obsessed earl.

Roxanne bounced on the bench like a child and began to laugh until she could barely breathe. As they wended their way down the lane, past the front of the estate, she clapped a hand over her mouth.

The entire lawn, which had been maintained with military precision just a fortnight ago was now riddled with the evidence of rodents who had churned tunnels with voracious fury.

Roxanne Vanderhaven, the Countess of Paxton in truth if not in spirit, jumped into his lap, the dairy book falling to the floor. "Oh, how can I thank you?" she said, nearly choking with mirth. "I was wrong, you know."

"About what," he murmured.

"Revenge *is* sweet. Look, I know it's evil to be so gleeful, but he had a very odd connection with that lawn."

He lifted his brow. "You are the only woman I know who would show such gratitude over a clutch of moles."

"But you see he loved that lawn so much that he wouldn't let anyone set foot on it except to cut it. He had two under-gardeners whose sole occupation was to water it, weed it, and cut it with more care than his own hair. Once, he even threatened to dismember Eddie if he ever saw him near it. And to think, all you had to do was hide a false map on my dog's collar and find a few lovely little moles. Heavens . . . this is so much better than the headstone. It's simply brilliant. It's—it's," the words spilled out so fast. "I—Oh, *thank you, Alex.*"

She leaned down and kissed him for all she was worth. He had to agree. Revenge was, indeed, sweet. Sweeter than anything he had ever tasted. Her fingers raked his hair, surely making a more authentic tousled effect than the one Jack insisted on foisting on him every chance he could.

That was the last thought in his rational mind as Roxanne began to explore every inch of his face with torturing little kisses. Every now and again a soft giggle would escape, and it set his body on fire for her. He was beginning to believe he would be willing to move heaven and earth to see that sort of happiness on her face every day.

Until she left, of course. Nothing ever remained the same. Change was inevitable. But he had learned to take advantage of every last morsel of goodness while it lasted. And then to put it all behind him. To forget was the only way to survive.

God. She fit so perfectly in his embrace. He loved the way her slim waist bent as he pulled her closer.

He loved the way she smelled—of warm honey soap, and something maddeningly elusive.

And now his breeches were uncomfortably tight in all the obvious places. He squirmed in his seat and her pert derrière only nestled deeper into his lap. He was so close to his limit that he had the vague sense that he might for the first time in his life embarrass himself. And he hadn't even touched her bare skin.

With a shout, the carriage stopped so abruptly that Roxanne nearly ended up on the floor. At the last moment, Alex gripped her tight.

Who would have guessed that it would be the Earl of Paxton who would save the Countess of Paxton from finding herself in a far more precarious predicament than the one she had faced a few weeks before?

Chapter 11

~~~~~~~~~~~~~~~~~~

"Hey, ho!" the driver shouted.

Alex glanced out the window only to see Lawrence Vanderhaven running toward the carriage by way of his ruined landscape, waving his hands in the universal signal to stop.

"Stay in here, and don't you dare say a word or move a single blasted finger," Alex warned her before loosening the carriage curtain from its roping. He quickly grabbed the book, opened the door, leapt from the vehicle without bothering to let down the step, and firmly closed the latch of the door.

He covered the placket of his breeches with the book and tried to think about anything except the long, slim femininity inside his barouche. He prayed that for just once, she would obey him. An obviously useless wish.

"Halloo!" The Earl of Paxton's fast gait was disjointed and as inelegant as a goose's waddle.

"Yes?" Alex replied as soon as the man was near.

Lawrence Vanderhaven leaned over his knees, breathing hard. "So glad I caught you. Saves me a visit."

Alex raised his brows and waved his hand. "Love what you've done here."

* * *

For the first time in many years, Roxanne was grateful to Lawrence. She was completely out of her depth with the Duke of Kress. The man scrambled her wits. She was sure he thought her a lunatic. One minute she was telling him she was leaving as cool as you please and the next she was attacking him with kisses and God knows what other silly romantic nonsense. And he appeared completely immune to her efforts.

Oh, he kissed her back, but he never let his tightly leashed emotions get involved, no matter how hard she tried. It only proved yet again what a failure she was in the game of seduction.

And her marriage had been the same. Lawrence had preferred hours spent with his plants, his books, his horticulture magazines, anything but time spent with her. And when he had come to her bed, less and less after the first year of marriage, it had been a perfunctory quarter of an hour. Then again, wasn't that the way it was done? And yet . . . She had once spied the Paxton stable master and the scullery maid in a passionate embrace behind a hayrick one summer afternoon. It was not at all what she had experienced with Lawrence. She had assumed that sort of exuberance was considered vulgar by the upper classes.

Until Alex.

As she slid down on the bench to hide any shadow she might cast, she wondered yet again if her marriage would have been different if she had conceived a child. She sighed.

"Do allow me the honor of asking you to join me in my library, Your Grace," her vile husband simpered on the other side of the carriage door.

Well, at least this would give Alex the chance to snatch the miniatures while she sat in this overheated carriage.

When she heard Alex reluctantly agree to her husband's request, Lawrence instructed the coachmen to move the barouche to the circular drive in front of Paxton Hall.

Roxanne had more than a half hour in the darkened carriage to contemplate the grave injustice Lawrence had done to her. She had thought she was done with revenge. She had thought she was through with finding answers. Why then did that little question still sneak past her defenses and plague her?

Why?

Why had he wanted her to die? It wasn't her money as Alex suggested. He was clearly courting Miss Tillworth, and her nonexistent dowry.

The carriage seat had become as hard as the wooden slat bench miners lowered into shafts. She wiggled against the discomfort. And the airless inside of the carriage caused her to become even more uncomfortable. She peeked past the edge of the curtain. There was not a soul in sight. And she knew it was the hour the servants took their dinner.

She nimbly descended from the barouche and whispered her intentions to the driver before she disappeared toward the west side of the mansion, where the library lay to tempt her.

She tiptoed up the four steps of the wide terrace, and rested flat against the brick wall adjacent to the French doors. She had not enough luck on her side. The doors were shut. But if she knew anything, she was certain they would be unlocked. One of Lawrence's favorite activities was to stand on the terrace and admire the landscape he had designed.

She eased toward the window of the French door and peeked inside. Lawrence was in his favorite chair, the back of his head just visible. The bald spot he had always tried to hide with boot polish was quite evident. It made her smile.

Her eyes focused on Alex, sitting across from Lawrence. All at once, Alex's brown eyes met hers and she dared not think what he would do when they were alone.

No matter. It would be worth it. She reached for the knob of the door and turned it slowly. Noiselessly, she eased the door open an inch.

"Your Grace, I knew you would understand," Lawrence stated.

"Oh, completely. I understand you have quite a bit of gall to ask to remove something from the Mount," Alex drawled. "It is my duty as the current duke to protect all that is entailed in the duchy's name. I cannot let anyone run roughshod over the grounds to dig up precious greenery no matter how much you desire to cultivate this rare white camp— Whatever."

"It's the white form of the red campion, actually. Surely there must be some room for negotiation, Your Grace."

"I told you not to address me so informally," Alex announced.

"But there is no more formal address." Lawrence's voice gained a squeak. "I could address you as 'Peter,' as you suggested the time we last met."

"Don't be ridiculous, why would I have ever requested that when my Christian name is Harry, the masculine form of Harriet, don't you know?"

"Please, I beg of you," Lawrence whispered.

"Oh, very well," Alex said with a convincing sigh, "as you said, we are the two most important people residing in Cornwall for the moment. I suppose we shall have to deal with each other. *Perhaps* I will see fit to accede to your request, but you must give me what I require in return."

"Anything," Lawrence breathed reverently.

Yes, this was the little man she knew, Roxanne thought with annoyance. She prayed Alex would find a way to secure the miniatures.

"You must answer a question."

The fine hairs on her neck rose.

Lawrence Vanderhaven leaned forward in anticipation. "And what question would that be?"

"Why did you kill your wife?"

Roxanne would have swooned if not for the fact that she had to hear Lawrence's answer.

"I beg your pardon?" Her demented husband's voice cracked.

"Your dearly beloved wife, the Countess of Paxton."

Lawrence half rose from his seat. "How dare you come into my house and suggest—"

"Because I happened across your wife's headstone the morning of the funeral. No, I require you to remain seated, sir. I was amazed you were able to have it carved so quickly"—Alex let that sink in before he tapped in the last nail—"and then a party from the Mount toured St. Ives yesterday and I took the opportunity to bring some flowers from your wife's dog to place on the hat's grave. Have you seen what has been done to the headstone?"

Roxanne would have given just about anything to see her husband's face just then.

Lawrence stuttered, "I—I—I don't know what you are suggesting, but I was informed that someone had vandalized my wife's—"

"Your *beloved* wife's," Alex corrected.

"Yes, yes. My *beloved* wife's memorial. It is being repaired as we speak. I can't imagine that it is still there. I asked for it to be removed several days ago. You say you saw this yesterday?"

"You have forgotten the more important question, Lawrie." Alex's voice sounded like that of a disappointed father chastising a child.

"Sorry?"

Roxanne could see her husband mopping his face with a handkerchief. *How cliché.*

"Why did you kill her?" Alex asked softly. He lifted his eyes from Lawrence and glared at her for a moment before returning his attention to her husband.

"How dare you suggest anything of the sort. I should not have to defend myself. Of course, I did not kill my wife. I loved her with every breath I possess. Your reasons for thinking such are a grave insult. I should call you out."

"Why don't you?" Alex's voice sounded thoughtful.

"I don't believe in such barbaric practices. That sort of thing should have remained in the dark ages—or in London, for hotheaded young blades who consume too much spirits. Something I would never do. I am a peaceful sort. In fact I am the magistrate in the district and I'm known for my generous forgiveness of sins."

"And so you forgive yourself first, then?"

"I don't have anything to be forgiven for."

Alex was accomplishing it. He was finally getting the earl angry. She could hear it in Lawrence's voice.

"In fact," her husband continued, "if anyone should require forgiveness, it is my poor wife."

Roxanne almost lost her balance in her desire to inch closer.

"Yes," Alex agreed. "I find most women to be deficient on many levels. There is even one I know who never, *ever* keeps her promise or does what she is told. What did your beloved wife do to merit forgiveness?"

Lawrence hesitated.

Alex urged him on. "I have yet to find a female worthy of any man. Don't you agree?"

That opened the floodgates. "To be perfectly honest, she was frigid," Lawrence gushed. "A most spiritless creature, and incapable of procreation. Everyone knew it. Reproduction is the main purpose of every living thing on this earth. Plants manage it perfectly, even brainless animals. She could not. And why are you so bloody interested in my wife? You never even met her."

Alex ignored the question. "And so you killed her. Your *beloved* wife?"

"No, I did not kill her," Lawrence said stiffly. "You asked me why my wife merited forgiveness. You suggested all women have faults, as we both know. Eve tempted Adam, remember? Why, I pitied Roxanne more than anyone, but I did not kill her."

"Really?"

"Really. Now, may I please remove a portion of the white form of the red campion on the Mount?"

"No," Alex said calmly.

"I beg your pardon?" Lawrence stood up suddenly. "And what do you keep looking at behind me. It's as if—"

Alex rose up from his seat, like a giant specter behind Lawrence, and whacked his head as Lawrence turned to look over his shoulder toward her. Her husband went down in a boneless, spineless fashion, but Alex caught him to silence the fall.

It all unfolded so quickly Roxanne had barely a moment to react. She had been frozen as solid as a Scottish icicle in January since Lawrence's words had floated through her, paralyzing her. *Frigid*. She had been deemed frigid and barren.

Her arm fell to her side, cracking the tension in her body and she stumbled through the French door.

"Is he dead?" she whispered with more than a modicum of hope.

"No. He's too thick-headed for a book about dairy cows to do any satisfying damage. Now's your chance to give him a good kick or three if you'd like."

"I just want to leave," she murmured, dejected, "before one of the servants discovers us." She turned to go, but he reached for her arm to stop her.

"Wait," he said in a serious tone. "You might be finished but I'm not."

She couldn't respond, but for once she did as he asked. She just didn't have the spirit required to banter with him.

And so she waited as he had bid her.

She watched as he pulled something out of his vest pocket and picked up Lawrence's limp hand. He jammed her tiny ugly ruby and diamond ring on her husband's pinkie which was more than a mite too large for the ring.

She tried to muster a smile.

"Now go outside and meet me in the carriage," Alex said. "Have a care and try not to let anyone see you."

"Where are you going?"

"I'll join you before you have a chance to plan your *beloved* husband's funeral."

She couldn't speak and so she nodded her agreement.

A thousand and one thoughts flew through her head as she waited for Alex in the carriage. A thousand and one times the word *frigid* echoed within her. She squeezed her hands over her ears. She was not even entirely sure what it meant, but she knew it was ugly.

And how dare he suggest she was barren? True, they had not had any children, but he had made very little effort if the local midwife's advice had been accurate. Roxanne had privately sought out the woman to learn the secrets no one dared speak of in polite company. She had learned that relations should be frequent—at least several times a week—if one was to conceive a child. It was also a fact that Vanderhavens were notoriously short on producing heirs, and notoriously long on handing down the title to distant relations.

Barren, indeed. She refused to be saddled with that particular shame her husband assigned to her. Then why could she not stop the flood of doubt raining down on her? She was going to leave anyway and—

Alex's voice, commanding the driver to make haste to the Mount, cut into her rumination. The door opened and his large frame was crowding her, forcing her to move to accommodate him on the bench again.

"There's more room on the other side," she muttered.

"Yes, but then I wouldn't be next to you." He knocked on the roof to signal the driver to move on.

"Why would you desire that?" she said, annoyed with the petulant tone she could not keep from her voice. "I'm prone to send a chill down a man, didn't you hear?"

"Sounds perfect. It's hotter than Hades during a midsummer's night in here," he said, his voice gravelly as he draped an arm about her.

She allowed him to draw her near, but she remained as rigid as Lawrence had suggested.

"I have something for you," he said quietly.

"I'll look at the dairy book later." She stared out the window at the passing scenery.

She was frigid and barren.

She felt rather than saw something slip onto her lap. She looked down to see the twin ovals of her parents. She swallowed hard.

She would never cry again. She was done with regret. Done with mourning. Done with the past. She silently closed the miniatures together and engaged the clasp. "Thank you," she said softly.

As the miles passed in quiet reverie, she pushed away everything that had been and forced herself to think only of everything that was to be her future. Yet a random reflection emerged from her torrent of thoughts. What she liked most about Alex was that he knew when to be silent. It was a talent few possessed. In fact there was not a soul she knew who possessed it, even her father. As she had the thought, Alex opened his mouth to discredit everything she had just deduced about the man beside her.

He spent the last half hour of the journey chastising her for exiting the carriage at Paxton Hall, and creeping about the estate. He reminded her of all the risks she had taken. He asked if she wanted Paxton to discover she was still alive. He continued the barrage of questions yet never waited for an answer. She intervened when she realized he was doing it on purpose—to stop her rumination of her failure as a wife.

"I don't see why you're making such a fuss. It all turned out perfectly well." She could pretend to be distracted if it made him feel better. She owed him so very much.

"Yes, if you consider a possible investigation for knocking your husband silly 'perfectly well.'"

"He didn't see you and I'm certain you explained everything in an exemplary fashion to the servants."

"You could show a bit more appreciation." He leaned down to her ear and nipped it.

"He might have seen me," she admitted. "I suppose I should have stayed in the carriage as you suggested." She waited for his agreement.

"I told the housekeeper that he slipped on the newly waxed floor and required aid. And then I asked her if the earl was a bit touched in the head since he insisted he had seen the ghost of his wife before he fell."

"Thank you," she murmured and then turned to look out the window again. "I'll show him a ghost all right."

"That's my girl." He kissed the top of her head.

After the exertion Roxanne had shown partaking in that evening's meal, she did not have any more reserves of false calm and good humor to endure another evening of cards, or billiards, or charades with the others, despite Barry's plea. Instead she slipped out for a quiet stroll to take the cool evening air.

She had not gotten much farther than the short privet hedge near the small cemetery on the grounds when a trio of ladies caught up to her.

The ladies on the Mount had naturally fallen into two groups. Those who were not desperate to marry, and those who were. The three who found her were in the former camp.

Isabelle walked slightly ahead of Candover's sister, Hope, as well as Lady Mary Haverty.

"You were very quiet tonight," Isabelle said, catching up to her first. "Is everything all right?"

"Of course," Roxanne replied, taking care to keep her voice even. "Is not the air particularly fine this evening?"

"Pardon me," Isabelle said with a smile. "But I do believe that is the first time I've ever heard you stoop to talking about the weather."

Hope and Mary, linked arm in arm, closed in on the pair.

"I've always found," Lady Mary Haverty inserted, "that when a lady speaks of the weather when there are only other ladies present then she is really thinking about a gentleman."

Hope laughed. "I suppose that means you think I only think of gentlemen. How mortifying, Mary."

"Oh, not you, dearest," Mary said, patting her friend's arm with her gloved hand. "You, I know, do not want to intimidate anyone by admitting that you are thinking of some terrifying mathematical concept that not a soul would comprehend, including your own brother."

"Pardon me," Roxanne said, not a little put out by the beautiful lady's outrageous suggestion regarding her banal comment. "I shall change the subject. Shall we not all discuss geometry, Hope?

I've always enjoyed theorems and drawing figures." She, of course, did not add that she had learned to love geometry and the architecture of every mine her father had ever built.

"Please forgive me, Miss Barclay. I'm sorry if I offended you," Lady Mary continued. "I only tease people with whom I sense I could share a friendship."

Roxanne felt Isabelle's hand clasp hers in the growing darkness. She squeezed back. "Of course, we shall become friends."

"That doesn't sound very promising," Mary Haverty replied with a low laugh. "I suppose I've gotten off on the wrong foot again."

"What do you mean 'again'?"

Hope released her arm from her friend to adjust her shawl as Lady Mary replied. "I'm not very good at befriending ladies. Most do not take to me at all. I've never understood it. I used to fawn and flatter, and try to fit in, but I finally gave up a long time ago. Ladies either love me or hate me. There is no gray area, you see."

"I know why," Roxanne said, unable to stop herself.

Three pairs of eyes examined her.

"We're all jealous. Except Hope and Isabelle. They're too kind to be jealous of anyone."

"Speak for yourself," mumbled Isabelle.

"Oh, that is very true," Hope said louder. "I was terribly jealous when I first encountered Mary. I wondered how God could be so cruel as to give over my portion of beauty to another woman. Then I realized he had also given her my share of wit."

"Enough of that, Hope," Mary murmured. "We shall not fall into a match of compliments for you know I shall beat you every time. Your reserves of goodness surpass everyone else's."

Roxanne and Isabelle murmured their agreement.

"Well, then," Mary said with a deep sigh. "Can we all stop complimenting each other and get to the more interesting topic? Who is in the forefront of the race for Kress? He is even more handsome than I had heard. Miss Barclay, what do you think?"

"I told you she was amusing," Hope said ruefully.

Isabelle squeezed Roxanne's hand again and then spoke. "I think he is partial to no one, actually."

Roxanne relaxed.

"Botheration," Mary Haverty said. "That's non-sense. I think he likes you, Miss Barclay."

Roxanne started. "What makes you say such a thing?"

"He thinks no one notices, but he could not keep his eyes from straying toward you during supper. Did not one of the rest of you notice?"

"It's only because we are cousins," Roxanne insisted.

"And when did that stop anyone from marrying in this day and age?" Mary came about in front of her, blocking her path. "Are you fond of your cousin, Miss Barclay?"

Isabelle interrupted Roxanne before she could form a reply. "You do not have to answer that, Tatiana."

"What a lovely name. Tatiana," Mary Haverty ruminated. "It's one of my own middle names."

"Well, I usually go by Harriet," Roxanne said, grabbing the chance to be contrary.

Hope began to laugh and finally Isabelle joined in.

"Are you laughing at me?" Roxanne looked from side to side.

"Not at all," Mary said, chuckling. "You see, I just knew we were all going to be friends. And Isabelle? Do you still fancy Candover?"

"Mary, stop," Hope said, laughing all the harder. "You cannot do this. It's the reason most ladies cannot form a friendship with you. You cannot be so direct."

"I don't see why not. Gentlemen behave in the same way behind our backs. They scratch their, ahem, breeches, and talk of nothing but cards, horses, and"—she paused for effect—"*breeding*. Why can we not do the same? Minus the scratching of course."

"Of course," said Hope trying to catch her breath.

Roxanne did not know what to make of this beautiful, outrageously honest creature in front of her. She wanted so much to dislike her and yet she also wanted to be just like her. She looked at Isabelle and shrugged. "Lady Mary—"

"Please, if we are to be intimate friends, let's dispense with the formalities."

"All right. Here is a question, Mary. What are your ideas regarding gentlemen and their thoughts concerning the fairer sex?"

"Oh, that is easy. Gentlemen are the simplest creatures on earth. They are ruled by lust, not any finer sensibilities. And they either fall all over themselves spouting ridiculous romantic love poems or they are devastating and silent. Some use their charm and wit to excite. But every type might or might not truly be in love with you. And you will never be sure if they really adore you for yourself or not—especially if you possess beauty or a fortune."

"We do not feel sorry for you," Isabelle said dryly.

Mary laughed. "I don't expect you to, Isabelle.

I have tried to tell you many times that I have no interest in James. I don't know why you choose to disbelieve me."

Isabelle grumbled, "I only dislike you because he *thinks* he likes you."

"I've never thought he does," Mary replied. "But you must admit I do nothing to encourage him. Shall I eat raw garlic and breathe on him?"

"Would you?" Isabelle said, hope threading her tone.

"If you would pretend to like me. I've found that if you pretend a feeling for a while it sometimes grows into the truth."

The lady was not only the most beautiful lady on earth, she was also the most accomplished wit Roxanne had ever encountered. It was impossible to find fault with her. "May I ask you something else, Mary?"

"Anything, dearest," Mary replied. "Did you notice I managed to please you by not mentioning either of your two names?"

"Stop!" Hope giggled.

Roxanne ignored her. She just had to know the answer to this question. "How do you know if or when a gentleman loves you?" This was as close as she could come to asking something so close to her heart.

Mary stopped and gazed toward the stars. "Ah, that is easy. You will know by his actions first. The all-important three words most women long to hear come much later. But the real question is how to know exactly when a man *stops* loving you. I learned this the hard way. In fact, they would rather chew off their own hand than ever admit their ardor had cooled toward a lady they formerly adored. They will just slowly pull away from you. First they will stop calling on you, then they will put in only a late appearance to any entertainment they think you will attend, and finally they might very well retreat to the country. The last blow will be when you hear a house party has been formed without you. Within a fortnight, an engagement will be announced. This will be the same gentleman who professed his undying love for you and asked you to wait for him." Her voice became a whisper at the end.

It was so silent after Mary's speech that only summer crickets could be heard on the Mount.

"I'm so sorry," Isabelle murmured.

"It doesn't matter," Mary said. "Perhaps it will serve as a lesson for the rest of you."

"If any gentleman can part with you, what hope is there for the rest of us?" Candover's sister bowed her head dejectedly.

"Silly goose," Mary continued, and relinked her arm with Hope's. "You are too smart to let anyone fool you with false promises. And besides"—she smiled—"you have a brother who would gladly slay any man who dares to hurt you."

"I wish I had had a brother," Roxanne inserted. "Not that I do not appreciate my devoted cousin."

She could not add that a pretend cousin was not at all like a brother. And worse, he appeared devoted only occasionally. The rest of the time he made it perfectly clear that while he might rarely choose to kiss her, or help her since it amused him, he would never ever lose his heart to anyone.

Why should she care, anyway? Nothing could ever come of it. And Roxanne would be gone within a week or less if everything worked in her favor. He was doing her a great kindness actually by offering comfort, protection, an occasional kiss when she demanded, revenge when she did not, and an emotional wall between them that was as high as the cliffs at Kynance Cove.

And that was why she could do the one thing that she should not do.

Tonight.

Before she lost her nerve.

Chapter 12

Alex's intuition had served him well his entire life. It had saved his neck when he was fifteen and he had begged Mémé to leave Mont-Saint-Michel with his brother the night before they had originally planned. It had saved his life many times over when he had assumed a new name and joined the Hussars under Napoleon from the age of sixteen to nineteen, before he had escaped to England. It had not served well only once—the night he had been captured by the Portuguese.

Tonight, however, it appeared his intuition would not serve him well once again. He had been certain Roxanne would seek him out. And so he had excused himself from the boredom of the after-dinner entertainments and had retired early to his apartments.

He was grateful his valet was in London so he could enjoy the solitude of undressing in peace. It was strange. He was coming to like the quiet of the Mount. The ceaseless rush of the waves and the rhythm of the tides. His sleep was never disturbed by the sounds of hooves on cobblestones, or curses from inebriated drivers, or revelers in London. He shook his head. He refused to like rustication.

It was impossible.

It was too much like before.

He examined his pocket watch and then laid it on the marble table near the massive mahogany bed in his chamber. He had decided he would not go to comfort her. That way led to temptation and complete disaster.

But he would not turn her away if she came to him. Yet, if she did come, he could not do what he dreamed of doing every sodding moment. She was far too vulnerable at this moment, even if she displayed a cool front.

He had wanted to throttle that idiot Paxton. Frigid? Roxanne frigid? Why, she was the most open and passionate female he had ever encountered— when she chose. Everything about her left him wanting more. But she would only scoff if he suggested it. It would seem as if he were lying to her to assuage her finer sensibilities. She would disbelieve him and tell him to go—

He cocked his head toward the door and then set aside the crashing bore of a book—*Cows of Southwest England*—that had served far better as an attempted-murder weapon. Footsteps. He had heard footsteps.

He flung back the bedcovers, swung into his dark dressing robe, and crossed to the exit.

He paused, listening, and then opened his door.

Roxanne stood there, in the simple pale blue satin gown she had worn that evening, her clenched hand raised. "I didn't knock," she insisted.

"All right," he agreed. "And I didn't open the door. Do you want to speak to me or not?"

She looked up and down each side of the corridor. "Yes, but not in the hallway."

"Then how about in here?" He grasped her clenched hand and pulled her into his room. He closed and locked the door.

She glanced toward the huge bed and then took several steps to sit on the stool in front of his dressing table. She took up his shaving soap brush and stroked the inside of her other hand. "What did he mean?" Her eyes did not meet his.

He didn't pretend to not understand. "He is *un imbécile*."

"Please answer the question." She lifted her huge eyes and tilted her head back, her pride in evidence. "There's no one else I can ask."

He drew up a side chair, and helped her turn on the stool to face the looking glass. He carefully extracted the first two pins from her simple coiffure. "It refers to a woman who lacks ardor." He exhaled and spit out the rest. "Or cannot find completion."

She remained silent as he pulled more pins from her hair. He glanced over her slim shoulder to see her cast-down eyes in the looking glass.

"You," he continued evenly, "do not suffer from what he suggested. He is an idiot, as I said. A complete fool. He shall be found out ere long."

"How do you know?" Her eyes met his in the reflection of the looking glass.

"Because idiots never get away with—"

"You know what I was referring to—how do you know I'm not what he said?"

Lord, he had hoped she wouldn't ask. "I know because I know you." He combed his fingers through her loosened locks and removed a final pin. He pushed aside her curtain of hair and gently kissed a pulse point on the side of her neck.

"I'm always cold," she muttered. "My feet are like icicles in bed, even during the summer."

"That's because you're a long, tall glass of water. It takes far longer for your blood to circulate to the tips of your toes than a short, stout female. And actually, I suffer from a similar condition. I know it's shocking but I will admit that I sometimes wear woolen stockings to bed."

"You had better not be lying to me," she murmured. "I need you to explain the other thing you said—the part about completion."

"Um . . . did not your mother ever discuss with you—"

"My mother died when I was ten. Of a lung complaint."

"All right," he said, massaging her head. "If a female cannot find completion . . . well, it is sometimes said—"

"Completion? Completion in what?"

He opened his mouth even though he had no idea what he would say.

She continued for him. "You mean if the husband is so repulsed he cannot finish the act?"

"No," he whispered. "That's not it. Roxanne, you are just going to have to take my word for it. You are not frigid. You are just the opposite. You had it right. You had a lying, murderous clod for a husband. We both know it. Do not be a fool by believing anything he says."

She dropped her head down, and her long blond hair fell forward and shone in the candlelight.

He couldn't stop himself from stroking her head again. That one sign of tenderness revived her.

She swiveled on the stool and faced him. "But I didn't particularly care about what he did to me—what husbands and wives do. It didn't repulse me, you understand. It was just a routine activity, rather like candlemaking."

Alex coughed.

"And I assumed he didn't really give much thought to it either for he rarely came to me, if what the midwife confided to me was true. So I agree he was at fault just as much as I for not conceiving a child."

"Yes," he said. "I think we already agreed that a man who prefers plants to women is a . . . Need I say it again?"

She was silent for a while and he retrieved the shaving-soap brush from her stiff fingers.

"Thank you," she murmured. "I only have one last question."

"Yes?" He wasn't sure how much more restraint he had. All this talk of completion and finishing and dipping candles . . . well, it was a good thing his robe concealed far more than his breeches ever had in her presence. He wanted to pounce on her and ravage her and prove to her that there was not an ounce of frigid in her lovely bones.

"If you insist I'm not what he said I was, then why do you find it so easy to keep your distance from me right now?"

"You keep reminding me you are married."

"And you keep reminding me I am dead."

She stood up suddenly from the stool. He slowly rose from his chair until she was forced to tilt her head back to stare into his face.

The candle flickered, and her golden hair shimmered in the low light. He cupped her face with one hand, and her waist with the other—and began walking her backward toward the door. He could not take her. No matter what she said. But he would not make her feel worse by suggesting she was vulnerable.

When they were two steps from the door he stopped.

"You know," she whispered, "you are ruining your hard-earned reputation by turning me away."

He searched her face long and hard. "Perhaps I'm just shortsighted," he murmured.

"Well, I'm farsighted. I think you wanted to go in the other direction," she said, urging him backward toward his bed.

And then, he lost any chance of a witty retort when she reached for the belt of his robe.

God, she had no idea what she was doing. Her knees were shaking uncontrollably. She had never behaved in such an outrageous manner in all her life. It was wicked to speak and act in this fashion. And yet . . .

And yet, she thought she might just very well shrivel up and fade away if she didn't do this. Tonight. With this man.

She was going away. But she would do this and then go away. And she would take this memory with her. It would mean very little to him. Just one more female in a long string of ladies. Maybe, the last one before he chose a wife. And this, most certainly, would be her last chance at intimacy before she moved to a remote corner of Scotland, where there was certain to be more gossip over who did what, when, where, and with whom than in the sprawling villages of Cornwall.

She had unknotted his belt. And with that movement he had repositioned her so that her back was to the bed. She forced herself to be bold. To do what she had seen the maid do to the stable master behind the hayrick. She ran her hands inside his charcoal velvet robe to circle his narrow, rock-hard hips and finally rested her fingers on his back. His muscles tensed through the fine linen of his nightshirt. A breath hissed out of him as she tucked herself inside his robe. He was so warm and she was so cold. Her body drank in his heat.

A moment later she felt his fingers and hands move to the short puffed sleeves of her evening gown. He eased down the wisp of satin and dipped to kiss her shoulder.

Oh, he was going to do it again. He was going to touch and kiss her breasts, something she had relived in the solitude of her bed almost every night since that evening by the pond. She had never felt anything like it. Just the memory of it left her dizzy with longing.

The stillness of the night was disturbed only by their breathing.

He eventually lifted his head and searched her face from half-shuttered eyes. She felt his fingers working the row of tiny unseen buttons on the back of her gown.

"Don't know why people ever complain about buttons," he murmured, dropping a kiss on her forehead. "It's all in the waiting, don't you agree?"

"I wouldn't know," she whispered, breathless.

He winked, and pulled apart the edges of her gown until it fell open to her waist. "Mmmm," he murmured, plucking at the ties of her corset, loosening them.

She wasn't sure why the prickle of mortification tickled her. It wasn't as if he hadn't seen her small breasts. It was just that before he had eased them above her corset and gown, making them appear larger than they were. She had always been painfully embarrassed by her coltish figure. Her father had always told her she was the son he had never had whenever he had seen her climbing trees and clamoring down into a mine.

Oh, a flurry of thoughts was getting in the way of living this moment. She turned her eyes away from his shoulder to meet his gaze straight on.

"What are you thinking?"

"Nothing," she lied.

"Nothing good I can see," he said with a lazy smile. "Do you know what I've dreamed about?"

She looked away. "No." Certainly it was not about a scarecrow figure of a woman's body.

"Your back." His hands turned her body so she was facing the bed. At the same moment she heard the sound of his heavy robe hitting the carpet. "You can tell a lot about a woman by her back. And you have this way of holding yourself. As if you could balance a book on each shoulder and waltz across a ballroom. I want to see it," he growled. He pulled the final lace from the corset and flung it to the other side of the room. A moment later he managed to disengage her arms from her shift and now she was bare to the waist, and colder than she'd ever been in her life. Her nipples hurt, they were so tight.

His hot palm traced the length of her spine and she shivered.

"Are you chilled, Roxanne?" Without waiting for an answer, he urged her body forward onto the plush draping of the huge bed.

"Not really," she breathed. She was glad he didn't turn her over. She clamped her eyes shut.

The bed dipped and she knew he sat on the edge of the frame. Again, his hand traced the curve of her spine, only this time his other hand joined the first. He singled out every last quivering muscle of her back to ease the tension. As she relaxed, his touch became smoother, and he traced the contours of her back over and over in a figure eight until she grew warm.

And then suddenly, he was pushing the chemise and gown gathered at her waist even lower, exposing her bottom.

She heard a muffled sound escape him. Every muscle in her back reengaged.

"Oh, Roxanne," he murmured.

She dug her face into the covers, mortified.

"You take my breath away. Truly, you do."

And then his mouth took the place of his hands before she could tell him again that she didn't fancy compliments. He was kissing every last inch of her back and her bottom, leaving a trail of gooseflesh in his wake. She turned her head to inhale a huge lungful of air.

She knew she should be lost to these feelings, but she was too busy wondering what he was really thinking and also what she should be doing to him. How could she even touch him if she was too shy to turn over and expose herself to him?

And then, she just didn't care. She remembered that soon he would never see her again. And she knew enough about a man's anatomy to know that when it came to the critical point, he would not be able to feign interest that was not there.

He ran his fingers through her hair, and she could

feel his breath on her back. Slowly, she eased over to face him and managed to somewhat gracefully cross her arms over her breasts at the last minute.

He paused and stared into her eyes. "Everyone has something they don't like about their physique, Roxanne. You've made it easy to divine yours." He paused. "Soon, you might guess mine."

His brown eyes had grown darker in the night. She silently released her breasts to grasp the sides of his nearly translucent white nightshirt and inched it up. He stayed her hands. "Not yet," he insisted.

"Why?" Her voice didn't sound like her own.

His voice was raspy. "Because I'm not done."

She knew nothing about turns. "Am I not to touch you?"

"Later," he growled, and then dipped down to taste her. She squeezed her eyes shut and bit her lip at the pleasure of it. She wanted to twist against him, but didn't dare because she didn't want him to stop. She curled her toes instead and could not stop a moan from escaping her lips. His warm palm massaged her other breast and tweaked the crest as he gently bit the other's tip. Her entire body convulsed on the bed and warmth flooded her womb. "Ohhhh . . ."

"Mmmmm," he murmured as he continued his torturous ministrations.

She could not stop herself from arching her back to get closer to him and he complied with maddening leisure, feasting on her for such long minutes that her flesh ached and became even more sensitive to his tongue. She crossed her legs and squirmed. And her hands clenched his arms, clasping him still closer. She was afraid he might stop, and there was something achingly elusive about what he was doing. She wanted him to continue but she also wanted him to stop.

As if he could read her mind, he glanced up at her, his mouth covering her nipple, and gazed at her with . . . with reverence. Yes, that is what she hoped it was.

All sensation was centered on her small breasts, and he would not stop the pleasure pain of it. It seemed forever that she strained against him as he touched her with his tongue, his mouth, his teeth, and his firm fingers. She was ready to scream from the white hot desire.

All at once, she realized one of his hands had drifted to her navel and then . . . lower.

He stroked the blond curls at the apex of her thighs, and she inhaled sharply.

Yes . . . That was where another ache had grown.

The candlelight flickered over the features of his beautiful face, which appeared strained.

He nipped her breast again and again and then soothed it with his tongue and his lips. Oh, was there a more wonderful feeling?

And then, just as he sucked hard, his hand slid fully between her thighs, and two of his fingers entered her, his thumb pressing higher.

She shattered into a thousand points of light, and cried out his name. He plunged deeper, and sucked harder and she convulsed, great pulses throbbing deep inside her, clutching his fingers, which moved within her relentlessly.

She couldn't breathe, afraid it might stop. Slowly, the last undulation echoed through her, and she gulped air inelegantly like a drowning woman.

He gently released her and drew her into his arms, rolling her until they were side by side. He was still clothed, while she was more naked than not. He pushed away the rest of her rumpled gown from her legs, using his foot.

"I've been a very patient man," he groaned, kissing the tip of her nose.

"Mmmm," she said, unable to speak coherently.

"I've been longing to see certain parts of you since the day I met you. All right, perhaps it was the next day when I saw you without all that dust."

She snuggled into the crook of his neck. "Don't be ridiculous. I know you never longed to see my breasts."

"No, you're correct," he murmured frankly. "I didn't have to fantasize about them as I became *un peu fou* after touching them the—"

"*Un peu?* That means *little*. You don't need to remind me of the size—" she interrupted.

"Hush," he interrupted right back. "I said they drove me *a little crazy*. And no, you are not to tell me I'm not allowed to give compliments while in bed," he insisted. "You must allow the Gallic in me to overcome the dour English, who cannot come up with an original observation at the point of a dagger."

She said not a word.

"It's hard to decide," he said, as if trying to decipher a complicated algorithm, "if I've wanted more to see your derrière or your legs, which I still have not examined, by the way."

"And why is that?"

"Because I had not paid homage to where you wanted attention."

"How did you know?" She was whispering so softly, he had to bend his head toward her.

"I knew. Every person secretly longs for someone to adore the one part they do not find attractive."

She was silent for a long moment before she spoke. "Your legs," she said softly.

"What about my legs?"

"That's the part of you that you don't like."

"I can't imagine why I would not like my legs. They are very fine legs for a man," he said with hauteur.

She smiled. "I'm sure they are."

"Well, then, why did you suggest I would be embarrassed by my legs?"

"To stop you from uttering some ridiculous compliment again."

"You're very sure of yourself now, eh?"

"Thank you," she said quietly.

"*Pourquoi?*"

"Please don't do that. French makes me nervous."

"Why did you thank me?"

"I finally understand what you were trying to explain to me earlier about completion."

"Good."

She wondered why he wasn't trying to cover her with his body now. He had far too much control over himself for someone who truly lusted after her. Well, she was done being embarrassed. She would address the issue straight on.

She grasped the side of his nightshirt and tugged it up.

He stopped her hand. "Don't you think that was enough of an education for one night?"

"Oh, my God. It's your—your manhood," she whispered, shocked.

"What about it?" His entire body tensed.

"What you're embarrassed about," she replied with compassion.

He immediately sat up and removed his shirt.

"No, bloody hell. It's not that. Good God, woman, don't you know enough to never, ever suggest something like that to a man?"

She looked at the gleaming sheen of bronzed, muscled flesh in front of her and swallowed. Dear Lord, he was perfect. She could see the fast pulse of a vein near his neck, and dragged her eyes down across the defined ridges of his chest and abdomen. There were so many ripples with each tiny movement. A sprinkling of dark hair dusted the planes of his chest.

She just couldn't bring herself to drop her gaze lower than his navel, and the defined V of his hips. There was a trail of dark hair . . . She jerked her gaze up to meet his.

He didn't know how to tell her that he wasn't embarrassed about a single inch of his physique. He could not care less about his form. As long as it accomplished the tasks he set out for it to do, he was satisfied.

The problem was that there was a certain part of him that he had pushed long past the task he usually assigned it, and he was as unsatisfied as a soldier on the march for two years.

He growled and reached down to lift her leg in the air and rolled away the stocking. "I knew it."

She pointed her toes reflexively.

"It's a bloody toss-up," he declared.

"What is?"

"I can't decide if I like better your lovely long legs, or your derrière. Both are perfection."

"You, Alex, are impossible."

"Then again," he continued, "there is the matter

of your breasts. Extraordinarily responsive. I think we should check on them again, don't you?"

"Enough! You must stop dishing out this muck. I'm immune."

"Ahem, I think we already proved you are not."

"Why can't I be immune, if you are?"

"Who said I was immune?"

"Well . . ."

"Oh, for bloody hell. How can you be embarrassed to say anything to me after tonight?"

"All right, why haven't you taken me in the usual fashion? Do you not want to?"

He rolled his eyes. "Are you blind?" He reached for her hand and guided it to his arousal. And then regretted it. "Oh God. Don't move," he ground out.

"I'm not a virgin. Remember, Alex? You seem in pain. Let me ease you."

"No," he insisted roughly.

"How ridiculous," she whispered.

"We've proved what you came here to find out."

"What? That I'm not frigid?"

"Exactly."

"Why are you considered a rake again? Do I have to beg you?" She searched his face, and he felt like the idiot he was. "I'm not leaving you like this."

"Just touch me then, *cherie*," he groaned. He covered her hand with his own. "Like this." He guided her for a few strokes and then he released her hand to clench his. He shouldn't have shown her. It would be over far too fast. But then, it would be better that way. He closed his eyes and tried to concentrate on all the stupid breeds of dairy cows in Cornwall.

In alphabetical order.

The Aberdeen Angus, the bloody British White,

and the . . . Devon . . . No, the *South* Devon . . . *Oh, God*.

He felt the warmth of her other hand cup his *bonbons* and he was lost in that delicious sensation tightening his lower back.

He was like a fountain under pressure, exploding in a never-ending series of long bursts. Warmth filled his veins as it continued in strong pulses. He breathed in as the pulses slowed to a stop. Alex felt lighter than air and couldn't move for the heaven of it.

After long moments, he finally gathered an edge of linen sheeting and swiped away the evidence of his spilled seed before grasping her close to him.

"I'm sorry," she said in all seriousness.

He bit back a smile. "I can't wait to hear why." Alex stroked her hair, and felt the strong stirrings of happiness in his chest. He pushed it away and tried to find humor in the scenario. He failed miserably as they stayed there, silent. He could almost hear the grinding of the gears in her head.

"I'm sorry I took advantage of you," she finally uttered. "I fear I only came here to prove Lawrence wrong. I might have used you to get back at him."

"You could just use the more traditional approach of lying, you know. You could suggest you succumbed to my virile charms," he uttered, not believing a word she said.

"If it makes you feel better, we could employ that excuse. Go ahead and add another notch to your bedpost. Who am I to deny you your measure of male pride?" She placed her hand over his heart.

"Actually," he admitted, trying to keep a lightness in his voice he did not feel. "It's only a half notch as we did not truly engage in relations."

"It was more intimate than anything in my woeful history," she replied quietly.

He nuzzled her head and kissed her lightly. Her hand was now caressing his chest and abdomen as she appeared lost in thought. She had no idea what it was doing to him. She had no idea what the mere thought of her did to him. He couldn't stop the groan as she traced the trail of hair down past his navel.

She abruptly stopped. Her eyes flew up to meet his and she smiled with surprise. "Don't tell me you require another half notch?"

His lips twitched on her neck, and then he lightly nipped her. "I'm known for my pride."

"Well, I'm not at all sure I can do this to you," she whispered in a light tone that did not match the seriousness of her eyes.

"Whatever do you mean?"

"I don't want to let you down. I fear I shall hurt you too badly when I leave."

"I believe I'm the one who is supposed to say that, *cherie*."

"No. You have too much male in you and would never dare say it—even if you feel it. It's a well-established fact that a man would rather chew off his own hand than tell a woman he has tired of her."

"Who told you that? It sounds like something that vixen Lady Mary would say."

She tried to look away but he would not let her. "We both know I'm leaving and I have another life to begin living as do you with someone on that marriage list. I told you I'm going away as soon as I recover my fortune. So . . ."

"So . . . what?" Her breast fit the palm of his hand perfectly.

She inhaled with a hiss when he pinched the tip.

"So I shall apologize now for any hurt I cause you later when I take my leave." Her huge eyes glittered in the candlelight.

Now he wasn't sure if she was acting or not. "All right. I'll play this game if you insist," he said evenly. "But I'm not certain I'll recover. I sense a decline in my future."

He had no earthly idea how those words would come back to haunt him in such a short period of time.

"I like you better when you are English. The French in you is *un peu* too inclined to spout nonsense."

"That's not how to say it, *cherie*." He whispered something wicked and incomprehensible in her ear while he did something very explicit with his hands.

She gasped.

But tonight's game would soon be over and they both knew it.

Chapter 13

She pursed her lips. Lord, how was she to withstand him?

She was *not* falling in love with him. She was merely in love with the idea of him . . . of an honest to goodness gentle man. A sheep in wolf's clothing.

Oh, she was a complete idiot and knew it. But there was nothing she could do to stop her emotions. Shouldn't a woman whose husband had tried to kill her nearly a month ago take a little more care to guard her heart?

But no. She never had, had she? It wasn't in her nature, or in the nature of her father. Love was everything. Love was grand. And she would rather love and then leave than leave without having loved.

Not that she would ever admit it. Mary had been wrong. It was a woman who would chew off her own hand rather than tell a man she loved him without knowing he loved her, too. And there was not a chance of her ever hearing those words from Alexander Barclay, the ninth Duke of Kress, the man who had locked away his heart more thoroughly than the Bank of England guarded the country's wealth.

But his pride was nothing to hers. When she left, she would leave with her head high, and her pride intact. Yes, it would be the only thing keeping her warm this winter. And she would refuse to spend a single second wondering about his future life with a well-chosen young wife.

There was only one thing that was certain. If she made the mistake of making love to him, she would lose herself in the process. Her heart might very well be already lost, yes, but not yet her soul. She must extricate herself before it was too late. He had been strong enough to stop her earlier, now she must be strong enough for herself.

"I'm sorry, Alexander," she whispered. "I just can't do this to you." *To me*, she wanted to shout.

He searched her face and tucked her into his arms. "Of course. But, I insist you stay here just a bit longer, won't you? You look so very tired."

She usually slept unevenly and woke at dawn's first light. It was a habit born of years working with her father and then of managing her own household. Papa had taught her the importance of keeping similar hours to the mine workers and the servants. And so she was surprised to wake with sunlight streaming through the gap of the heavy curtains.

Good Lord. She was still in the Duke of Kress's bed. She turned her head quickly only to find he was gone; the indentation of his head imprinted on the long bolster they had shared was the only indication that he had been there. Her eyes noticed a teacup resting on the walnut table next to his bed. She dragged herself to his side and noticed a note.

> *The door is locked. The tea is for you.*
> *See you at supper.*
>
> *A.*

That was it . . . The most extraordinary night of her life, and all that remained was an impersonal note of three sentences left on a bedside table. It might as well have said, "Wonderful to see you. Do take care. So busy, must go."

She sank back into the bed and pulled the sheet over her head. Oh, why was she surprised? Really, what did she expect? Flowers, a solution to her impossible situation, and a grand proposal?

Why, she had practically forced herself on him. Had he not made it perfectly clear that he did not believe in love? Had he not told her the very first day they had met that he was under orders by His Majesty to marry a rich, titled heiress? And had she not told him a thousand times that she loathed compliments and that she was leaving? And there was no need to add that she was married and dead.

She had no one to blame but herself. She must lock away her sentiments in the coffer of her soul and throw away the key. It was the only answer.

She pushed down the sheet, struggled into an upright position and drank the stone-cold tea in one long gulp. Then she fell out of the bed and recovered all her articles of clothing strewn about the room, save one. She searched high and low before she finally spied her corset hanging from a wall sconce.

Oh, for heaven's sake.

Fully dressed in evening satin, she tried to arrange her hair in a simple chignon with little success. Her hands were trembling as she remembered what she had done with the duke this past evening.

She listened at the door before gaining the nerve to turn the key in the lock and peek into the hallway. She silently rushed to her apartment, three corridors east of his. She felt dizzy and realized she had forgotten to breathe while she dashed.

Never so grateful that there was no maid assigned to her, Roxanne calmed herself by taking a cold sponge bath and then dressed in the clean, newly mended gown she had been wearing when Alex had found her hanging on the cliff of Kynance Cove. She didn't dare ruin any of Mémé's. But she was going to need help if she was to succeed in the endeavor she must face today.

Time had run out.

She had gotten as much revenge as she was ever going to get by seeing Lawrence's ruined lawn and gardens. And more importantly, she had the answer to why Lawrence had tried to discard her from his life. Now she must go, if only to avoid the awkwardness of hiding her sensibilities from Alex.

By the time she finished her toilette, her hands had stopped fluttering. She stared at her reflection in the looking glass, and there were roses in her cheeks. There was no doubt who had put them there. She felt more womanly than she had ever felt in her life.

And more alone than ever before.

Roxanne wended her way down the servants' stairs and stopped a footman to ask the whereabouts of Isabelle.

"In the music room, ma'am."

The music room? Roxanne was certain Isabelle had said she didn't play any instrument. She stopped at the room's entrance and heard one of the worst renditions of some sort of sonata on the flute. She made her presence known.

Isabelle stopped instantly. "Oh, thank heaven you've come to release me from my delusions of talent."

"But you loathe playing instruments. You told me."

"Yes, well, that was before *someone* mentioned his admiration of music and the woman who played with amazing flare."

"Don't tell me Mary has talent in that corner as well."

"All right, I won't. I shall only say that she plays the pianoforte like Mozart and sings like an operatic genius."

"I really don't like her."

"Oh, stop it. We all like her."

"She's impossible."

"Impossibly perfect."

"Nobody likes perfection."

"Except Cando—"

Roxanne interrupted. "He doesn't. Oh, do let's stop. We could go on all day and I have something important to ask you."

"Yes?"

Roxanne retraced her steps and closed the music room door. "Isabelle, I'm sorry to ask this of you, but may I share a confidence? It is something gravely important, and I would require that you not speak of it to anyone. Ever. And it will likely change your opinion of me forever. But I have no other recourse."

Isabelle's eyes grew round with excitement. "Oh, I adore secrets. Does it have to do with your cousin?

He's proposed? Or did he . . ." She clapped her hands and covered her mouth with glee. "You can count on me. I shan't tell a soul."

"No," Roxanne said sourly. "It has absolutely nothing to do with him." She grasped Isabelle's hands. "Look, my life depends on this. Truly."

"Tell me."

And following those two breathless words, she told Isabelle who she was, where she had lived, to whom she was married, the person she was indebted to for saving her life and hiding her, and finally that she would be leaving very soon to create a new life but needed her help.

"So, if I have the right of it, you're really Harriet somebody?"

"No. Roxanne Vanderhaven. The daughter of Cormick Newton of Redruth."

"Hmmm . . . Roxanne. I've always adored that name. Much lovelier than Tatiana, which never really sounded very English."

Roxanne sighed.

"And you're a tin miner's daughter, not Kress's third cousin four times removed? And the countess of an idiot."

"Precisely."

"And you're in love with Kress."

"I beg your pardon? I never said that."

"Perhaps," Isabelle said slyly. "But I knew it."

Roxanne sighed again. "So will you help me?"

"Do what?"

"Recover my fortune. I can't do it alone. And I do not trust anyone but you."

"What about Kress?"

She looked at her feet. "I'd rather not."

"Well, then," Isabelle said. "Let's be off."

"Really?"

"Really," Isabelle insisted. "Let's take the servants' entrance so no one will see us."

"I shall forever be in your debt," Roxanne said, taking up her friend's hands. "You are the first noblewoman who doesn't seem to mind the smell of tin."

"Tin? Really? I've always thought you smell like honey if anything."

"That's just soap," Roxanne said quietly. "Thank you, Isabelle. Thank you so very much."

"Oh, botheration. Let's go now before Mary comes and makes me feel even less capable of producing music with this bloody instrument than I am."

Roxanne smiled and pulled her toward the door.

Within a half hour they were dashing across the shingle path to collect the horses they would need. As they rode toward the home of her childhood, Gwennap near Redruth, Roxanne felt a great calm settle over her. They took the older, forgotten lanes to avoid notice. But when the familiar scent of fresh, hot pasties drifted from a lone miner's cottage, Roxanne begged Isabelle to go inside to buy two while she hid behind a stand of trees.

Isabelle bit into hers and moaned with delight. "Like apple pie. Mmmm."

Roxanne grinned. "You started on the wrong end."

"Whatever do you mean?" Isabelle mumbled as she took another inelegant, large bite.

"You're supposed to start on the savory end— with the meat and potatoes and peas—and then you work your way to the side with the fruit." Roxanne sniffed one end and bit into the flaky crust.

"How convenient," Isabelle said, not at all following Roxanne's directions. "But I shan't stop now. I think I now prefer dessert first. One never knows if one will have room for it. True? Who cares about peas and potatoes when one can have something sweet?"

Roxanne adored Isabelle. She had never had a friend like her. Oh, the wives and daughters of the miners had enjoyed her company, but Roxanne had had to follow her father's instructions to always remember that they were employees, and so to always be friendly and respectful, but never to confide anything of importance. Isabelle was the first lady with whom she could be fully herself.

"So where are we going?" Isabelle dabbed at her dainty mouth with the cloth Roxanne handed her from the saddle pouch.

"Very few people go to this place, Isabelle," she warned. "For good reason. It was a mine my father started two decades ago. But it was abandoned after an accident. Miners refused to work it, saying it was haunted by those whose lives it claimed."

"That is where he left your fortune?" Isabelle's eyes were huge in her face.

"Don't worry so. You're not going down there," Roxanne said with a smile. "I am."

"Aren't you afraid?"

"Not at all. I know all the mines very well, even this one. While there is an old wives' tale suggesting women in mines are bad luck, that never stopped me from going with my father. I was always fascinated by every aspect of the trade."

Roxanne took up the reins again and clucked to urge her horse forward. Isabelle followed suit. The petite duchess asked an endless number of questions the rest of the ride to the deserted Wheal Bissoe mine.

Roxanne knew her father would have left everything she would need, as his attention to detail had been unparalleled. Indeed, when she drew closer to the narrow, stone engine house, and the smaller structure which housed the miners' dry goods, she could almost sense her father's spirit hovering nearby. In his old locker, she found a set of canvas jacket and trousers along with traditional wooden-soled boots, and several felt tulle hats hardened with pine resin. He had not forgotten to leave beeswax candles—one at each end of a very long wick. She swung several about her neck.

"I forgot the clay in the saddlebag, Isabelle," she said to her friend, who appeared more terrified than Roxanne had hoped. "Don't worry. It will only take an hour or so to negotiate the ladders. I'm certain my father accounted for the varying level of the water. The pump was destroyed by the blast, but not the series of platforms and ladders at the top.

"Why do you need clay?" Isabelle was desperately trying to act much calmer than she was.

"I'll show you."

Isabelle didn't need any further hint to fetch the packet. Roxanne peered into the dark entrance to the mine and took a deep breath as she mumbled an old Cornish mining prayer.

Placing a dab of clay on top of the hard felt hat, Roxanne stuck one of the candles in the middle to secure it before lighting it.

"How convenient," Isabelle murmured, biting her lip. "Are you certain it wouldn't be better to have Kress here? What if you should require help?"

Roxanne dragged out a huge coil of rope. "See those two pulleys over there? I'll thread one end through them both and all you'll need to do is let out the safety line when I tell you. I might really need it depending on what I must haul out of there."

"Why don't you attach it to your waist?"

"Because it would be too easy for it to become twisted and catch on something and I can't take the risk of getting stuck. But I can try to keep it free. Please don't worry. I know how the platforms and ladders are positioned."

"Well, I refuse to continue on like a mother hen. It's obvious you know what you're doing, Tatiana."

"Roxanne." She looked at Isabelle pointedly.

"I think I've the right to call you whatever I want at a time like this—when you've asked me to watch you possibly fall to your death."

"Good point," Roxanne said with a grin and tugged the rope through the pulleys. She then took a step down the first ladder. "And by the way . . . thank you, Isabelle."

Her friend was flustered, and biting her lip, but refused to say another thing. Her clenched hands on the rope said everything.

Roxanne nimbly felt her way down the ladder, taking care not to look down as was a miner's way. As she descended the second and third series of ladders, the light from the mouth of the entrance grew dim and her candle only shone enough light for her to see her hands. She counted the rungs, knowing exactly when the next platform would be reached.

There were eleven ladders to negotiate. The scent of stone and minerals invaded her nostrils as did the damp from the water below, and the sweat from the mine's walls. It grew hotter with each level down, and she remembered how wonderful and brave the mining families had been who worked in her father's mines. She began to hum a song to calm herself.

Every now and again Isabelle would call down all the while feeding out more line. Her voice echoed and Roxanne would reassure her. "You're letting the line out too slowly, Isabelle!"

Roxanne couldn't make out Isabelle's reply, but her tone was annoyed.

On the ninth platform, Isabelle again called out, more faintly this time, and Roxanne lost her concentration. She failed to test the rung of the ladder before placing her full weight upon it.

The wood had rotted, and down she went, the force of her fall wreaking havoc on the rest of the rungs of the ladder. As she lay panting on the tenth platform in total darkness without the flame of the candle to help, her mind reeled. She could hear Isabelle shouting to her, but all Roxanne could do was lie there gasping, the wind knocked out of her.

And now Isabelle was crying and saying she was leaving to find Kress.

All Roxanne could do was rasp, "No! I'll be fine." But she knew it was a futile effort. She could barely hear herself. The oddest thing was that she wasn't scared. Her father had taught her long ago never to be afraid of the dark. As she regained her breath and tested out her limbs, she knew she was not gravely injured. Finally, she sat up, her arms tingling.

Disentangling a new long candlewick from around her neck, she reached for the small flint box in her pocket. The flame from the beeswax candle confirmed that the arms of the canvas jacket had ripped and Roxanne's arms now had more splinters than she cared to think about. Her head ached, but she was fine. She peered over the edge of the platform and wondered if the last ladder was safe. Of course, Isabelle had fled without letting out more line, and it hung just out of reach.

She was going to be sore tomorrow, but she was going to retrieve her fortune today. Inching down the ladder, Roxanne took more time than was necessary to descend to the eleventh platform. She removed the new candle from her hat and looked for a crack on the mine's wall. Her father's whispered instructions floated in her mind. Spying a fissure, Roxanne retrieved the chisel from her pocket and wedged it at an angle. Quickly, she popped open the inch-thick stone face hiding a carved out space beyond. Relieved beyond measure, she reached inside.

"She did what?" Alex said, his guts falling to his toes.

"Don't have time," Isabelle panted, barely able to talk. "Come . . . get to the boat . . . waiting."

Alex picked her up like a child and began running down the steep path from the dairy on the Mount, his carefully drawn plans for the soon to be renovated structure fluttering behind them.

"Put me down, Alex!"

"No, not till you catch your breath."

He nearly tossed her into the waiting boat as he spoke to the oarsman. "I'll double your wage if you take us back in half the time."

"Aye, aye, yer Highness." The man had but one tooth in his gummy smile.

Isabelle tugged on his sleeve. "She might be dead," she whispered, her eyes terrified in her pretty face. "We must prepare ourselves, Alex. I shouldn't have let her do it."

"Hush." He couldn't manage anymore. He was already plotting out a scenario for something he knew nothing about. "Is there rope or do I need to secure some?"

"There's quite a bit of rope."

"But is there enough? Think, Isabelle."

"I told you, there's rope. There's so much rope in the building next door, it could probably reach China, for God's sakes. Oh, Alex . . ." Tears welled in her eyes.

"Don't you dare, Isabelle." He had the sudden memory of Roxanne and how she had not shed a single tear when he had saved her.

"Fine," she said raising her chin. "I told the stable master in Penzance to prepare his strongest animal for you since Bacchus is at the Mount. Another fresh horse awaits me."

He couldn't respond. Could barely say anything— his mind was racing. "How deep is it?"

"I don't know."

"How much rope did you drop into it?"

"I told you, I don't know."

"How wide is the mine's mouth?"

"Maybe five or six feet? I—I don't really know."

"Well, what do you know?" He refused to shout, but he felt like jumping out of the boat and swimming to shore. The damned oarsman was grinning like a fool, and rowing far too slowly to his way of thinking.

"Alexander Barclay, you cannot talk to me like

this. It is not my fault. I tried to talk her out of it. I told her it would be better if you were there."

"You just told me it was your fault."

"You were supposed to disagree with me."

"Has she been giving you lessons?"

"In what?"

"Talking in circles?"

"Well, I like that." Isabelle crossed her arms and turned in the other direction.

Neither said more than three words to each other the rest of the awful journey to the mine.

Alex had lost the habit of prayer long ago. Half the inclination had left him when he watched Mont-Saint-Michel go up in flames. The other half disappeared during the war when he had lied about his age and served as the youngest Hussar, only to face a terrible test and nearly lose his sanity.

As he threw himself off of the gelding's saddle and ran toward the entrance to the mine, without waiting for Isabelle to dismount, he began to pray. But he could only envision one thing. And it wasn't Roxanne.

It was that dank, dark-as-pitch prison cell, where he had been held for four long months during the Peninsular War. The Portuguese renegades didn't care when he insisted he was half English and half French. They only saw his uniform and threw him in that small hole to rot, instead of wasting a bullet on him. It had been a miracle he had survived long enough on his keeper's scraps to have been rescued. He had never told a soul about his ordeal. He had never wanted to think of it ever again. It was better that way.

But now . . . Now, he was about to live it all over again. His future was now the hell of his past. He prayed he could face it with courage he knew he did not possess.

He crawled to the edge, his legs cramping already. The first time he tried to shout her name, it was barely a rasp. The second time he bellowed her name so loudly surely they would hear it on the Mount. He closed his eyes and cupped his ear to listen.

"Alex?" Her faint voice was like cool water flowing toward a parched and dying man.

Isabelle limped forward, breathing hard. "Did she answer?"

He nodded, unable to speak in his relief.

"I'm fine, really, just fine," Roxanne's voice bubbled up from below. "Tell Isabelle not to worry."

Alex exhaled roughly and then turned to glare at the duchess. "She said you should worry."

"She would never." Isabelle placed her hands on her hips.

"She said she might strangle you for letting her go down there in the first place."

"Well," she huffed. "If this is how you're going to go on . . ." She turned to head for her horse.

"Enough, Isabelle. Get back here, for Christsakes. I *might* need your help. Even if it is only to get more help should I happen to fall and kill myself." He was having a difficult time drawing air into his lungs.

She stopped in her tracks. "This is not the way I expected to spend the day. But, yes, I shall help both of you and then I am going to return to London where people do not insult me, and I can sit in bed and eat bonbons and *read* novels about heroines and heroes who fall down rotting mine shafts instead of watching them!"

"You're a wonderful woman," Alex replied, but did not dare show her his face. He was even more worried he'd be unable to peel his hands off the edge.

He saw her shadow fall near him. "Are you going in after her or not?"

"Do I have a choice?" He couldn't hide the hitch in his voice. "Of course I am."

"Look, she said something about platforms. Yes. She said she was going down eleven ladders with platforms at the bottom of each ladder. She wouldn't let me tie a rope on her. She said it might snag and would be too dangerous."

"Then why is there a bloody rope dangling down there?"

"Don't you yell at me, Alexander Barclay."

"I'm sorry." He dropped his head.

"Hey, are you all right?" Isabelle knelt beside him.

"I'm bloody fine. I'm going."

"Isabelle?" Roxanne's faint voice called out. "Lower the line another twenty feet."

Alex shook his head. "If we survive this, remind me to never, ever, ever let her out of my sight ever, ever again."

"Of course," Isabelle whispered and laid her hand on his shoulder. "Do you want some candles? I know how to affix them to the hats in the dry room."

He nodded.

Moments later, he pried his hands from the edge of the mine and lowered himself onto the first ladder. He looked up at Isabelle as he plunged into darkness and thought it might just be the last thing he saw for all of eternity. Her eyes reflected the gnawing terror engulfing him. The raw nerves he'd spent a lifetime trying to bury overtook his rational mind. Unconsciously, he took a step down to his own private hell.

And another . . .

Chapter 14

⌒~⌒◯◯⌒~⌒

The descent into the mine was his nightmare come to life. His only lifeline was Roxanne's voice growing stronger with each level he descended. She was pragmatic, giving advice about every detail. He could not utter a syllable in return. With each rung, his nerves unraveled a little more. Sweat flowed down his brow, and his hands grew unsteady. Two platforms down, and he was back in the tiny, dark Portuguese prison cell, starving, and waiting for death.

"Alexander?" Roxanne's concerned voice reached him. "You know, I can do this on my own now that I have the rope. Don't come down any farther. I can find my way out."

He couldn't reply. Three platforms down, and he was wondering how he was going to go on. He remembered the trick he had used sometimes in the cell. He would close his eyes in the dark and recall an entire day on le Mont of his childhood, from dawn until dusk. But he couldn't do that here. He had to concentrate on not falling.

At least he had the small glow of the candle. By

the sixth platform, his breathing was irregular and he was dizzy with fatigue.

He stumbled halfway down the next ladder.

"Alex?" Roxanne shouted. "Stop! I told you not to come down any farther. I'm perfectly able to get back to the top on my own. I'm just using the rope and climbing the one—"

He croaked out a curse. "Don't bloody move." He made it to the seventh level and didn't even stop to ponder his state.

"I don't want you to go another step," Roxanne said, and then paused as if deciding what to say next. "I know what I'm doing. *And—and you don't.*" Her voice had taken on a morbid, humorous edge.

Damn it to hell. "Right," he retorted, stronger now. "Just like you knew what you were doing when you fell off the cliff." The eighth ladder was slippery, but for some reason he was able to focus on his grip.

"This is a mine. It's like a second home to me. I know exactly what to do. Just as I know exactly what to say in every predicament," she said indignantly. "Unlike you."

"And what is that supposed to mean?" He ground out an oath.

"I don't have any need of you or any more of your stupid notes. I can see to myself very well."

"My notes? What in hell are you yammering about now?" He had reached the next rocky ledge without even knowing what he was doing.

"I refuse to discuss it. I'm leaving anyway," she said, sounding much closer. "There are no rungs on the tenth ladder. I broke them."

He ignored her in his indignation. "You're the one who brought it up. What was wrong with my note?"

"You mean the one that said, drink your tea and be on your way since I've got so many more important things to do, and I don't want to have to face or talk to you this morning?"

She was so close he could hear the effort of her breathing. She had not listened to his instructions and had obviously ascended the rope.

"You are like every woman from time immemorial. You say you don't want something—in your case, compliments and romantic nonsense—when in fact you crave the reverse." He could see the tiny light of her candle growing brighter with each platform.

"You know, I've changed my mind. I've figured out your physical fault and it's—"

"Don't want to hear it," he interrupted. "And by the way, you snore."

"Is it a long gurgle, with a loud snort at the end? Kind of like the noise you made all night long?" she asked sweetly.

"I do believe now would be the proper time to tell you that you are, indeed, frigid."

"You also drool," she retorted. "Hold the rope steady, I'm almost up to your level. And grab on to the one length of the broken ladder in case I need it."

He did as she asked, muttering loudly about females who did not do as they were told, and damning all well-meaning notes and compliments to hell.

When she shimmied to his platform, using the rope and the ruined ladder, he had to lean in close to drag her onto the flooring. He finally gazed into her eyes in the soft glow of light radiating from his candle. He could see her eyes. There was great concern reflecting out of their blue depths.

For him.

And that was when he knew . . .

Roxanne had recognized the voice of a person in trouble and out of his league. She'd heard it before from time to time—usually it was a young man on his first trip down. But Alexander's voice had held something else in it. It wasn't simple fear. It wasn't desperation. It was paralyzing agony.

She didn't know why, but she did know that the only thing that had kept her sane when he had hauled her up from certain death on that cliff earlier in the summer was the levity in Alexander's voice after he saved her. And now she was returning the favor. "Hey . . . it's you," she murmured nonsensically. And then she slowly slid into his arms, taking care with the candles.

His chest was solid as a tree trunk despite his labored breathing. Roxanne wracked her brain for more nonsense.

"And just think," she said, voice steady, "when we get to the top, you shall have the rest of the afternoon to shower me with lectures. And all the while you'll have the added pleasure of knowing I prefer them to false compliments. Oh . . . ouch!"

"What is it?" His composure was stretched to the limit.

"Splinters. Lots of them. You'll be able to torture me while removing those, too."

He was silent, his arms still encircling her.

"Alexander?"

"Yes?"

"Let's go. I need you to ascend first, to test the rungs as some are not sturdy." She could not trust him to follow her.

He didn't move. He had a death grip on her. It was time to pry him from whatever was keeping him there.

"Look, I have bad news. And more bad news."

He instantly pulled away to look at her. "Are you hurt?"

"No." She tugged him to the rickety ladder and urged him forward. Before he could stop on the higher platform, she had him reaching for the next ladder. "My fortune is not where my father said it was."

"Who cares about your bloody fortune," he said tightly.

She smiled in the darkness. She might just have to love him even more.

The next platform, she remembered, was not as sturdy as the others. "Careful, step to the left," she said. "I care about my fortune. Someone obviously stole it."

"I refuse to talk about this now."

"Well, I want to. I have to see Dickie Jones, the only man my father ever trusted. He'll know who took it." They were on the fifth level, and she touched his arm to see if he was still shaking.

"Please tell me you won't go down any more mines," he retorted.

"I won't as long as you promise never to write another stupid note to me."

"Agreed," he said immediately.

They ascended the next two ladders rapidly.

"And I will leave within the week. I've placed us all in jeopardy."

"How so, aside from nearly causing me apoplexy?"

"I caused you to nearly kill Lawrence, and surely he is beginning to wonder if I really died since you gave him back my ring. Not that I blame you, you understand. I adore that you shoved that tiny, hideous thing onto his finger. But even Lawrence can be a little smarter than I give him credit for at times."

They tackled the next ladder in silence. Roxanne's stinging arms were so tired, she could barely feel them, and her chemise and clothes were soaked through from her exertions in the heated shaft. The hole of light was growing very close and she had to hold Alex back from bolting toward it.

"And I hate that I took Isabelle into my confidence. It is too much to have asked of her."

"You're absolutely right," Alexander retorted.

Thank God he had reverted to his old self.

She plucked at the back of his coat just before he reached for the last ladder. He turned his head and she could see his profile. "Thank you, Alexander," she whispered. "You're one in a million."

"The feeling is entirely mutual," he ground out. "And in case you are wondering, that was not a bloody compliment."

As the cooler air rushed down to meet their last few steps, Roxanne strangely felt elated. She wasn't sure of the why of it. She only knew that instead of being terrified at the knowledge that her father's fortune might be lost to her forever, she didn't seem to care. She felt alive. And she felt free for the first time in her life.

She ran into Isabelle's waiting arms, and closed her eyes to the luxury of the other woman's friendship.

But when she opened her eyes, while still hugging her petite friend, she did not expect to see what she did.

Alexander's back was to her as he stalked toward

a chestnut gelding grazing near shrubs of mauve heather and gorse in full bloom. He threw aside the felt hat, snatched up the horse's reins and swung onto the animal's back. In an instant, he was galloping away from the mine without a single backward glance.

Alex had the unnerving sensation that he was running away. He had never run away from anything. He prided himself in facing up to every hellish situation no matter what the cost. He would rather die bravely than live as a coward. But right now he felt chickenhearted even when he had no reason to feel anything of the sort.

He had gone down that hellhole and he had seen her back to safety.

And everything she had said was correct. She had placed them all in jeopardy. She shouldn't have brought Isabelle to the mine. She shouldn't have gone there at all. At the very least she could have told him her intentions. Not that she ever did anything that did not suit her. Roxanne Vanderhaven had become a plague on his existence. He was glad she was leaving.

And he was going to marry one of Prinny's favorites. What did it matter, really? There was no question he would have married at some point in his life. Not that he could say precisely why he knew that. It was one of the unspoken rules noblemen could not avoid: birth, baptism, marriage, death, and a variety of arcane taxes along the way. And really, what did it matter whether he wedded now or later?

But he'd be a mewling nodcock if he allowed anyone to continue to dictate the way he was living right now—with an insufferable mockery of a house party and a woman who was causing him to do things he had sworn never to do again.

It was all going to end this very night.

And so it did.

Candover didn't know what awaited him that afternoon when Alex sauntered into the famed portrait gallery, which echoed every sound from its hallowed walls covered with more brown-eyed Barclays than should ever exist in one place in Christendom.

"What in bloody hell? I won't have it," the other duke retorted.

"Don't care," Alex said, calmly leaning against the great yawn of the marble mantel seated in the middle of the long, ancient hall. "We're culling the herd. Within the hour. I've informed the maids and valets to begin packing, and I've sent the Cossack ahead to St. Ives where it's being arranged for all of you to spend the first night of your journey to Town."

"You can't do it," Candover seethed. "Have you forgotten the Prince Regent's orders and all that? And it's bloody discourteous to the ladies and their families, who were ordered here by His Majesty not so very long ago.

"Give over. It's been an age." Alex clenched his hands. "All of them are to go, except those on this list." He extracted a piece of paper from his vest and handed it to Candover, whose sour expression bespoke of years of practice.

"You want my older sisters to stay, and Isabelle? Oh, and of course, Mary Haverty. No huge surprise there. Hmmm. But you want the rest to depart . . . including *me and Barry*?"

"You read very well."

Candover's eyes narrowed. "Your hospitality almost moves me to tears, Kress. And here I thought I had grown on you."

"Oh, you've grown on me, all right. Like a barnacle on a ship's arse."

Candover's expression darkened. "If you think I will leave you alone with four innocents, two of whom are my sisters, you're more daft in the attics than I thought."

"I'm willing to compromise," Alex began, stroking his chin. "You may take yourself off along with your sisters, but I shall personally invite Isabelle and Mary to stay on."

"Isabelle will not accept," Candover ground out.

Alex smiled. "If you think you have a chance of convincing a duchess in her own right to do as you say, be my guest."

Candover's expression turned thunderous.

Alex continued smoothly, "My cousin will act as chaperone as will my great-aunt." No need to inform him that Roxanne Tatiana Harriet would be leaving sooner versus later. Nor was it a good time to reflect on his great-aunt's blindness, which seemed in question most of the time.

"Oh, I'll go all right, Kress. If only for the pleasure of informing His Majesty of your complete disregard of his orders and your abysmal *progress* on the matrimonial front. But you have forgotten the archbishop. He will stay."

"The archbishop," Alex echoed, amused. "Ah, yes, the archbishop. That gentleman is so bloody quiet, I've yet to see him anywhere on the Mount. I suppose it will be an age before he finishes his reflections in the chapel for the sins he committed the night of our revelry. Poor man."

"Yes, it's too bad you fail to show even a hint of the same remorse."

"So you are on your knees in the chapel every morning?"

Candover ground his molars to bits. "The archbishop must stay. Especially for Isabelle. You are not to come within ten feet of her or you shall face my sword."

"How chivalrous of you. I shall be certain to tell her of your theatrics and devotion. Really, Candover, you should try just a mite harder to curb your jealousy. It's an ugly trait. Shows a lack of confidence in one's abilities, don't you think?"

The richest duke in England shifted on his feet and Alex was hoping for a good explosion. He'd never seen Candover shed his cool façade. It was impossible not to try and flummox the most famous stiff upper lip in the land. But Alex was not to be satisfied tonight.

"You know, Kress, it's often said that what one most despises in another is the very trait he himself possesses in abundance." Candover smiled.

It was only the second time Alex had ever seen the other man's teeth. "Yes, well, thank God we will not have to put up with each other ere long. And by the by . . ."

"Yes?"

"I have one last favor to request."

Candover's brows rose to the roof.

Chapter 15

Alex figured it was best to get it all over with in one fell swoop. He'd faced down Candover, who was already presumably barking orders for his servants to prepare to depart, and now it was time for Alex to conquer a greater adversary . . . Roxanne Vanderhaven, the most audacious countess who had ever lived and breathed fire on mortal mankind. The passion, humor, and fury she could inspire in his breast during one single twenty-four-hour time span was dangerous to anyone's health. He felt no need to justify his actions. None at all.

Really.

After throwing back a shot of that abominable malted whiskey his forbearers had stacked in the cellars as if preparing for the last siege on earth, Alex decided he would march to Roxanne's far-flung chamber and he would calmly, coolly, coax her through a vast maze of vague suggestions, which would lead her to her own decision—that she would prefer to leave the Mount as soon as possible. To-night even. She kept saying she was going to leave, but had she?

He threw back another shot and stared into space,

examining the dust moats floating in the late afternoon light streaming through his study's window. An uproar of noises filtered past his doors every now and again as the minutes ticked by.

He drank another shot. The malted whiskey was not as bad as he'd previously thought. The frequency of scurrying feet slowed as did the number of times people knocked on his locked door to obviously take their leave.

He couldn't seem to muster an ounce of *politesse*. He refused to acknowledge it was unusual for him to behave thusly. Why, there was no more courteous a people on Earth than the French when it came to manners. The English might think they had the corner on silent grit, but they had nothing when it came to etiquette.

He finally dragged himself to his feet, without a single inch of swagger. He was stone cold sober despite it all. He rather thought it would take, in his current state of mind, a barrel of malted whiskey to settle his anger.

A few minutes later found him staring at the door to her small apartment. Hmmm . . . He might just trespass the other, darker road. Alex cleared his throat and opened the door without a single polite knock.

Her head bobbed up from her task near a basin. She sat in profile, her arm extended with a trickle of blood dripping down.

He exhaled roughly and went to her. "What happened?" He examined her limb.

"Just a few splinters. Remember? I got them when the ladder collapsed."

"I don't remember anything," he lied.

"All the better for you," she replied.

"You're doing it wrong."

"It's hard to see underneath," she replied, attempting to twist her arm.

With a mind of its own, his hand flipped up and opened its palm.

She placed the needle in it. "What was all that commotion earlier? Is everyone gone to tour Penzance?"

He dabbed at the blood with linen and then positioned her arm higher. "No. They're for London." He silently dared her to say one bloody word.

She said not a syllable.

He stopped short of cringing. She had dozens of splinters embedded in her tender flesh. "Is the other side the same?" He could not stem his annoyance.

"Perhaps a few more." She didn't meet his eye, instead she held up the other arm for his inspection.

He inhaled. "I shall arrange for a doctor tomorrow."

"I don't need a doctor. And besides, I know all the doctors in Cornwall. It would be too much of a risk."

"A risk," he murmured, before raising his voice. "A risk to see a doctor? You're killing me, Roxanne. A risk is what you took this morning—not the doctor I will arrange to see you."

"May I have the needle back?"

"No, you may not have the bloody needle back."

"For someone who does not like the Duke of Candover, you are suddenly acting remarkably like him."

"Familiarity breeds familiarity."

She pursed her lips, and it infuriated him that he could not tell if it was from contempt or to keep from laughing.

It would not do. He could not go on like this.

He concentrated on extracting the worst of the splinters first. "Hold still."

Wordlessly, she obeyed him. She flinched not a muscle as he quickly plucked out most of them in silence. He reviewed his work and satisfied, took up her other arm, and completed the task.

"I'm leaving at first light," she murmured.

He inadvertently stabbed her. "Yes, you keep mentioning that."

She barely moved and made not a sound.

"Sorry," he mumbled. "You may leave after the doctor sees you."

"Alexander?"

"Yes?" He dabbed at her red flesh after pulling the last splinter from her arm.

"I'm sorry."

"For what?" His voice was deep and low. "For nearly killing yourself and me? For ranting about some bloody note I left for you? For causing nothing but trouble since the moment you got here?"

A flush rose from the bodice of her modest gown. "Yes. And . . ."

"And?"

"And for never taking the time to properly thank you for all you've done. That's what I'm trying to do, very inelegantly, I agree. But I do realize the best way to thank you is to just depart straightaway so you can begin your new life as required by His Majesty."

"Really," he said, dryly. "So you propose to just skip along the sand flats to Penzance and then walk to Scotland, where you will eke out a living doing what exactly? Harvest blighted potatoes? Start up a henhouse with filched birds?"

Her chin rose a notch. "You do not need to worry about me any longer. Besides, I have a plan."

"Oh, you have a plan? *Mon Dieu.* How many damned times do I have to tell you that plans never work? Life mangles every well-laid plan. Nothing goes according to sodding plans. Oh, but you, the scrappy tin miner's daughter, have a fail-safe plan. Let's hear it."

"No."

"No?"

"No," she replied. "I might owe you my life, among many other things, but I do not owe you an explanation since I'm leaving."

"Oh, you owe me, all right. You promised to pay me for your upkeep, remember?" *What was he saying?* He wanted her to go. For the first time in his life, he could not keep his lips from flapping.

"And I shall repay you. I might not be able to right now, but I shall repay you. I think you know I will not rest until I do."

"I don't want your bloody money."

She sighed heavily. "Well, then, what do you want?"

He paused. He had no bloody idea what he wanted. He had no idea why he was so furious with her. He had meant to lead her to the door—to make her think it her own idea. And she had already decided without his leave.

He was glad. He *should* be glad.

She had learned the answer to the question she had sought, she had had her revenge, and now she must find her own way. Just like he had had to do time after time throughout his life. And yet, here and now, with the opportunity to be rid of her handed to him on a silver platter by the woman herself, he was being as contrary as a sodding adolescent. He wanted her to go, hang it all. She wanted to go. And so he would let her.

He opened his mouth and then shut it. Alex placed the needle on the table, turned on his heel, and crossed to the door before he did something stupid like kiss her senseless.

Before he could open it, a soft tap filtered through the door. "What?" he shouted.

"It's me, Isabelle."

He opened the door and the duchess stared back at him, disapproval brimming in the depths of her golden eyes. "Everyone is gone, just as you ordered. I cannot believe you actually—"

"Not another damned word," he interrupted, irritated beyond measure.

"Don't you dare bark at me, Alexander Barclay," she said tartly. "You know, you sound and look just like Candover right now."

"If I hear one sound minutely resembling a laugh from the person behind me there will be hell to pay," he retorted. He turned to look at Roxanne only to find her flushed face downcast.

Roxanne finally met his glare with compassion. "Isabelle, would you give us a moment?"

"Of course, but it will need to be quick for I have something important to impart." Isabelle exited and closed the door behind her.

"Alex . . . I think it right to tell you before I go that I finally figured out the part of you that you don't like."

"I don't know what you're talking about."

"Yes, you do," she whispered as she loosely wrapped her arms with clean linen. "Just last night you mentioned that everyone was embarrassed about something regarding their physical selves."

"I told you that to make you feel better about yourself. You have nothing to hide. Your physique is perfect just the way it is. Women are uniformly obsessed about insignificant things that men never notice. We're too happy to have captured you in a bed, you see. We're nothing but dogs."

She stared back at him, not giving an inch. "It might have taken me a while to figure it out, but I know." She waited for him to ask her to reveal it, but Alex refused to say another word.

The silence in the room was deafening.

"Well," she continued, "since you obviously don't want to know, I won't force it on you, as I have done everything else. But I shall share a woman's perspective on love, since you just gave me a man's view on sexual congress," she said quietly and then paused before continuing. "Most women would rather live with half a heart and have loved than to live with a whole heart that has never been touched. Most gentlemen, on the other hand, never allow their hearts to be breeched. They find it easier to say goodbye and leave unscathed before the messiness of sensibilities sets in. But, I'm beginning to believe, men have the right of it."

"Are you suggesting—"

Isabelle knocked on the door with more force than a miner striking a vein of gold.

"Do not come in," Alex shouted without taking his eyes off Roxanne.

Isabelle opened the door. "Alexander, the Earl of Paxton is pacing the hall downstairs and insists he will come searching for you himself unless you come down spit spot. Something about ghosts and kidney vetch, whatever that is."

"I shall be gone by dawn," Roxanne murmured. "I'm sorry you must face Lawrence yet again."

He was at his limit. "Enough. We'll continue this after I see to bloody Lord Kidney of Vetch."

She wanted to follow him, but knew it would be too much for either of them to bear. Isabelle came forward and took her in her arms.

"I know I'm supposed to pretend that I didn't hear anything, Roxanne, but I cannot," the duchess murmured.

"I suspected you did," Roxanne choked.

"I have a favor to ask you," Isabelle said.

"I'll do it," Roxanne replied instantly.

"Really? But you haven't even heard what I was about to propose."

"It doesn't matter. You are my friend and I would do anything you asked. Especially after this awful day."

"I know you want to leave. And we both know you love him. And that he must marry someone else since you are already married. We also know it's not going to be me."

"Mary," Roxanne said, standing straighter.

"That's my guess too," Isabelle said, not able to meet her eye. "Look, you must put aside your pride and allow me to help you. And really, you would be helping me even if you would never admit it. I need a lady experienced with running an estate whom I can trust to advise me and live with me. My father's old steward hates having to answer to me. My idea was to find a new one, who would train under the ancient crone, and then at a certain point, I would put both myself and my father's steward out of our misery by giving him a generous pension. This is just one of the innumerable tasks I must address and—"

"Isabelle," Roxanne squeezed her friend's two hands. "I refuse to be a burden to anyone. I'm just not capable of it. I've never had to rely on anyone's generosity and I'm too old to learn how now."

"But you would be helping me. I'm so very alone on my estate. It's a huge burden. And you know so much about . . . Oh, I see you are too stubborn to listen. If you refuse to stay with me then you must allow me to lend you the money to go to Scotland to find a suitable living, or something." Isabelle was out of breath.

"Or something," Roxanne murmured. "Oh, Isabelle, I had to wait a very long time to find a true friend. But now the wait was worth it because I found you. I thank you so much for your kind offers, but I have a plan."

"A plan?" Isabelle looked stunned. "It doesn't involve going down another mine does it? Because if it does I'm afraid I—"

"No," Roxanne laughed. "It involves a man by the name of Dickie Jones. You would like him very much."

"Forgive me, Roxanne, but you must take Kress with you when you go to see this man. He will never tell you he wants to go. But it is the kind thing to do. He will not rest easy until he sees you off safely. And if this Mr. Jones cannot help you, then you must show Kress the gold guineas I will force you to borrow from me before you go—whether it be to my estate or Scotland."

* * *

Lady Mary Haverty was the sort of female Alex Barclay knew very well. Assured, beautiful, accomplished, rich, and certain of her elegant charms. Every man on earth typically fell to his proverbial knees in awe of her.

Lawrence Vanderhaven was no exception. The earl was transfixed and didn't even seem to be aware of Mémé, who hovered near both of them, hampering any chance of flirtation.

This was how Alex found Lord Paxton in the gold-and-white-striped drawing room. The familiar fish-emblazoned coat of arms for both the French and English Mount was prominent in the center of the room.

"Good evening, sir," Alex said with not an ounce of good in his manner.

Paxton reluctantly turned away from Mary the Vixen. "I've come to have a word, if I may be so bold."

"One can hope this is of some importance, Lawrence. I was given to understand that you were in such a state of apoplexy that you were near to death. How goes the head?"

"About that fall—"

"Still seeing ghosts?"

"Your Grace . . . I mean, Peter, or—"

"Why is he calling you Peter?" Mémé interrupted.

"That's what he once asked me to do," said the earl defensively.

"*Mon Dieu*," Mémé said with hauteur dripping from her rigid posture. "Well, I suppose that means I must allow you to address me as Antoinette."

Alex sighed.

"I would be honored, madam."

"I said to call me Antoinette," she said peevishly.

"As we are all to be so informal, please address me as Josephine," Mary Haverty purred. "Mary is such a common name, and Josephine is the pet name I allow my true friends to use."

The earl's head bounced from one person to the next and so on. He could not seem to form any retort.

Alex decided that was how he liked the earl best. "So?"

The earl stammered. "Uh, may I beg a word alone . . . ?"

" . . . *Peter.*" Alex helped him along. "Or Harry, if you prefer."

"Yes, blast it all. May I beg a word alone, Peter Harry?"

"No," he said, studying his fingernails. "Whatever you have to say can be said in front of Antoinette and Josephine."

"You are all uniformly mad," the earl whispered.

Alex raised his eyebrows. "Really? That says something coming from you."

"What is that supposed to mean?" The earl's voice ascended an octave.

"It means, get to the point of your call. I have a table full of wilted lettuces, braised beets, roasted asparagus, tender baby corn and carrots, and an apple and apricot tart waiting," Alex said. "Actually, perhaps it might be best if you join me at table to discuss what you are so hell-bent on saying. Antoinette? Do be so kind as to inform the chef of our additional guest."

"He will not like it," Mémé said, shaking her head. "He does not like changes."

The Earl of Paxton was dumbfounded.

"Oh, do join us," Mary purred. "I will sit at the

other end of the very long table with Antoinette. My hearing is very bad, and—"

"And I can't see," Mémé inserted.

"So, we will leave you to your privacy," insisted Mary Josephine.

Lawrence Vanderhaven appeared to wish he had not come. "Uh, you are all very kind, but I must insist . . . or rather"—he said weakly, mopping his brow—"I would very much appreciate if I could just have ten minutes of the duke's time . . . uh, *Harry Peter's* time."

Alex glared at him. "You may stay until my stomach growls. What is it?"

The other man desperately tried to put a few steps between himself and the ladies. After a long sigh, Alex finally complied.

"Yes, Paxton?"

"I know something is afoot."

"Really? Is it about Sydney Vetch or some other ridiculous person or flower you mentioned this morning? You know, I have no time for this nonsense. Plants are for eating, not revering."

Paxton staggered back, then tried to collect himself. "It's Kidney Vetch, but no, that was just an excuse for your overly large footman . . . No, I'm here to inform you that I saw my wife just before I slipped in my haste to reach her. You were gone before I could tell you."

"You mean your *beloved* wife. Or rather your *not so beloved* wife according to the headstone."

"Yes, yes, whatever you say, Peter Harry. Did you see her as you left my estate, perchance?"

"I saw no one. I saw only a few dozen moles taking tea under a chestnut tree," he said with as much detached disdain as he could muster. "But in your delirium before I left you in the care of your servants, you kept muttering something about *Roxy*. Your beloved wife I presume?"

Lawrence paled. "I've come to ask your help in locating her. I'm afraid she has gone mad. She must have injured her head in the fall from the cliff, and perhaps she does not even know who she is. I fear she might even need to be in an asylum."

"Well, Paxton, you might very well be right. A man knows his wife better than anyone, and I would take your word for it if we ever find her. But what made you draw this conclusion?"

"She left. She must have seen me fall trying to reach her, and yet she was not there when I was revived."

"Forget the countess, man. She'll come around when she gets hungry. Most females are funny that way, don't you think?"

"Or she might just try to murder me in my sleep if she is as insane as I believe."

"Yes, I find that the best ones do try that on occasion."

Lawrence's eyes bounced around in his head with worry. "Look, I just have one more thing—"

"Something more?" Alex wore his best put-upon expression. "Isn't one ghost story enough? And . . . yes, I hear my tummy now. Must see to those rare baby lettuces I had beheaded this afternoon."

Lawrence blanched to the color of baby lettuce. "You—you asked me some nonsense about killing my wife this morning. I hope this does not mean she came to you in her altered state and suggested . . ."

"Suggested what?" Alex's innocent face was one he had perfected in childhood.

"I don't know. I just started piecing together a few things. And you have her dog."

"I rather think the dog has me," Alex sighed heavily. "Or had me."

"That's odd . . . Uh, did you just say, 'had me'? Is Edward no longer here?"

"Truly, it was the strangest thing, Lawrie. A woman appeared at my door this morning and the Cossack couldn't get rid of her. Edward went wild when he saw her. She said something about living on St. Clement's Isle for the last month."

The earl's face became as gray as ancient parchment. "You gave her the dog?"

"Yes, well, I didn't want to, but I couldn't get the mutt away from her. I think Edward was looking for a new owner. Was tiring of the vegetable diet, I suppose."

Lawrence's Adam's apple bobbed.

"If it helps, Lawrie, the lady said she had relatives in Gwennap. Then she said something about visiting someone named Dickie Jones, who would put her up so she could get a proper night's rest before visiting some mine. What was it called? Yes, I'm certain she said the Wheal Bissoe mine would solve all her problems."

His eyes grew to the size of a cow's before a butcher. "What was her name?"

"Tatiana. Or was it Harriet?" He turned toward the two ladies. "Antoinette and Josephine, do you remember which?"

The two women drew near and quickly raised and lowered their shoulders in a uniquely French style that indicated they knew not what he asked.

Alex continued. "The only thing that gave me pause was her gown. It was completely in tatters."

Mémé's vacant eyes took on a gleam. "I would not say her dress was in tatters," she harrumphed. "It was ruched in blue silk, with the most divine little matching half-shawl lined in French satin. Indeed, it looked very much like one I once—"

"How would you know, Antoinette, since you cannot see?" Alex interrupted. He adored when Mémé became contrary to confuse visitors she did not like. Hell, she had probably invented the game of cross-purpose.

"Josephine tells me everything," Mémé said with her usual nonchalance.

Lawrence wrung his hands. "Does it really matter what she was wearing when—"

"Of course, it matters," Mémé interrupted. "Her name was Tatiana. Such a common name on the Mount these days. She appeared very French to me, don't you think, Josephine?"

"Yes," Mary said, a single giggle marring the farce. "Although more than anything she appeared like a ghost out of the morning mist, except she was angrier than one would imagine a ghost could be."

"I will admit," Alex added, "she seemed a bit touched in the head." He assumed a theatrical pose. "Why, do you think it might have been your beloved wife, Paxton?" Could the earl be as stupid as he hoped?

Paxton immediately put his hands behind his back. "You have been so very kind and I cannot disturb you any longer. I thank you so very much for your time. I think I shall go and ponder all you've told me."

Good boy, Alex thought. "Is your finger all right, old man? It looks a bit swollen." He reached out his hand, demanding to see the other man's hands.

"It's nothing really. It's just a ruby ring I found this morning."

"Let's have a look, shall we?"

Lawrence Vanderhaven reluctantly stuck out his swollen pinkie. The small ring had restricted the circulation and the finger was now three times its size and resembled a beet.

"How very fetching," Alex uttered. "And it fits perfectly. I say, 'finders keepers.' "

"Actually, it's mine. Or rather, it was Mother's."

"Really? Hmmm, I admire a man who wears his mother's ring. Antoinette," he continued, "fancy lending me that opal and pearl ring great-uncle gave you? You can't even see it anyway."

Lawrence was just about nearing the end of his last shred of sanity. His upper lip was beaded with sweat, and his face had taken on a nervous tic. "Have you all gone about the bend? I'm sorry to disturb, but really I must take my leave of you. Must go to—"

"My dear Lord Paxton," Alex interrupted, "I regret to inform you that we have two witnesses present, and they might be willing to testify to the local magistrate that it is you who have gone a bit around the bend. I fear that fall you took has caused your brain to swell. Ghosts? Your irrational thoughts this morning and now that ring? Why, I would be willing to swear on a bible that I've seen that ring before today."

"I—I am the magistrate."

"Really? Hmmm. Doesn't seem quite right that a duke answers to an earl, does it? I shall have to talk to Georgie about it."

"Georgie?"

"Yes, my dearest friend in the world, the Prince Regent. I shall present you when we go up to London."

"I'm not able to leave Cornwall at present. But,

thank you kindly. 'Tis the height of the growing season and—"

"But your gardens are all a-jumble. And this further proves my point. I fail to understand why a famed horticulturalist such as yourself would ever allow his grounds to fall to ruin."

"I am not to blame," sputtered Paxton. "I fear someone is plotting to damage my estate, my reputation. Indeed, my very person is at stake." The sheen of perspiration was not attractive on his upper lip.

Alex cocked a brow. "Paranoia is the first symptom of madness. Have you fallen into a decline since killing your beloved countess? Lawrie? Perhaps I should call on a skilled physician to diagnose you. What was the name of that asylum you mentioned?"

The two ladies had moved closer to surround the earl. At that moment, the unmistakable high whine of Eddie pierced the air.

An unseen hand opened the door, and the mutt raced into the room carrying something in his mouth.

Chapter 16

~~~~~~∞∞~~~~~~

Roxanne had the most irresistible urge to run into the chamber behind Eddie. But for once, she resisted. Perhaps it had something to do with the death grip Isabelle had on her arm.

Asylum? He was going to try and put her in an asylum if he found her? She clenched her hands.

"Don't you dare," hissed Isabelle. "Don't ruin it for Alexander."

"For *him*? I was the one hanging off the cliff."

"Just give him another minute," Isabelle begged. "What's in your dog's mouth?"

"A coin purse."

Isabelle quickly turned her face toward her. "Whose coin purse?"

"Yours," Roxanne said with true regret. "But I promise Eddie will return it. He has the softest mouth. He will not ruin it."

"Roxanne Vanderhaven, did you steal my purse from my reticule?"

"Um. No, I just borrowed it, since it is identical to the one I used to have and Lawrence will recognize it. And by the way," she hurried on, "I accept that position you offered."

"Oh, so now I'm expected to take on a confirmed thief for a companion?"

"Is that not expected of an impoverished servant?"

"You might as well tell me more about Mr. Jones and your new plan, because I'll find it out. I'm much better at following you than Alexander will ever be."

"And why is that?"

"Because I can sleep in the same suite of chambers as you without ruining your reputation."

"My reputation? I'm dead. At the very least that means I don't have to worry about my reputation any longer."

"Oh!" Isabelle whispered. "Shush. We're missing the best part, I'm certain. I hear them all coming. Must hide . . ." Isabelle was already tugging her out of sight, behind the curved staircase outside of the drawing room.

"No need to rush off, Paxton," Alexander said as he and Lawrence exited the salon. "The evening is young."

Lawrence mumbled something incomprehensible.

"Very well, suit yourself," the duke replied. "Take your leave if you must. Our paths shall cross ere long. Yes, I suggest you prepare for Town straight away. What say you to the day after tomorrow? Georgie will be so pleased to make your acquaintance and I'm certain he will want to hear all about this business with your beloved wife or her ghost."

"I'm not afraid of you," Paxton suddenly sneered and, like a mad dog, went on the offense. "His Majesty will undoubtedly be very interested to hear all about the truths circulating Cornwall. We know a French loyalist when we see one. And you've done nothing to fortify the Mount."

"Oh, by all means, don't let me stop you, Lawrie,"

Alex drawled. "That is one of His Majesty's favorite subjects. And you might help your cause if you gift Prinny with a few bottles of his favorite brew: absinthe."

Roxanne wished she could see her damned husband's expression, but Isabelle blocked her with a force that surprised Roxanne.

She could hear but one pair of quickly retreating footfalls. Isabelle relaxed her hold and they fell into view of the others who stood on the black-and-white-checked floor of the wide hall.

Several pairs of eyes looked in her direction. It felt more like twenty-four pairs since two columns of Greek philosophers carved of gray marble also stood in judgment of her.

Someone finally spoke—Mémé, of course. "Roxanne?"

"Yes . . ." She hesitated. "Antoinette?"

"How ridiculous," Mémé said. "Everyone knows my name is Jacqueline."

"Of course it is," Roxanne replied softly.

"And how long do you suppose it was before I knew your name was Roxanne Vanderhaven, daughter of famed copper and tin miner Cormick Newton, and wife to a fool?"

"Here we go," muttered Alexander.

Mémé did not wait for an answer. "Less than a day."

Roxanne looked away.

"Do you know how lucky you are, Countess?" Mémé harrumphed. "If a blind woman could discern your secret in a day, how long did you intend to try and keep it from the rest of the world? *Your death* has been reported *to death* in this area of England."

"It was foolish, I agree," Roxanne said quickly.

"And I will leave early on the morrow. I am very sorry—"

"Not sorry enough," growled Alexander.

"Hush," said Mary steadily. "Let her speak."

"I'm sorry for not confiding in you earlier," Roxanne said. "Please understand I did it for one reason alone. It was bad enough that Alex had to be involved. I did not want the rest of you drawn into this sordid affair as well."

"Too little too late, my dear," Mémé said sourly. "And I would have you know that I enjoy watching sordid affairs unfold as much as my great-nephew. Runs in the blood, I suppose. It's the reason I allowed you to steal that chisel from the armory and let you flounder on your own until now. But this has gone on far too long. Alexandre, what are you going to do? You're not really going to London, are you? Prinny will have your head."

He looked at Roxanne, his dark eyes curiously blank.

Isabelle nudged her, and nodded toward Alexander. "Go on, tell him."

"I would be indebted to you if you would escort me to see my father's dearest friend, Dickie Jones." She looked at Isabelle who silently urged her to continue. She reverted her gaze to Alexander. "Mr. Jones will arrange for my safe passage to Scotland, and help me begin again there, I am certain. You will not have any reason to worry about me after I see my father's friend. And I am so sorry for all the trouble I've caused, and the risk you are taking."

He murmured gruffly, "Delighted to help you."

"So it's settled," Isabelle said as perky as usual. "And"—she continued with a *I am not to be disobeyed on this'* tone, "Roxanne has agreed to stay at my estate up north for a bit before continuing on her journey to Scotland."

"Of course, Isabelle. I would not disappoint you for the world."

"Perfect," the duchess replied. "Now what was that nonsense about beets and lettuce? Ladies do not live on beets alone. And Mémé, I am certain your delightful chef prepared the most intoxicating menu."

"Mémé's chef is anything but delightful," Alex muttered.

"And by the by, did you recover my favorite coin purse, Alexander Barclay?" Isabelle held out her small palm.

"Your purse?" He scratched his head. "The way Paxton stared at it, I was certain it was Roxanne's. But it's Edward's now. He dashed through the French doors before the earl could wrest it from his crocodile-like jaws."

Isabelle condescended to give Roxanne a look. Roxanne attempted an apology before being cut off by Mémé.

"But what is to be done about that toad, Paxton?" Mémé fluffed out the skirts of her gown.

It was the question that was on every person's mind in the hallway. It was the question no one had an answer for save one.

"I shouldn't waste too much more time thinking about the Earl of Plants," Alexander murmured.

"Really? Why?" Isabelle's expression grew worried. "You're not suggesting that you will . . ."

"No. I've grown weary of his uninspired villainy. If he cannot provide more sport, how long must I continue playing with a mouse who is already dead?"

"I agree. I think he'll die of greed in that hellish mine," Isabelle murmured.

"Let's give him the meager remnants of the next day or so to dig himself deeper," he said, while his expression spoke of something withheld.

Roxanne studied Alexander's bored air closely. It was impossible to tell if he told the truth. She just wasn't sure if he would take it upon himself to actually kill her blackguard husband or not. She prayed he would keep a cool head, but feared very much that today had been the tipping point.

She glanced at Mary, who was looking at Alexander, indecision radiating from her cool, unguarded expression.

The two of them made for a most beautiful couple. Yes, Roxanne thought, she was looking at the future Duke and Duchess of Kress, who would produce the most beautiful heirs together and thereby allow Alexander to follow his dream to return to London in His Majesty's good graces once more.

And now it was her turn to keep an eye on him. She was slightly worried he might actually do something they would all regret—all in the name of the innate chivalry he refused to show the world.

The long day's events had left everyone exhausted to the bone. Isabelle had insisted that Roxanne move to the chamber that connected to hers. And Roxanne had slept like the dead, despite her worry over Alexander's potential revenge. She had had a long word with the silent Cossack, who had agreed with a single nod of his head to keep Alexander from leaving the Mount.

So much for waking at dawn. It was more like nine o'clock when she yawned and opened one eye.

Roxanne stopped in midstretch, her arms aching from the splinters. Beyond the open connecting door, Isabelle conversed with her lady's maid.

A knock at the door leading to the hall explained why Roxanne had finally woken. A maid poked her head in and announced an apothecary had arrived to wait upon her.

More than anything, Roxanne wanted to scramble down to the sideboard for she suddenly realized she was starving just like yesterday, when she and Isabelle had stopped for the pasty. Roxanne had lost her appetite nearly a month ago on Kynance Cliff and finally, thankfully, she had regained it. No one but she had noticed the growing gauntness to her already thin frame. That would change from this day on. She was not going to waste another moment of her precious days worrying about the future and wishing for justice. She was finally prepared to forget the past and forge the next chapter of her life.

Isabelle must have read her mind for within a half hour, they were both dressed, coifed, and finished with two breakfast trays that had been sent up. A very young apothecary from Penzance examined her arms and applied a licorice-smelling poultice while Roxanne finished her tea and ate the last morsel of toast and poached eggs.

The man looked at her above his spectacles while he closed his black bag. "His Grace asked me to inform that he awaits you in his study."

"Go," Isabelle said, making a waving motion with her hands.

"But my affairs are not packed."

The man looked between the two ladies and shook his head before departing.

Isabelle rolled her eyes. "Do you really think

Alexander wants you to leave today? Surely you will settle everything with this Mr. Jones fellow and then you will return for at least one final evening. You must give Alexander . . . and the rest of us," she added, "a little time to get accustomed to the idea of you leaving."

"He wants me to go."

"Of course he thinks he wants you to go, but he does not. I'm certain of it."

"Well, I think he only says what he means. He's rare in that way, Isabelle. And nothing can come of it but pain. You don't know him as I do."

Her friend's eyes grew wide. "You *know* him? As in, he *knows* you?"

Roxanne bit her lip. "No. He knows me as I know you, for example."

"Well, I know you very well," Isabelle retorted. "You slept nearly in the same chamber as I last night. And I know that you snore and that you—"

"I do *not* snore," Roxanne insisted.

"Yes, you do. I even heard Alexander tell you in that mine that you snore, which only proves—"

"I cannot be blamed for what I do in my sleep. And by the by, you talk in your sleep."

"I do no such thing!"

"You do," Roxanne continued. "You raved about some sort of French bonnet with grapes and leaves on one side and three feathers trimming the other. It did not sound very fetching in my opinion."

"You know," Isabelle said as she sighed, "you are an expert at changing the subject."

"I learned from the best," Roxanne replied.

"Well, I outrank you and I insist that you return tonight after you finish with Mr. Jones. And then I shall pack too and we shall go to my estate together. I decided it all when you kept me awake half the night with the fear you would slip away."

"Well, at least it wasn't due to my snoring." Roxanne's insides tumbled with happiness. She hadn't realized how much she dreaded the idea of leaving everyone behind. It was going to be bad enough saying goodbye to Alex.

She smiled and hugged Isabelle. "Nothing could make me happier than traveling with you. And it has nothing to do with your well-padded carriage."

Isabelle drew back for a moment and studied her. "Oh, I can think of one thing that would make you happier. But I won't torture you any longer this morning."

By the time Roxanne and Alexander left, the sun was overhead and the tide was fully retreated. When they approached the Mount's stable to secure two horses, there was but one minor adjustment to his plan.

Bacchus was missing. And the stable hand knew naught of it for he had been off island to arrange for a feed delivery.

Alexander turned to her, and she hated having to owe him once again.

"I'm sorry. Lawrence must have borrowed him. He hates to walk, and I believe he came here by boat just as the tide was receding."

He smiled. "Actually, I rather think that horse was made for your husband. I think they shall get on together. Well, at least until Bacchus breaks down one of Paxton's stall doors to get at the earl's last inch of lawn."

Roxanne mounted a pretty gray mare, and released the skirts of Mémé's riding gown to cover her legs. "How does your great-aunt manage to ride?"

"Someone is always there to lead her," he replied. "It's you, right?"

"Sometimes." He swung his muscled leg over the saddle and settled himself on the back of a bay gelding as if he had been born to the saddle.

They started down the hill separating them from the shingle path. "Were you ever a cavalry officer?"

Alexander was ahead of her and she saw his shoulders flex. "Why do you ask?"

"You have that look in the saddle," she replied.

After a long pause he finally replied. "Hussar."

My God. He had fought for the *French*? Did the other dukes know? Did His Majesty know?

"Go ahead," he continued. "Spit it out."

"What?"

"I know what you're thinking."

"And what is that?"

He halted his horse and turned his torso to look back toward her. "That I must be a traitor."

"I never thought that."

"Really."

"I don't care if you are."

"Well, everyone else will if you say a word."

"I would never. Not after everything . . ."

"I know. It's the reason I told you."

That was it of course. He could tell her because she owed him so much—not because they shared any sort of true intimacy.

He was silent a while before he continued. "I joined to earn enough francs to smuggle my brother and Mémé to England after we escaped Mont-Saint-Michel by the skin of our teeth. The jewels only went so far. Later, I joined them when I had saved enough to leave myself."

He said naught of supporting his great-aunt or of putting his younger brother through Eton's lesser collager program. Of course not. He was a hero. Had he ever been anything else since the day she had met him?

"Why did your father's family not help you?"

He shrugged his shoulders. "I've told you. You cannot count on anyone in the world except yourself. I'd hoped you'd learned this lesson by now."

As they arrived at the last bank leading to the now-exposed path, she forced him to continue on topic. "Did you develop a fear of enclosed spaces and the dark while a Hussar?"

"I am not afraid of the dark, thank you very much."

"So you've only a fear of small spaces?"

"Does it matter? It's not the sort of thing I must worry about from day to day. It's only when someone decides to climb into a sodding mine," he muttered darkly.

His annoyance didn't bother her any longer. She realized it might just be a sign that he could find his ease with her and was capable of dropping his constant façade of cool wit. "You didn't have to try and save me," she said softly.

He clucked to his horse and moved to the side of the path. After a long silence, he finally spoke. "The Portuguese captured me while I was holding documents containing English troop movements and numbers. I spent several months in a small pit deep underground." He stopped abruptly.

She felt ill. Her imagination conjured all sorts of vile images: bugs; muddy, crumbling walls; dank air and little food. God, what he had endured. He was a stronger man than she had ever guessed. Yet, she knew nothing she could say would alter his emotions, so she said the only thing she could muster. "I'm so sorry."

"It was war and to be expected. It's in the past, and what's more important is the future." He peered sideways at her.

She spoke quickly before she could think. "Will you marry Lady Mary Haverty after I leave?"

He pointed to a huge tangle of seaweed in the middle of the path. "Careful here. I shall have to ask John to arrange for someone to tend the path each day. Have I told you I've decided to have John apprentice as my steward? The Mount fell to ruin when my forebear failed to take any interest in finding a new man when the former steward died a decade ago."

"I see."

"It will be the blind leading the blind leading a blind French comtesse, but then when I return to London, I will leave the Mount in good hands."

"Absolutely," she agreed.

"And Mémé will be content here as long as she doesn't realize she's in her dotage."

"You're absolutely right," she replied.

"You can disagree with me, you know," he said without turning his head toward her.

"It's your heart, Alex."

"I beg your pardon?"

"Your heart is the part of yourself you're embarrassed by, but it is my greatest hope—"

He was on the verge of an explosion when he interrupted her. "You haven't the bloodiest idea what you're—"

She interrupted him right back by raising her voice over his. "But it is my greatest hope that you will give it to someone. Maybe to Mary? She deserves it. And so do you."

He halted his horse and she did the same. They stared at each other. Her own heart was in her throat. And it was breaking. She had no choice but to set free her dreams. She wanted him to be happy, and to open himself to the possibility of love. It was the only way she could stomach the future without him.

She knew then that her last real shred of hope had died. Lawrence would win in the end, even if Alex actually tried to force the issue in London. It would always be her word against Lawrence's no matter what Alex, Isabelle, and Mémé said. No one would take the word of a tin miner's daughter over that of an earl, not even the Prince Regent. And Alexander had no choice but to heed the future king's demands for a scandal-free existence.

And so she finally moved ahead of the man she loved and turned her face into the wind to gallop toward the opposite shore so he would not see her face. It was the wind rushing against her eyes that caused them to water.

Dickie Jones had been the best friend of Roxanne's father, Cormick Newton, since their childhood. They had roamed the cliffs near Falmouth together, and had withstood the rigors of various tutors when their parents had forced them on them. Their friendship was no surprise given that their fathers had been the best of friends as well.

The only difference in their lives was their respective wealth. Fate had dealt a good hand to Cormick's paterfamilias by way of a Scottish lass of good fortune who had fallen in love with the Cornishman. Jones's father had been blessed with a wonderful wife of little means. It was for this reason that the latter went to work for the former as his accountant, and Dickie had followed in his father's footsteps by becoming Cormick's accountant when the two outlived their fathers.

This also explained why there were few people, save his own wife and children, who Dickie Jones had loved more than Cormick Newton and his daughter Roxanne.

While Roxanne knew that Dickie Jones would never understand why she had rarely visited her old friends and father, she also knew Mr. Jones would always protect a Newton.

And she was the last Newton in Cornwall.

She was also the last person Dickie Jones would ever dream of seeing again. Yet when she appeared outside the window to his study in his small, but comfortable house on the edge of the largest of all of her father's former mining enterprises, Dickie Jones did not turn a hair.

He had always had the ability to conceal surprise. Dickie Jones carefully placed his quill beside a document and wiped away the ink on his two fingers before he pushed back his chair with a long squeal and slowly rose to cross to the window.

"Hello, Countess."

"Roxanne, please," she said quietly. "Hello, Mr. Jones."

Alexander stepped into view.

"Allow me to present Mr. Richard Jones to you. Mr. Jones, His Grace, the Duke of Kress."

Dickie Jones bowed to Alexander and then nodded to her. "Are you coming in then or what?"

"Is anyone in the house, Mr. Jones?"

"No."

"Could we enter through the back?"

With a single nod of the head he disappeared as did she and Alexander. Assembled in his study, with the shades now drawn, Roxanne found her voice, and then lost it before she could even start. "I'm so, so sorry," she rasped.

"About what?" the man of few words replied, seating himself behind his plain desk and indicating with his bony hands that they should sit across from him if they chose.

"To bother you, Mr. Jones."

He tugged on the ends of his waxed salt-and-pepper moustache in the same manner she remembered. He cleared his throat. "You have never bothered me before," he said gruffly. "Actually, you only ever bothered me when you became a high and mighty lady and never bothered to bother me anymore."

"You are very familiar to me," Alexander cut in, narrowing his eyes. "Have we met before?"

"Not formally, Your Grace."

"At the funeral," he said. "I saw you standing at the edge of the grave. You were the only one who appeared in mourning for the countess's hat."

He stared into the space above their heads. "I knew it was a good sign that the sun was shining."

Roxanne finally allowed herself to smile.

"Everyone knows that the soul of the departed cannot arrive in heaven unless it is raining," Mr. Jones continued.

Alexander looked at Roxanne with curiosity.

"It's an old Cornish superstition," she explained.

"A Cornish *truth*, if ever there was one. You're sitting in front of me now as cool as you please, aren't you?" Mr. Jones puffed out his thin chest.

"I am."

"And why has it taken you so long to inform me you are not at the bottom of the sea?"

"Because . . . Well, because, I didn't want to—"

"If you say you didn't want to bother me, I might say something we will both regret," Mr. Jones interrupted.

She couldn't stand it anymore. She had to go to the man whom she hadn't seen in almost seven years.

Roxanne stood abruptly and walked around his desk at the same time Mr. Jones came to her. She folded herself in her father's best friend's arms. "Oh, how I've missed you, Mr. Jones." He smelled so familiar. Like pipe tobacco, and moustache wax, and stone dust.

"I've missed you, too, Countess."

"Don't," she insisted. "Don't ever call me that again. I hate that title." For long moments she drank in the warmth of his thin arms.

"And why is that?" Mr. Jones finally pulled back and looked down from his great height.

"Because it took me away from you and everyone else, forced me to cut my ties, and made me see how foolish I had been to wish to marry above myself."

He studied her. "And?"

"And the *gentleman* whose sole gift to me was his name and title left me to die when I fell a portion of the way down Kynance Cliff," she choked out.

Mr. Jones's hands gripped her shoulders.

She explained the rest of her predicament in a

stream of words. Roxanne came to a stop when he sagged and finally sat, his head in his hands.

"The bastard. The blue-blood bastard." Mr. Jones shook his head. "I shall challenge him since your father is not here to do it," Mr. Jones said, angrier than she'd ever seen him.

"You cannot," Alexander finally spoke. "Only a gentleman can challenge another gentleman."

"Well, then, why haven't you challenged him, Your Grace?" Mr. Jones stopped short. "Or does a tinner's daughter not require justice?"

Roxanne cringed. "Mr. Jones, the duke has done so much for me already. And he is under orders from—"

"I think I can answer Mr. Jones's questions all by myself, if I choose," Alexander interrupted dryly. "At present I choose not to reply. Mr. Jones, did the earl pay a call on you yesterday evening or this morning?"

"No."

"Hmmm," Alex murmured. "Then perhaps he went to Wheal Bissoe mine straightaway."

Mr. Jones's gaze immediately sharpened. "And why would Wheal Bissoe hold any interest for the bloody earl?"

"Just before he died," Roxanne rushed on, "my father told me he secreted his fortune inside a hidden space carved into the rock face of the eleventh platform there."

"Did he, now?" Mr. Jones said hollowly.

"Yes. And when we went there it was gone," she said.

Alexander stared at Mr. Jones with a strange intensity.

"And I was hoping you might be able to help us

learn where it is. Perhaps my father told you? Or perhaps you know someone who might have found it or taken it when they heard I was dead?"

"No. No. And no," Mr. Jones replied stonily.

"But you knew Mr. Newton had a fortune when he died," the duke argued.

"I knew no such thing," Mr. Jones retorted. "Cormick Newton was a very generous and benevolent man. In his will, as Roxanne knows, he gave his entire fortune to the mining families in his company."

"Including you," Alexander added in a measured tone.

"What are you suggesting?" Roxanne felt ill. "You don't know Mr. Jones. And of course, my father gave him a portion of his wealth. He was his best friend as I told you."

Both men continued to stare at each other.

Mr. Jones broke eye contact first. "Roxanne, you know I shall always provide for you, although not in the manner of your father or your life at Paxton Hall. What is your plan?"

Alexander sighed heavily and wordlessly shook his head.

Roxanne gave him a look, and then turned to Mr. Jones. "I should like to go to Scotland. To the village my father always spoke of—where his mother was born. I shall endeavor to find work there to lessen the financial burden. Perhaps," she turned to Alexander, "Isabelle and your great-aunt will provide references."

"Certainly," he said dryly. "For Tatiana Barclay, I presume?"

"No. I think Harriet is a better name for the sort of work I will seek. And I shall take Mr. Jones's surname for he is more like a father to me than anyone else."

Mr. Jones returned his attention to the duke. "And you see no reason to bring the earl to justice? If anyone could do it, it would be you, no?"

Roxanne rushed in. "In the end it would be my word against the earl's, Mr. Jones. You know that. And no amount of the duke's interference could change it. And furthermore, I do not want to become known as the infamous tin miner's daughter whose noble husband possibly tried to murder her. I would rather retire to Scotland and live the life I choose."

Mr. Jones scratched his head. "It's cold in the highlands. It's not for the likes of a warm-blooded Cornish lass."

"It's what I want," she said firmly.

"What have you to say about all this, Your Grace?"

"Me? Does it matter? This is a female with a plan."

"His Grace must not become embroiled in any hint of a scandal, Mr. Jones. And he must marry an aristocratic heiress with an immaculate reputation by order of the Prince Regent," she added.

"Yes, I receive issues of the *Morning Post*— eventually. I know the story of the debauchery by the royal entourage. And the stew of fruit thrown at the Prince Regent each time he leaves Carleton House. And everyone knows His Grace lost his fortune and was sent here in disgrace."

"Not disgrace exactly," Alexander said softly. "More as a punishment—for what could be worse than living on this edge of wilderness while I acquire a diamond and gold leg-shackle?"

Roxanne knew a lost cause when she saw it. Mr. Jones would never take to the Duke of Kress. And Alex would not like anyone who did not like him.

She spoke before either of them could wring the other's throat. "I had hoped to leave as soon as possible, Mr. Jones. It is too dangerous to remain any longer. My husband is searching for me and my nonexistent fortune. Please be careful. He might be a little mad."

"A lot mad," Alexander corrected.

Mr. Jones looked at her with a question in his eyes.

"His Grace hit him on the head with a book when Lawrence chanced to get a glimpse of me. And the duke also accused the earl and insisted they should go to London and speak to the Prince Regent about the whole sordid affair."

Mr. Jones was not impressed. "A bullet to the brain box is a better idea, and I—"

"Mr. Jones," Roxanne interrupted, "I will be leaving Cornwall along with the Duchess of March. There must be no more talk of murder. I will not see you hung or languish in a prison because of my miserable rat of a husband."

"Well, then." Mr. Jones reached into a drawer of his desk and removed a metal box. Inserting a key and extracting a substantial amount of coin, he placed it in her palm. "Once you settle across the border you must send me your direction and I shall forward you a bank draft each quarter."

"I don't know what to say, Mr. Jones, except, thank you. And I shall endeavor to repay you when I'm able."

"I should warn you that she owes me first," Alexander said dryly. "She probably owes everyone in town."

Chapter 17

In the end it took two additional days than had originally been planned for the ladies' departure. Isabelle blamed it on the intricacies of folding her numerous gowns into a staggering number of trunks.

"You have not the slightest idea how long it takes to place pieces of tissue between the sleeves of each gown to maintain the integrity of the fine silk, Alex."

"Oh, I know precisely how long it takes to send a female packing," he muttered. "No longer than a half hour, at most."

"You know, Alex," Isabelle continued with a sniff, "you used to be the most good-humored gentleman. I can't imagine what has caused this unpleasant shift in temperament."

Roxanne hovered, and remained silent.

Mary watched all with a knowing smile.

The archbishop remained conveniently repentant and invisible in the chapel, or in the replenished wine cellar, or possibly even in his apartments. No one was certain.

And Mémé ate every morsel the chef so lovingly

prepared for her, and pretended to read the three London newspapers she had arranged to be delivered via the Mail Coach. Or perhaps she actually *was* reading them. Sometimes one could catch the smallest of smiles quivering on her lips when the scandal sheet was exposed.

Alex retired to his study to reread an express from the Prince Regent, who was furious. First and foremost His Majesty called him every grievous word in the dictionary for not having settled on a fiancée. He boldly reminded Alex of the vast sum of money that would have to be repaid to the royal treasury *with interest*. The note would become due within the next two weeks, unless, of course, a bride was put forth on the sacrificial altar of marriage.

Candover had obviously taken great delight in painting as black a portrait as possible when he had returned to Carleton House at breakneck pace. Yes, he had even had the audacity to speak of Roxanne, for the future king added a postscript—"And you shall cast aside any idea regarding a questionable, poverty-stricken relation who Candover refuses to name." Alex had an unholy desire to put on a Hussar uniform and slay both Candover and Prinny with a French blade.

Alex rubbed the ache between his neck and shoulders. Well, Mrs. Plan of Planningville had her ducks all in a row, while he, who had so diligently, yet unconsciously, balanced a delicate house of cards all in a goddamned scheme for the first time in his life was watching it crumble to dust. And the worst part was that he had no sodding idea why he had attempted it when he had sworn never to attempt to twist fate ever again. This after he had told her his motto—Life Never Goes According to Any Plan—the day he met her.

Impending disaster was upon them all for there was the telltale frisson of tension in the air. And if Isabelle didn't ready her trunks within the next hour, Alex would have every servant on the Mount cart her half-packed valises to Penzance to be loaded onto her carriages. He had no idea how they would secret Roxanne to the conveyance, for surely the Earl of Paxton had arranged a watch on everyone coming from and going to the Mount. The man might be a fool, but he was a terrified fool now. The earl had not even responded to Alex's note putting off their journey to London for one week.

During the last month, Alex had periodically sent the Cossack footman out and about to learn everything he could about Paxton. The footman had proved to be as good at sleuthing as he was at remaining silent and using his superior strength at a moment's notice. The Cossack had learned that Roxanne and Paxton had not lied when they'd each independently suggested the earl had ties to every lord and man of importance within a seventy-five-mile radius of Cornwall. Apparently, gentlemen especially valued the earl for his superior magisterial judgments against poachers and people of the lesser classes. But Paxton was even more prized for his excellent connections to every smuggler and their cache of ill-gotten goods. There was not a man of worth who would not stand for Paxton as a character witness. It was enough to make Alex want to take a tour of the armory himself. He pushed back his chair from the desk and—

A knock on his door sounded. "Come."

John Goodsmith, his fine dark-chestnut hair carefully combed and parted, entered, wearing the new clothes Alex had arranged for him. His shoes squeaked.

"Pardon me, sir."

"Yes, John?" Alex sat back down. "What have you there?"

The young man came forward and carefully laid a new ledger in front of Alex. "I made notes of the animals purchased, and the additional grain and feed requirements. The reconstruction costs are excellent—below the initial estimate, you will see."

Alex studied the neat handwriting. John had been well educated by the last and only monk the former duke had allowed to continue on the Mount during his lifetime. "And the books we discussed acquiring?"

"All part of the plan, sir."

"John?"

"Yes, sir?"

"Please don't ever use that word in my presence again, all right?"

John looked at him quizzically. "Which one?"

"Dukes are allowed their quirks, and the word *plan* is mine. We may decide on clever endeavors, or concoct ideas, but that is all. We are not to count on the future."

John scratched his head. "But how are we to better the Mount and ourselves without plans? Pardon me for being outspoken, sir."

"No, you are right to ask and I don't wish to dim your optimism. You have much of your life ahead of you to accomplish that," he said kindly but with his signature dry wit.

"My father always said you can't count on things

going your way, but you must dream. For if we have no dreams then we have no purpose, do we?"

Alex felt a rush of pain invade his gut.

"If I may be so bold, sir, what is your dream?"

"No, not mine," Alex said gently. "But I should like to hear yours."

"You have already helped fulfill part of my dream, that of bettering myself. But I also dream of this castle restored the way it once was. The way it was when my grandfather was young. He and Father spoke of it often. And I dream of good people inhabiting it always, like you, sir, and the Comtesse de Chatelier, and Miss Barclay. And I hope to see it filled with happiness for as long as I live. All we can really do is try to leave this earth in a better fashion than we found it. That is what I dream."

"That's all?" Alex spoke quietly.

"Well, I dream of love, of course, doesn't everyone?"

"But you are only seven and ten."

"Love comes when it chooses. You don't get to say when and you don't really get to say who. I was lucky to have the love of my father, my grandfather, and Father Fielding. I hope to give and receive more if I'm allowed the chance. I guess the only choice you have is whether to say yes or no when it knocks on your heart."

"Who told you this?" Alex's voice was hoarse even to his own ears.

"I learned it from my father."

"And your mother?"

"I didn't know her, sir. Father said she died when I was born."

"I see," Alex inhaled deeply. "Well, you were, indeed, lucky to have such a wise father. My father had similar ideas." He did not add that he now felt ashamed for probably the first time in his life. This young man, who possessed so little, had lost his only relation in the world at the tender age of twelve, if Alex had the right of it. But John had had a great enough heart to retain his optimism, while Alex had lost his parents at the ripe age of fifteen and then he had immediately thrown optimism on its ear. Despite having Mémé and his brother, he had taken the easier pessimistic path. "John, I should warn you I am a cynic and am not to be taken seriously. I see life as a farce that rarely works in one's favor."

John smiled. "But Father Fielding taught me that the Greek cynics were virtuous and masters at self-control. Their only flaw, according to him, was that they were fiercely independent and thought they could do everything on their own."

"Fielding taught you well, but that last part was not a flaw."

"Perhaps not, but I prefer the joy of being surrounded by others. I am so grateful to you, sir, for coming here and bringing the Mount to life again. And for allowing me the privilege of serving you."

Alex hated the ball obstructing his throat. "Go along, then, John. You are doing an excellent job. Your talents were wasted on the chickens," he added dryly.

"I love every aspect of the Mount, sir," John said with a smile so wide his dimples were revealed.

Alex shuffled the papers in front of him. "Of course you do. Now, please inform the architect that I should like to go forward with the reconstruction of the dairy."

The young man bowed and appeared very well pleased by the news.

Alex opened his pocket watch and glanced at the time. Isabelle had less than a quarter hour before he would boot the pretty, young duchess out with the suddenly quiet Mrs. Vanderhaven. He would then allow himself only five minutes after they departed before he would pack away his Greek cynic's view and attempt with all sincerity to make Lady Mary Haverty the happiest bride in Christendom.

Mary Haverty, he did not know, would have a far better idea, since a heroine-in-waiting always has a better *plan*.

Roxanne Vanderhaven, née Newton, but with a host of aliases, the newest being Harriet Jones, calmly stood by the shadowed rear door of the Mount. She'd said her goodbyes to the servants, and to Mary, who had looked like a cat who had got into the cream in the larder. Mémé had not been nearly as collected when Roxanne had found her in the music room playing a Chopin concerto on the pianoforte. Her thin, proud frame swayed as the notes flew from her nimble fingers. Edward sat on a plump feather cushion Mémé had had made for him.

The comtesse stopped suddenly when Roxanne entered on tiptoe. "Yes?"

"I've come to take my leave, ma'am." Roxanne had been unable to use the grand lady's informal moniker as she owed her a deference she could no longer ignore.

"Mémé, please," Alex's great-aunt insisted, her back arched.

"I must be allowed to thank you for everything you've done for me," Roxanne said as she went to stand beside the pianoforte.

Mémé stared straight ahead, beyond the music on

the stand. She reached into her pocket and extracted something. "Come here, my child."

Roxanne drew close and placed her hand in Mémé's outstretched palm. She felt a cool object slip onto her finger. An extraordinary ring with tiny diamonds scattered in an intricate confection of spun gold rendered Roxanne nearly speechless. She had never seen anything like it.

"Why would you—" Roxanne began.

"Hush. Every lady requires at least one piece of jewelry. And I have no need of this."

"But—"

"It was given to me by a suitor I eventually spurned in favor of another with better taste."

Mémé was being every bit as absurd as her great-nephew.

"My dear, I wish for you to have something to remember me, just as I would request something of you of far greater value."

"And that would be?" Roxanne's heart sank.

"Edward."

"My dog? But Eddie is all I—"

"I know," Mémé interrupted. "But I must face facts. He is most likely the only male who will occupy my bed for the rest of my life, whereas you . . . Well, I have great hopes for you, *cherie*."

Roxanne felt ill. She could not part with her dog. He was all she had left.

"Your husband will guess you have left if Edward disappears," Mémé continued. "And he is far too unusual-looking and would be noted by anyone who sees him if Paxton searches for you. You must leave him here and I shall take excellent care of him. Cook dotes on him. And each time the earl dares to show his face, I shall set Edward on him to take *un gros morceau*—a, ummm, fat bite—from his ankle."

Roxanne swallowed. She crossed to Eddie's side to pet him. Her adorable dog cocked his head and then rolled onto his back for a tummy scratch and she complied. For the first time, Roxanne noticed her dog would not keep Mémé out of his sight. When she stopped scratching, Eddie jumped up, trotted to Mémé, and jumped into her lap. "I think," Roxanne said with a small hitch in her voice, "he's telling me what he wants."

"And when Alexandre marries, Edward and I shall pay a long visit to Isabelle. I hope you will be there, too. We shall make it an annual affair."

"Please call him Eddie."

"I assume you know that Edward means 'guardian of prosperity' in Latin." Mémé paused to allow Roxanne to regain a measure of composure. "And after my visit with Isabelle, I hope to travel with you to Scotland to help you settle there if you still insist, Roxanne."

"I should like it above all things. But I must warn you that my living quarters will not be what you are used to."

"Ah, but *cherie*, they will serve as an important reminder of my own new start when I arrived on this wretched island. Your residence will seem palatial in comparison, I assure you."

They both laughed. The younger a little less than the older.

"It's a lovely idea," Roxanne murmured, twisting the ring on her finger, "but really I cannot accept—"

"Don't be ridiculous. It's a token of gratitude, Roxanne. And if you cannot fathom for what, I shall not tell you. And no, it is not for Eddie. Now go. And leave by way of the servants' entrance. Arrangements have been made for your departure."

Roxanne raised Mémé's hand to her lips and kissed it before bringing the older lady's hand to her cheek. "Thank you, Mémé. If I could have chosen a great—"

"You mean a mother."

"Or a sister." Roxanne smiled. "It would have been you."

"Of course, it would have been me." Mémé withdrew her hands and shooed her away. "Off with you now. I must continue my practice. And this is not a goodbye, for I shall see you again very soon."

Eddie snuggled deeper into the older woman's lap. He was a born lap dog, it appeared, and not the rabbit hunter Roxanne had raised from a pup. He had changed, just like she.

Roxanne looked at Mémé's profile for a long moment and then crossed the expanse of the room. As she walked through the doorway, she did not see the tear on the other lady's cheek.

She made her way to the appointed exit with a feeling of calm entering her mind. She had nothing left of her old life now. And with the exception of leaving behind her beloved dog, she was at peace. Almost everything she had wished to accomplish since that awful day on Kynance Cliff had transpired. And it was all due to Alexander Barclay.

The Cossack footman appeared at her side and silently opened the servants' door. An enormous trunk lay on the ground. He motioned for her to enter it. Roxanne realized she had never heard the faintly exotic-looking man speak.

"You want me to get in there?"

He grunted.

"But I will suffocate."

A familiar voice floated over her shoulder. "It's a wonderful, calming feeling." It was only fitting that he would sneak up on her one last time for their final goodbye.

She forced a smile to her lips as she turned. "I am not afraid."

"I know. That's what worries me."

"I thought you didn't ever worry about anything."

"Times have changed. I've learned one must change too or be frozen in time."

"Very impressive," she replied.

"I'm capable of adapting," he said, a smile forming on his handsome face. One dimple even made a rare appearance.

She cast her gaze from his face. "I'm about to reveal something, Alex."

"Not another secret? I'm not sure I can stand another."

She tried very hard to maintain her smile. She was proud of her success. "I'm not very good at saying goodbye."

"Surely you're better than Paxton at the very least."

She was grateful that he was trying so hard to make it easy for her by keeping it lighthearted. "Yes, there is that at least."

"Well, then. We shall not draw this out."

"Thank you, Alexander."

He held up a hand to stop her.

"No, don't brush it off."

"Actually, I don't think I shall. I think I've earned it."

She managed a chuckle. "Allow me to wish you

every happiness, and I shall endeavor to assure it by
never interfering in your life again."

His dimple disappeared.

"But I shall write a letter to your great-aunt to tell
her of my safe arrival."

"I shall require your directions so any news of
your husband can be sent to you."

She looked at his boots. "You must inform Isabelle who will write to me."

"So you will not give me your directions?"

She stepped into the trunk. "Are there any holes
for air in this coffin?"

"It depends on your answer," Alexander replied
with a forced smile. His hands were clenched at his
sides.

"Who needs air, when I shall have the comfort
of darkness?" She folded herself into the trunk, and
nodded to the hulking footman who reappeared to
help close it. Thank God, the Cossack shut it quickly.

She heard Alexander murmur something, but
could not make out a single word.

"Goodbye . . ." she whispered.

Her head was so full of pain that she barely noticed the trunk was rising from the ground. She
had thought the Cossack alone would carry her to
a waiting dog cart at the Mount's path to Penzance.
It took her a few moments to realize that the trunk
was being carried by both the footman and Alexander. She knew it not from any words, since they
were silent, but the trunk tipped from side to side
unevenly.

She tried to think of anything but the man outside of the confines of her tiny, dark space, which
smelled of him. The starch of his shirts, and the
unique scent that was his alone invaded her nostrils.

She tried not to think at all, but a collage of the many versions of his face invaded her mind, unbidden. His great wide, even smile, framed by dimples, and his warm brown eyes filled with mischief at the best of times, presumption and annoyance at her antics at the worst. The remembrance of the fine texture of his brown hair running through her fingers when they had shared kisses and much more filtered through her torrent of memories, torturing her. She would allow this now—now before they reached Isabelle's carriage. And then she would compress these thoughts far back into a deep corner of her mind, only to be released for brief periods when she was alone and in Scotland and could torment no one but herself with her sadness.

She refused to cry, however. There would be no more tears ever again. She had found love, and shared love even for a brief period, which was much more than many people ever had in an entire lifetime. And she had her freedom, something she had never thought to ever have again. She was free of Lawrence, free to start a new productive life.

The trunk pitched too far forward and she almost fell on her face.

Chapter 18

❧

S he lost her breath as the trunk was dropped to the ground with a rough curse. They had not gone nearly far enough. Surely, the path to the Mount's harbor was a little farther at the very least.

A cacophony of loud voices competed against one another. Roxanne was certain she heard Alexander's voice, along with Isabelle's and also three other men's voices. Thank the Lord she did not hear Lawrence's distinct nasal voice.

Blinding sunlight met her eyes a moment later. And with it, a far more bitter future than she could have ever imagined fell into place.

When she sat up and her eyes focused on the three gentlemen confronting Alexander, her stomach dropped to her toes. They were Lawrence's three closest allies, Lord Milford, Lord Ramsbothem, and Mr. Crosby.

"I knew it," Lord Ramsbothem shouted. "I told you she was behind it all."

"What have we here?" Alexander looked at the Cossack. "I thought this was the Duchess of March's trunk."

"Sneaking off like a thief in the night, are you, Roxanne Newton?" Lord Milford continued without regard for Alexander's words. "You dare to think we would not find you out?"

"Need I correct you by informing it's full daylight?" Alexander replied. "And her name, by the by, is Lady Paxton."

"And you," Mr. Crosby dared to point at the duke. "You are her accomplice."

Alexander raised his eyebrows. "Her accomplice? In what, pray tell?"

"Don't play the innocent with us. We know what you've done to Lord Paxton."

"What?" Alexander said lazily. "Scaring her husband to bits? He deserved it and more."

"So you admit you harrassed Lord Paxton?"

"Why not?" Alexander said as he crossed his arms over his wide chest.

The three gentlemen's faces turned various hues ranging from magenta to purple. Their tight-vested bellies puffed out like three plump roosters.

"What have you to say, Roxanne Newton Vanderhaven?" Lord Ramsbothem spat out.

She had always despised this particular gentleman more than the rest of Lawrence's friends. He always laughed the loudest, and refused to leave long after all of Lawrence's other cohorts had departed. "I have nothing to say to you, sir."

"Well, you might not have to answer to me, Tinner, but you will answer to a magistrate."

She started. "Whatever for?"

Alexander held her back with his arm in front of her. She was prepared for fisticuffs as these awful men had always been unkind.

"Yes, do tell us why you dare to come to the Mount without invitation," Alexander's tone was full of eloquent contempt.

"One needs no invitation to arrest someone," Lord Milford said snidely.

"I fear you have no sense of direction, sir, for the Earl of Paxton resides far north east of Penzance. He's the man you want."

"Actually, the earl lies less than an eighth of a mile from here, face down in a remote patch of sand."

Roxanne inhaled. "He's dead?" Her voice barely worked.

"And you are mysteriously alive," Mr. Crosby replied.

"What does the untimely death of Lord Paxton have to do with Lady Paxton?" the duke retorted.

"And you," Mr. Crosby added.

"Your black beast," Lord Ramsbothem continued, "was found not forty yards away from Lord Paxton's body. The stallion was happily feeding at the edge of Farmer Gilbert's hayfield. We found a small bag containing a root ball of some sort in the saddlebag. It's common knowledge that Lord Paxton has a penchant for collecting plants."

"He's a damned thief is what he is," Alexander seethed. "He took the kidney vetch or red something or other after I told him he could not have it."

"So you admit he was at the Mount," one of the lords argued.

"Of course. How else could he have stolen my plants and my horse?" Alexander shook his head in disgust.

Roxanne noticed the tension behind his expression as full shock set in. She was unable to believe

Lawrence was truly dead. "Well, Lawrence's transgression against me takes precedence."

All five men present, including the Cossack, turned to stare at her.

"He tried to kill me," she whispered, desperately attempting to regain a measure of confidence. "Lawrence Vanderhaven saw me fall from the cliff of Kynance Cove and then left me there to die."

One of the men snorted. "No one could survive a fall from that cliff."

"I only fell part way," she said defensively. "And Lawrence was with me and said he was going to get rope, but he never returned."

"Really?" Mr. Crosby said with sarcasm. "Or were you merely faking your own death in order to lie in wait and murder him before you would then run away and hide like a fox in a den?"

"You thought you'd planned the perfect murder, Roxanne Newton, didn't you?" Lord Ramsbothem added. "Although how you managed to use your wiles on the duke to aid you is a mystery."

"Then again, don't forget she used her vulgar trickery to mesmerize Paxton in the beginning. She must be some sort of witch," muttered Lord Milford.

Out of the corner of her eye, Roxanne spied Alexander about to spring on Milford. The Cossack inched in front of him.

"By order of the magistrate in the next county we are arresting both of you for the murder of the Earl of Paxton," Ramsbothem said with a small smile he couldn't hide.

"How ridiculous," she replied. "Surely you are joking. Clearly, Lawrence took His Grace's horse without leave, mind you, and then suffered the unfortunate consequence of a bad fall. There is no evidence of murder."

Ramsbothem's eyes narrowed. "You shall have to do a better job at lying, my dear. The only real question is which one of you shot him while he was on the brute."

Lord Milford continued. "No one is above the laws of our land."

Alexander turned to her, his enigmatic eyes blank, as if this was an epic comedy of errors instead of a nightmare come to life. "Did I not tell you the same thing? And you didn't believe me."

"Now is not the time to—" Roxanne was interrupted by Alex.

"Now is precisely the time."

"To do what?" Milford asked with a sneer.

"To tell the three of you that you are trespassing on my property."

"We have the right to go anywhere we so choose in the name of justice," Milford retorted. "And—"

Alexander raised his voice a notch. "Unless you have a proper writ from the House of Lords demanding our presence, my footman and I shall *kindly* escort you from the Mount. And by the by, I do believe you are standing on my Liver Vetch."

"Kidney," Roxanne whispered.

"Kidney, liver—whatever," Alexander replied waving his hand in the manner of a monarch. "It's all valuable."

The three men eyed each other uneasily.

"If you think . . ." Mr. Crosby stalled.

Milford took up the cause. "If you think you are above—"

"Repetition breeds reiteration. Look," Alexander said in a tone one would use with a simpleton, "I *am* above you. Remember? It's mister, esquire, knight, baronet, baron, viscount, earl, marquis, duke, prince, and king. In that order. I thought you would know that at the very least, Milfool."

"*Milford*," the lord seethed.

"As such," Alex continued full of condescension, "we are under no obligation to answer to anyone except His Majesty or the House of Lords."

Ramsbothem narrowed his pig eyes. "It makes little difference whether we arrest Roxanne Newton and you today or tomorrow, or even in a week's time, Kress. Suffice it to say, until then, we will have all of Cornwall's eyes and ears focused on the Mount. And since you are too hen-hearted to come along today to face the allegations along with the tin whore, then we shall—"

Roxanne stepped forward at the same moment Alex pulled her behind him with lightning speed and then slammed his fist into the fleshy cheek of Ramsbothem. Alex's other fist struck the fat lord's stomach with such force it raised the man off his feet.

Roxanne grabbed one of Alexander's arms with all her strength and tried to pull him back, all the while asking the Cossack for help.

"No," the footman grunted with his odd accent.

She felt as though she was attempting to control a three-ton bull. Roxanne let go when she realized he did not intend to do further damage. His focus was so great, he probably had no idea that she was even trying to hold him back.

Crosby and Milford helped Ramsbothem, who was gasping, to his feet.

Alexander's expression was now the bored one she knew so well.

"I do hope you will spare us the usual clichés while you take your leave," Alexander said, readjusting his coat sleeve with the arrogance of the duke he was.

But the three gentlemen had not the self-control to do as they were bid. And Alex had not the tolerance to stay and listen as they promised retribution they were ill suited to mete out.

Roxanne looked at Alexander's even, strained profile and silently placed her arm on his when he turned to offer his to her. The Cossack followed behind them with the empty trunk as they ascended the long path with silence belying the flurry of words coursing through at least two of the three minds.

It would be a long time before they would have the luxury of silence again.

"It's never too early to panic." Isabelle's eyes bespoke twice the worry her words suggested.

From a nearby window seat, Alex watched Roxanne pace the carpet in the middle of the huge stone hall, where he had ordered a fire lit to chase away the first coolness of a summer evening.

"And I say, there is nothing to gain by worrying," Mary insisted. She was even more gray about the gills than Isabelle.

"While I appreciate everyone's concern," Roxanne said, halting in front of the fire and stretching out her palms to warm them, "I want none of it. And it's not Alexander they want. It's me, I assure you."

Alex heard Mémé make an inelegant sound for the first time ever. "And you think to deprive us of besting those ignorant, unsophisticated rustics?"

Alex watched a tiny smile creep onto Roxanne's

lovely face, and it warmed his heart. He hated to see her in any way anxious.

"Alexandre," Mémé's voice held a particularly plaintive quality, something he had not heard in many years. "What say you to all this?"

"I should like to hear from the archbishop," he said, not moving from his cold, hard seat.

The plump, little man appeared almost as ill as the morning after Candover's botched-up affair. "I cannot speak for His Highness. We must wait for his answer to the express I just sent."

"If it were me," Mary said quietly, "I should make a run for it. The both of you together."

"That's a terrible idea. It would appear as if they were guilty," Isabelle insisted. "Don't you agree, Alexander?"

"The only one guilty here, aside from Paxton, Devil take his soul, is my horse. If Bacchus had only left the scene of the crime," he said with as much dark humor as he could muster. The frown had returned to her face.

Roxanne turned to him. "I am going to them tomorrow. Your footman may escort me. There's nothing to be gained by waiting. It only adds to the appearance of guilt. I shall dash off a note this eve to Mr. Jones, who will help me face the outrageous charges. They have no evidence I did this. I don't even know how to shoot a pistol. I only wish I could guess who did it."

"Who do you think could be behind it?" Isabelle asked anxiously.

Alex could see she didn't want to say. He could guess she was worried it might very well have been Dickie Jones. He did threaten to do harm.

"It could be any number of people," she stated.

"I heard the servants whispering more than once that a group of smugglers was tired of Lawrence's stranglehold on all of them. And then there was the large number of local poor and dispirited creatures who earned harsh punishment each time they were brought before Lawrence on small charges, like poaching one rabbit when they were clearly starving."

"One can only imagine what he would have done if they had been caught eating one of his apples," Mary said with disgust.

He refused to dignify any of this with a comment. And there was not a single thing any of them could do tonight to answer the question. He would have to do it all himself. But his primary concern from now till doomsday was very simple. He could not let Roxanne out of his sight for a moment. And he'd be damned before he'd let her go to those lesser Cornish nobles. She was an innocent and knew not how savage men could become when the promise of violence stirred awake the dormant primal beast.

Everyone turned to him. He yawned. "The prawns were a bit off tonight, don't you think, Mémé?"

They all looked at him incredulously.

"I can't imagine why you would say that, *cheri*," Mémé retorted. "They were perfection. And Monsieur le Pique's *sauce moutarde*?" She kissed the tips of her pinched fingers. "*Simplement exquise.*"

Roxanne eyed first Mémé before turning to him. She sighed and shook her head. "I shall bid you all good night, then. And thank you again for your concern. But really, this is the most ridiculous allegation and I refuse to be cowed by it. Everything will be brought to light in the name of justice. I am only sorry any of you might become involved." She glanced at him. "I won't bore you with another apology. I fear there is nothing more I can say to—"

Isabelle rushed to grasp her hands. "Hush. Don't you dare turn away. You are one of us and we help our own."

"Thank you," Roxanne murmured, squeezing the duchess's hands.

"I think that's enough wretched theatrics for one day, don't you agree, Mary? My stomach can only take so much *sauce moutarde* and the other. I'm for bed with a nice warm bottle of Armagnac. I suggest everyone do the same."

"Perfect idea, Alexander," Roxanne said with false brightness. "Everything will appear so much worse in the morning."

"My thoughts precisely," he murmured, glad to see she had not completely lost her humor. They would both need it to see them through to the gross end. And that was about as much optimism as he could muster for a man who had taken a vow to change his point of view of the world.

Alex finally acknowledged to himself that he had known what he would do the moment he had learned Paxton was dead. Somewhere deep inside the muscle of his brain, he had always known his final course no matter what. He feared he had even probably known the afternoon he had pulled the gray and dusty statue-come-to-life form of Roxanne Newton Vanderhaven past the lip of Kynance Cove cliff.

And he would not change his decision. No, to be true to himself, it was only fair to admit it was not a decision. It was a godforsaken, stupid, ill-conceived, not a chance in a million *plan*. He would only need time, something he feared he had little of, to see it through.

But to achieve it, or at least to attempt to achieve part of it without her interference, he would put Roxanne in Isabelle's connecting apartments, along with Mémé for good measure, bar the windows, and place the Cossack between the two chambers' doors.

Then he plunked a well-padded leather chair from his study at the end of the long hallway where Isabelle's chamber was located. And he sat his derrière down to wait out the night. He was not taking any chances. He knew her far too well now.

Two hours passed with only the interruption of the grandfather clock two floors below clanging the hours. The Armagnac served to clear his mind instead of calm it. He used the time wisely, carefully reexamining his past, the present, and what he wanted for the future. He was determined to live a good life. A life of duty, even if everything was lost to ill chance. It was the only way he could die in peace in the end, whenever that was. There would be no more living on the sidelines of life, watching it unfold without attempting to right a wrong. His life might be in complete tatters at this moment, yes; he might very well face murder charges, and be unable to save himself, or worse, Roxanne. And he would be so out of favor with the Prince Regent now, that he could very well lose everything.

But it was amazing to him that if he concentrated solely on doing his duty to the best of his ability, focused only on protecting others—protecting *her*—to right a wrong, then he could let everything else fall away. He would—

First the Cossack slumped to one side, and just like a horse, fell asleep on his feet. A quarter hour later, Alex watched the chamber door open slowly. He dropped his head to one side and pretended to be asleep.

He heard her light, fast footfalls coming toward him. At the last moment, he stuck out his boot.

She tripped and he grabbed her before she could fall forward. He pulled her into his lap and chuckled softly. "Cherie . . . Really?"

"I beg your pardon," she said with a put-out air.

He stood up and gripped her arms and legs to keep her from pushing away from his grasp.

"Put me down," she said halfheartedly.

"Ah . . . *non*," he said quietly. "That I will not do. You must come with me now and accept your punishment. It's been a long time coming."

She stopped wiggling. "Botheration. What you call punishment might very well be a reward in disguise." She smiled finally. "You think you know everything when gentlemen know actually nothing."

He was walking as quickly as he could toward his own chamber. "Really? Hmmm. How much do you weigh anyway? I think you'd better stop ladling the *sauce moutarde* for a while."

"And I think you'd better have another bottle of spirits in your chamber."

"Of course I do."

"Good. All the better to bash your head with it."

"You certainly took your time trying to escape."

"I thought you once told me anticipation is half the fun."

He rolled his eyes. "I refuse to remember ever saying that."

He awkwardly opened his door, carried her inside, and locked it while almost dropping her.

"Let me down, Alexander."

"No." He proudly carried her to his bed and placed her in the center, feeling just like an animal guarding his supper. He dropped to one knee, snatched her slippers off, and tossed them over his shoulder.

He thought he might have heard a giggle, but perhaps it was just the sound of her trying to wiggle away from him.

"Not on your life," he murmured. "Be a lady about this."

"As long as you don't plan on tickling me, I'll accept anything you do."

He ran his hands up her calves and then suddenly stopped.

She rose up to her elbows, a small smile on her face. "What is it?"

"How far did you think you'd get in your night rail?" He had only just noticed what she was wearing. "You were going to run away in this?"

She smiled knowingly and it warmed his gut.

"I told you, gentlemen know very little of anything."

"I know how to run away," he murmured, "and it doesn't ever include flimsy nightclothes." He ran his hands higher and higher, allowing her fine cotton night rail to follow his fingers.

She inhaled raggedly, but failed miserably at appearing undaunted by his actions. "Well, at least you admit running away is your strong suit." She pulled her foot from his grasp. "You just don't know how to stay."

He retrieved her foot and stretched out her leg again. "Where exactly did you think to go at three o'clock in the morning?" He lazily caressed her beautiful firm limb.

It brought the prickle of gooseflesh to her skin and he felt her shudder. He leaned closer and turned her ankles out to kiss the tender skin of her inner calves.

"I, um . . ." She was breathing too fast. "I was . . . Oh, I can't think when you do that."

He stopped for a moment and smiled to himself.

"But don't stop. Oh, God—please don't stop."

He smiled wider and could not dam the growing trickle of happiness he tried so hard to stop all his life. "Tell me where you were going." He began to kiss her legs again when she spoke.

"To this very chamber, you imbecile."

"I must teach you more refined terms of endearment, *cherie*. And just why were you coming to my chamber?" He had reached her pretty knees. He turned them out as well.

"I told you. To find . . . spirits."

He nipped the inner flesh of her thigh.

She jumped. "Ow."

"That, by the way, is never a sound a man likes to hear in bed. And you haven't answered the question."

She giggled that beautiful, deep laugh of hers and the trickle of happiness flowed faster. He lowered his head back down to continue the feast in an uphill fashion.

She spoke in a jumble. "Well, I'm no longer married. And I think the world knows I'm not dead. And I will only spend one more night here before I go. So . . ." Her chatter stopped and then she inhaled a shocked sound before scooting farther away from him and drawing her legs back under her gown.

"Where do you think you're going?" He stood up, pulled the end of his neckcloth, and then divested himself of his coat and vest before pulling his shirt over his head.

"That's what I was going to ask." Her blue eyes were incandescent in the huge chamber. A single flame from a glassed-in candle illuminated his apartment.

He crooked his finger toward her. "Come back here, my little flower. You are not going anywhere. Tonight or tomorrow or any other day." He tugged off his evening footwear, and tossed them over his shoulder as well. His stockings followed in their wake, leaving him in satin knee breeches, which he did not remove.

"I'm not sure I really like this new domineering habit you've assumed. And you cannot tell me what to do."

"I can't?" he growled.

"No. And by the by, it's not very romantic. I'm certain Frenchmen don't seduce women like that. It's not very smooth or—"

He jumped on the bed and pinned her down; his hands gripped her arms and his legs encased hers. "You, *cherie*, talk too much."

"I know," she whispered. "I think I do it when I'm nervous."

He placed a gentle kiss on her forehead. "I know." A flush crested her delicate cheeks, and he brushed a stay strand of hair from her face. "It's one of the things I tolerate from no other woman except you."

"I'm not sure if I should say thank you or not."

"Hush." He placed a finger to her lips. "Now, we are going to go somewhere far, far away right now and forget for just a little while what happened today. Will you let me take you?"

She nodded.

"Will you not question me?"

"I can't promise that."

"Good," he chuckled. "But will you trust me?" He'd asked her that same question a very long time ago. This time he received the answer he had never wished to hear before.

"With my life."

"As I do you with my own," he said gently.

Alex gathered her in his arms, protectively, his shoulders flexing over hers. Slowly, ever so slowly he lowered his lips to hers and deeply kissed her, inhaling the honeyed sweetness that was hers alone. He could feel how fast her heart was beating . . . for him.

He nibbled the edge of her mouth to seek entrance. When she parted her lips he twined his tongue with hers. Her kiss drugged him and he could not get enough of her. He wanted to shred the barrier of her night rail between them, but instead he forced himself to slow down—something next to impossible. The incessant throb of an arousal had taken hold of him the moment he'd placed her on his bed.

But it had to be a long, leisurely dance for what he had in mind. He wanted to unleash the innate power of her, and he would do it. Even if it was for this one night only. Change was inevitable, but he'd be damned if he'd not live every moment with her while he could still breathe.

His hands almost trembled with the need to take her, and yet he moved lower to kiss the soft lobe of her ear, the column of her neck, and the length of her collarbone. And all the while the hard length of him pulsed with the need to be inside her.

She arched her strong, lithe back and sighed as he pushed down her neckline and settled between her breasts, paying homage in the fashion he knew she loved. He would stay here all night if that was what she wanted. He licked. He swirled his tongue and suckled her. He lightly bit the tender crests until she almost sobbed for him to stop.

With the sweep of his hands he pulled her forward for a moment and swept the gown over her head, leaving her fully revealed before him for the first time. Good God, this was heaven. It must be.

She was a slender, long, perfectly formed siren. She was lean and strong, with small breasts, slim hips, like a girl entering womanhood who liked climbing trees and clamoring down mines instead of taking tea and eating pastries. Yet, she called to him like no other. She was simply irresistible and he would never want another ever again even if it meant a lifetime without.

He twisted a long strand of her blond hair, which was loose, and brushed her lips and then the tips of her breasts with it. Watching the ruched tip tighten more made the tension in his groin nearly unbearable.

"Now, where was I?" he gritted out. He touched his finger to her lips when she opened her mouth.

Slowly, he moved lower, trying not to think about the exquisite pleasure-pain, the friction caused beyond the fall of his breeches. His feet touched the floor again and he stared into her darkened eyes, and gently, but deliberately spread her long legs apart. This was what he had wanted to do for so long but had never dreamed of actually achieving. He kept his eyes on hers, while he ran his hands over the tops of her lovely slim legs. Again and again he caressed her, first with his hands then with his lips, all the while watching her imperfectly perfect face.

Her head finally dropped back and her breathing became uneven. He slowed his movement until his hands stopped at the juncture of her thighs. Gently, he pushed her legs even farther apart and raised her knees. He could feel her tension but she did not resist him.

Her breathing turned ragged when he kissed the inside of her thigh. "Lovely, so very lovely . . ." he murmured between kisses.

He stole a glance at the tiny dark blond curls at her juncture and felt a primal guttural sound come from him.

Enough.

He could not hold back a moment longer.

He had to touch her. Had to taste her. Had to take her, until they were intertwined as one.

Chapter 19

Roxanne thought she knew everything about the act of procreation. This was not like anything she knew.

It was an act of pure passion in its rawest form. Every touch of his seared a memory of him deep within her. And he was doing things she didn't understand. Things she'd never experienced in her entire life. She didn't question. She didn't have to, because she trusted him with every fiber of her being.

She wanted to tell him that she loved him, and yet, while her mind sped a thousand miles an hour, she could not. She didn't care if he didn't love her back. She just wanted him to know that he was loved unreservedly.

But this . . . his hands were all over her legs. And his mouth was following his hands, inching up her ankles, her calves, her knees, and now her thighs. She felt as if she was burning and freezing at the same time. And she could not stop shivering.

"You're cold," he murmured between kisses.

"No," she whispered.

"Do you want me to stop?"

"No," she answered breathlessly.

She felt the day's growth of whiskers on his face shift on her inner thigh, and she knew he must be smiling. It made her smile, too. Until . . .

At first she thought his hands had closed the distance. But no, she clenched her eyes shut. His palms were pushing her inner thighs still wider apart.

And then he was kissing the top of her mound and the crinkle of her hair. Only now he inched lower. She nearly shot off the bed when she felt his tongue stroke her center. Her hands clenched the linen sheet.

His hot breath fanned her sensitive flesh and she moaned. Every nerve in her body was on fire, and her mind froze. He worked the sensitive center of her and she cried out, uncertain. Immediately, he captured the peak of her cleft, and suckled her, while his hands held her in place, despite the jumble of sounds flowing from her throat.

And just like before, it became obvious to her that he would not stop until he was satisfied that he had pushed her to the pinnacle.

Mindless, she took a deep breath, and held still to give in to the growing maelstrom, shattering into a kaleidoscope of lights and a great pulsing release.

"Mmmmm," he growled while still clamped to her tender flesh.

As the tidal pulls within her slowed, she became light-headed and realized she'd forgotten to breathe. Roxanne gulped in air and released the sheet to reach for him. She urged him up and into her arms.

Never had she experienced such peace and yet felt so empty. Her body wanted his fully. His weight came down on hers and it felt so right. So perfect.

His eyes were dark with desire as Roxanne ran

her hands down his immense shoulders to the sensitive small of his back. Her fingers caught on the band of his breeches, as her mind registered a long ironlike length beneath the black fabric against her thigh.

"Come to me," she whispered. She fumbled with the falls until he pushed aside her hand and undid an ivory button on one side.

His arousal sprang free and he smothered a curse into her shoulder as he tried to yank the opening wider. It took far longer than was necessary to disentangle himself. Roxanne giggled.

She felt so young and carefree, and full of happiness. This was not at all the practiced seduction she had feared. She didn't want this to be that. She wanted it to be joyful and warm and intimate.

He fell back on her and the heavy weight of his sex imprinted on her thigh, shocking her with heat and sensation. She was certain he could feel her racing heartbeat, as the tension coiled inside of her again.

"I want to be inside you," he groaned.

"Yes," she whispered. "It's where you belong." His weight was delicious.

He grasped her knees and pulled them high above his hips. He rested his forehead against hers and didn't move for a long moment. She wasn't sure why he was waiting.

Her smile disappeared as she felt him move slightly and the blunt end of him slid to the center of her wetness. He rose up on his elbows and gazed at her as he paused at the entrance to her. The moment felt like a benediction.

She leaned up to kiss his cheek softly.

It broke him. He plunged into her, past the tight

ring of her, and her clenched muscles, past everything, until she felt completely filled in every direction. She was gloriously stretched, and wanted the moment to never end, as he invaded the deepest recesses of her being. He was so hard, and he tested the limits of her with his hot length.

Nuzzling her neck, and gulping for air, he reached to cup her bottom, holding her firmly in place as he began the long, slow push-release. Roxanne wrapped her arms around his back, hugging him closer to her, while the sparking lights of pleasure swirled in the darkness behind her eyelids.

She desperately wanted to climb higher with him, and pushed her body to meet him stroke for stroke. She clenched his ironlike back, his muscles rippling under her fingers. The deep, wet, hot glide of him teased her senses until she reached a peak, and remained stock-still. The quicksilver pleasure was elusive until she realized he was drawing out the ecstasy to the outermost limit for them both. She could not move until he met her at the summit, and took her over the edge as a deep growl tore from his throat.

The two of them fell through space and time together, entwined in the fashion of two eternal lovers entering paradise. Wild pulses of light showered about them; his great surges melded with hers, and she couldn't stop the cries leaving her lips.

The rampage rained over them, until he collapsed on top of her, breathing hard, his hands gently massaging her sore hips, before he eased back onto his elbows and caressed her face.

Her breath evened slowly as she stared at the overly large pupils of his eyes. She reveled in his protective expression. She didn't need the security he offered, but she loved that he wanted to give it to her nonetheless.

He cupped her shoulders with his large hands and she stroked his hair, which had grown too long since she had met him.

She was shocked by the intensity of her reactions and his. Roxanne would never have known what love could be like if not for the man above her.

He bent down to kiss her lightly on her eyelids, her cheeks, her forehead, and finally her lips. As he finally pulled back, his brown hair fell forward and his dark eyes looked down at her.

"I love you," she whispered, peeling away the last layer protecting her heart.

"Roxanne . . ." he murmured.

"No, you must let me say it. It's not a simple thing, you see. I loved you even before I met you. I loved the idea of you," she said quietly. "And to think you existed all this time. And it only took that horrid moment when everything went wrong for the both of us for our paths to finally cross. I would fall off that cliff again and again for the promise of you."

He caressed her cheeks and dipped to kiss her forehead before she continued.

"And I love how you took me to the Mount—even when you didn't want to and had your own set of problems."

"I love me for that, too," he replied.

She smiled.

He leaned in for a long, leisurely kiss.

"So . . . do you love me, too?" She was certain what he would say. But as the silence dragged, doubt snuck in.

"What do you think?" he murmured.

"Is that a yes or a no?"

"Why do you ask?"

She grasped the pillow resting beside her head, and hit him on the head with it. "Just bloody tell me and put me out of my misery," Roxanne pleaded. Really, had he no idea?

"It will only make it worse," he whispered.

"No. It will make it better."

"I doubt it."

"Please," she said grasping his hand. "No matter what happens. It is better to know it. And to say it."

"Well, then . . . I love you," he said, staring at her. *"Je t'adore. Bloody hell, cherie. Je t'aime."*

"Have I told you how much I love French?" She smiled.

"You are adorable."

"Really?" Her heart overflowed and she kissed him back. "I've never felt adorable. Only awkward and too tall and . . . Oh, enough. Now look, we must form a plan to—"

"I agree," he interrupted.

"You do?"

"Absolutely. First, I am going to tie you to the headboard of this monstrous bed. Then I'm going to take a feather from one of my valet's ridiculous hats and use it to tickle you. And then . . ." The rest of his words were muffled as she began to kiss him for all she was worth.

Oh, they were in love. Truly, madly, deeply. This was what it felt like. And it was not a love that was the work of a minute—a fast spark that would fizzle. It was the love of a lifetime.

Well . . . at least she would have this moment for the rest of her life no matter how short it might be.

* * *

There was no more talk of schemes the rest of the predawn hours they shared intimately together. It was as if the two of them did not dare mar a moment of the time they had to give to each other without reservation.

And so they made love to each other. Repeatedly. Desperately. Slowly during some moments, and furiously the rest of the time. He murmured incomprehensible phrases in French that sounded unbearably erotic and all the while he challenged her to do things she did not know could be done to drive one another to distraction. And she delighted in his every groan and mutterings as she dreamt up ways to deepen his own rapture.

Many times he made her cry while she laughed, or perhaps . . . she laughed while she cried. It was only when he fell asleep with her cradled in his arms that she sensed true doom. And worse.

They had managed to push away the reality that awaited her in this time out of time. But now it was rushing toward them, like the never-ending tide.

But she reminded herself that at least she had had this one night with him. She was a romantic and would go to her grave a romantic. Was it not better to be so—than to be a realist?

As the night lightened to dark blue, then lavender, she forced herself to face the harsh truths that awaited them. They might not be able to avoid a cruel future. Pale pink, and orange limned the great chamber and she slipped out from under his heavy arm draped over her and tiptoed from the huge bed.

"Where are you going?" he rumbled. His brown hair was tousled and his great bronzed chest bare.

"To make myself presentable. My gown is in Isabelle's chamber."

"Come back here and keep yourself warm while, instead, I find a gown in your chamber."

She returned to him and snuggled into his warm embrace. Within moments he was hovering over her, his arms straining. "You must be sore, my darling. I don't want to hurt you," he murmured.

"No," she whispered. "I want you. I will always want you."

And he kissed her just like he had a thousand times during the night, and drove his hard length inside her. She matched him movement for movement, wishing she could turn back time forever and a day as they stared at each other with the knowledge of all the love being forged between them.

The memory seared into her mind as they soared together.

Roxanne only allowed herself to surrender to lassitude when Alexander unwound his large form from her reluctantly, and pulled himself free of the mound of bedclothes. He dragged a hand through his disheveled hair, and yawned. When she thought of all they had shared, and of what he had caused her to feel, a well of happiness overflowed in her heart.

He disappeared beyond the door, but for a moment and then reentered with a pitcher of steaming water and placed it on a washstand. He poured out half and splashed himself before using a clean length of cloth, and then in that amazingly short time only gentlemen need, dressed himself in his usual impeccable attire.

"The rest of the water is for you, *cherie*."

When he disappeared, she quickly made use of the soap and water and then stepped into her chemise. She couldn't find her stockings . . . until she looked up and saw one caught in the gilded chandelier. The second was under his armoire. He loved to throw her clothes across the chamber in wild abandonment. It was a habit of his of which she could grow quite fond.

She could not stop the smile spreading over her face despite the worry that darted between every other thought. The curtain fluttered in the breeze and a small shard of dawn's first light fell upon her. Roxanne moved toward the curtain, drew it back, and halted.

Oh, God.

A troop of three dozen or more horsemen were trotting toward the Mount.

She ran out of the chamber and didn't care about the spectacle she was making. She called to the footman at the end of the hall, alerting him to wake the ladies.

She was looking over her shoulder as she ran in the other direction, and collided into a hard object . . . Alexander.

"They . . ." she stuttered. "They've come. And they have torches."

When he heard that last word, his heart hardened to stone. He could not feel anything beating in his chest. Roxanne's hands cupping his face did not even register.

"Hey . . ." she said worriedly.

"Mon Dieu," cried Mémé, clutching her robe together as Isabelle guided her. The four of them stood in the hallway as the Cossack came up behind them.

"You want I shoot them?" The huge footman said the very thing Alex wanted to do. It was the first time Alex had heard the man say a full sentence.

"*Absolument,*" Mémé replied.

"No," Isabelle said at the same moment.

"Alex?" Roxanne asked.

He said not a word as he turned on his heel and took the stairs two at a time, leaving everyone behind him scrambling to dress.

It was time for him to do what he should have done long ago.

Not a quarter hour passed before a disorganized crowd stood just outside the entry to the Mount's great hall. By then, Roxanne, Isabelle, Mary, Mémé, the archbishop, the Cossack, the new housekeeper, even the French cook, and an assortment of maids and kitchen underlings had assembled behind him.

Alex stood rooted in the entryway, scanning the crowd of nobles and not so nobles outside. At least a dozen of them appeared to be pirates or smugglers. "I told you that you'd best have a writ from the House of Lords before you return," he said loudly.

The barrel-chested Ramsbothem, whose ire Alex had obviously inflamed, stepped forward. "So you did, Kress. You, we shall return for soon enough. But we need not wait to arrest the common tinner hiding here with you."

"Unless you enjoy eating your own teeth for breakfast, Ramsbothem, I suggest you consider re-phrasing your last comment. Lucky for you, I'm certain I did not correctly hear you. And I always like to think I'm fair-minded, and will always give a man a second chance. You know very well that a countess, just like a duke, does not answer to a common magistrate—only to the House of Lords."

The lord's face became mottled with purple patches. "We're taking the murdering tinner. We have our own set of rules in Cornwall for upstart commoners who murder one of our nobles. We're taking her now."

"I think not." Alex showed his pistol and the Cossack did the same.

Ramsbothem looked behind him, and jerked his head toward the door. A dozen firearms rose in response. At least none of them was foolish enough to use them. Instead a fury of fisticuffs, and the occasional flash of a blade erupted. Alex's faithful servants, and all the others, even blind Mémé, held them off for as long as they could, but the numbers were against them. Two dozen poorly armed men and women were no match for twice as many carrying pistols and swords.

In the end, there was no question that Alex would surrender along with her, despite Roxanne's soft plea to the contrary. He had sworn never to leave her side, and he would not.

Ever.

Unless . . .

Chapter 20

And just like he had always said, it did not go according to his plan or hers.

Roxanne and he were torn apart and wrestled over the shingle path to waiting carriages in Penzance. All the residents of the Mount, who were able, scrambled after them. Alex cringed as he heard Mémé's impassioned pleas followed by elegant French curses calling their handlers every animal name his great-aunt knew.

The primitive nobles of Cornwall were an altogether different species than any Alex had ever known. They were not English. They were not Welsh. They obviously prided themselves on being an amalgamation of pagan natives who thrived on superstition and ritual. And, God, how they loved ritual. It was unnerving how much they reminded him of the savage commoners of the French Revolution. The thought made the ice melt in his veins.

He tried unsuccessfully to enter the same carriage as Roxanne, but was blocked by Ramsbothem, Milford, Crosby, and three oafish-looking men who smelled of the salty smuggling trade.

The carriage holding Roxanne started forward

and Alex was finally able to shrug off the arms holding him back. He shouted to the Cossack to bring him a horse, but before the loyal footman could move, Alex found himself shoved into the second carriage and an ominous sound proved the door had been barred from the outside.

Hang it. They were such idiots. Did they not know he *wanted* to go wherever they were taking her?

He had a long time to contemplate where they might be going, every possible way this disaster could unfold, and every action to stop it. And for once in his godforsaken life, he knew he would not rest until he had freed her, and he could return her to where she belonged.

By his side on St. Michael's Mount.

The last shred of his cynical self fell away. He would not fail. He knew it. He had paid the price and now he had earned happiness. He only needed to yank it away from the evil in the world which had so far prevailed.

He leaned his aching head on the cracked black leather squabs of the poorly sprung carriage. God, he prayed she was not now suffering overmuch with worry. And he prayed she had not been harmed in the melee. He would break apart any man limb from limb if they had dared harm a hair on her head. His last view of her tore at his heart. She was pleading with them not to take him. She was the bravest female he had ever known.

The ritual began on the border of Cornwall and Devon in the small town of Lamerton. A magistrate waited on them in a huge town hall half filled with curious, gossiping friends and neighbors from both counties.

Alex, walking between Ramsbothem and Milford, made his way down the center aisle of the main chamber. Behind him, he heard the sound of many footsteps. He glanced over his shoulder only to find the giant Cossack making a path through the throngs for Isabelle, Mary, Mémé, John, and even Monsieur le Pique, the chef. Behind them, the gaunt, dignified frame of Mr. Dickie Jones led a group of mining families in his wake.

By the time Alex was jostled into a seat on the bench in front, the entire chamber was filled to the brim, and many voices erupted in a fever pitch of arguments for and against punishment. Vile suggestions of retribution contributed to the ugly scene.

Alex ground his teeth and forced himself not to spring up as soon as Roxanne was led into the chamber from a side entrance.

She was in shackles. *Shackles, for Christsakes.*

Her eyes were downcast.

Behind him, he could hear Isabelle weeping, and Mary trying to hush her. Mémé said not a word, but he knew she was there with them. He felt a hand on his shoulder, and he peered sideways to see John Goodsmith's face, which appeared oddly calm. The Cossack, twice John's size, was beside the lad and he nodded.

The amity he shared with these two men was unparalleled, he realized absently—aside from his friendships with his valet still in London; his oldest friend, Roman Montagu, now nowhere to be found; and Alex's brother, William, whom he rarely saw. And hang all the other dukes in the royal entourage. Where were they when one needed them? Alex reverted his attention to Roxanne.

Her head was held high, but she still refused to meet his gaze. He knew she had seen him. She was escorted to the lone chair in front of the ancient, shrewd-looking magistrate, his white wig of the last century slightly askew. Roxanne descended onto the hard seat as elegantly as the heavy manacles on her wrists allowed.

"Roxanne Newton," the magistrate stated with a pronounced accent from the south. "You are charged with the murder of the Earl of Paxton. What have you to say in your defense?"

Alexander immediately stood up. "You will not answer him, Lady Paxton. A peeress only answers to the House of Lords."

The older man's jowls flapped as he pounded the gavel loudly to silence Alex as well as other outbursts in the chamber. "There shall be order. No one shall speak out of turn unless they are prepared to be removed from here." The magistrate pointed his gavel at Alex. "Do you understand, Your Grace? Unless of course, you want to come forward and sit beside the accused murderess?"

He immediately stood up and came forward. A bailiff brought forward a second chair and he sat down next to her.

Roxanne still refused to look at him.

"You asked me a question, sir," she said, staring straight ahead. "May I answer it now?"

"No," Alex said under his breath.

She ignored him. "I did not kill Lord Paxton. It was the other way around. He saw me fall from Kynance Cliff and left me to die. He—"

The magistrate cut her off. "Yes, yes, I know all about your unfounded claim. But your assertion could very well be lately fabricated since you did not come forward sooner. We do not stand by allegations without evidence in my chamber. Do you have proof that Lord Paxton tried to harm you?"

Alex knew it would not help either of them, but he refused to let her go down this path alone. "I do."

The magistrate raised his bushy white brows. "I have not given you leave to speak, Your Grace, but I am a tolerant, patient man. You have something to say?"

"I found Lady Paxton clinging to the side of the cliff, just as she stated. I was witness to Lord Paxton's criminal behavior that day."

The older man scratched the stubble on his chin. "Criminal behavior, you say, Your Grace? So you saw Lord Paxton watch her fall and leave her? Or are you merely taking the word of this woman who was born a commoner? I shall warn you that if you do, you would be supporting her ill-founded claim over that of the Earl of Paxton. His lordship went to Lord Ramsbothem, Lord Milford, and Mr. Crosby the afternoon before he died to inform them that his wife was alive and was conspiring to kill him."

"Lady Paxton speaks the truth," Alex stated.

The rumble in the chamber grew and again the magistrate pounded his gavel.

"Well," the gentleman chuckled. "We can all guess why you are willing to defend her, now can't we, Your Grace? No. Don't answer that. Let's start over shall we? For I have testimony, and I must disclose that this testimony is from my third cousin four times removed, Cynthia Leigh, Lady Roth of Devon, just twenty miles north of here."

Alex wanted to explode from the insanity of it.

"Did you or did you not, Roxanne Newton Vanderhaven, suggest to Lady Roth that her daughter,

Lady Katherine Leigh, should ride the duke's horse, Bacchus, when all the while you knew the stallion was a most dangerous creature?"

She answered truthfully. "No. I suggested Lady Katherine should ask His Grace to *show* her Bacchus, not ride him."

"And did you not arrange for the stable hand to saddle this same horse for Lord Paxton, knowing the tide was coming in?"

"No!"

The magistrate adjusted his spectacles and reviewed the long set of notes in front of him. "Did you not deface the tombstone your husband, Lord Paxton, had made for you?"

"Yes, of course. I was not dead, you see. It was a tombstone for my hat and—"

The magistrate interrupted. "Did you not go to your husband's estate to haunt him?"

"Well, not precisely . . . All right, yes, I did," she said resolutely. "He left me to—"

"Did you or His Grace, the Duke of Kress, strike a near mortal blow to Lord Paxton's head?"

Roxanne would not stop. "It was a book about cows, sir. Not very thick and certainly not—"

"Did you not pretend your own death, Lady Paxton?"

"No!"

"And did you not steal Lord Paxton's dog, Your Grace?"

"It was *my* dog!" Roxanne interrupted Alex when he opened his mouth to finally speak.

"Madam," the magistrate said, "as a wife, you have no possessions. Any dog residing on the Paxton estate belonged to Lord Paxton. Even you belonged to him, or did you not know that?"

"Yes," Alex admitted. "I stole the dog. His baptismal name is Edward von Dogged, by the way. Eddie is his preferred name. And Paxton succumbed to my murderous book, *Cows of Southwest England*, quite satisfactorily."

The magistrate stared at him, dumbfounded.

Alex continued. "You have forgotten to ask about Paxton's gardens. About how I set loose a clutch of moles on his prized lawn and falsified information about where Lady Paxton's father might have hidden a fortune from the lazy dolt of an earl."

A new roar erupted within the chamber. Another pounding of the gavel, which had less of an effect than before. The crowd finally quieted themselves to hear more of the words they would repeat for the entertainment of generations to come.

"Did you not concoct a scheme with Roxanne Newton Vanderhaven to blackmail Lord Paxton? Going so far as to threaten him with a trial in London? Did you dare to suggest he had murdered his wife all without a shred of proof, Your Grace?"

"Uh, I didn't have proof of her death because, you see, she is still very much *alive*," Alex retorted. "You forgot to call Lady Paxton his "beloved" wife, by the way," Alex added caustically.

"And did you not have an adulterous liaison with Lady Paxton?"—a raw outburst of shock erupted and the magistrate boomed louder—"Did she not convince you to go after Lord Paxton and put a bullet through him?"

"No," Alex said, jumping to his feet. Except for one lone cough, the chamber quieted to hear his retort. "There was no intercourse." He'd be damned if he would admit to what had happened *after* the lecherous swine had died. "And no, I know noth-

ing about how the ass managed to acquire the bullet
he richly deserved." He snatched a glimpse of Roxanne's profile and she was as white as parchment.
She appeared close to fainting.

"Sir," Alex insisted to the magistrate, "I would request a brief recess—"

His words were lost to a pounding at the heavy
wooden doors at the opposite end of the chamber.

The entire proceedings had become slightly out
of focus. Roxanne feared she might, for the first time
in her life, swoon, which was really the most boring,
clichéd thing to do. She tried mightily to stop the
dark weight. It was too stifling hot, yet she felt colder
than death.

And there was a great hammering behind her.
As she turned in her seat like everyone else, the
dark rim of her vision closed and she was suddenly
lighter than air. Floating, floating . . . far, far away . . .
so happy to leave . . . only the landing jarred her
more than expected.

She was so lethargic. Why wouldn't they just
leave her to sleep? Someone was talking too loudly
and jostling her. She tried to tell them to leave her
alone but her mouth refused to work. She drifted
back toward bliss until a terrible acrid scent invaded
her senses. Her wits returned in a painful explosive
rush and she shoved aside the hand near her nose.
Many arms moved her to a seated position before
she was ready.

"Give her a minute," Alex's gravelly voice insisted.

At least it was much quieter here than where she
had been.

She tried desperately to clear the fog in her head
as her eyes regained focus. She looked about her.

They were in a different, smaller chamber. Alex was beside her and *Candover* had mysteriously appeared and was standing next to a very fat man wearing the most ostentatious fashionable clothing, and an enormous, ornate royal *collier* necklace. She closed her eyes. Lord above, it was the Prince Regent.

"Don't faint again," Alex said, his deep voice quiet with concern.

She snapped her eyes open wide.

"Your Majesty," Alexander began, "may I present Roxanne Vanderhaven, the Countess of Paxton?"

"No, you may not," His Majesty replied haughtily. "You also may not kiss my ring, nor say another word, Kress. You will be at the lowest level of disgrace, facing expulsion from England, if the crowds outside Carlton House catch a whiff of the goings on here."

Roxanne sat as still as a statue before the Prince Regent.

"Now, then, Kress," His Majesty continued stiffly. "I understand from our dear friend, Candover, that far from staying the course and following my imperatives, you have done nothing but buy an inordinate amount of expensive quarry stone to rebuild an unimportant tower, purchased flocks of exotic chickens, and placed an order for a great herd of dairy cows. Did I or did I not demand you to fortify the canon emplacements and secure a bride? Evidence of a new duchess in breeding would have been the coup that would have softened my heart, Kress. Instead I find you championing this, this *lady* you dare to introduce to me without even a by your leave. A lady who might very well have killed her husband. A lady who was hiding at St. Michael's Mount, with your knowledge?"

Out of the corner of her vision, Roxanne could see Alex open his mouth and then change his mind and close it.

"Finally," His Majesty said. "So glad to see you've learned how to quell your defiant nature, Kress."

Candover mumbled something.

"Speak up." The Prince Regent adjusted the long gray wig he wore and scratched his belly. His fat fingers were covered in rings with jewels of every color and shape.

"To be fair, Your Majesty, he did try to select a bride," Candover said stiffly.

Roxanne watched Alex's eyes widen.

"But I refused his request for one of my sisters," Candover lied convincingly. "And all the other ladies were unacceptable. Even I would not have been able to stomach them, Your Majesty."

It was a first. The Duke of Candover thawed? Unheard of. Even the Prince Regent was without words.

His Majesty gazed at the grand duke for a long time before switching his gaze to Kress, and finally to her. He pursed his fleshy lips, then closed his eyes and shook his royal head. "I cannot allow it. You know not how bad it goes in Town. I cannot allow you to marry an accused murderer, Kress. You must take on a lady from the original list."

Kress bowed his head.

A long silence reigned.

"Look, Kress," His Majesty continued, "as soon as you agree to a bride, I shall arrange for this lady to be released. I understand she seeks residence in Scotland. This will be secured. And none of this audacious scandal shall be known in London if we quash it right now. I shall have a word with the magistrate and a promise of something for all who attended. They can be bought, without question. And you may remove to London, where we all know your heart resides."

She wanted to speak. To tell them that she would see to her own welfare, but she knew enough to say not a word.

Alex had a different idea.

"Lady Christine Saveron," he said quietly.

Roxanne squeezed shut her eyes in horror. Lord God, he had chosen the worst of the lot as a sign to her. So she would know his true sensibilities.

The Prince Regent preened. "I knew you would see reason, Kress. In fact, this proves you are loyal to me, and I shall herewith consider all those odd rumors about your fidelity during the early war years completely false. Indeed, libelous. You have my word on it."

She would not let Alex do it. "No," she whispered. "No," Roxanne said firmly. "No!" she shouted and jumped from her chair.

Candover started forward. Alex instantly flew behind her and restrained her arms.

"Hush," he whispered.

"No, I will not hush," she said loudly. "I have always followed the rules generations of lords have chosen to set. I have broken no laws. My husband tried to kill me. If His Majesty believes otherwise, then I shall accept the justice the magistrate orders. But I will not go quietly into the night—to Scotland. I will take gaol or worse. I will tell the truth, and accept my fate. And . . . and . . . and . . . " The audacity of her outburst silenced her finally.

"No. Pray continue, Lady Paxton," His Majesty said amused.

"I beg your pardon, Your Majesty, but it is not

right to allow the Duke of Kress to marry Lady Christine Saveron. They would not suit."

"I see. And who would you choose for him?"

"Someone worthy of him. He should not be used as a scapegoat or tie himself to a woman he does not like."

The Prince Regent's jaw dropped and his head tilted back in his shock. His wig slid off, revealing his regal half-shaved head. About a quarter of an inch of salt-and-pepper-colored stubble graced one side and shoulder-length gray hair fell from the other.

How she managed to make not a sound was a miracle. She turned to glance at Alex, who was as slack-jawed as the Duke of Candover, not due to the future monarch's bizarre coiffure but at her audacity to speak to His Majesty with such unreserved impudence.

For a long moment, Roxanne held tight to hope before . . . it was lost when the Prince Regent regained the use of his tongue and the lashing began.

Alex finally understood where true happiness could be found. It was not a place, and it was not a person. It was devotion to a cause greater than oneself. In his particular case it was held in his desire to save this vibrant, brave woman who would not play by the rules but would accept the consequences, all in the name of truth.

When the royal three and common one returned to the main chamber, the magistrate was in the midst of pounding his gavel so hard, Alex was certain it would splinter.

Lord Ramsbothem, Lord Milford, and Mr. Crosby stood, facing the magistrate.

"So be it," the old magistrate insisted in his booming voice. "I have reviewed the evidence and, again, let it be known that Roxanne Vanderhaven, nee Newton, has been found guilty of conspiring to murder her husband. There is no evidence to convict His Grace, the Duke of Kress, of course, except for perhaps the minor offense of withholding the animal known as Edward von . . . hmmm, the name escapes me. However—"

"Edward von Dogged," Alex said as he strode forward with Candover. Roxanne remained behind the Prince Regent as she had been told to do. Her moment of daring had faded with the prince's ultimate decision.

Alex stopped in front of the magistrate. Candover did not halt. Instead, the premier duke stepped around Alex and stopped within inches of His Honor.

Alex could not hear what Candover said, but the magistrate did not take kindly to it. He half stood and peered around Candover, and pointed toward the Prince Regent. "Let it be known before all and sundry present that I cannot be swayed or bought by our monarchy. And I daresay, Your Highness"—the magistrate took on an ugly sneering tone—"will find few if any supporters here, given the well-known debauchery of the Crown. I will not—"

A great rustling in front caused the magistrate to stop mid-sentence. Alex watched Roxanne step beside the Prince Regent to see better.

Young John Goodsmith had come forward to the middle of the chamber. "Excuse me, sir, but I have something to say."

The magistrate's bleary eyes widened. "Bailiff. I want that man removed from—"

"I did it," John said loudly enough for all to hear. "I killed Lord Paxton. I found a pistol—"

"He lie. I kilt the flower-loving bastard." The Cossack was crunching a lot of observers' feet as he tromped past the seated people down the pew.

The magistrate lifted his gavel to pound it again, but Candover stepped forward and grabbed it before it could be lowered. The duke turned to the crowd, who immediately quieted. "By my order," Candover pronounced, "the chamber shall hear any and all comments before an official sentence is rendered."

"Well!" the magistrate huffed. "I will not toler—"

Mr. Jones stood up. "They are both incorrect. I killed Lawrence bloody Vanderhaven, because Roxanne Newton's father could not. If you are going to—"

"*Non.* I will not have any more of you kind people of Cornwall—how would you say?—*play roulette for me*?" Mémé said, jumping to her feet. "I did it. I took my little French *pistole*, and took careful aim and—"

"Don't listen to her, everyone," Alex ground out. "She is blind, for Christsakes."

Mémé lifted her shoulders. "*Beh, alors* . . . If they can say it, why cannot I? Pfffft." Mémé's Gallic exhale drew a few giggles as she regained her seat and Isabelle rose.

Candover spoke before she could open her mouth. "The Duchess of March absolutely did not do anything. Isabelle, sit down."

"You cannot speak to me like that, James. I know when to admit a wrong. I killed Latimer Vanderholden."

"*Lawrence Vanderhaven,*" Candover said dryly.

"Right. Whatever his name was. He deserved

it." Isabelle's lovely pink gown poufed out as she whirled to sit down.

And then, the oddest thing happened. A huge number of observers in the chamber slowly stood up. The fact that they wore traditional, simple miner garb was not obvious to any except those of the trade. "I dids it," shouted one. "No, I done it," yelled another. "No, 'twas I," shouted a third. "Me sister did it," brought a wave of laughter that grew and grew until Candover himself stood behind the seated magistrate, and hammered the gavel to restore order.

"Well, sir, I do believe this proves that the accusations against Roxanne Newton Vanderhaven are unfounded."

"No, it only means that justice has not been met," the magistrate whined. "And it is the fault of the one person truly above me for the time being who refuses to—"

"My dear sir," Candover drawled. "If you are so against our sovereign state, which is treason by the by, I'm certain you would agree to a free and democratic vote. All those in favor of freeing Lady Paxton, please say aye."

A chorus of "ayes" echoed from the walls of the large room.

"All those in favor of continuing this baseless drama," Candover called out with disgust.

Four voices rang out, "Aye!" (If one cannot guess who those four be, then careful attention has not been paid.)

"So be it. Please join His Majesty in removing all charges against Roxanne Vanderhaven. She may now return to Paxton Hall. Or Scotland. Or wher-

ever she chooses, including the dower house at
Paxton Hall."

Roxanne started. Return to the estate? Why, she
never wanted to set foot on Paxton property ever
again. Well, perhaps just one last time, if only to collect her gowns. Mémé's were lovely, but the neck-
lines were very risqué. Her thoughts were jumping
hither and yon, unable to find a rational train of
thought in her shock. A warmth spread from her
shoulders down to her toes.

Oh . . . the mining community did still like her—
accept her—despite her rude removal from them
upon her marriage. Perhaps not all of them, judg-
ing by the number of people still sitting. But she
recognized all the families who had worked for her
father. They had stood by her. She would never let
them down again.

Chapter 21

The return to the Mount was accomplished at sixes and sevens. Cheers broke out from time to time and the conviviality brought forth spirits and the spirits brought forth song and the songs gave the inhabitants of the carriages and the men on horseback a great sensibility of hope and justice well served.

Especially Alex Barclay, the ninth Duke of Kress, who was still grinding his teeth at the overwhelming bustle of people who had managed to keep him from entering a carriage with Roxanne. He had been able to see her only in the distance, handed into the simple yet large carriage of Mr. Jones.

He mumbled a choice French curse and removed his hat to shove the rim between the leather straps on the ceiling of his carriage. Alex felt the bulge under his vest and removed the documents Candover had transferred to him while in the chamber with the Prince Regent. Mémé leaned forward to pat his knee. Isabelle did the same to his other knee, only harder. "Alex?"

He turned his focus to the petite, lovely duchess, and wondered how he could contrive to force Candover to give over and do right by her despite their huge gap in age. "Isabelle, *cherie*, you know I adore you, don't you?" Kress stated.

"Of course. It's not every day a duchess stands by her friend, even risking death for her and for him. Although, I must say, I was more worried when we were at that awful mine. You are going to somehow manage to get her to stop doing things like that, right, Alex?"

He stared at her. "We are not having this conversation."

"All right," Isabelle murmured. "Mémé and I will have it, then." She looked at the older lady in question. "Don't you think they make an adorable couple, Mémé?"

Alex could barely hear the two ladies banter. He had unfolded the documents and began to scan them. *Mon Dieu. Mon Dieu. Mon Dieu.*

Mémé clapped her hands together again. "Oh, *absolument.* As lovely as you and le duc Candover, *ma petite chou.*"

Isabelle giggled and kissed the older lady on her cheek. "One day someone will have to explain to me why the French find cauliflower an endearing pet name."

Kress knocked loudly on the carriage's roof. It came to a bone-jarring halt and Alex popped open the door to leap out, narrowly missing an oncoming cabriolet. He stood in the middle of the wide lane as soon as he spotted Mr. Jones's vehicle, which slowed.

Alex quickly opened the door of the boxy vehicle and jumped inside, where Roxanne sat across from Mr. Jones. The carriage pulled forward again.

"Well, well," Mr. Jones said with the smallest of

smiles in evidence. "The very man of whom we were speaking."

Alex nodded the correct amount despite the confines of the carriage. "Delighted to see you again, Mr. Jones."

"I am happy and surprised, I can say the same," the lowborn but modestly rich man replied deliberately as was his style.

"And why is that, sir? Have I finally met your expectations? It would be a good thing, actually if I did." Alex glanced at Roxanne. "*Ma cherie*, please, may I ask you very kindly to put your hands over your ears and hum a few bars of the French anthem?"

"Of course, Alex. I've had to hear it so often from you, I fairly know it by heart." She began to laugh. And for the first time since he had met her, she did exactly as he bade without a single question. The notes were as poorly rendered as was humanly possible and he loved her all the more for it for some ridiculous reason.

The entire situation was surreal and a bloody miracle in the making. He was not foolish enough to think the spell would last long.

"Mr. Jones, you are the person who comes closest to a father for Roxanne. I would ask your permission for the great honor of Roxanne Newton's hand in marriage."

A tiny smile crept on her face, which was turned to the carriage window.

"Louder, *cherie*," he requested.

She obeyed, but the smile remained.

"And just how do you mean to provide for her, Your Grace?" Mr. Jones demanded.

"As best I can. There will be blunt from the dairy

and the chickens and eggs at first. But over the course of the next twelve months, I have every expectation of improvement in our living circumstances. However, most of the monies at the start will go toward the improvement of the Mount."

Mr. Jones's lips twitched. "I don't think that would work, Your Grace. Roxanne is not accustomed to living in straightened circumstances."

Roxanne stopped her awful humming and frowned at Mr. Jones. Both men glared back at her. She resumed her off-key rendition. And then abruptly stopped as the carriage lurched to a halt.

The door opened once again and Mémé was helped inside with the aid of Isabelle. Before the door could be closed, Candover, out of breath, leapt inside, too. "Finally," he ground out.

"We were wondering and worrying what had become of you, James," Isabelle said sweetly.

"Perhaps. But I cannot be sure since no one cared enough to stop and learn I'd been forced to accept a lift from a cart full of the most animated crowd of miners," he said haughtily. "They even provided spirits more vile than that god-awful absinthe."

"And where is Mary?" Isabelle asked.

"She refused to leave the cart," Candover muttered, a rare rueful expression revealed momentarily.

Everyone laughed heartily, making them aware just how tight the carriage had become with the six of them crammed inside.

"So where are we, Alex?" Isabelle asked. "Have you asked Roxanne to marry you yet?"

Roxanne bit back a smile. "No, I do believe I have to get to the anthem's refrain again before a hint of a proposal will be heard. So please do be quiet, dearest, for it's taking an age."

Mémé clapped her hands in delight.

"Oh, good! We didn't miss it," Isabelle said, a huge lovely smile overspreading her face as she tucked Mémé's skirting away from Mr. Jones's boots.

Candover had regained his senses and said not a word. He was looking as far away from Isabelle as he could.

Roxanne's insides were twisted in anticipation. This simply was not possible. How could she have gone from knee-weakening horror to overflowing happiness in such a short period of time? She only wished Mr. Jones would spare Alex any further pain. Did he not know that she would be willing to work the mines herself if it meant more money to satisfy Mr. Jones's protective nature?

Mr. Richard "Dickie" Jones glanced at the circle of people in his carriage. "As I was saying, His Grace is unable to support Roxanne in the fashion she is accustomed, and so I would turn down his kind offer, except for one thing."

All eyes bore down on the gaunt man.

"Yes?" Candover finally spoke.

"Well, Roxanne is an heiress, and of age, and as such, she should be allowed to make her own decision," Mr. Jones replied. "If you will pardon me for saying so, Your Grace, only idiot peers require their womanfolk to be sold into bondage. So what say you, Roxie? Do you want this fool bloke? He be a pretty one, to be sure, but perhaps a bit too froggish for a practical bonny lass such as yourself, no?"

"I am not an heiress in any way, Mr. Jones, as you well know. And by the by, I don't take kindly to compliments, except perhaps French ones on rare occasions."

To his credit, Alex said not one glib word. His lips did twitch, however.

"Roxanne," Mr. Jones said in all seriousness. "My dearest and only goddaughter, you are, indeed, an heiress. When word of your death reached me, I did as your father bade me on his deathbed. I retrieved the fortune and hid it in a new place."

"Why did he ask you to do that?" Roxanne's mouth had gone dry.

"He worried Paxton would follow you if you ever dared to retrieve the fortune. And he worried he would try to harm you. If anything happened to you, your father wanted his money to go to the mining families."

"Of course," she whispered.

"He also suggested," Mr. Jones continued in the shocked silence, "the distribution should not be done quickly for fear that Paxton would question any change in the mining community's spending habits. And so I was to hide the fortune, and wait a year before slowly apportioning his wealth."

"But then we arrived on your doorstep," Alex ground out. "And you said not a word to her."

"Of course not. I knew her father wouldn't want me to give Roxanne a shilling if any shenanigans were at play. And you, sir, are a known fortune-hunter, just like that blackguard Paxton. I would have given it to her eventually."

"But now you've changed your mind about him," Roxanne said softly.

"You certainly took your time about it," Alex added dryly.

"Well, it's a lot of blunt," murmured Mr. Jones.

"*Et bien, dites donc.* How much?" Mémé's

lightning-fast response did nothing to aid her pretended nonchalance.

Mr. Jones glanced around the faces surrounding him. "She didn't tell you?"

Alex looked at her.

"You never asked." She shrugged her shoulders.

"One hundred ten thousand pounds," Mr. Jones replied.

Alex and Candover froze in shock. Isabelle burst out laughing and clapped a hand over her mouth.

"What is it?" Roxanne said, looking at her dearest friend.

"Why, I do believe you are richer than I!"

Alex blinked.

"I told you I'd repay you," she whispered to him.

Mémé clapped her hands like a young girl. "Oh, do let's order new drapery for all the chambers. And new carpets. Furniture . . . oh, and the wine cellar, my darling Roxanne. And then we shall plan a grand wedding."

"No," Alex ground out.

"No?" Mémé and Isabelle asked, their voices echoing in the confines of the carriage. The vehicle swayed and hit a bump in the road, leaving half of them on the other half's laps.

Roxanne was now in Alex's arms quite conveniently. She wrapped her arms around his neck. His eyes were very dark in the night and he said not a word.

She touched the ends of his hair. "I take back my request that you go before the House of Lords to ask them to look into the condition of the roads. They're quite conveniently pitted. But, please, I really would like to help with the reconstruction of the Mount. It is only fitting considering everything you have done for me."

He sighed. "I will not take your money. It is yours to do with as you choose, but it will not be spent on the Mount. I, too, have plans and they do not include spending your money."

She smiled.

Mr. Jones smiled.

Alex met her eye to eye. "And I'll agree to only one female's wedding plan. Yours."

Mémé exhaled. "Oh, do tell him, *cherie*! We must begin right away if you are to be married within two months. I fear that's the limit of my great-nephew's patience. I shall have to house you in my adjoining chamber to keep him from you. And—"

Roxanne laughed. And laughed all the harder when she realized all eyes were upon her.

Alex cradled her head in his hands and whispered in her ear. "Will you have me, then, *cherie*? Whatever you like, I will do. Just tell me."

"At the Mount," she murmured.

He pulled back slightly to examine her face.

"As soon as we arrive," she continued.

It was his turn to smile.

"It's a perfect plan, actually," Roxanne said. "The archbishop is there, as will be all our friends. And I don't want anyone else. And I don't want wedding finery. I just want . . . you."

"And so you have me, *cherie*," he said as softly as he could manage despite the fact that everyone could hear him.

"And what of the Prince Regent?" Candover asked quietly. "His Majesty is going to demand some sort of repayment at the very least when he learns of her fortune. It will take a miracle for him to agree to allow the two of you to marry as it stands."

"I rather think, James," Isabelle replied, "His Majesty will have little choice."

"What know you of what Prinny will require when he hears this news?"

"I know enough that if His Majesty follows our advice," Isabelle suggested softly, "and that of all the other dukes we can muster—such as Sussex, and Barry—that he will not say no, especially if we suggest the populous might very well adore the idea of a commoner marrying one of the royal entourage. This might endear the monarchy to commoners unlike anything else."

Alex looked at Candover. "When are you going to realize, *mon ami*, that women rule the world?"

Mémé smiled. "Of course we do, *cheri*. You always were the most intelligent male of the *famille*. You get that from me, I think."

"And do you know what I got from my father?" Alex murmured.

"What?" Roxanne asked with much curiosity.

"The ability to search out an extraordinary soul willing to take a risk beside him, all while discovering a heretofore unknown great need to protect her, nurture her, and bring her enough joy to last for a lifetime."

"How lovely," she murmured, sinking her nose into the warmth of his neckcloth. "Your English compliments improve hourly."

Candover exhaled. "Yes, well, I daresay compliments will not suffice for Prinny. Have you no other plan, Kress, if Isabelle's notions are not sufficient to bring the Prince Regent around?"

Alex kissed the top of Roxanne's head, in front of all of them, and could not keep his eyes off of her as he replied to the premier duke. "You do realize we will be great friends, James, after all, don't you?"

"I beg your—"

"It's taken an age to make out your character, I'll admit. You might enjoy playing the cool, condescending, watch fob–jangling, quizzing glass–peering premier duke, but I know you better now and I like you. And you may have already forgotten that you performed the one and only favor I requested of you long ago when you took your leave of the Mount, but I have not." Curiosity piqued in the heated carriage as Alex stroked her hair, in the fashion she adored.

Candover raised his quizzing glass but then lowered it as he realized he was playing into Alex's description. He raised his chin a notch instead. "I did not take my leave voluntarily. I was nearly kicked out of—"

Alex interrupted, amused by Candover's inability to accept gratitude. "I refer to the favor in which you retrieved the Letters Patent from my solicitor's office in Kensington and then took the trouble to give them to me whilst I was in that chamber with Prinny back in Lamerton."

"Well, of course I did. You asked it of me. What has that to do with it?"

Roxanne's neck began to prickle in the way it did before something interesting unfolded.

Alex's eyes kept boring into hers alone. "While Mémé and Isabelle chattered in our carriage, I perused the Letters Patent I requested from James, and found a tiny clause specifying that in times of war, the owner of the Mount may rely on the sovereign to provide funds to rebuild any damage to key outposts. And"—he held up a hand to keep from being interrupted—"furthermore, Kress House in London is unentailed, something I did not know. I shall sell it. Roxanne will be far happier here, and . . . so will I. The monies will go toward fulfilling our plans at the Mount."

And for the first time in Roxanne's life, she heard Mr. Jones laugh. It was a lovely, deep sound that came from the bottom of his lean stomach. Slowly, everyone joined him, and Roxanne clasped her beloved closer and reveled in the happiness that had eluded her for so long.

"So it is settled, then?" Isabelle said. The duchess's eyes sparkled with excitement. "Will you at least allow me enough time to pick a bouquet for you, Roxanne?"

"Only if it is kidney vetch," Alex replied.

The carriage filled with the sound of laughter. Mr. Jones scratched his head as the excitement subsided. "Perhaps this is the time to clear my conscience," the older man said with resignation replacing his happiness. "I fear I must turn myself over to whoever is chosen as the new magistrate in our county."

Alex scrutinized the man. "If you are going to try and tell us that you were the one who shot Paxton, Mr. Jones, I suggest you save your breath. I killed him."

"You most certainly did not," Roxanne insisted. "I did."

Candover shook his head. "Enough. There will be no more talk of Lawrence Vanderhaven. A man who leaves his wife to die doesn't deserve this sort of scrutiny. Any sort of investigation will be halted." The premier duke pursed his lips and added, *"By me personally."*

"And I assure you, Mr. Jones, that I, and the rest of the royal entourage, will ensure it," Alex added.

Dickie Jones, one of the most respected and honorable men in all of Cornwall, sighed deeply in relief. He'd done what his best friend, Cormick Newton, had asked him to do on his deathbed. He'd protected Roxanne with his own life, and much to his astonishment, it appeared he would be none the worse for it. Praise the Lord.

By the time the weary travelers reached the Mount, darkness was well entrenched and the first chill of autumn lurked afoot in the castle's mysterious corners.

"Perhaps we should wait until morning, Alex," Isabelle said. "How will I ever find that vetch at this hour? What time is it anyway?"

"It's merely half past four in the morning," Candover said with a yawn so wide, everyone assembled in the great hall could hear his jaw crack.

Mémé leaned against Mr. Jones, yet had not one hair out of place. Only Alex and Roxanne were wide awake, the joy that was upon them keeping them from any sign of exhaustion.

"Come along, Isabelle, I shall help you find that organ vetch, for we've not a chance of talking them out of it now," Candover muttered.

Isabelle was so shocked by his suggestion that the petite duchess placed her arm on the tall duke's arm with nary a word.

The archbishop appeared asleep on his feet as he mumbled something that sounded remarkably like a curse as he searched the book of prayer for the wedding vows.

Roxanne went on tiptoe to whisper in Alex's ear. "John isn't here. Nor is Mary."

"Mary, I daresay is happily enchanting a clutch of spellbound tinners. And John? He will return in a moment, *cherie*." Alex looked down at her with the blinding light of happiness, and something else in his eyes. "He's merely retrieving something for me."

Mémé moved closer to them, her arms out in front of her. "Roxanne, I must thank you. *Merci, cherie*. You are truly the daughter I never had."

"Great-niece," Alex chided.

"Yes, yes. Great-niece, niece, daughter, sister— *c'est la même chose*. The same thing . . . Family."

Emotion welled in Roxanne's heart.

"Ah, ah, ah," Mémé reproached softly. "Tears of joy are insupportable. Remember?"

"Of course, Mémé." And she quoted her soon-to-be great-aunt. "Tears of joy are boring. One should shout when joyful."

"*Exactement*. You are very quick. I like that."

Mémé reached out her hand at the same moment that John walked up to Alex and handed him a small box. Mémé's fingers touched John's hair.

"Thank you, John," Alex said.

"John," Mémé murmured, "your hair is so soft. Just like . . . What color is it?"

"Brown, ma'am."

"A very nice dark chestnut, actually," Roxanne inserted as she gazed at her beloved.

"And your eyes?" Mémé would not leave off.

"Brown. Very common."

"I see," Mémé said, not seeing at all.

The archbishop ambled forward, one hand rubbing his eyes. "Well, then, are we ready?"

"Do you really want the kidney vetch?" Alex's eyes were filled with emotion impossible for Roxanne to fully absorb. She could not deny him another moment.

"Maybe they won't return in time." She hoped they did not. She hoped they would find their own small piece of paradise in the kidney vetch patch.

"Now, then. Let us begin." The archbishop yawned yet again. "Although this is highly irregular. Marriages are not to be performed at night."

"Of course," Alex said with a warm smile. "We would be happy to wait here in the Hall for another hour if you prefer."

Moans all around, most notably from the archbishop, halted that argument.

"Where is the groomsman?"

"John." Alex turned to the young man who was nearly his own height, without yet the brawn. "Would you be kind enough to stand up for me?"

"You do me a great honor, Your Grace."

Alex nodded with encouragement.

"What is your full name, then?" The archbishop had hoisted his spectacles to his round face. "I shall need it for the marriage documents."

"John Petroc Goodsmith, sir."

Alex started at the same moment as Mémé.

"Mon Dieu," Mémé whispered. "Alex, *touche ses cheveux*. His hair . . . touch it."

"What is it, Alex?" Roxanne was so cold suddenly. Worried.

"My name . . ." Alex halted.

"Yes?" Roxanne pleaded.

"Is Alexander *John Petroc* Barclay," he finished.

The younger man looked to the older, and the ladies stared at the two of them.

"John," Alex said, "do you know who John Petroc was?"

"Yes, sir," he said with his head bowed.

A long silence ensued.

"Alex, please," Roxanne begged. "Tell us."

"He doesn't need to tell me," Mémé murmured. "I know all the names of the relations, remember, *cheri*? John Petroc was the given name of the last four Dukes of Kress."

"I didn't want you to know," John said sadly.

Alex laid an arm about the younger man's shoulders. "John, are you my cousin? Are you family?"

"I'm a bastard," he murmured. "My mother and the last Duke of Kress . . . It wasn't her fault. It was . . ."

"You don't have to explain it, John," Alex said quietly.

"She was the governess here. The duke took advantage of her one night. She would have been ruined if my true father had not married her. I shall always consider William Goodsmith my real father, not the other," John insisted.

"Of course, you should," Alex murmured. "But will you allow a Barclay to be your cousin?"

John Petroc Goodsmith smiled, and Alexander John Petroc Barclay smiled back.

The archbishop yawned. "Such a delightful bed-time story. Do you, Alexander Bar—"

"Alexander *John Petroc* Barclay," Alex corrected.

"Yes, yes, yes. Will you take this woman, Roxanne what is it—Tatianà? Harriet?" The archbishop was in misery.

"Roxanne Newton will do," she said with a small giggle.

His holiness's shoulders sagged in relief. "Do

you take this woman in sickness and in health, for richer, for poorer, in—"

"Yes," Alex said cutting the man off.

"And I will take him, too," Roxanne said with a huge smile. "But, I won't obey, if that is all right with you, Alex."

"I know better than to try and change you now."

"But I would die for you, if need be," she said anxiously.

He chuckled. "There's to be no more dying for husbands. Although . . ."

"Yes?"

"Although I would ask you to wear a ring."

"A ring?" She looked at him skeptically. "But I don't particularly like . . . What I mean is that Mémé already gave me a lovely ring."

Mémé cleared her throat. Loudly. "*Et bien, cherie,* since you will remain here with Edward, perhaps I should ask for it to be returned."

Roxanne sighed and shook her head. Mémé stuck out her hand, palm up.

Alex tugged off Mémé's band only to replace it with . . . *simply the most extraordinary ring.* She inhaled in surprise. An enormous rectangular diamond was flanked by two luminous sapphires. "It's—it's . . . exquisite," she breathed.

"Admit it"—Alex smiled and his eyes sparkled— "for just the merest moment, you were worried it might be hideous."

She shrugged her shoulders casually in his French manner and then gave up all pretense and threw her arms around his neck. "I should have known you had a plan," she whispered ruefully for his ears alone.

Eddie suddenly dashed into the hall, his nails not

gaining much purchase on the final curve before he jumped into the couple's arms, and began barking and howling his approval.

It was the most perfect wedding ceremony Roxanne could have ever envisioned. And she had no doubt the supreme clergyman would verify it no matter how abbreviated it had been.

The archbishop slapped the book closed and trundled off to bed, wondering once again why he had ever chosen this profession.

He also wondered why in hell there was none of that particularly wonderful stuff called absinthe to be found in the cellars here. He had but one last cellar to check to be certain.

He went off not knowing that he would hit the mother lode that very night.

And Roxanne and Alex? Was there any question what became of them?

One thing was certain. They had both paid hell twice over in their lives. From this day forward there would be no further torment—only heaven on earth for the two of them—surrounded by the oddest assortment of relations, friends, and canines, which no one would ever deny are the very best sorts to love for a lifetime on a magnificent mountain of granite pulled from the sea, with little plant life to tend.

Now you know what happened to Alexander Barclay, the Duke of Kress, after the most extravagant royal bachelor party of all time. But what about his friend Roman Montagu, the Duke of Norwich?

Roman has two rules: never marry, and never go to sea. So he's stunned to find himself the morning following the party aboard a storm-tossed ship and locked in the arms of a proper lady.

Esme March, the Countess of Derby, has two rules too: never give away your heart, and never let anyone get in the way of your life's deepest passions. But Esme cannot resist Roman when all seems lost at sea. Yet when their ship returns to London, everything will be forgotten . . . as long as they can keep their secret from the Prince Regent. For if the future king commands them to marry, all their fondest dreams will be ruined. But where love is concerned, some rules are made to be broken . . .

Turn the page for a sneak peek at *The Art of Duke Hunting*, the second book in the Royal Entourage series by Sophia Nash, available April 2012 from Avon Books!

Roman Montagu, the seventeenth Duke of Norwich, knew he would end up at the bottom of the sea. He'd known it for almost two decades.

Yet, he never complained about his fate. For God sakes, no. Why, he had cheated death longer than most of the devilishly long line of Norwiches before him. He even considered himself lucky.

For a Norwich.

Indeed, almost everyone in England knew why there had been a dizzying number of Norwich dukes in two hundred years. They were cursed. Every last one of them had found death prematurely.

It was said the first bloodthirsty duke had damned the family by publicly accusing a young lady of witchcraft after she had refused his ham-handed offer of marriage. But really, who could blame her for her less than enthusiastic response? The duke had not brought jewels to profess his affection. No, he had brought a half dozen ill-plucked fowl to her family and proclaimed her the luckiest lady alive due to the honor he would bestow on her. That did little to impress the young lady, or rather, the young witch, whose powers might not have saved her from persecution, but had managed to damn each and every Norwich thereafter.

Roman had learned to live with this familial noose by adopting the blackest sense of humor concerning his forebears' early visits by the Grim Reaper. Indeed, he could recite the family's history by rote.

1. The first duke stuck his spoon in the wall when
    he choked on a giblet in his favorite duck stew
    not two days after his not-so-beloved burned
    at the stake, while cursing all Norwich dukes.

2. The second unfortunate duke ate grass for his
    last breakfast when a bolt of lightning struck
    his duck blind in which he was silently perched
    at dawn in the pouring rain. It was then that
    the whispers of the curse began.

3. The third, fourth, fifth, and sixth dukes vowed
    to give a wide birth to all birds to stay alive.
    Instead, they dampened their insatiable thirst
    for hunting by pursuing the dangerous fairer
    sex in London's ballrooms. While they might
    have been well-endowed with passion for the
    wives and daughters of their class, sadly, they
    were not well-talented with dueling pistols or
    swords borne by the husbands and fathers.
    The line devolved to a far less romantic branch
    with better aim.

4. The seventh duke tried to avoid the curse by
    daily readings from Johnson's sermons. He
    tumbled from the rolling ladder in Norwich
    Hall's famous, but mostly unread (especially
    by dukes III through VI) library while looking
    at an illustrated guide to geese hidden between
    Johnson's pages.

5. The adventurous eighth duke tossed away all
    sermons and took his dirt nap after sinking in
    a Scottish bog in search of a rare merganser,
    which barely looked like water-fowl at all. He
    had wrongly assumed the curse would not
    cross the border.

6. The ninth, tenth, and eleventh dukes were
    never seen or heard from again when they

heroically went to war against the French. At least they were brave. Then again, when you knew you would die young, why not embrace your fate and die like a hero instead of a demented bird-brained predator?

7. The twelfth duke refused the call to arms. Indeed, he refused to put one toe out of bed in an all out effort to avoid his fate. He cocked his toes in an acute case of gout within a twelve-month. Most said it was the duck paté enveloped in goose fat.

8. The thirteenth duke knew he stood not a ghost of a chance given his number and family history. He went out in a blaze of pleasure, at full cry, with one of his seven mistresses, who tickled him with duck feathers.

9. The foppish fourteenth duke sacked a host of valets before he inadvertently strangled himself whilst fashioning a new knot for his Widgeon-colored neckcloth the scandal sheet dubbed "The Norwich Noose."

10. The fifteenth duke decided to confound the curse by befriending the enemy. He raised a pet mallard, who quacked on command and followed him everywhere. But whilst taking a short lie-down under a willow tree, a poacher aimed for the sitting duck and killed the dreaming duke instead.

Only Roman Montagu's father, the sixteenth Duke of Norwich, had lived past his fourth decade. Some said it was due to a tragedy of which he never spoke, or his avoidance of all spirits and hunting. Indeed, the stern aristocrat refused to sin in any fashion whatsoever.

But Roman knew better. The man had avoided a premature rendezvous with his maker by sheer bloody pigheadedness. Yes, the sixteenth duke had been nothing if not inflexible. But even the most wary and stubborn Montagu man could not avoid his destiny. At least Roman's father's death had been dignified. It was hard to find humor in a fall from a horse. Then again, the sixteenth duke had not possessed a shred of wit. Roman never told his sister or his mother that there had been feathers nearby, indicating his father's horse had most likely bolted from the sudden appearance of a migrating flock.

And so Roman Montagu, "Seventeen" to his intimates, did not worry overmuch about his future since it was already written. He would be the first Norwich to sink to the ocean floor—just like his elder brother before him, who should have been duke. He did not know how a duck would cause it, but of his fate he held not a feather of doubt. The other point on which he was decided, was that he would be the last—*the very last*—Norwich. There were no males left in the line—not even a fourteenth cousin twenty-four times removed.

And so, Roman Montagu went about the process of life in a simple manner. He avoided ducks, and he did not enter bodies of water larger than his bath. The rest he left to chance. He worked on his grand schemes, and seized every moment of every day with gusto for who knew when the lights would go out.

But at this very moment in time, it appeared he was about to break the record of shortest title-holder. Well, at least it did not involve a damned duck.

Or did it?

*   *   *

Sheer unadulterated terror rained down on Roman Montagu, the Duke of Norwich. He was in the grip of a hellish nightmare—on the one thing he had vowed never to set foot on again . . . a ship. He shook his head, and it seemed to spin endlessly in the gale wind. Seawater lanced his eyes as waves crashed and retreated over the railing, while clips rattled against the masts over the roar and whine of a storm.

Hell and damn. 'Twas not a dream. His brother was not some ghostly figure haunting him. No. Roman was wedged in the windward corner, unable to move. His fingers clawed the quarterdeck, only to find one hand tied to the sodding taffrail. His blood seized and stood still in his veins.

Blindly, he freed his wrist, and managed to crab-walk away from the stern. The vessel rose and violently shifted on a massive wave and he slammed into the mizzenmast. The blow sent a shower of white hot pain sparking through his brainbox. He lunged for the aft mast again. It was his only chance.

Safety was up in the rigging, where he would wait for the hair-raising crack of the deck's wooden beams giving way to shoals—when the sea always won her game with foolish mankind who tried to tame her. Up one of the three masts, he would be the last to lose.

As the ship violently creaked and rocked in the kaleidoscope of the summer storm tumbling through the inky darkness, he tried mightily to make the muscle of his brain flex. He had not one particle of an idea of how or why he was on this bloody wreck in the making. Flashes of insane evening revelry with his fellow dukes in the Royal Entourage crackled through his mind as he was tossed away from the mast.

Well, damnation, he knew how to swim. He'd once proved he could outswim fate. Maybe he could do it again.

It was worth a try.

Esme March, the Countess of Derby, peered out of the rain-riddled porthole of the door leading to the ship's deck. She was probably the only passenger not terrified or ill. Yet.

Well, at least she was not afraid. Never would be after the last year. But she feared she might become as green as a pea if she didn't inhale a few gulps of bracing sea air instead of remaining in her small cabin. Her gaze swept the murky seascape as she gripped the door handle to keep her balance.

For a moment, she could have sworn she had seen something odd—likely just a poor sailor whose task it was to secure a line. The deck would be impossible to negotiate given the pitch and sway.

There he was again. A ghostly image of a man, his hair whipping his face in the storm. She inhaled sharply as he slammed into a mast and fell back.

Good God. The man regained his footing and swayed dangerously as an enormous wave crashed over the railing. He reached wildly for the mast but the wave dragged his body toward the edge of the ship.

Esme bolted past the door, knotted a line about her, and dashed for the man about to be lost to the sea. She couldn't breathe for the ferocity of the wind and the freezing sheets of rain.

She grasped the man's wrists just as he would have been tossed into the deep blue. Esme prayed for strength. His hands gripped her arms as another

wave crashed over them both, the white foam glowing in the darkness.

As the seawater receded, for just a moment hanging in time, she chanced to see his face; harsh lines
etched the corners of his mouth and forehead. But
it was his translucent pale eyes that frightened her.

She recoiled. It was the only time she'd ever spied
death. The ship pitched to advantage, and they were
hurtled in the direction of the door to the cabins.

For some odd reason, the gentleman appeared
to pull away from her. She used the last remaining
strength she possessed to navigate him over the
threshold before he sagged. She had but a moment
to open her door before he lost consciousness.

Esme struggled to move his leg from the door-
jamb, and then shut her cabin door and locked it. She
paused, dripping puddles on the bare wooden floor.
She pushed back her wet, tangled hair from her eyes.

Lord, he was so deathly pale; his lips waxy and
almost blue. Wind-whipped strands of dark hair
threaded with premature gray plastered his noble
profile. He looked like a weary archangel felled to
earth while she probably looked like a drowned rat.

He could not be dead. It would be too much to
witness twice in one year. No, his chest was rising
and falling. Without thinking, she slipped the door
key into the top of one of her sodden calfskin half
boots.

She grasped his nearly frozen hand and felt for his
pulse. Not that she'd know what to do if she found
it. She had not an idea if it was too fast or slow. She
was tempted to slap his face to revive him since cold
water would obviously not work on someone who'd
just endured a wall of seawater.

Just then, with a rushed gulp of air, he came full awake, scrambling like a wild animal looking for escape. The unearthly pale blue eyes that met hers were intensified by an intriguing web-like line weaving through each iris. Lurching to one knee, he flinched away from the touch of her hand and half crawled toward the door. He wrestled with the brass lever.

For some absurd reason, he wanted to get out. Thank God she'd hidden the key just as she had on so many other occasions with Lionel. But this man was another case altogether. She had not a chance of holding him back. He might be her height, but his torso was immense and he was clearly as strong as a bull stampeding the corridors of Pamplona in August.

"Hey," she said, gripping the back of the one sturdy chair in the cramped cabin, "wait a minute."

He again rattled the handle, his shoulders flexing with the effort to rip the door from the frame.

She had a terrible thought. "Is there someone else out there?"

"Key," he shouted. "Where is the bloody key?" They both stumbled sideways when the ship heaved starboard.

"But you'll die out there." There was not a single melodramatic note in her words—just stated fact.

He didn't deign to turn to face her, but at least he paused, a sign he was finally listening to her. He then jammed down the brass lever so violently, a screw gave way and the handle failed to return to its position. The oath he swore was so blue it almost made Esme cringe.

"Fool," he gritted out, still not looking at her. "Death is in here, not out there."

Esme stared at the back of his coat. The stitches at the center seam were stretched to the limit. The drenched blue superfine clung to the striated muscles of his shoulders.

"Please look at me," she said quietly.

"I'll find it myself," he choked, finally turning to stare at her. His eyes swept down her tall frame.

"Who are you?" She'd never backed down from a threat in the past, and no matter how intense his glare, the clothes of a gentleman were a good calling card.

He marched toward her, his black riding boots with the arched outer edge molded to his calves. The seawater-soaked leather soles made smacking sounds as he walked. He extended his palm.

"All right," she said softly. "I'll tell you where it is if you tell me who you are and what you were doing out there."

"I'll have the key and then I *might* tell you." He grasped her arms and Esme felt the strength in him as his hands squeezed her. He was a mere half inch taller than she, so she looked almost directly into his light blue eyes that almost glowed in the static air.

"Are you going to growl now?"

His eyes narrowed.

"Look, the storm is waning. There's no need to go out there." And, indeed, it was true. Even the howl of the wind seemed muted.

He released her abruptly, but the wildness in his eyes did not disappear.

"You've a cut on your forehead."

He refused a reply.

She continued her tried and true methods of speaking calmly in the face of insanity. "I'm freezing." She reached for her two blankets and offered him one. "You must be too."

He muttered something incomprehensible and didn't take the blanket. She set both back down.

"Oh pish. Do tell me what's going on, Lord . . . ?"

"Grace . . ." He barely paid her any attention.

"Lord Grace? Hmmm, I've never heard of a Lord—"

"No," he sighed, "Duke."

Ah. That explained it. All dukes were insane. Too much power. Too much deference. She raised an inquiring eyebrow. Too much inbreeding.

"For Christsakes . . . I'm Norwich."

"I see. Are we sure?"

He sighed heavily. "Roman Montagu, *not* at your service."

She smiled inwardly. "Really? How lovely. I didn't know we had such refined company on board."

Again he muttered.

"Would you be kind enough to speak louder, Your Grace? I guess I must be becoming a bit hard of hearing in my advanced years."

When he didn't refute her, it irked her, which annoyed her even further.

"I said," he enunciated clearly, "I didn't know such refined company would be aboard either."

"I'm merely a countess, Your Grace. I'm—"

He interrupted. "I was talking about me."

She frowned. "Of course you were." She lowered her voice. "It's what dukes do best."

"I beg your pardon," he replied. "What did you say?"

"I see old age has affected you, too, sir," she said sourly. She would not kowtow to him. He hadn't even thanked her for saving his life. That reminded her. "I saved your life."

"I beg your pardon?"

"I'll enunciate better, Your Grace. I. Saved. Your. Life."

"What is your name, madam?"

"Esme March, Countess of Derby," she dipped the smallest curtsey possible, "at your service even if you aren't at mine. May I see to that gash?"

"No."

She raised her eyebrows. "It's the least you could do since I saved your life."

He rolled his eyes. "Look, I'll tell every last sodding person in London you saved my life if you give me the key." His voice rose with each syllable.

She smiled and hoped it didn't appear sincere. "But the winds have died. So, why are you acting so oddly and what is so bloody important to you out there?" She was proud of herself for swearing. She so rarely had an opportunity to try it unless she was in private. And as Lionel had used to say, blaspheme was much more fun with two.

He stared at her and those strange eyes of his bored into hers with an intensity she felt down to her toes.

"Ships sink." He shrugged his shoulders. "If you can swim, you are far less likely to drown if you're on deck. You won't be able to open that door"—he nodded to her—"with the weight of water pushing against it."

His words made a small amount of sense, and so she locked away the schoolmarmish tone from her words. "Of course. But I really don't think we have anything to worry about now. Don't you agree? The Drake is new and well built—such fine craftsmanship."

He closed those unnerving eyes of his. "The Drake? This ship is named The Drake?" He almost seemed to moan.

He might be a handsome devil with that oddly ancient noble mien, but his wits were obviously scrambled. Right. She walked to the secured water jug, poured a good portion in a bowl and dipped a piece of linen in it. Crossing the space, she faced him. "May I?"

He didn't move. She wiped his face with clean water and dabbed at the cut on the upper edge of his forehead. She almost recoiled when she noticed a very familiar licorice scent almost oozing from his being. Absinthe. One of her beloved deceased husband's poisons of choice. She held her breath and forced herself to say not a word lest she lose her grip on common civility.

When she was done, she dropped the linen and he stepped on it so she could upend the bowl over his head to sluice the salt from his face and clothes. Silently, she repeated the steps to cleanse herself. After scrubbing her face dry, she offered him a new scrap of linen too.

"Are you ever going to tell me what was going on out there?" she finally asked quietly.

"I was preparing to die, madam. You must be one of the few in England who hasn't heard of the Norwich Curse."

"Oh . . ." She widened her eyes. "*The Duke of Duck Curse.* Of course."

He pokered up. "We prefer the other reference."

The vessel immediately dipped ominously and both stumbled sideways. His eyes glazed over as his face paled. He looked ready to lose his bearing again and so she dragged him to the sole bunk in her cabin to urge him to sit.

And suddenly, she remembered. Remembered hearing what had happened to him all those years ago. He had every right to be terrified, especially since he obviously had not an idea why he was on the ship. If she had to wager on it, she would guess it had something to do with the Royal Entourage, the infamous rapscallion band of dukes who walked hand in glove with the Prince Regent, and of which he was a member. Yes, Norwich had very likely rubbed along with Lionel at some point during her husband's high-flown days. Several of these gentlemen had even drunk Lionel under the table, and probably helped him stumble into an early grave if she was to hazard a guess.

But none of that mattered right now. No, this gentleman needed help. And while she had always given comfort freely to all those who required aid in the past, she had sworn that when Lionel died, it would be the last time she would put herself in that position. It was just too heartbreaking. And this man, no matter how high his title, was on the road to ruination if she had to wager her eye teeth.

Well.

The black despair she spied in his face broke her. She sat on the bunk beside him.

Next month, don't miss these exciting new love stories only from Avon Books

A Week to be Wicked by Tessa Dare
When a confirmed spinster and notorious rogue find themselves on a road to Scotland, time is not on their side. Who would have known that in one week such an unlikely pair could find a world of trouble, and maybe . . . just maybe . . . everlasting love?

The Art of Duke Hunting by Sophia Nash
On a ship in a storm-swept sea, a duke with no desire to wed and a countess who swears she'll never give her heart away find desperate passion. But they must forget their moment of folly, for if the *ton* were to learn their secret, all their fondest dreams could be ruined.

Confessions from an Arranged Marriage by Miranda Neville
It happened the usual way. He had no plans for marriage, she abhorred his wastrel ways...but a moment of mistaken identity, an illicit embrace, and the gossiping tongues changed everything. Will their marriage be one of convenience . . . or so much more?

Perilous Pleasures by Jenny Brown
Lord Ramsay has long awaited his revenge. But when the daughter of his sworn enemy is delivered into his hands, he isn't prepared for the vulnerable, courageous woman he finds. As passion burns as bright as a star—Ramsay and the bewitching Zoe will be bound together in a desperate struggle that can only be vanquished by love.

At Avon Books, we know your passion for romance—once you finish one of our novels, you find yourself wanting more.

May we tempt you with . . .

- **Excerpts** from our upcoming releases.

- Entertaining **extras**, including authors' personal photo albums and book lists.

- Behind-the-scenes **scoop** on your favorite characters and series.

- **Sweepstakes** for the chance to win free books, romantic getaways, and other fun prizes.

- Writing **tips** from our authors and editors.

- **Blog** with our authors and find out why they love to write romance.

- **Exclusive content** that's not contained within the pages of our novels.

Join us at
www.avonbooks.com

AVON

An Imprint of HarperCollins*Publishers*
www.avonromance.com

Available wherever books are sold or please call 1-800-331-3761 to order.

978-0-06-209264-9

978-0-06-208478-1

978-0-06-211535-5

978-0-06-204515-7

978-0-06-207998-5

978-0-06-178209-1

Visit www.AuthorTracker.com for exclusive
information on your favorite HarperCollins authors.

Available wherever books are sold, or call 1-800-331-3761 to order.

ATP 0312

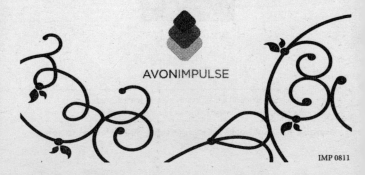